Paula McGregor

BLIN

Diana took a long gul[
wanted to talk to you
been asked to produce that I need a researcher
on. I thought of you; it will help to get you out
on the trail again.'

I speared a potato. 'I like researching. What's the
programme about?'

Diana chewed, then swallowed, then answered,
'Dating agencies.'

My fork was almost to my mouth. Dating agencies?
Forget it. No way was I going to join one of those,
and certainly not to please Diana. That was not the
kind of research I had in mind. A candlelit dinner
was as far as I was prepared to go to keep anyone
happy.

Diana, being a quicker eater than I am, had emptied her plate. She placed her cutlery together with
emphasis. 'Producers have scoffed at the agencies
and made fun. But some of them I'm convinced
are genuine and give a good service. I'm especially
interested in those ones that specialize in trans-
ocean couplings. American men are apparently very
keen on English women, and you can find out
why.'

About the author

Married and divorced twice with three grown-up children, Philippa Todd has lived in Australia, Greece, Jamaica, Italy, France and Spain. Amongst other things, she has worked as a catwalk model, landscape gardener, dressmaker and interior designer.

Blind Date

Philippa Todd

CORONET BOOKS
Hodder and Stoughton

First published in Great Britain in 1996
by Hodder and Stoughton
A division of Hodder Headline PLC
First published in paperback in 1997
by Hodder and Stoughton
A Coronet Paperback

10 9 8 7 6 5 4 3 2 1

British Library Cataloguing in Publication Data

Todd, Philippa
Blind date
1.English fiction – 20th century
I.Title
823.9'14[F]

ISBN 0 340 68023 7

Typeset by Palimpsest Book Production Limited,
Polmont, Stirlingshire
Printed and bound in Great Britain by
Mackays of Chatham PLC, Chatham, Kent

Hodder and Stoughton
A division of Hodder Headline PLC
338 Euston Road
London NW1 3BH

For Alexander, my first and cherished grandchild

Grateful thanks to my family for their encouragement, to my agent for her faith and to my editor for her support.

ONE

No longer were Sundays the days when I, Camilla Cage, felt blessed, and Sundays alone in London, Lord, how I hated them. But the one that fell on 5 May, two days before my forty-third birthday, topped them all and I would not have wished it on a rabid dog.

Deep panic swamped me as I stood outside my own front door on the sixth-floor landing of my apartment block. The key I held in my trembling hand simply had to fit the lock because I'd used it hundreds of times before, and had double-locked the door quite successfully when I went out earlier. What a stupid decision that had turned out to be, what a lulu! Talk about being in the wrong place at the wrong time, and not once but twice in one afternoon. Not bad going for an outing I need not have taken.

Waking earlier to the realization that it was Sunday, and a grey and dreary one at that, had driven me out of the flat. That, and the aching desire for Marcus, made worse by my sexual dream, was more than I could handle all alone.

He'd held me to him with my legs wound around his hips and my weight supported on the edge of the table. He'd teased my mouth with his tongue as he thrust deeply in between my thighs to our familiar rhythm, and we moaned, softly. I was climaxing alone as I came out of

1

my dream and I pulled the bedclothes over my head as
though to hide my shame.

The coffee had not tasted right at breakfast. I'd run out
of orange juice, and my cat, called Kat, had turned up her
nose at her special Sunday treat of poached cod. A short
outing to the deli for fresh bread, antipasti, cheese and
gherkins seemed like a sound idea to me. Especially as I
had only recently become comfortable with buying items
for one. Until then I'd purchased for two, and to hell with
the expense, just to show that, like everyone else, I had
a mate waiting for me at home. (Show whom, I ask you,
the check-out girl? She couldn't have cared less.) And
maybe, while I was out, I'd rub shoulders with a few
living, breathing, friendly even, human beings. Besides,
I thought, why should I work at my desk on a Sunday?

The mail I should have opened on Saturday before
going out to lunch with my daughters could have spoilt
the treat, seeing as how it was mostly in window envelopes, and on one the print showing through was in red.
If just one envelope had looked remotely like containing
a friendly letter from a faraway place, or a cheque for
a change, that would have been different. Sometimes I
wondered if my agent believed I wrote for amusement,
like doodling on message-pads, or as a therapy to combat
suppressed anger, instead of to feed and clothe myself and
to pay off the mortgage on my godawful flat.

Some days are worse than others since Marcus left me
(dumped me, I call it, to really pick at the sore) and as
for Sundays, forget it. Even when my best friend Diana
Bingham asks me out for a pub lunch, as she sometimes
does when having a rare Sunday off from her high-flying
job with HTL television, somehow going back to an empty
flat seems worse than not having left it in the first place.
Sundays can affect the most spirited of us like that. They
are just different from other days, especially when you
are grieving.

When Marcus and I were married, and had the big old house in leafy Hampstead, and the children were under our feet, Sunday was my favourite day. Together we would spread the morning papers on the kitchen table and digest them with our coffee and the croissants Marcus took the kids out to buy when he collected the papers. I haven't been able to enjoy a Sunday paper since. In summer, on fine, bright Sundays, we would have breakfast in the garden, and use the honey pot, the butter dish, and whatever else came to hand to anchor the papers when the wind blew.

Marcus and I did not always agree on what we were reading, and sometimes it could get quite verbal. My views were to the left of his extreme right ones. Not that I'm a political person, and getting the Sunday joint in the oven on time turned me on more than an argument on whether the Prime Minister could win another general election.

Family Sunday lunch, what a long time ago that seems. And not a single Sunday dawns without that nostalgic smell filling my nostrils and making my heart ache. I can conjure up the aroma of roasting meat whenever I want to. And they all agreed, my family, wasn't I just the best cook in the whole world. Those were heady times for a woman who'd never bothered with a cookery book in her life, and invented her own recipes as she went along.

Now, here I was in a slough of despond, locked out of my own goddamned flat, bloody-kneed, jeans torn beyond repair, my head hurting fit to split and a swelling the size of a gull's egg still growing above my right ear.

As I drove from the deli I thought, once again, about losing Marcus, the only man I had ever loved. He's not lost, only mislaid, Diana says sometimes, to cheer me up. But that is not true, and I wish that I could face it.

I try, please believe me. I'm not a wimp by nature, and self-pity has never rested on me for long. Some days even

I can see my old spunk returning. But then it goes, and leaves me to flounder.

I slowed down to allow a cute young couple, arms entwined, to cross the road, and to envy them kissing as they reached the pavement, when Marcus, can you believe, in a city of nine million people, took the corner wide from a junction, in his pearly-white Porsche 928S, and swiped my nearside wing. In a narrow street there he was, his eyes locked on mine and his face crimson with embarrassment.

Even while I stared at him and braked to a halt as my front fender coupled with a tyre, I could see the awful Angie person, wearing long shiny drop-earrings and ridiculous turquoise contacts, sitting there beside him. The brass-faced woman didn't even have the grace to look perturbed, she just looked at me with a vacant expression and fingered her long blonde frizzy hair.

The adrenalin coursing through my veins made my head spin. I thought I might be sick and wished that I couldn't smell the gorgonzola cheese in the bag on the back seat. Marcus pulled up further down the street than was necessary. I wound my window down and through the wing-mirror watched him coming towards me. I looked at those long legs that had always made my heart beat faster, encased now in designer jeans (how often had I tried without success to get him into jeans when we were married?). Those sexy legs were what had appealed to me most when I first met him, and they were definitely his best feature.

'I'm sorry, Milla,' he said breathily as he reached me and leaned in through the open window.

I stared into the face of the man I loved and inhaled his warm breath. My cheeks were hot, my heart was racing, and I found it hard to look aggrieved. It was a shared moment of closeness and I hoped that the hooker-lookalike girlfriend was watching.

It didn't last long. Anger engulfed me. I pushed him aside as I flung open the door and I flailed at the front of him with fists clenched as tight as a world-class boxer's. Of course, it didn't get me far. He grabbed at my wrists and held them still, and I swear he was near to laughing.

'You should take more care in that lethal machine,' I said, 'you could have killed me.'

He went to look at the damaged bumper. I followed him. We stood close and I wished that I'd splashed on the dregs of his favourite perfume before I left home.

He bent down and wrenched the bumper into position. I noticed the veins swelling on his neck at the effort and hoped that his heart was okay. I'd made him have regular check-ups when we were together, should I ask if he was still having them? Maybe the designer jeans that stretched so tightly over his gorgeous backside were too tight.

'It's not so bad, you'll be able to drive it now,' he said, straightening up.

'Gee, thanks,' I answered sarcastically, and got back into the driving-seat. I slammed the door shut, wishing my heart would stop pounding. How could he still affect me like this?

His head was through the window and I hoped that he wouldn't smell the cheese. (He hated cheese, and had a nose for it like a ferret with a rat.)

'For God's sake, Milla, it's only a scratch . . .' That was Marcus, attack to defend. 'Send me the bill,' he said, and looked at his watch.

It was a bad move. I was used to that gesture and knew that it had nothing to do with wanting to check on the time. Slowly I looked up at him. Jesus, if it was only the money, if it was only the car. But standing there in the street, how dare he dismiss twenty-five years of my life as a mere dent in a car for which he was willing to pay? I took a deep breath.

'I'd hoped I would never see you with that younger model you turned me in for,' I said.

He groaned and turned up his eyes. Until now he'd hoped that only the car was the issue. 'I didn't turn you in for anyone, Milla. Especially not her, and you know it.'

If only I could kiss his cheek, I thought. Or run my fingers through his now greying curls. I had a right to, did I not? We'd been lovers for more years than he would care to remember.

'I should hope not,' I said slowly, looking at him.

'What's that supposed to mean?' It was bitter comfort that he had to look away. But at least I had his attention.

'I'd heard about her, of course,' I said. 'Name and everything. Your children call her the poison dwarf.'

I could see the signs of anger as he flushed, and I loved it. 'They would. I expect you encourage them.'

'She's a tart,' I said. Couldn't he see that I was almost out of control with jealousy?

'Of course she isn't.' He was on the defensive, now that his taste in women was challenged.

'She is,' I persisted. 'It shows.'

He didn't want to, but he couldn't help asking, 'What do you mean, it shows?'

'Who else but a tart would wear drop-earrings on a Sunday?'

He shook his head and started to laugh. He was laughing at me, but I hoped, and totally without angst, that the Angie person could see and would think that we were sharing a joke.

I knew that I must leave before I made a further fool of myself, or tried to beat him up again, and I started the engine. He placed both hands on the edge of the window. I selected first gear clumsily. Marcus hung on to the door and winced at the sound of the grinding metal.

'Milla, don't be like this, it's stupid. I'll get it repaired for you if you like . . . save you the trouble.'

As I moved forward he walked beside the car. 'Milla . . .'

'Go to hell,' I screamed as I felt the old familiar burning sensation behind my eyes and the veins in my neck pulsating.

He loosened his grip on the door. 'Don't forget to send me the bill,' he called out. But it was only his way of dismissing me, and he might as well have said Merry Christmas.

I put my foot down hard. I was damned if I would let him see that I was in danger of crying. But dear God, how I loved that man. Two years apart, twenty-two years together, and he still made my juices flow. I would never get over him, never. I knew that I would not. Forget about one couple in three splitting up, and divorce becoming a way of life. I could never love anyone else. It's pathetic, ridiculous, lamentable, I know. But it was true. And I tell you, that day I saw no hope for me, and no future.

By the time I reached the parking places at the back of my block and had turned into a vacant space, I felt numb all over. I switched off the engine, got out slowly, took the paper sack of groceries from the rear seat lethargically, and locked the car. As I walked away, lost in my own dark thoughts and staring at the ground, numbness was slowly replaced with awareness. Something had alerted my senses. I was being followed.

A tingling sensation crawled from the top of my head down over the nape of my neck and along my arms. I looked around and saw nothing. There was not much noise, more a chilling silence really, but someone was out there among the cars. I stopped. So did the other footsteps.

I walked on again, so did whoever was following me. I was frightened now, and the basic instinct for survival that is in all of us made my heart pound against my rib-cage. Should I run without hesitation, or should I turn, face the aggressor, and show some spunk? Not before finding the door-keys, the inner voice said. I carefully took them from my jeans pocket as I hurriedly walked on, and with one hand selected the key to the entrance of the block. Of course, I dropped the damned things and had to stoop to pick them up. Behind me I heard laughing and without cogent thought I started to run. Thank God I was wearing my trainers.

'Nice arse,' a voice called. 'How about a fuck?'

Jesus Christ, the footsteps were gaining on me. If only Marcus would swing into the parking lot in his killer machine and rescue me I would forgive him every-thing. I would condone him having a mistress, not argue if he stayed out at night, and never question why he did not like me wearing red. But, come to think of it, why hadn't he taught me what to do in a situation like this, husbands were supposed to, weren't they?

Utter fear made my stomach churn and bad-tasting saliva filled my mouth. Don't ask me why, but I stopped, turned, and faced the enemy. There were two of them, shaven-headed, dirty-jeaned, heavily booted, and almost too young for hair to be growing on their leering faces. They stopped too.

'Boo,' one of them shouted. The other one laughed.

With strength I didn't know that I possessed I hurled the paper sack of groceries at them. The one with a tattoo on the back of his hand caught the bag, and the contents spilled at his feet. A tin of cat food rolled under a parked car. I turned and ran like an athlete towards the door marked Entrance. They ran too, laughing and shouting obscenities.

'I always wanted to fuck an older woman, didn't you, Kev?'

'Yair,' Kev answered. 'And she can suck my dick. She won't give no trouble when she sees this.'

There was a distinct click, and I knew without looking that it was from a switchblade knife. I thrust my key, held so tight in my hot and sweating fingers, into the iron door and bolted through it. The door crashed shut behind me. Mental overload thankfully put my brain into neutral and fear temporarily left me. Even seeing the lift door still open at the top of the six concrete steps, probably meaning it was where I'd left it, probably meaning there was a dearth of residents in their flats that weekend, failed to faze me. My heart seemed to have settled down even though I was breathing hard and my chest hurt, and I walked sensibly and positively towards the steps.

Then it happened. As the youths put their shoulders unsuccessfully to the iron door I missed my footing on the fourth step and fell. My knees took the impact of my weight on the edge of the step and my head hit the wall with a crack like a pistol. I felt no immediate pain as I picked myself up and bolted on into the lift.

It seemed to me to take an age for my arm to raise to allow my finger to press the button. And I was sure that the doors closed more slowly than usual. Then my brain returned to thinking mode and my heartbeat quickened again. I'd passed through the second floor where the doors always rattled, there was no other noise, it was deathly quiet. Had the louts given up and gone off to terrify some other unsuspecting female, I wondered hopefully, or were they racing silently up the stairway ready to push their coarse and ugly faces into mine when the lift doors opened on sixth floor? What in God's name would I do then?

They'd rape me for certain, cut me, torture me, even kill me, and leave my body to be found on Monday. And how would Marcus feel then? With luck, he'd never know the joy of a good night's sleep ever again.

I stared at the plain metal doors and began to feel the searing pain in my knees and the warmth of blood trickling past my ear. The small round indicator light showed a six and the doors opened slowly with a sinister sound. The landing was empty. I stepped out quickly on trembling legs propelled by fear. The silence was heavy, and the jangle of my keys resounded in my throbbing head with the volume of church bells.

Then, horror of horrors, the door to my flat would not open. As I examined the errant key I thought that my chest would burst as my heart thumped painfully against my ribs. I had to get in, and fast, my flat was my refuge. My reinforced, triple-locked door would keep anyone and anything out, I was convinced. I pressed my eyelids hard together, then opened them wide for clarity. The door stopped spinning. I tried the key again, this time slowly. It slid into the lock on oiled wings and turned without a murmur. I burst through, slammed the door shut, relocked it, bolted it and engaged the security chain before collapsing to the floor to rest my head against the cool wood, without the strength to push back my untidy brown hair as it hung over my face. Kat ran up to me in welcome and wound figures-of-eight around my ankles.

Anger came first. Anger at myself for being curled up on the floor, so cowed and so defeated. Tears came next, quietly at first. Then my shoulders began to shake and noisy sobbing took over. I wanted to move away from the door, take off my jeans, bathe my knees, but my brain refused to communicate the message to my legs. I wanted to telephone my children, my mother, Diana, anyone, just so I didn't feel so utterly alone and abandoned. And I supposed it would make sense to inform the police. My sobbing reached hysteria. I was drowning in salt water. Mucus from my nose mixed with the tears from my eyes and ran into my mouth.

'Marcus, you bloody bastard!' I shouted through my

sobs. 'Why have you left me all alone to live like this? I hate you. I hate you.'

I wiped my nose with the back of my hand, then wiped my hand on my jeans.

'It's all your fault. You don't give a shit, you really don't. You don't care what happens to me. I hate you for it, I really hate you.' Now I was truly out of control.

I struck the door hard with a clenched fist. 'I hate you, do you hear me, you bastard?'

I beat the floor with my fists. 'I'll never forgive you . . . never . . . never . . .' I sobbed into the carpet.

The telephone rang. On the fourth ring the answer-machine took over. I could hear my own voice saying no one could come to the phone at the moment and would the caller leave a message. On my last word there was a click. The caller didn't bother to speak. Not even a short message. No one cared what happened to me. No one cared at all, they really didn't . . . Kat cared, though. She looked up and mewed, then hunkered down to stare at me and patiently wait for the crisis to pass. Who knows how long it took, but, with brain and limbs frozen in shock I vaguely remember eventually tottering painfully towards my bedroom.

I could see Marcus quite clearly through closed wet lids, and had total recall of the order of events. He'd said he was leaving me at the end of a day when I'd been feeling particularly relaxed. It was two months to the day after the last of our three children had left to go it alone. It was fun, we'd both said, being just Marcus and me after twenty-two years of bringing up children. That morning I'd tried out a new recipe and thought it good enough to add to my collection for the cookbook I hoped to get published one day. I'd also looked at the guidebook I'd bought on good eating in France, for those special weekends when we could get away without feeling guilt. And I'd marked off at least three places.

He was unnerved by my shocked silence as he faced me. I could tell that he was thrown by not being able to answer the question he was sure I would ask.

'There isn't another woman,' he said quickly, anticipating that I would eventually have to ask.

I could not think of a single thing to say. Had I not been giving him enough attention? Men often complained about not getting enough attention when there were children involved. It certainly had been difficult for me at times dividing my love between four of them. But I always let him know that he came first, and he'd said he understood. Told me not to worry, said that I was making a good job of it all.

'I'm depressed,' he said. 'I'm restless, Milla. You must have noticed.'

I stared at him blankly. The truth was, I hadn't. Was he just trying to jolt me into showing emotion? Should I run into his arms, be the adoring little wife, tell him I loved him so much that it hurt? Should I press myself to him, suggest we discuss it in bed? In the confines of the bedroom it could all be made better, surely?

'It's midlife crisis,' I said nervously at last, relieved that the situation didn't sound as serious as I first thought. Then, can you believe, I followed that inane remark with, of all things, and too late to stop the words tumbling out as they do when I'm nervous, 'They don't call it *men*opause for nothing, you know.'

He turned away, his shoulders hunched. 'I still care for you,' he said, ignoring the midlife crisis bit. 'We don't need to be enemies. And we can meet to discuss things, now and again. Have dinner, even.'

I watched him closely. He couldn't really mean what he was saying, could he? Not to me, his wife, the mother of his children? Had he flipped his lid, or what?

'I don't want a divorce,' he said, his back still to me.

I wondered if it was just a bad dream, and if so, could I please wake up? Perhaps he felt wronged, I mused. Husbands often did, I'd once read in an article on marriage problems. You know the ones I mean, those that couldn't possibly apply to you.

'Well, that's a relief,' I said archly, feeling annoyance and fear changing the sequence of my heartbeats.

He was pacing the length of the sitting-room. 'I simply have to go, I really do. Before it's too late.'

Suddenly, with a rush of blood to the brain, I was really angry. Didn't he care how much he was hurting me? Couldn't he see that he was causing me unbearable pain?

'Why?' I asked sharply. 'Has your sell-by date run out?'

He spun round on his heel. I jumped. He had never hit me, but there was always a first time.

'Don't be flippant, Milla. You know I hate it when you use that journalistic flippancy.'

I picked at a loose thread on a corner of the settee for something to do with my hands. 'I hate it when you say you're leaving me.' Suddenly I felt gutted, a failure, useless, a burden.

He watched my nervous hand as I twined cotton around a finger. 'I've been trying to tell you for some time, that I want to be on my own.'

Why did he sound so exasperated? We'd only just begun to talk. The angry feeling settled on my chest.

'Don't tell me you're aping the kids and want your own bedsit. You can't recapture your youth, you know, if that's what you're hoping for.'

His face was red. 'Milla, don't shout. I hate it when you shout.'

I could feel a nerve twitching under my right eye. 'There seems to be a lot you hate about me suddenly.'

It dawned on me then. He wanted to ease his guilt with a quarrel, and I was playing into his hands.

'We all get fed up with being married at times,' I said, working on keeping my voice low and the octaves in place. 'I've sometimes felt like quitting too, but I haven't worried you with it. And I've never considered running away.'

He couldn't look at me, and he began his pacing again. 'You're stronger than I am,' he said.

'That's bullshit!' I shouted.

He turned at the end of the room and stood looking at me. 'I know you'll be fine. Most likely even enjoy the peace once you get used to not having me around!'

Damn the twitching under my eye. He must be able to see it, I knew.

'I will not. How can you say such a thing?'

'Because that's life, Milla. You'll take up your writing again.'

I hated that patronizing tone in his voice . . . probably I wouldn't even miss him and stuff like that. Did he think that he was speaking to a child? I folded my arms around my chest in the vain hope of finding comfort. How could he make changing our entire lives sound so normal? His face became blurred as hot tears filled my eyes.

'You can write another book,' he said lamely, stuffing his hands deep into his trouser pockets.

I felt cold. 'I can do that with you here.' I took a step towards him. 'Don't run away, darling. Don't punish me like this. I love you so much. Can't we mend whatever's wrong?' How could I be such a crawling wreck?

His face was still flushed and he sucked in his lower lip, the way I'd seen so often when things weren't going his way. I sat on the arm of a chair and looked up at him. 'I thought we could have such good times now, the two of us. Go away for weekends, stay in bed when we want to, that sort of thing.'

It all sounded so pathetic. I wished that I could think of something profound to say. Marcus headed for the door, needing to escape. 'I've told you, I need to be on my own. We'll discuss it again tomorrow.'

So this was only the first round. I jumped up and moved towards the door to cut off his exit. 'You can be on your own. I'll give you space. I'll stay quiet. You don't need to leave me.' God, I hated myself for the subservience.

He was close to me now. I could see the dampness on his upper lip.

'I do,' he said. 'Please don't make it more difficult than it is already.'

I felt more desperate than I thought possible. Worse even than when I nearly miscarried with Kate, our firstborn. 'There is another woman, isn't there?' Couldn't he see that he was breaking my heart?

He held my gaze. 'Not really. Certainly no one I care about.'

How dare he sound so in control? I reached out for his hand, and he let me take it.

'Then is it something I've done? Are you feeling resentful about me? Is it because your mother doesn't like me?'

He smiled forlornly. 'My mother doesn't like anyone.'

I lifted his hand and pressed it emotionally and firmly to my cheek. 'I didn't know that I was so dreadful to live with. You've never told me. I'll try to change. Just tell me where I've gone wrong.'

Was this really me sounding so obsequious, so cringeing? I'd always thought that I was self-effacing, uncomplicated, and certainly not servile.

He took his hand from mine, and pushed by me. There was a look of helplessness on his face as he turned his head away. And I was sure that there were tears in his eyes.

But he wouldn't really go, would he? He was just

sounding off, surely? Checking that I really cared for him?

He couldn't go, could he? That would be ridiculous. And anyway, I wouldn't let him.

TWO

I awoke to a room as dark as a tomb and a heavy weight resting on my chest. When I moved, Kat, lying across me and purring, touched my face with her paw. That told me who I was and where I was. Not an overly welcome realization. I turned my head to the digital clock and saw that it was seven in the morning. Brief rational thought told me it was Monday, and that I'd slept my way well and truly out of Sunday, thank the Lord.

As I flicked the light switch, Kat jumped off the bed and mewed in anticipation of an overdue feast. Painfully and stiffly I lowered my legs to the floor, surprised to find that I was still wearing my jeans. Threads of torn denim, stuck now to my raw and bloodied knees caused extra pain and made me wince. I ached all over.

As I numbly contemplated my feet, noticing that I had a bruise on one of them, and Kat rubbed her head on my ankles, I smelled a familiar maleness. It touched a nerve and looking down I saw that I was wearing Marcus's sweater, the one I had stolen from his suitcase when he was leaving me, and hidden in my closet to wear, or smell, or hug, or whatever when my need of him was too much to bear. I tore it off in horror at my irrational and unheeded action, and threw it across the room, where it landed beside my abandoned trainers, lying apart on their sides with smudges of blood on them.

Philippa Todd

My head throbbed without mercy. Steadying myself
with a hand on the bedside table, I saw a scattering of
blue sleeping capsules and the pill bottle lying there,
empty and stopperless. Small wonder, I thought, that
I'd slept for so many hours, helped along as I must have
been by the blue dolls I hadn't remembered taking.

Cautiously I picked my way towards the kitchen,
staggering like a drunk. Kat pranced ahead and with a
semi-cartwheel landed expertly on a counter-top, where
in anticipation of food her upright tail quivered as she
circled gleefully.

I filled the kettle absently and threw a tea-bag into my
favourite mug, a blue one, the survivor of six Marcus
had once bought for me in Italy. As the kettle whined
I stroked Kat.

'You're next, poor no-name baby,' I said huskily. 'Just
wait while I make tea, my throat is killing me.' She
jumped down to stand by yesterday's empty dish and
stare up at me.

Leaning heavily with my back against the counter, I
watched Kat devour her food and sipped at my scalding
tea. My feet were cold on the tiled floor and I placed one
over the other for comfort. I felt miserable, but mindless
somehow, unable to bring the horror of Sunday to the
forefront of my brain. Mercifully, I supposed, nature had
numbed my distressed mind and robbed me temporarily
of the energy to fret.

'I must get cleaned up,' I said aloud as I rinsed my mug
under the tap.

Then, all of a sudden, I looked at the mug and threw
it, positively at the wall. It broke into three pieces, which I
retrieved and placed in the bin. Not much of a gut gesture,
I know, but at least it made me feel better.

Kat looked up at the sound of breaking china, mewed,
and then resumed her meal. I tottered towards the
bathroom.

While the scented gel made a mound of bubbles as it mingled with the steaming water, I sat on a stool and soaked the shredded denim from my knees. Then I carefully eased off my jeans, threw my soiled clothing into a corner and painfully lowered my aching body into the healing water. My wounds began to sting and smart and I held my breath as I ducked my head under the foam.

A psychiatrist friend once told me that the best cure for heartbreak or fear was to bring it forward in the mind and face it, not to suppress the agony and try to be brave. And most of all to talk about it. So being all alone I did some hard thinking aloud and discussed recent events with myself, while I gingerly rubbed shampoo around the lump over my ear and wondered if I should show it to a doctor.

It had, though, no question, been the worst Sunday in my entire life. Worse even than I could dream up on a good writing day to put in a story. Still, now it was Monday, and life would go on, like it or not. Best of all, it was six whole days before next Sunday.

I had a dog of a controversial piece to write on incest being on the increase in the provinces with a deadline for Thursday, and the *Weekend News Mag* wouldn't want to know about my threatened rape or a possible blood clot on the brain as an excuse for late delivery.

Shortly I could telephone my children. They would listen intently to what had happened to their mother, be appalled at what they were hearing, afraid for me. They would offer to call round, bring me flowers or invite me over. I'd phone best friend Diana too, an altruist of the first water. She would lend a comforting ear and to change the mood would cleverly make me laugh, even throw in some aphorisms about my imminent birthday.

God, yes, my birthday, tomorrow, my forty-third. Yuck!

I stared at the wall and slowly began to wonder if Marcus would remember what happened on 5 May . . .

I closed my eyes and distinctly saw him lean over me in bed as I lay in a froth of white pillows. We were divinely married, and he was holding a large tray and spread on the white damask cloth was a collection of breakfast goodies, amongst which nestled a bottle of chilled champagne and two frosted glasses.

'Happy birthday, darling,' he said lovingly . . .

Stop it, you stupid bitch, I yelled at myself. Some bloody hope. The sonofabitch never once brought you breakfast in bed. It was time to pull the plug.

Not on my birthdays, not to celebrate giving him two adorable daughters or one heavenly heir. Nor at any other time, I argued as I wrapped my sore head in a towel. Once, I remembered, I'd asked him if he knew that it was 14 February and he looked at me vaguely and said he thought that my birthday was in May! So, Camilla Jane Cage, cut the crap . . .

Carefully I strapped my knees with medical tape and put on a long clean T-shirt. I was hungry, food not having come my way since Saturday. Not knowing if it was shock that made me shake or the after-effects of the sleeping pills, I decided to take breakfast back to bed and to include a small brandy. Purely for its medical properties, of course!

After comfort food of Marmite toast and milky coffee with the brandy added I felt tired again. Should I shrug it off, I wondered, take advantage of it being early and get to my desk? Or maybe take one of the 'uppers' Diana once gave me and prance happily through the rest of the day? Best not do the latter, though, last time I'd taken one I was still on the wall thirty-six sleepless hours later. I laid back my head, intending to doze till the hour was respectable for phoning my nearest and dearest . . .

Hadn't I been a fool when Marcus was leaving to ask

him, with tears on my cheeks, as he struggled with
his suitcases at the door if he still loved me? What
a half-witted question, what a moronic idea! Was I a
crawling nit-wit, or what? Does a man leave a woman
he's in love with?

'Yes, I do,' he said, avoiding my eyes and making heavy
going of the overstuffed bags.

But even worse than that, hadn't it been chronically
embarrassing for both of us the night I asked him if I'd
failed him in bed? He felt the need to put his arms on my
shoulders and look into my troubled eyes.

'There has never been anyone better than you in bed,'
he said.

I stiffened then, and my cheeks went instantly pink. He
realized his mistake right off and moved away. So there
had been others, after all?

'You must,' he said eventually, to cut off the silence,
'have had someone on the side, now and again?'

My anger was instantaneous and came from deep in my
stomach. Someone on the side? What a naff expression.
And some hopes. Convenient of him too to forget how
possessive he was. I turned on him.

'Someone on the side?' I asked, pacing myself to move
slowly round the room. 'Other men, you mean? When
would that have been, I wonder? On the way home
from chauffeuring your children to school perhaps? Or
against the sink with the plumber as a respite from peeling
potatoes?'

I barely paused for breath now that my Irish was up.
'Oh no, wait a minute. How about a quickie at my ailing
computer when I wanted to do some writing without
feeling guilty because the vacuum cleaner was at the
mender's and I couldn't clean the carpets? You know
how attractive that technician was.'

'Milla, please,' he said, placing a hand on his brow in
mock pain.

'Or how about when the children were on holiday at my mother's and it would have been easy to pick up a willing stranger?'

Marcus sat down in his favourite armchair that would not be his for much longer. He looked weary, not to mention showing that he wished he was somewhere else. Back in his mother's womb perhaps, or on a plane heading for Africa . . . I didn't care. I was hurting. And I was trembling with anger.

'And certainly I could never have met a man in the evenings. Remember how you flipped the first time you arrived home to an empty house? When I came in you looked as though your world had come to an end.'

'I don't recall,' he said, not looking at me. How convenient again.

'No, I bet you don't. Well I do,' I persisted. 'You hated an empty house, you said, it reminded you of how your mother always seemed to be away from home when you were a child. You'd probably never get over the creepy feeling of an empty house, you told me . . .'

Marcus held his head in his hands and sighed. 'Milla, please, I didn't mean it like that.'

I felt as though the air was being torn from my lungs. Hot, angry tears filled my eyes. I was ready to break things. Jesus, the man was leaving me, making himself believe, for his own convenience and feelings of guilt that I'd probably, and with a bit of luck, been unfaithful.

'And I, stupid halfwit that I am,' I continued with a painful intake of breath, 'made certain that it never, ever happened again . . .'

I was sure that Marcus had not in all truth thought that I'd had other men. He was not the sort to keep silent about it if he had. Besides, our sex life together had been perfect, or at least I thought so. Full of passion and satisfaction, and plenty of it. On Saturday nights when the children were small, Marcus would put a stencilled notice outside our bedroom door when we went to bed, for them to see next morning. NO ADMITTANCE TILL INVITED. IT'S SUNDAY, it said. Often we made love for hours. Till the sun came up, or so it seems to me now. Till we were sated and weak and the bed smelled like a brothel when the fleet was in. Such bliss it was. Never had a woman felt more fulfilled than I did on a Sunday.

I phoned Emma first, hoping that on this of all mornings my daughter would not be feeling sick.

'Hello, Mum,' she said weakly as she lifted the receiver, 'I feel dreadful, I've thrown up twice already.'

I proceeded with caution. 'Oh, you poor darling. Have you tried nibbling on a dry biscuit?'

'Don't even mention the word biscuit.'

I sighed. 'It won't last much longer, it never does.'

'Mum,' she started, 'you said you had morning sickness for the whole nine months that you were pregnant with William . . .' (There went my big mouth again. Would I ever learn to button it?)

'Well, it won't happen with you, believe me,' I said motheringly.

'So how about this? Yesterday I was still throwing up in the afternoon.'

Emma always had been a whinge first thing in the morning, pregnant or not. She got it from her father.

'Yesterday was bad for me too,' I said. 'First of all—'

'I tried phoning you,' she cut in. 'I needed some comfort and you were out for hours. Good lunch, was it?'

'I didn't have lunch—'

'Neither did I. I was too ill to cook. Poor Gareth had to get himself a McDonald's.' (My dear, how dreadful. Poor Gareth. More calories yet to assist his widening girth!)

'First I saw your father with that hideous woman of his, the awful Angie—'

'Yes, Daddy phoned us,' Emma interrupted. 'Hearing his voice was the highlight of my day.' (That didn't take the sonofabitch long, I thought. No doubt he phoned the rest of the family too.)

'Did he tell you what he did to my car?' I asked, trying not to sound petty.

'Of course he did, he was very upset about it. But there wasn't much damage, he said.'

I was sinking fast into the quicksand, and could be lost without trace if I wasn't careful.

'No, there wasn't, but it upset me too. And then I had a nasty exper—'

'Sorry, Mum, I must dash.'

'Why so fast, I wanted to tell you—'

'I'm going to be sick again.'

The phone went dead.

'Hello, Katie.'

'Hi, Mum, I was about to call you,' she said lovingly with her mouth full of food.

The lump on my head was throbbing something awful. Maybe when I told Kate she'd insist on coming right over and putting a bag of frozen peas wrapped in a towel on it, after she'd put me to bed, of course.

'I suppose your father spoke to you yesterday?'

'Daddy? Yes, he telephoned. Imagine, in one of the largest cities in the world he has to bump into you. Hey, that's a pun!'

'Very funny.'

'Sorry, Mum. It's a bit of a bummer about your car though.'

Inwardly I was screaming. It wasn't her fault. But Sunday's events, for me, at least, had been more than a bit of a bummer or a pun.

'He was with that dreadful woman, you know, the poison dwarf . . .'

I listened to the silence. Was Kate about to get rid of me too?

'Yes, he said you were angry about that . . .'

'And he was wearing tight designer jeans.'

Katie laughed, but not unkindly.

'Mum, it doesn't matter. It's a phase he's going through, he thinks it's cool.' (Now give her twenty seconds and sure as eggs she would change the subject.)

'Then,' I said, 'I had a bad experience in the car park, two—'

'Don't tell me. Another crash?'

'No, just a mugging, and a touch of rape—'

'Mum, you are funny. Anyway, tell me tomorrow. As it's your birthday, Wills and I thought we'd take you to see *A Perfect World*. You know, it's a movie.' (Of course I knew it was a movie. Where did she think I'd been living, on another planet?)

'Kevin Costner is in it. And you liked him in *Dances with Wolves*. You said he reminded you of Daddy. But he hasn't got any Indians with him this time . . .'

That could be two good reasons, I thought, for not wanting to see him again. 'That sounds brilliant, darling. How nice of you both.'

'And we thought we'd eat Chinese first. We've found the greatest Chinese restaurant in Soho. Full of Chinese people.'

Was that so unusual, I wondered, that it merited saying? Maybe I did live on another planet, after all . . .

'So that shows you how good it is. Their wonton and their Peking duck is to die for. Then we'll take you to the Häagen Dazs ice-cream place after the film for dessert.'

Kevin Costner without Indians, Peking duck to die for, ice-cream, sore knees, an aching head . . . and all I wanted was to tell her about what had happened to me yesterday.

'Darling, how lovely. I shall look forward to it . . .'

'Must get to work now, Mum,' she called out. 'Love you. Bye.'

There was no answer to William's phone. He must have stayed over with the current girlfriend. It was all right for some.

Diana's answering service said that she was not available till after nine-thirty. Sleeping late, I supposed. It must have been a good Sunday. As I said, it was all right for some . . .

It was a fact of life. No one wanted to listen to sob stories, no matter who was doing the sobbing. Marcus had not injured me with his car. I had not ended up in traction. The booted thugs had not caught me. Therefore no story.

Marcus no longer lived with me. Therefore, how he lived his life, what sort of idiot he made of himself was no business of mine. I must, and I would, try to stop thinking about him. The way I let him get to me lacked intelligence, and spunk. I must, and I would, start going out more. I must, and I would, put my failed marriage behind me. I was a strong woman, everyone said, with lots of stored-up energy. I was one of life's fighters. So I would make it.

I looked at the digital clock. Time to get up again and face the day. If only I didn't feel so lethargic. Could I still be suffering from shock? It really had been a nasty fall. Maybe ten minutes more with my head on the pillow would make a world of difference to my attitude. And afterwards, what the hell, why shouldn't I risk one of Diana's uppers to give myself a kick-start?

Twenty-three years of marriage and now I was supposed to accept gracefully that Marcus had a life that was no business of mine. What a load of cobblers, was everybody barking mad? The idea was absurd.

Maybe I should call on him, ring his doorbell, tell him

how much I still loved him. Invite him to come back, point out that no one could ever adore him like I did. I would wear a sleeveless T-shirt, and lots of perfume around my armpits, and when he let me in I would put my arms seductively around his shoulders. He'd often told me how sexy it was to feel my bare arms on his neck.

Once when we were driving back late from a country restaurant in summer, he'd touched my bare arm and that was all that was needed. I was pregnant with Kate at the time and my skin was particularly velvety, I remember. We pulled up in a narrow lane and made love on the front seat, passionate, tender, heavenly love. Afterwards, he drove slowly, steering with one hand, his other holding mine. He told me how he could not bear to think of ever having to live without me. I mustn't die, he said, sometimes he had nightmares about it. And would I promise, he asked, positively promise, not to die, whatever happened, before he did?

The telephone rang. I reached over and picked it up quickly.

'To use the royal we,' Diana said, 'and run the risk of sounding like Madam Dizzy Tits, how are we on this fuck-awful Monday morning?'

Could it be that she knew I'd had a bad Sunday? Could Marcus have phoned her too? I sat up. 'Well, not as bad as yesterday . . .'

'Oh, darling, much worse, surely. Have you looked out of the window? It's piddling down.'

'I don't think I'll bother, thank you.' I could hear her exhaling smoke.

'Doesn't sound as though the Lord's day was any great shakes for you either,' she said.

Why bother trying to tell her? 'That would be one way of putting it.'

She took another drag. 'I should have met you for

lunch, my day was awful too. My date was that silly old fart Damien Tring. What a crashing bore he is. No wonder his wife left him.'

I examined my knees. 'Poor you. My whole day was a crashing bore, you might say. I very nearly was—'

She blew smoke down her phone and cut in with, 'Ah well, tell me about it when I take you to lunch next week.'

'Lunch next week?' I repeated, blankly.

'Of course lunch, silly, don't you remember our date? It's my belated birthday treat, and anyway I want to talk to you about something. Can't see you sooner because I'm off to Munich for the BBC.'

'Lucky you,' I said lamely. I could hear the rattle of gold bracelets.

'A heavenly present will arrive tomorrow. I couldn't really afford it, but as it's for you . . .'

'I know, and I'm your best friend . . .'

I smiled to myself. It was probably another fluffy bath-robe from Harrods, like most years. Maybe this year they'd let me exchange it for perfume.

I could not settle. I paced the flat like a newly caged tiger. I tried to count my heartbeats and they didn't seem regular. I tried to find the gadget that Marcus had frequently used for taking his blood pressure, and then remembered he would have taken it with him.

I looked at my watch for the umpteenth time. I really had to start some work. Maybe another bath would help to calm me and take the soreness out of my knees. After all, it was three whole hours since the last one.

I lay in the extravagantly perfumed water with bubbles nudging my chin and smoothed herbal creampack on my face for something to do that was positive. Bette Midler sang tunes from *Beaches* on my portable tape-deck which was balanced on a stool beside the bath. My freephone was within reach. I soaked folded tissues in witch-hazel lotion and placed them over my badly swollen eyelids.

There was no doubt about it, I discussed with myself, I was not an avid Believer. All my adult life I'd struggled with the guilt of not being Godly. I could come to terms with Something being in charge of us, driving us on, deciding who was good enough to die young, who should be left to rot in hell, that sort of thing. And I talked about God and called out to Him in adversity like everyone else. But as a male figure, sitting in judgment way up above the clouds as the religious freaks wanted us to have it, now that gave me trouble.

It was evidently also my downfall. Yesterday, I thought, would not have happened if I'd been a religionist. God was punishing me.

I removed the tissue pads for long enough to pour more witch-hazel on to them and then returned them to my eyes.

Anyway, God, I said to Him, you need not have gone so over the top. Banged-up knees and a thump on the head was a bit extreme for someone like me. I would have taken the hint if I'd just been dumped on by a pigeon. That would have been enough of an indication of Your wrath for me. After my confrontation with Marcus, and having to lay eyes on the awful Angie person, bird crapola in my hair would have been enough to make the day a nasty memory, and to have made me feel suitably punished for my agnosticism for the rest of my natural existence.

The telephone rang. I considered letting the call go on to the answering machine, then thought better of it. On a Monday morning, fingers crossed, it could be about work. I groped for the receiver. It was my agent Daisy Tibbs (or Dizzy Tits as Diana called her).

'Camilla, I called you yesterday and spoke into that

ghastly machine. You didn't call me back, you naughty girl,' she drawled in her phoney Sloaney accent.

'No, I didn't. Sorry.' Here we had the last person in the world to try a sob story on.

'What are you doing?' she asked bossily. 'I can hear water sounds.'

'That's because I'm in the bath.'

'In the bath,' she barked, as though I were a pervert. 'At this hour?'

It was only ten-fifteen, for God's sake, it seemed like the perfect time for having a soak to me. Especially if you'd had the kind of Sunday I'd just experienced. I blindly wiped facepack off the receiver as it began to set like drying concrete and reluctantly felt my way to the volume control on the tape-deck.

'I overslept,' I said.

'Camilla, dear, is something wrong?'

Wicked thoughts formed in my mind. I edged further into the water. 'Far from it. I'm lying here with the most handsome man you ever saw.'

'Camilla!'

'It's true. And he's exciting the hell out of me with his big toe.'

I could not believe what I was saying, especially to Daisy. My God, was it the bump on my head, had a blood clot really formed on my brain?

'Well, dear,' Daisy said, trying to sound casual, 'I'm glad you're having fun.'

'*Was* having fun, you've spoiled it now, we've gone off the boil. So tell me, how's my favourite godson?'

'He's fine,' Daisy trilled, relieved that I'd changed the subject. 'He sends his love.'

I doubted it, from three-year-old Tom. And what a terrible handle to burden a child with, Tom Tibbs. Do parents have no imagination, I wondered? Lucky for him their surname wasn't Cat.

'In fact,' Daisy was saying, 'I'm phoning to ask you to tea next Sunday. Put it in your diary, then you won't double-book.'

The word Sunday did bad things to me. The bath-water seemed colder and I became aware that the herbal pack was setting like cement on my face.

'Just me, by myself?' I asked quietly.

I could hear another telephone ringing in Daisy's office and then a whispered conversation on the side.

'Of course just you, darling. Who else?'

Something similar to a missed heartbeat happened in my head. A reaction to that upper, perhaps? Slowly I eased myself up from the suds and took off my eyepads. 'No, thank you, Daisy.'

Daisy showed surprise, someone was actually telling her no.

'What do you mean, no thank you? Do you already have another engagement? The following Sunday then.'

'I don't think so.' I could feel the facepack cracking as I talked.

Impatience fairly leaped into Daisy's voice. 'So what is it, Camilla? Don't you love us any more?'

I slid back down into the water and turned on the hot tap with my big toe. It was turning into a long conversation, no point in getting cold.

'I would rather come to your next dinner party, Daisy. Surely that must be coming up soon?'

I could hear Daisy breathing, it whistled softly on the line.

'Well, of course. But that way you don't get to see Tom. I thought you liked to see him?'

I softened the facepack with a wet hand. 'I do like to see him. I'll come early, before the other guests arrive, and read him a story in bed.'

A bump on the head, or the result of uppers, no matter, something that had been bugging me for ages was out.

Philippa Todd

There was a heavy pause before Daisy asked quizzically, 'Are we a little tetchy this morning?'

Bloody right, I felt like saying, but didn't. I turned off the hot-water tap with a reverse thrust of my toe.

'Maybe. But I've asked you to my dinner parties, Daisy. Not as grand as yours and not as often, but usually interesting and always fun. And all I get from you these days is tea and no company.'

Daisy gave a painful sigh. 'So what is it you're trying to tell me, Camilla? I really don't have much time.'

Suits me, lady, you're ringing me, remember, I resisted the urge to say, and blew suds from around my breasts. How could I tell a woman like Daisy that I was shit-scared without Marcus and still loved him like breath, and needed all the help I could get?

'That I'm lonely, I suppose. That I need to be in a room full of people sometimes, have interesting arguments, a few laughs, mental stimulation. Unless you don't mind having a writer with an addled brain on your books.'

Curiously I felt a strong sense of relief at saying it all, because I was telling myself something. If I was asking to be invited out, I must be feeling ready to go. Was the beginning of the trail to recovery in sight?

'For goodness sake, Milla, we are in a bad mood this morning,' Daisy chirped. 'I phoned because I was thinking of you. What more do you want from a friend?'

Sweat from my brow was undermining the facepack and getting into my eyes. 'From a friend?' I repeated. 'A bit of understanding, I suppose. I've been through two years of hell, Daisy, and yesterday . . . well, yesterday you wouldn't even believe how awful that was . . . oh, shit, and now you're making me sound petty.'

Daisy switched to her matron's voice. 'And so you are being petty, Camilla. Hurtful, too. Really!'

Understanding and sensitivity were not Daisy's forte. Married to Basil, a man who hung on her words as though she were a prophet, while he paid all the bills and danced to her tune, Daisy was used to the best of both worlds. I used the now warm eyepads to wipe sweat and facepack away and stop both from blinding me.

'Yes, you're right, Daisy, so I am being. And I mustn't keep you from your work any longer. Give hugs and kisses to Tom.'

Daisy did her best to adopt a softer tone. 'So does that mean you'll come to tea on Sunday, dear? It would do you good to go out.'

I sat up and reached towards the tape-deck to turn up the volume. I preferred Bette Midler to Daisy Tibbs on any Monday at 10 a.m.

'No, Daisy, it doesn't. But I'll telephone you next week to see if you're still speaking to me.'

THREE

Postponing it could not be done, ignoring it would have been impossible. I could not remember having so many cards before, certainly not when I was happily married. I took them all to the kitchen table to open and read, then I put them out of sight. Marcus, of course, did not send me one.

The doorbell rang. On the security screen I saw a florist's delivery boy standing in the street. As I let him in my heart began to beat a little faster. Maybe the flowers were from Marcus. Last birthday he'd forgotten and when he phoned to apologize it hurt more than if he'd ignored it, because I knew he'd been reminded by one of the children.

I remembered well my fortieth birthday, when he still loved me, and he'd taken me to Paris for the weekend. What a glorious time we'd had. After lunch on the first day we went to the Louvre. In the middle of looking at fine art, with the heady afterglow of champagne coursing through my veins, Marcus put his lips to my ear and tickled it with his tongue.

'I want to fuck you, Mrs Cage,' he whispered. My stomach tightened as I turned my smiling face towards him.

'You mean right here, in front of these Old Masters?'

He looked at me sexily. 'If we do it in the street we might frighten the tourists.'

I felt my juices flow. 'Then let's get back as fast as we can,' I said, and we legged it hurriedly through the halls.

In the taxi he put his warm hand up my skirt and stroked my thigh. In the Hôtel Crillon, in the lift, he pulled my knickers down and I tore them on the heel of my shoe as I hurriedly stepped out of them. In the suite we ran to the bedroom, pulling off our clothes. In the huge four-poster we romped and rolled, we clung, laughed and moaned for the rest of the afternoon. Sweating and spent, he told me I would never know how much he loved me. He said sometimes it frightened him, and would I promise to be his for ever?

Taking my face away from his damp chest, I looked up at him and kissed his chin. 'Make me happy again like that, Mr Cage,' I said, 'and I promise I'm yours for the rest of my life.'

I snatched at the card buried in the basket of freesias. 'From Your Favourite Son, With Love Wills,' it said. I felt a warm sensation in my stomach that almost made up for them not being from his father.

Fifteen minutes later a bottle of pink champagne arrived nestling in a satin-lined box, and a small jar of caviar tied to the side. Too much thought had gone into the gift for it to be from Marcus. It was from a drama critic called Richard Newcombe. Dear Richard, dull as a puddle, shy and short and not a bit like Marcus. If only I didn't mind about the handicaps I need never be lonely again, I knew.

I relented about the birthday cards and placed them around the flat, and Kat followed me, as though in appreciation of it being a special day.

Two more bunches of flowers arrived, one from Emma and Gareth and one from my mother. I arranged them with care, felt lonely, and opened a half-bottle of Spanish champagne that I'd bought in the supermarket, with which to drink my own health.

The chopsticks and loaded dishes were placed on the table by a po-faced Chinese waiter.

'Tuck in, Mum,' Katie said. 'It's not posh nosh but you'll love it.'

I was happy to have two of my children with me, and counted my blessings for them. I wondered if they met up with Marcus and the poison dwarf on his birthday, but lacked the courage to ask, fearful that I might not be able to handle the answer.

While we waited for Chinese tea to arrive after the meal William slipped me his present, a gold chain attached to which was a pendant in the shape of a gold ingot. On the back was inscribed a simple 'With Love From Wills'. I chided him lovingly for spending so much money.

As we unwrapped the fortune cookies and giggled over the maxims, Katie handed me an envelope. 'From Emma and me,' she said. 'Don't hold your breath, though, it's not a first-class ticket to Australia.'

Carefully, wary it might be a jumping jack or something else jokey, I pulled out an invitation to a dinner at a house in Mayfair. Embossed in a corner of the gold-edged card was a five-stemmed candelabra of which Liberace would have been proud.

'What is this?' I asked, hoping that I didn't already know.

'Isn't it obvious?' Kate said. 'It's an invitation to a dinner party. You know, an organized one where professional men and women meet each other. A poor relation of royalty has started running them. It'll be brilliant.'

I felt my hand moving of its own volition to my throat.

A frown of impatience creased Katie's brow. 'It will

be good for you,' she said. 'You've been in mourning long enough. My workmate Lucy Bainbridge's mother has been to two of them. She's already dating someone she met there, and she's not as good-looking as you.'

I stared at the invitation as though it were a high-court summons. 'I'm pleased you think so,' I said. 'But should one's children be procuring men for their mother?'

Katie refilled the tea cups. 'Oh, come on, Mum, lighten up. You don't have to go out with anyone unless you want to.'

'But what would your father say?' There it was, out before I could stop, and what a stupid remark. Katie could hardly say, casually, off the cuff, that she really didn't think he'd give a damn.

'Besides,' I said quickly, 'they'll be total strangers.'

'Mum,' Katie said, trying to be patient, 'if you're lucky enough to meet someone you like, he'll only be a stranger until you get to know him.'

Help! I was trapped. 'Well, I'm not at all sure,' I said weakly. 'I mean, paying money to meet a stranger seems unnatural. Not that I don't appreciate the thought.'

'Dad was a stranger the first time you met him,' William said with misplaced wisdom.

How right my son was, though. I would never forget that night in the taverna when Marcus pressed a glass of ouzo into my hand and I took it, feeling overdressed, square and shy as my fingers accidentally touched his. How I wished I owned a topless sheath like the girl eyeing him from her perch at the bar. Or at least that I possessed a honey tan, instead of freckles on my nose and pink on my forehead.

'I'm Marcus Cage,' he said with that luscious timbre to his voice I later took for granted. 'Have you just arrived on this swinging island?'

It was all too much. The ouzo, I mean, and the hot

night and the stars. It was heady stuff, the music, the Greek dancing and the plates being smashed around me. I looked at my watch. Better I slipped away, I thought, for no real reason. He ran after me along the beach.

'Breakfast on the port,' he said breathlessly. 'Nico's Place, that little café at the end, ten-thirty. Can't stop, I'm supposed to be helping run the bar. What did you say your name was?'

I stared at William. 'You mean you think I should go to this dinner thing? I'm certainly not looking for a husband. I'll always be married to your father, in my head anyway, you know that.'

He asked for the bill. 'I think you should give it a try,' he said. 'I'm sure the girls didn't have marriage in mind. More like someone for you to have dinner with.'

I was not sure that I liked the idea at all and I looked across to Katie.

'I've never considered anything like this,' I said. 'I mean, parting with money for a woman of forty-three to find a man. It's unreal.'

Katie leaned over and kissed me on the cheek. 'We know how lonely you are, Mum. And you're only eighteen hours past forty-two. Arthritis won't set in just yet.'

I smoothed out the strip of paper that was hiding in my second fortune cookie. DO NOT LOOK AT LIFE WITH AN ACCUSING EYE, it said. What did the Chinese know about it, that's what I would like to know, I thought, oppressed and hounded, and living in Red China? What gave them the right to tell me how to look at life?

As William paid the bill, with too many ten-pound notes, and we waited for change, I wondered if I should try to get the dinner-party money back on the grounds of ill-health and buy myself a handbag instead of a man.

I thought that the young boy in *A Perfect World* was the

best child actor I had seen in a long time. Katie leaned over me in the cinema and said, 'You never know your luck, Mum. You might sit next to someone at dinner who looks just like him.' She meant Kevin Costner, I think, not her father.

After the ice-cream they took me home. In the lift William put his arm around my shoulders and gave me a hug. There was no doubt about it, I did have nice children. Surely, then, I couldn't be all bad? Well, not as a mother, anyway. Just as a wife, then, I supposed.

At the door they kissed me goodnight. William said, 'You must start having an enjoyable life again, Mum.'

Katie said, 'There are a lot of nice men out there, I'm sure.'

An enjoyable life? With nice men? It all sounded so easy. What it was to be young.

'You're a good-looking broad,' William said, tucking my hair behind my ears as I shyly lowered my head. 'Lots of the boys at my school had the hots for you. And that wasn't so very long ago . . .'

On the doormat, face down, were two envelopes from the late delivery and I snatched them up. Just possibly one was from Marcus. The writing on the top one was my sister's. Hallelujah, for once she'd made it on the right day with the birthday card. And the other? That was the gas bill.

The sun poured in through the glass-domed roof and the restaurant was a riot of flowers. The table was the best in the room, Diana always managed such things. Champagne was waiting in an ice-bucket. I felt good in my beige linen trouser suit and my blue silk shirt. So I'd best watch out, I doubted it could last.

Diana was waiting, a glass of bubbly in front of her. She wore a black suit, with nothing but a black uplift lace bra beneath, and the cleavage was awesome. At her throat, on her fingers and on both wrists gold was in abundance, and together with a whacking great Rolex watch the gleam seemed to add extra sunshine to the room. She stood up to kiss and greet me, and to leave bright lipstick on my cheeks, which she then scrubbed off with a red-taloned thumb.

She raised her glass, 'To the best-looking forty-three-year-old I know.'

Why suddenly was everyone commenting on how good I looked, I wondered? My looks hadn't changed – well, not for the better – and they were not good enough to keep Marcus wanting me. So it must be obvious to everyone that I needed an ego-booster. I blushed.

'From your lips to God's ears.'

The bubbles tickled the end of my nose as I sipped. (Marcus always swore he saw my nose wiggle when that happened.)

Norman Hampster the newspaper columnist came over and asked what we were celebrating, and without waiting for an answer asked Diana if she had seen his gossip piece on Donald Mergesson.

'That randy old polo-playing fart,' she said, 'who cares about him?'

Hampster ignored the slur on his column and managed a hollow laugh. 'And what about you, dear heart?' he said to her, ignoring me. 'Anything worth printing on your scene?'

She looked innocently into his face. 'Yes, I'm pregnant by the Duke of Abercrombie. We're getting engaged next week.' She winked at me.

'Are you really?' he asked earnestly.

'No,' she said sweetly, 'but that shouldn't stop you from printing it.'

I looked at my champagne. I wanted to take another sip and hoped that the flamboyant Hampster man would not be asked to join us.

As if reading my mind, Diana said, 'If we give you a glass of bubbly will you toddle off like a good boy?' She beckoned to a waiter for another glass, and Hampster did as he was bid, with a wet-looking kiss on both cheeks for Diana and a nod for me that said I didn't merit more.

'You look lovely today, Milla,' she said when he was gone. 'But with knees like yours you should try wearing a mini-skirt.'

An opportunity to tell her had loomed at last. I looked earnestly into her lovely eyes and prepared to have her gasp in horror at my tale of woe.

'Not today you wouldn't, they're grazed and horrid and have scabs on them. I had a nasty fall two Sundays ago. Some thugs chased me . . .'

The waiter interrupted with the menus. Diana wasn't even listening, she was flirting with someone across the room. I stared down at the white damask cloth feeling somewhat disadvantaged. Like a junior schoolgirl vying for attention with a sixth-form prefect. So I thought about Marcus, champagne did that to me, I doubted I would ever drink it again without thinking of him. He knew his wines, did Marcus, especially champagne. If you can't afford a good champagne, he'd say, don't drink it at all. His children were no end impressed!

I heard Diana order the wine as if through a wall. I felt the warmth of her hand over mine, and I looked up. Her lovely face, framed by her naturally blonde curly hair, quite belied her power and her intellect.

'You have to let the old bugger go, put him firmly in a secret box and close the lid. It's your only hope.' She watched the mist in my eyes.

'So you heard what happened with him on the awful Sunday?' I asked. 'God, my kids have big mouths.'

Diana patted my hand. 'They worry about you. *I* worry about you. You seem one minute to be at peace, at least on the surface, then wham, you see that man and you're an instant wreck. Whatever happened to the funny, spunky woman I used to know?'

I tried to keep my eyes on her face. 'She got lost when her lover left her. And she can't get over him going, that's all. But she tries. She really does.'

Diana shook her head. 'That man is a double-crossing, egotistical, pompous prat, and not worth your tears.'

I could not stop my face from flushing, as anger worked its way up from deep inside. 'Don't say things like that, or I won't stay,' I said.

She squeezed my hand. 'Sorry, hon, but I know what it's like to be dumped by a man, remember? Believe me, you're better off telling yourself what a no-good sonofabitch he is. And bin the good parts.'

The wine waiter refilled our glasses.

'I can't remember how long it took you to recover,' I said, wanting to take the heat off Marcus.

'Not as long as you, darling. I took on a few lovers, slept around a bit. It worked wonders. It always does.'

I stared at my glass, seeing his face among the bubbles. 'I'm not ready . . .'

'Not ready to order lunch?' she asked. 'Or not ready to sleep around?'

'Both.' I opened the menu. Diana looked at me over hers.

'You could have a lover in Richard Newcombe. He told me he made another effort on your birthday and you thanked him politely and then refused an invitation to dinner.'

I felt defensive. 'Richard's boring. And he lives in the past.'

Diana laughed. 'That's a choice remark coming from you.'

I looked down at my menu. 'Anyway, he's too short.'

She leaned forward. 'They're all the same in the dark, my dear.'

I laughed. 'I don't think I can believe that.'

She sampled the wine and nodded her head to the waiter.

'Of course,' she said, 'I keep forgetting that dear Marcus deflowered you and that you've never had another man, you old-fashioned thing . . .'

I adjusted my napkin and hoped that the waiter had not heard.

'I'm not going to defend my lack of carnal knowledge by numbers,' I said hotly.

I could remember when Marcus and I first made love as though it were last week. It was five days after we met and we'd sailed in a small boat with a picnic in search of a remote cove on the other side of the island. The brilliant blue water was crystal-clear and we dropped anchor halfway there, put on masks and snorkels and went in search of things to see. Marcus brought up a blue starfish for me and I made him take it back down again, then screamed when he returned with a baby octopus held between his teeth. We ate our picnic in the boat and drank retsina.

We pulled up the anchor and sailed for a cove, not having seen another boat since setting out. A farmer was washing his herd of goats in the sea in the first cove we came to, and we sailed on to the next. We hauled the boat up on to the beach and ran into the water to wash off the sand. Marcus took my costume off in the sea, hung it on his arm and carried me up the beach.

You wouldn't believe how I worried on that journey across the sand, Marcus with his lips on mine and his tongue in my mouth letting me know what was in store. Don't get me wrong, I was a willing participant, but I hadn't been with a man before. Curiosity at an early age led me to explore my anatomy with the aid of contortions and a mirror and it had all looked so complicated I wondered (hasn't every young girl?) if something about me was different. However, Marcus seemed to think that I was normal, and by the time my initiation was complete and the mysteries had unfolded I was convinced that if this was sex it was too good for most people. Imagine Attila the Hun experiencing such joy! Just reliving it in my thoughts was enough to keep me awake at night for quite a time . . .

'But you are making excuses,' Diana was saying across the table. 'Not every man is blessed with long legs, and some short men have incredible brains, and are good lovers.'

'And come up to my shoulders when they stand up,' I answered, feigning a serious study of the menu.

'But you know what,' Diana persisted, 'lying in bed it doesn't matter how long they are, well, not in the legs anyway.'

A waiter placed a dish of Greek olives, a round crock of butter and a basket of French bread before us.

'You haven't even sown your wild oats yet,' she said with an olive in her mouth. 'Going from child-hood to motherhood the way you did with the dear departed Mr C.'

'Are you ready to order now, ladies?' the waiter asked.

Diana looked up at him beguilingly. 'We'll start with the warm smoked chicken salad,' she said, without consulting me.

I took a wedge of bread from the basket. French bread, Normandy butter and juicy black olives were my idea of heaven and reminded me of how Marcus and I bought them for picnics in France.

'I think I may have offended Dizzy Tits,' I said, anxious to change the subject, spreading the butter thickly on a pull of bread.

Diana stopped chewing. 'That thick-skinned old broad, impossible.'

Philippa Todd

'I'd taken one of your uppers, and I told her I was in the bath with a man.'

'And were you?' Diana asked, hopefully awaiting details.

'No, not a chance. But she believed me.'

'She must have been wetting her knickers with excitement?'

'I don't think so. She touched a raw nerve when she asked me to tea next Sunday and I told her to forget it, I'd rather come to dinner.'

The first courses arrived. Diana picked up her fork.

'I don't get asked to dinner alone either. You know why, don't you?'

The smoked chicken was divine. 'Social lepers?'

'In a way. I call it the untidy table syndrome. Some hostesses cannot cope with uneven numbers. Especially more women than men.'

I sipped my wine. 'Sounds pathetic.'

'But true,' Diana said with her mouth full. 'And of course they're not at ease with unattached women, they think one of them may run off with the honoured guest and his wife will never forgive them. You should do a piece on it, only don't give it to Dizzy Tits.'

I had chosen the main course for myself, sweetbreads with sorrel sauce (they were Marcus's favourite dish too).

Diana talked about men, then she took a long gulp at her wine and said, 'I wanted to talk to you about a programme I've been asked to produce that I need a researcher on. I thought of you, it will help to get you out on the trail again.'

I speared a potato. 'I like researching. What's the programme about?'

Diana chewed, then swallowed, then answered, 'Dating agencies.'

*　　*　　*

My fork was almost to my mouth. Dating agencies? Forget it. No way was I going to join one of those, and certainly not to please Diana. That was not the kind of research I had in mind. A candlelit dinner was as far as I was prepared to go to keep anyone happy.

'It's been done before,' I said more sharply than intended.

Diana, being a quicker eater than I am, had emptied her plate. She placed her cutlery together with emphasis.

'Everything has been done before,' she said, 'but this will have a new angle. Producers have scoffed at the agencies and made fun. But some of them I'm convinced are genuine and give a good service. I'm especially interested in those ones that specialize in trans-ocean couplings. American men are apparently very keen on English women, and you can find out why.'

'It can't be for their money, so it must be for their incredibly good looks,' I said tartly.

'How about good in bed?' Diana asked.

I swallowed my last mouthful. 'Aren't American women better in bed, less inhibited?'

A rather bored couple at the next table listened intently. I could tell they were listening by the way they didn't look at us.

'No, no, not at all,' Diana answered loudly so as not to disappoint them. 'American women are ball-breakers.'

I wondered how she was so well informed and what, since it smacked of mallets and nut-crackers, the saying actually meant.

'Well, they're not going to find how good English women are in bed from me,' I said quite sharply.

Diana reached for her cigarettes, slowly and deliberately. 'You won't mind if I smoke?' she asked in a voice that made a statement more than begged the question. Then she smiled sexily at the first of two waiters who descended, lighters at the ready.

'Six agencies will be enough, I think,' she said, snorting smoke. 'You can select them yourself and let me know.'

A waiter brought the dessert menus. I wished that we were in the non-smoking section as I tasted exhaled smoke from across the table.

'Do you mean I would pose as a client?' I asked, adding quickly, 'If I become involved, that is.'

Diana produced a notebook as if by magic. 'Of course, and no one must know what you are doing, not even your children. And especially not Dizzy Tits.'

She told the waiter to bring her chocolate mousse on a raspberry coulis and I chose cappuccino ice-cream with hot fudge sauce. (I'd not had that since Marcus took me to The Ivy . . . oh, stop it, for the love of God . . . !)

'But first I must think about if I can do it.' (No point in giving the impression I would take on the job just because she expected me to do so. And second, I must remember to ask what the pay was.)

Diana took the top from her gold pen and began making notes.

'No computer-dating rubbish,' she said, 'leave those places for the peasants. I hear some even advertise clairvoyants now to satisfy the customers.' The desserts arrived. 'There's an agency on the south coast which only handles overseas datings. That, as I said, is the angle . . .'

I could feel a frown growing between my eyes. 'I'll probably accept,' I said, 'and I'll certainly start it off if you want me to. But I don't know about blind-dating.'

Diana was by now wearing her producer's look. 'You'll have to go on blind dates, Milla. How else can you write about it? Don't be naive.'

I felt foolish and resented being called naive. 'Just casual dating, then,' I said casually.

Diana stubbed out her cigarette and the ashtray was immediately replaced with a clean one.

'I shall not ask you how you go about it, just deliver the goods on time. You'll use a pseudonym, names will be changed for the programme, and professional actors will replace the clients.'

We ate our desserts in thoughtful silence until coffee was delivered.

'Milla, don't you see I'm trying to help you?' Diana said patiently. 'I know how lonely you are, the assignment will force you into meeting people. And besides, I'm going to tempt you with money.'

Funny how I felt wimpish and not at all attractive any more. Even my beige suit had developed wrinkles.

Diana stirred cream into her coffee. 'As you know, there are a lot of hardworking girls who would love me to invite them to do this. You're my first choice because you're my best friend.'

I must have looked contrite, because I felt it. 'I'd like to do it, honestly, thank you for asking me.' (Perhaps now she would discuss salary, and save me having to ask.)

'I thought ten thousand, plus expenses, would be fair.'

'Yes,' I said, hoping that I was looking thoughtful. 'Yes, that would be very fair.' (Wow, what I couldn't ever do with that. I could have a new carpet in my sitting-room . . . get a new video machine . . . a few facials . . .)

Diana reached over and squeezed my hand. 'Be in my office at ten o'clock tomorrow with some names and addresses of suitable agencies. I may come with you for the first interview.'

I sipped my coffee. 'I thought it was supposed to be a secret? You'll be recognized from the telly. Or do you want to be there to make sure I operate correctly?'

She lit another cigarette. 'Not at all,' she answered without conviction. 'And I'll go in disguise.'

'Disguise?' I repeated. 'I've never seen you in disguise.'

She laughed. 'That's because you didn't know that it was me.'

I accepted more coffee and munched on a chocolate mint. 'Would you go through an agency to meet a man?' I asked, adding quickly. 'If you needed to, that is.'

Diana examined her long red nails. 'Of course I would. But working with men in the media and propping up a few wine bars in my spare time has filled my cup, you might say, up to the present.'

'You might not believe this,' I said, 'but last night I went to an organized dinner party for professional women to meet intelligent men – ha ha. It was my birthday present from the girls.'

'I don't believe it,' Diana screeched. 'And you actually went? You're kidding me.'

'No, I'm not. I felt silly at first, and then, well, later on, I felt sillier still.'

Diana laughed. 'Any dishy men there? That's what I want to know.'

I looked into my coffee cup. 'One or two were not so bad.'

'Did you sit next to someone nice? My God, Milla, getting information out of you is like pulling teeth.'

'I met a man who was interesting,' I said. 'He wants to see me again.'

It was a rather grand house in the heart of Mayfair. I wondered if Countess Blomfield had rented it for the night or if she really lived there.

A butler asked my name at the doorway to the reception room.

'Camilla Cage.' It sounded weak, so I coughed, and repeated it.

The butler called it out to the large, regal lady in purple standing by a grand piano the size of a country cottage. She quickly consulted her notes, then smiled her most bewitching smile and extended her hand. 'Camilla,' she purred, 'I'm Edwina Blomfield. How perfectly sweet of you to come.'

The dear old girl didn't look as though she needed to do this sort of thing, but who was I to know if she was down to her last van Gogh?

'You're a writer?'

I tried to find my voice. She'd done her homework, of course, from her list, and my devilish daughters had helped.

'How clever of you,' she said a trifle condescendingly as she peeled a tiny self-sticking label with my name on it from a white clipboard on the grand piano and smoothed it expertly on to the lapel of my red silk jacket. 'You don't mind, do you, dear, it makes it easier.' Already she was looking towards the butler for the next introduction.

What in hell's name am I doing here, I asked myself as I felt panic setting in. The place oozed arrogance and snobbery, and there had to be at least thirty total strangers in the room, all holding near-empty glasses and all looking as bewildered as I was.

I took a glass of mediocre wine of the worst Chilean variety from the footman with the tray, smoothed down my red silk skirt with my free hand and hoped that the squares of medical tape on my knees were not showing. I looked around for a friendly face.

And to think I'd really groomed myself for this, spent hours at it like a teenager, and money too. Nails, hair and new sheer tights. What on earth had I been thinking of? I'd never felt more alone, I simply had to escape, I could no longer bear it. Maybe I could faint, get carted off on a trolley, anything. My daughters had better not ask if I enjoyed myself.

'Good evening, scarlet lady,' he said, and his gaze went from my face to my label. He offered me his hand and I quickly switched my bag and my glass and shook it.

'I am Gus Hidvela,' he said with a deep foreign accent, ahead of my reading from his lapel, 'and you are Camilla Caggee.'

I giggled (I hate myself when nerves make me do that). 'You pronounce it Cage, actually.'

He laughed. 'Am so sorry. I live in London for five years and America for long time too. I should learn better the language by now.'

I smiled a bit thinly, not to be too enthusiastic. 'It isn't important, really.'

He was tall, with dark blue eyes and thick greying hair. But then – how's this for rough justice? – he was ushered quite forcefully to one end of the table, and I was shown to the other.

My run of luck too, there being more women than men at the party, I was firmly sandwiched between a mannish large female barrister and an arrogant male stockbroker. The barrister was fun, with a keen sense of humour, the stockbroker was short and ugly. He also had a tendency to lock one hand onto my knee while he ate with his fork in the other.

The food was awful. Countess Edwina gave a speech with pudding and said snobbishly how important it was to have socially equal friends to stimulate one's brain. I wondered how the stockbroker next to me could stimulate anyone's brain when his own was housed in his trousers.

The tireless Edwina suggested that as coffee was self-service, wouldn't it be jolly fun to circulate? That was my cue, it was time to cut and run. I was out of my seat with the stealth of a cat, intending to slip out of the nearest door, down the front steps and into a taxi. Someone else had the same idea, and he held the door open for me to bolt through.

'Better not look in so much hurry,' he said. It was the man called Gus.

I blushed with guilt. 'I really have to get home,' I said. He walked beside me down the steps.

'You have babysitter waiting?' Dear, sweet man, keep talking like that, I thought, and I may linger long enough to listen. I shook my head.

'Would you like to have coffee? Is good idea after a meal.'

I looked at my watch for no reason whatsover, it was a nervous tic that came from those years shared with Marcus.

Gus spread his hands. 'Just suggestion. We could walk down to Dorchester Hotel. Is nice night, no?'

I almost overbalanced on the thick and expensive hotel-grade to-last-for-ever carpet and sank heavily into an over-stuffed armchair in the well-furnished and softly lit lounge. I tried to cover my knees but my tight skirt refused to oblige.

'We have brandy with coffee, yes?' Gus said with European old-world charm. I thanked him.

'Why lovely lady like you go to thing like that?' he asked with the bluntness of a foreigner. 'Is okay for me, I little bit bald and not so young.'

I giggled again. (It had to stop. Try some deep breathing and relax, I told myself quickly.)

'It was my daughters' idea of a treat for my birthday. I'm divorced and I've been rather unhappy, not getting on with my life, that sort of thing.'

He nodded gravely.

'What is your excuse?' I asked. 'Apart from little bit bald and not so young.'

His smile was attractive (his mouth was like Marcus's, maybe Marcus would look like him in ten years' time). 'I lonely,' he said. 'My wife she unhappily dead.'

I lowered my eyes. 'I'm so sorry.'

He spread his hands again. 'Is gone now, the sad. I've been widow for three years.'

Lucky you if the sad has gone, I felt like saying. But it did bear out my theory about being allowed to grieve properly.

'These things take time to get over, don't they?' I said. 'And it's widowER, actually, for a man.'

'Thank you,' he said with a twinkle, 'always something to get wrong with English language. You have many children?'

'Just three. And you? You look like a man who has lots.'

'Is shame, but none. We not lucky there.'

There went my big mouth again. I sipped my coffee and stayed quiet while he warmed my brandy glass in *his* palms.

'Are you Romanian?' I asked. 'I can't quite place your accent.'

'Almost right. Hungarian, actually, as you would say.'

We laughed and he handed me my brandy. 'Why you have sore knees? Something bad happen?'

I looked down. 'Sort of, but very boring, not worth telling.'

He poured more coffee from the silver pot left on the table by the waiter. 'I think you want to tell someone,' he said gently. 'I doctor, actually. I like that word actually, will always make me think of you.'

I put down my glass. 'I had wondered if you might be in medicine. Something about you.'

'Not medicine,' he said. 'Psychology, actually . . . and I good listener.'

I settled back and crossed my legs. Could it be I'd died and gone to heaven? Someone was going to listen at last . . .

Half an hour later I looked sheepishly across at him. 'I'm sorry, I didn't mean to talk so much. It's what happens when you live alone.'

He spread his hands. 'Is all right. I notice you were

not very happy when I first see you. Another brandy, perhaps?'

I shook my head. 'I really must be going.'

'I like take you to dinner. Soon, tomorrow maybe, or next day?'

I hesitated. 'It will have to be next week, I've lots of work to do. I have a deadline in two days.'

'Somebody dead? So sorry. You say when and where you like to go.'

'Can we make it lunch?'

He looked at me kindly. 'Of course, if you feel safer that way.' I opened my mouth. He held up one hand. 'I understand, lunch fine with me. Where you like to go?'

How could I say? I didn't know what he could afford. 'You decide.'

'Okay, Claridges. Day after you bury your deadline.'

Claridges, my God, what would I wear? And what if Marcus saw me? Then he'd never come back. Still, I could always cancel.

He gave me his card and asked for my phone number, writing it down slowly in his little book. 'Is a date, lovely lady. I telephone you and confirm.'

He had the doorman call me a cab. I thanked him for the coffee, the brandy and the chat. He kissed my hand. I felt warm inside, he seemed a nice man. And what a relief it had been to exorcize that bloody Sunday, even to a stranger . . .

I slept well that night.

FOUR

Rose O'Reilly tucked a duster into her pinafore pocket and fixed me with her pale, watery eyes.

'So I said to himself, I said, if you think piles are bad you should have my woman's thing, then you'd have real cause for complaint.'

I looked at my watch prudently, not wishing to hurt her feelings, and I had brought the diatribe on myself.

When Marcus and I were together Rose was lucky to get more than a good morning from us, and Marcus went ape if she became intimate about her ailments in front of him, which she was inclined to do at the drop of a spoon. She worked in the house full-time for us then and I knew that it was only her loyalty that kept her coming to do for me twice a week in the flat. And these days I quite looked forward to Irish Rose being around, humming 'Danny Boy' and talking to herself. It made me feel less lonely, and even Kat seemed to appreciate her company.

'So I said to the doctor, I said, this is worse than if I'd had all my babies at the same time. He said he understood, but how can a man understand, stands to reason? And they don't care, do they, these doctors? You might as well talk to the wall.'

I looked into her thin, careworn face as I began to edge away. 'I'm sure your doctor cares about you, Rose. Have you been given a hospital date yet?'

Philippa Todd

She rubbed at her thin arm through her shapeless pink cardigan. 'No, and you know what will happen? When they send for me, himself will turn round and say they'd better get the knife to his piles while they're about it, or he'll die, so why don't we go in together? As if we could.'

I side-stepped towards the door and waited for a brief lull in her verbal flow. 'Goodness.' (I'd had to train myself not to say God or Jesus in Rose's hearing or she would cross herself.) 'Look at the time, I must fly.'

It was a heavenly day, more like the middle of summer than late spring. I put on a T-shirt, struggled into new blue jeans, tied back my hair with a rubber band, grabbed a jacket and ran. I wasn't late, but I would have been if Rose had cornered me again.

Montrose International Introduction Agency was housed in Eastbourne, on the third floor of a soulless modern block. The logo on their office door was of two life-sized hands stretching out to each other with three wavy lines beneath depicting the ocean.

Diana and I bought a picnic lunch and indifferent white wine and consumed both on the beach prior to my appointment. I had psyched myself up to believe in what I was about to do and I was as nervous and apprehensive as any woman about to invest money to be found a mate.

Diana came out of the ladies' room on floor three and stopped in her tracks at the look on my face.

'Don't look so worried,' she said, 'you won't have to agree to marry anyone. Well, not today, anyhow.'

We fell about laughing. 'It isn't that. It's your black wig, and those glasses. You still look like you.'

Her eyes shone with devilment. 'To you maybe, darling, but they won't know. They're all thick as planks, these kind of people.'

I pressed the bell. My stomach was on the move and I hoped that it was my nervous state and not food poisoning from the cockles Diana had insisted we buy on the sea front for our picnic. Hurried trips to the loo might not be appreciated within those hallowed walls.

'Don't you dare to overdo it when we're in there,' I said.

Diana raised her eyebrows. 'Why not? I'm your pushy friend who's concerned about you, and you're a divorcee who is lonely.'

I pressed the bell again. 'Just like real life, then. But I know you, you'll say something wicked and embarrass me.'

The door opened eventually by remote control and we walked cautiously through it. A white-faced girl with dark red lips and long, thin black hair sat at a table, almost hidden behind a large computer. She had a surprised look on her otherwise empty face.

'Are you our two-thirty?' she asked in a whisper fit for a church.

I gave her my best smile. 'I'm Annie Lloyd.'

The girl checked her book, then pointed to two wooden kitchen-type chairs. 'Will you sit there? Ms Pilbeam will be here in a bit.'

'Ms Pilbeam,' Diana repeated in a stage whisper. 'What a bloody stupid name. Can it be for real?'

I sat down in a fit of panic, my blood freezing as it flowed. My God, it couldn't possibly be her, could it? Not my fourth-form maths teacher from school? She'd frightened the hell out of me for one whole year as a child, and no way was I staying if this Ms Pilbeam was she.

A nun-like, colourless girl in a Laura Ashley mid-calf dress appeared at the far end of the room and advanced towards us, hand extended. She was not the maths Miss Pilbeam and my heart slowed to a near-normal beat. I stood up with a feeling of relief and shook the weakly proffered hand.

'I'm ... Annie Lloyd.' I stumbled over my pseud-onym and lowered my voice as it seemed to bounce off the wall.

'And I'm her friend Mary,' Diana chipped in pointedly.

'I'm Mizz Pilbeam,' the vision said, 'would you like to come this way?'

She pointed to the far end of the open-plan room. It was cheaply furnished with a modern metal desk and several wooden chairs. The walls with which she blended so perfectly were painted cream and the only picture was a poorish print of a Turner seascape.

In a mystical way, Ms Pilbeam reappeared already seated at her desk.

'Would you care for cups of tea?' she whispered.

'No, thanks,' Diana answered loudly, then I noted that she too lowered her voice. 'I hate tea.'

'Coffee, then?' Ms Pilbeam said.

'Instant?' Diana asked.

'Oh yes, Mary, it's the most popular, is it not?'

'Only if you believe the adverts.'

I glared at Diana. The telephone rang and Ms Pilbeam whispered into it. Diana leaned towards me. 'She doesn't look as though she gets much sex. Doesn't augur well for her agency.'

Ms Pilbeam replaced the receiver and pressed a button that set off a buzzer on the desk of the girl beside the door. The girl looked up in alarm.

'No more calls, Monica,' Ms Pilbeam screamed in a voice above the normal pitch of a mere mortal. Then, reverting to the monastic whisper, she folded her hands on the top of her desk and looked at me with her pale eyes. 'May I call you Annie?'

'Of course,' I said.

'Well, Annie, I understand you wish to meet one of

our American gentlemen with a view to a permanent relationship?' She said it as though her gentlemen were men of the cloth.

'Yes,' I said, before Diana had the chance to speak for me. 'That would be nice.'

'Or more than one,' Diana said, unable to leave it to me.

After staring into space for an unnerving length of time, Ms Pilbeam slowly and silently opened a drawer. 'First of all I need to know your requirements,' she said. 'Perhaps you would like to fill in this form. Less embarrassing than talking about them, don't you think?'

I fished noisily in my bag for a pen. Diana asked if she might see a form too, and Ms Pilbeam surveyed her as a definite intrusion before handing over the relevant piece of paper, excusing herself and silently leaving her desk.

'We'd better not talk or Ms P. could get us for cheating,' Diana said.

Under the main heading of Requirements were listed Preferred Height, Weight, Colouring, Profession and Age. This was followed by Preferred Hobbies which only required a tick or a cross beside Sailing, Tennis, Golf, Model-making, Cards, etc. etc. . . .

Then there was a narrow space in which to name Dislikes. I was about to write short legs and beards against this last item, when I remembered that my needs were not for real.

A space towards the bottom of the page was left blank for Special Requirements. I could not think of any.

Diana slipped her form into my lap. Under Special Requirements she had scrawled big dick and lots of dough. Under Dislikes she'd written bad breath, pot-bellies and flatulence.

Ms Pilbeam appeared by magic sitting again at her desk and I guiltily stuffed Diana's effort into my bag.

It was time to look at photographs of the American

gentlemen, attached to which were lists of their most intimate details. I was told that for my initial fee I could have a choice of six men to contact.

All the men smiled at me benignly from their pictures. There were round faces, red faces, beards and designer stubble. There were muscular biceps, lost waistlines, brown skins, pale skins, misfits and midgets. Not one admitted to being under five feet ten inches tall and each one called himself attractive.

There were doctors, dentists, bank clerks, musicians, actors and entrepreneurs, red-necked midwest farmers and deathly pale New Yorkers. Most had been divorced and some of them often. I wondered why they were looking for yet another woman after coping with all that alimony. They were choosing English women, they all said, because they were caring and understanding (about alimony, perhaps?).

Diana looked over my shoulder and stabbed at some of the pictures with a long fingernail, saying, 'He's not bad,' or 'Ghastly, for God's sake,' and 'He might merit a one-night stand.'

Ms Pilbeam looked down her nose at both of us. I was sure that she expected more respect.

'You will, of course, Annie, send a photograph with each letter you write,' she said. 'And may I suggest a flattering one, one that makes you look younger, perhaps.'

I could not call to mind a photographer with such skills and decided there and then that holiday snaps would have to do. I wrote out a cheque for £600, thinking that £100 a shot seemed a lot to pay for some unknown Yank who might or might not reply to my letter, and hoped that Diana would honour my outlay quickly. Sweet Jesus, what a way to earn a living!

Two evenings later I penned six identical letters in a

light-hearted manner to six different men. I looked out five differing snapshots of myself (couldn't find a sixth) and sealed them in with the letters.

I chose a full-frontal of me in a bikini, at least four years old, for a New York artist called Bradford Delman. And a nice-sounding chap by the name of Hunter Lee McNab, who was a lawyer, got a discreet head and shoulders. He lived in Chicago, and was far and away the most classy. About Charlie Diamond from South Carolina I was not at all sure. He was the one who didn't get a snap. In the picture of him his eyes looked too close together – but what the hell was I worrying about, it wasn't for real. Tod Bradshaw lived in Los Angeles, and so did Bernie. Tod was sent a fuzzy number of me looking surprised, sitting on a rock, and Bernie would not find out till later that his tiny offering could have been of anybody. I never did get a reply from the sixth, but he lived in a place called Mobile, and I was not the least bit sorry later at not having to visit it.

As I stuck on the airmail stamps the telephone rang. There was silence the other end, but the sort of silence when you know for certain that you are not alone on the line.

Please God, I prayed, don't let it be another cerebral flasher. Last time it happened the disturbed character on the other end said he was a doctor doing a survey and would I like to tell him what I thought about when I masturbated. After two more of his calls on similar subjects it was suggested by the telephone gurus that I either change my number or encourage him to talk more to enable them to get a fix on his whereabouts. I chose the former.

'Milla,' Marcus asked at length, cautiously, 'is that you?' (Was it possible that he had forgotten how I sounded when I said hello?)

My heart began the usual rapid rhythm as I heard

his voice. 'Of course it's me. Why are you talking so quietly?' (Could it be that the poison dwarf had just left the room?)

'I forgot your birthday again.'

'Goodness, did you?' (sarcastically).

'I'm sorry.'

'I accept your apology' (nicer).

'Did you get your car repaired?'

'Yes.' This was getting boring.

'You haven't sent me the bill.' He was talking more urgently now, Angie must have been coming back.

'Don't worry, I will.'

'Yes, do. Well, goodbye, Milla.'

'Goodbye, Marcus.'

I threw all six letters on to the floor, shouting damn, damn, damn, and Kat leaped from the top of the computer (where I was convinced she got a buzz from the static) and beat it through the office door.

Why did Marcus have to do this to me? It was exactly what I meant about not being able to get over a break-up because you weren't allowed to grieve in peace.

For a week I had hardly been hurting. I'd put my mind to my new job, I'd stuck by my lunch date with Gus and resisted the urge to stand him up. Daisy Tibbs had sold two of my articles, I'd received some money and I'd bought some new clothes. And I was working hard at getting Marcus into the correct pigeon-hole in my mind (I never expected to get him out of it). Gus had offered to counsel me and I had agreed to let him. ('It take time, dear lady in red, but for sure you will get there.')

And now that thoughtless ex-husband of mine had the crassness to telephone me and that was me finished and done for. I need not have bothered with trying at all. I looked down at my hands, one clenching at the other.

'Blast you to hell, Marcus Cage,' I cried. 'You're so cruel, so bloody thoughtless . . . so . . . everything.'

I picked the letters up off the floor, threw them on the desk and flew to my closet. Now my night's sleep would be ruined unless I took a pill. And at best I didn't get more than an hour or two before dawn.

I could smell him, I could see him, feel him, hear him. And, dear God, I wanted him so badly suddenly in my heart and in my body it was unbearable. I found his sweater and pulled it on. Then I sat on the floor and opened an antique wooden collar-box I had salvaged at the same time as the sweater and sorted through the secret detritus of cuff-links, evening shirt studs, a signet ring, a crumpled love note he'd once written on my typewriter, a topless fountain pen, a silver toothpick, and, for some reason long forgotten, one half of a black bow-tie.

I wound the tie around my wrist and tied it in a knot, and sat back on my heels smoothing out the love note. It was one of several on-going letters from the early years. Marcus would start it by putting a piece of paper into my typewriter and typing the first line, leaving it in the machine. This note said, Marcus loves Milla and will come home to lunch just to be near her.

Before I left the house that day I added the line, Milla loves Marcus but will be in the gynae stirrups over lunchtime getting her coil removed.

Marcus then added, Because Marcus loves Milla more than ever he'll take her out to dinner. Why removed?

I was in the bath when he came in from the office, soaking my sore tail, but I'd typed another line saying, Milla loves Marcus more than ever too, and that is why she's had her coil removed!

After tearfully feeding Kat, I locked and bolted the front door, poured a long glass of wine and swallowed two Valium that I'd hidden from myself at the back of the bathroom cabinet. I got into bed and Kat settled beside me on the pillow.

It was a long, dreamless night that left me next morning with my head in a vice and fungus growing on my tongue. But I posted the letters and attended to my work and tried not to think about Marcus.

The Lavinia Lomax Marriage Bureau was a world away from Ms Pilbeam's hands-across-the-sea affair. For the serious fee of £1000 Lavinia put lonely people with healthy bank accounts in touch with one another with a view to tying the knot.

Annie Lloyd, alias me, explained her penchant for the American male and her longing to marry again. Lavinia wrote down the details by hand in a large ledger and I settled back in the comfy armchair provided.

'Could I interest you in a rather nice viscount?' she asked.

Would a pig like to fly, I nearly answered, and it must have shown on my face because she laughed in a way that should have been set to music.

'Naturally he's not from America, but you never know, he may change your mind.'

I had to think. Diana, the boss, had said Yanks only. But cutting my molars on a viscount wouldn't be such a bad idea, now would it?

Lavinia looked at me from under her lovely dark lashes.

'He's sixty-five, but I must say he doesn't look it. He's tall and quite good-looking, and he still has his hair. He has a large house in Fulham and a castle in County Wicklow.'

It all sounded hunky-dory to me.

'Why don't you let me arrange a dinner date?' she said. 'He'll take you to the Savoy, I'm sure. And I seem to remember him saying that he owned a Rolls Royce.'

It still sounded okay, but why should a Rolls Royce-owning viscount with a castle in Ireland and his own hair want to pay out money to find a mate? I wondered.

Anyway, what the hell, at sixty-five he sounded safe. I had to start somewhere and he'd be William's idea of someone to have dinner with. Also, an English viscount wanting to buy a wife might be an interesting way of rounding off a TV programme.

'Done,' I said, smiling sweetly at Lavinia and moving on to my next appointment.

Priscilla, at Introductions for Discerning People, was an ace businesswoman, showing plenty of leg, wearing a tight black skirt topped off with a fine white silk shirt, cuff-links, and large pearl stud earrings.

'We don't mess about here,' she said, flashing an enormous instant smile. 'If we fail to fix you up in six months we send you away to paddle your own canoe. But that almost never happens.'

'Fair enough,' Annie Lloyd answered, thankful that her fix-up was only a job of work.

'I have a delightful young man from Boston, temporarily living over here,' she continued. 'A trifle younger than you, but very handsome. I think that you should meet him.'

She pushed the Terms of Agreement form under my nose.

'How much of a trifle younger?' I asked.

Priscilla gazed in a businesslike way at the details on the computer screen before her.

'He's thirty-five. You'll hardly be a cradle-snatcher.'

I experienced a moment of alarm. Thirty-five sounded very young to a mother of three voting-age children.

'What does he do?' I asked, mostly to give myself thinking time.

'He goes to the City every day,' she said nonchalantly.

(So does the number 94 bus, Annie should have said, but she had no more bottle than I did.)

'May I give him your telephone number and then you

can start right away?' Priscilla said, edging her chair away discreetly from her director's desk.

Start what right away? I very nearly shook my head, but then I thought about Diana's wrath if I did, remembered the rather handsome salary I was working for, and agreed.

It had been quite a day. I opened a bottle of Château Latour 1980, one of three that Marcus had forgotten to take when he packed up, and took it with a glass to my bed. Alcohol in bed was becoming a habit.

I was a real working girl now, a hoofer, not one of the walking wounded. I was an active trouper, like the content of the assignment or not. And right then, it beat the hell out of sitting at home writing with only the cat for company. Six agencies had Annie Lloyd on their books, four contacts were in the bag, and six letters would drop into six US of A mail boxes at any given moment.

It was hardly the undertaking that would collect a Woman of the Year Award, but it was good honest work (well, almost honest). And maybe, I thought, when Marcus saw my name in the list of credits as he watched the programme on TV he might wish that we could start over being married.

It was a typical English summer's day, dull, windy and cold. I put on a brown winter skirt and a cream silk shirt under my one and only designer jacket. Surely that was good enough for lunch at the Ritz (or was it the Savoy?) with a viscount.

Ludgrove (I never did learn his first name) had telephoned. He had a frightful stammer and sounded older than Lavinia had said. Still, upwards and onwards, I was on my way, having persuaded him, with the sixth sense that made Marcus call me a witch, to make it lunch instead of dinner.

I motored to Fulham, and found the square where he lived to be rather rundown. The gardens in the centre were an obvious haven for dogs and the houses had long since succumbed to the results of neglect. There didn't seem to be a number 29 and I was annoyed with myself for the feelings of relief I felt. It meant that I could return home without a sense of guilt.

I had driven past the house three times without knowing it. Graffiti blurred the number on the gateless entrance and the house itself looked derelict. (Even in down-town Montego Bay it would have looked derelict.)

I would have chickened out on the last lap of the square and sped away had not a tiny old man like a gnome leaped into the road outside number 29 and flagged me down. Obviously, he was the old retainer, and anyway, didn't lots of aristocrats live in rundown houses and never give them a lick of paint or a new front gate?

I drove into the circular rutted driveway, careful not to run over the old retainer as he wildly indicated where he wanted me to park, and I pulled up behind a filthy van that had wooden blocks supporting the rear axle where the wheels should have been. There was no Rolls Royce around, and no garage in which it could be safely hiding.

The old boy hobbled forward on shoes so large that either they belonged to someone else (the viscount perhaps?) or they were orthopaedic specials. His fraying grey flannel suit had soup stains down the front and the collar of his blue checked shirt showed a brown rim. The six or seven white hairs on his otherwise bald head were sent skywards in the wind, giving him the cartoon look of a startled elf.

To my surprise he gripped both my hands in his as I stepped from my car and seemed to be trying to say something. 'Th-th-thank you f-f-for coming, A-A-A' ('Annie' I said for him), and he guided me towards a

front door from which the paint had peeled a dec-
ade ago.

I did my best to appraise the situation. Could this poor
old bundle of rags possibly be the viscount's father? In
which case that would make him an earl, impoverished
though he was, and I would voice the opinion when I met
the viscount that he should take more care of his pater.

He shuffled me past the front door and headed for the
side of the house and a basement entrance at the foot of
a set of dirty, steep stone steps, half-covered in moss and
mildew.

'C-c-careful,' he said, 'the-the steps are a t-t-t-trifle
d-dangerous.'

The door was stuck at the base. Elfman gave a draconian
chuckle, steadied himself against the frame and kicked it
free with the toe of his boot. It was then that I noticed
the length of his fingernails, so overgrown that they
resembled claws.

The gloom in what I supposed was the entrance hall
was consummate. He took my reluctant hand into his
ice-cold one and tugged me into the darkness. How can
the landed gentry keep their servants in such a place? I
asked myself. They wouldn't keep a self-respecting gun
dog in it, even though it did smell like a kennel.

Ludgrove's father, the old retainer (whatever) gave up
flicking at a discoloured brass light switch beside the door.

'T-t-tiresome,' he said, 'there d-doesn't seem to be any
electricity today.'

We staggered on with my eyes becoming accustomed
to the gloaming, and as we entered a room at the end of
the long hall my partner fruitlessly flicked at yet another
light switch.

'Welcome to my d-d-drawing-r-room,' he said with the
panache of a king, 'my sons let me l-live down here,
they've let the rest of the house as s-something strange
called b-bed-sits.'

I decided there and then that I was definitely going to have a word with the viscount about these awful conditions. I could not think of anything to say in answer, so I coughed, which wasn't difficult, helped as I was by the dust. One can hardly comment favourably on a room that resembles a pig-pen, can one?

Old rugs were thrown over two decrepit settees and the dirty carpet covering the concrete floor was down to the string. In the fireless black iron grate sat dried flowers heavy with dust and age, nestled between a set of antique andirons. In front of them there was a two-bar, well-aged electric fire with its frayed flex disappearing behind an old armchair sagging dangerously in the seat.

'Have you lived here long?' I asked eventually when I saw that he was staring at me hopefully, with his hands cupped behind his ears to catch the sound, in the manner of someone hard of hearing.

'F-fifty years,' he answered, moving towards a nasty-looking metal trolley on which stood several near-empty bottles and one beautiful antique crystal decanter containing three fingers of a dark brown liquid.

'Would you c-care for a sherry?' he asked, stammering less as his confidence grew.

I nodded my head. What else could I do to a seriously deaf old man who, I began to realize, read lips?

He handed me a small liqueur glass half-full of the brown gravy from the decanter. 'S-sit down, d-dear girl,' he said.

I'd hoped that he wouldn't invite me to do that, the settees for sure were on the point of collapse. I sat down gingerly and so did he, facing me at close quarters.

He raised his glass. 'G-God bless you. Shall we drink to a l-lasting r-r-relationship?'

Wait a minute, hold it there, I said to myself, freeze the frame while I think. Could there possibly be the remotest chance that this bundle of old bones was the

71

viscount himself? Get away, not a hope. Lavinia would never have put this person sitting before me now into that important-looking ledger.

He patted my knee and gave a chronically wheez-ing laugh. 'You th-thought I was y-y-younger, didn't you?'

(And that's the very least of it, old buddy!)

'Um, well . . .'

'Hee, hee, hee,' he wheezed, 'we c-certainly fooled that l-lady called L-Lavinia. Just a h-harmless l-lark, you understand.'

Some lark. Lavinia was lucky I didn't carry a mobile phone in my bag like the phoney power ladies do or I would have been punching out her number there and then.

'N-no point in saying I was eighty-three n-now, was there?'

I looked him in the eye as he scratched at the long lobe of his ear with his claws.

'You didn't go yourself to the agency, d-did you?' (He had me stammering now.)

He slapped his bony thighs. He was convulsed with laughter and his yellow teeth rattled. 'Th-that was my younger brother. G-good-looking d-devil. I m-m-must confess. I was amazed wh-when his ch-cheque didn't bounce.'

He jumped up with surprising ease, grabbed my glass and clattered over to the trolley to dispense two spots more of the sherry.

It was then that I saw, dulled with years of grime, the large painting on the wall of a very beautiful woman dressed in the fashion of the twenties.

'Is the beautiful painting of your wife?' I asked.

'God bless her, yes.' He turned, and held out his glass towards her. 'She died riding to hounds two years after that painting was finished. Bounder of a horse clipped a gate. They both broke their necks. All very sad.' He didn't stammer once while talking about her.

'Wouldn't you be happier in your castle in County Wicklow?' I asked him before, hopefully, I could excuse myself and run. No way was I going to risk driving up to the Savoy with this old tramp, even if the Rolls Royce did exist.

'Oh, th-that's long s-since gone, d-dear girl. But you American wo-women will do anything for a t-title.' He squeezed my knee. 'You are American, are you n-not?'

I had this desperate urge to bolt. 'Actually, no.'

I stood up, so did Ludgrove.

'You're not l-leaving me, are you? We are g-going for a sp-spot of lunch? Lavinia p-promised.'

The mother in me settled it. I had to get out fast and breathe some fresh air, the smell and the gloom were getting to my brain and unravelling me, but I'd have to take him with me. He looked so pathetic standing there with his head hanging down and a dewdrop of mucus at the end of his nose. And if he'd been promised, how could I leave him behind?

'All right,' I said briskly. 'But can we go now?'

He straightened his stringy knitted tie, smoothed back his few white hairs and did a little jig.

'I've booked at a d-darling little place in the High Street. The c-cod is the best you'll ever t-taste. Chips are g-good too . . .'

As we passed each light switch he flicked at it again in the vain hope that some electricity was seeping through.

'Your car or mine?' I asked.

He took my arm. 'Oh, bless your heart, I haven't owned a c-car since the w-war. Can't park 'em anywhere in L-London, my sons tell me.'

We walked. I felt the urge to hurry and he clattered beside me keeping up. As we reached the restaurant I noticed that the dewdrop was dropping and his nose was deep red.

He attempted with grace and breeding to hold the door open for me. But the spring was too highly sprung, and I ended up holding my weight against it to prevent us both from being crushed.

A waitress with a cloth over her shoulder came within earshot.

'T-table for t-two, dear girl. I have booked, I'm Viscount Ludgrove,' he said with a mien that would have sufficed at Maxims.

'Oh yair, an' I'm Madonna,' she answered. She then called to another waitress, 'There's an old codger 'ere says 'e's royalty.'

The other waitress came up to us and smiled into Ludgrove's face. 'You are royalty, 'ain't you, luv? Usual table?'

The Viscount followed her like a King Charles spaniel with me in his wake. He pulled out a bentwood chair and waited for me to be seated. The pink oilcloth on the table was patterned with large red roses. The chairs were decidedly uncomfortable and I wondered if they would hurt the old boy's fleshless buttocks.

'Did that w-waitress say her n-name was Madonna?' he asked me. 'Pretty n-name, what?'

The menu stood ramrod-straight in a metal stand. As the viscount pulled it out it became slightly stuck and the stand clattered to the floor.

He took an old and frayed spectacle case from his breast-pocket and tremblingly took out a pair of gold-rimmed spectacles of the kind with wire pieces to fold around the ears. They seemed made for a larger man.

'H-have the p-pea soup, dear heart,' he said, 'it's s-simply delicious.' He ordered what he called his usual wine and it came in a screwtopped bottle. It was urine-yellow, and do I need to mention how it tasted?

The pea soup could have been spread on bread. But Ludgrove secured his pink paper napkin under his chin and tucked in as though it were nursery porridge. I did what I could with mine, but pea was never my favourite. Then the viscount asked if he might finish it, and dropped a large gob into his lap.

The cod and chips were pretty good, and the scoffing of them by my partner was uneventful apart from the battle of wills he had with the top of the ketchup bottle. I was suddenly starving and so there were no scraps left on my plate for him to finish this time.

He appeared to be in seventh heaven. 'You m-must have the b-banana split, old thing,' he said. 'It's a poem.'

His hand was resting on the oilcloth. I placed mine on top, feeling the dry skin and arthritic joints beneath my palm. He curled with pleasure at my touch. Did no one show him affection? I wondered. Didn't his children care?

'You're very kind, but really, I couldn't. I don't have room.'

If I had known what was in store for me I might have persuaded him that he was full too.

He had asked for extra cream, and when it came his plate was awash with the stuff. He tried to cut through the unripe banana with his spoon. I grabbed a knife and tried to cut it for him. He carried on eating, which only added to the drama. Cream trickled from his chin on to his tie, and I stared in disbelief as his glasses fell off his face and into the middle of his cream-flooded plate.

'Don't move,' I shouted, and then added, 'Please.' I snatched paper napkins from wherever they lay on unused tables and took a jug of water from nearby. Ludgrove sat quietly as though I were his nanny and he was about to get a thrashing. I retrieved the cream-soaked specs and dropped them into the jug of water, then tried to clean him up. He was now stammering badly and trying to apologize. I crooned as softly as I was able that there was nothing to worry about. (I was overheated and overventilating, but that was my problem.) Then I washed his face, dried his specs and returned them to his nose. He was back into his pudding before I could say 'Cut your banana with a knife.'

For a respite and to get the smell of cream off my fingers and a blob of it from my jacket, I retired to the ladies' lavatory. I sat on the loo lid, leaned my head against the wall and seriously considered absconding.

When I returned to our table I found him counting out numerous coins from a tiny black twist-top purse. I wondered if I should offer to go dutch. But as though reading my mind, the waitress waiting to be paid looked at me and said as an aside, 'You have to let the poor old bugger keep his dignity, don't you? But it must be a trial for you looking after him. Is he your father?'

I decided not to tell her that he was my blind date from a top dating agency. If she'd believed me, she might have sold the rights to the story to the press. (But just you wait, Lavinia Lomax, till I reach home.)

As I delivered him to his side door, he leaped through the air like a fawn, made a grab at me and pulled my head down towards his own. I felt his sour, dry lips on mine before I could pull away. He was smiling at me I suppose, but his top row of false teeth had parted from his gums, making him resemble a gargoyle.

'I l-l-love the l-ladies, I w-wish you w-would come in. We could play the schoolroom game,' he said as he moved against me and reached up my skirt. I felt the claws on my thigh, and grabbing his hand, held firm.

'I'm going now, and you just behave,' I said crossly, only just managing not to wag a finger.

He leered again. 'Only if you p-promise to take me out again. Tea t-tomorrow, ah y-yes, t-tea tomorrow . . .'

Promise him anything and get the hell out, the inner voice said. I noticed a face appear at an open window on the second floor. 'What's the wicked old devil up to this time?' the woman called down, and laughed.

'Tea then, next week,' I lied as I locked myself into the car.

'I l-love l-ladies,' he called to me as I narrowly missed a cyclist while reversing out of the driveway.

When I straightened up the wheel and headed at a fair lick down the road, I could see the viscount through my rear-view mirror. He was standing in the road blowing kisses to the woman in the window. Then suddenly he stopped, bent over, and appeared to be searching the ground.

Well, he hadn't been wearing a solid gold pocket-watch that might have hit the tarmac. Could it then, by any chance, have been his top teeth, do you suppose?

FIVE

It had been a bloody and revealing quarrel in Diana's office. She'd called the meeting for eight in the morning, and as I hadn't slept all night, it showed.

'I've made an appointment for you with Marriages Made in Heaven,' she said, not looking at me. 'It's an Australian agency, I've decided we'll try that angle too.'

'Fine,' I answered nodding listlessly in approval.

'You're not recruiting men quickly enough,' she said across her vast desk, lighting up at the same time.

This put me on the defensive because it was unfair. 'I'm doing my best,' I answered.

She fixed me with her china-blue eyes. 'You haven't put your mind to the job enough. You know that there's a November deadline.'

I could feel my face flushing, she could be such a cow. 'Then maybe you should find someone else. I can't force the Yanks to answer my letters. A thing like this takes time to get going.'

She switched tack to the personal and blew smoke out of her nostrils. 'And look at you, you're a mess. Have you been up all night?'

I didn't think I looked that terrible. But the insult hit home and I smoothed my hair and tucked it behind my ears. 'Not all night. But I had another phone call from Marcus after I'd turned in, and it upset me.'

Diana drew on her cigarette extra deeply. 'Jesus H. Christ,' she said. 'I thought that this man Gus, or whatever his name is, was helping you to let go of your past. Or are you incapable of doing that?'

I was beginning to tremble, with rage really, more than fear. How dare she think that she could speak to me like that?

'He is helping me, and don't say his name like that. God, you can make anything sound like an insult.'

She kept her eyes on my face and did not even blink. 'Shall I give you something to hurry the process of recovery?' she said. 'From one good friend to another?'

I could feel doom approaching. My anger was being replaced with foreboding. 'I don't think I know what you mean.'

She took another drag and leaned forward. 'This is not giving me pleasure to say, Milla, but Marcus was not faithful to you for years. Everyone knew. I'm only amazed that you didn't.'

My first reaction was to leap out of the window. My second was to leap on Diana, close my hands around her throat, and squeeze.

'That is not true. You're trying to upset me,' I yelled.

'Milla, look at me.' She waited for me to lift my eyes to her face. 'Do you want me to name names?'

I shook my head and thought that I might be sick. She was destroying the last threads that held my universe together and the pain was unbearable.

'How do you know?' I hated myself for asking, and longed to say that it didn't matter.

She stubbed out her cigarette, and the smell, so early in the morning, was horrendous. 'Everyone knows. Get wise, Milla, grow up. Why do you think I told you to bury him?'

I hated myself for asking the next question. 'Even my

kids?' If this was heartbreak it was the worst kind of agony I had ever experienced.

The telephone rang and she reached out towards it, hovering for a moment with her hand over the mouthpiece. 'I suspect they know. But I suggest you don't try to corner them, it will only work against you.'

While she was in conversation on the telephone I walked out. My driving, going home, was appalling.

Going up in the lift those slow six floors I began to shake. The doors were barely open before I thrust myself out. Inside my flat I slammed the front door shut, threw my bag on a chair and headed for my wardrobe.

Rage, I think, is what I felt the most. But the pain I felt in my chest seemed to herald a heart attack. I found the sweater and began to wrench it apart. I hurt my hands. I used my teeth till they hurt too. The wretched thing would not tear. Blinded with anger and emotion, I snatched up a pair of long pointed scissors kept for sewing, then I hacked, cut and stabbed at the sweater. I nicked my thumb in the process quite badly but I did not stop until that sweater, and all that it meant, was in shreds. Then I started on the old wooden collar-box.

'You enjoy *Hamlet*?' Gus asked during our post-theatre supper.

'Yes, very much. Thank you for taking me.' I was so comfortable with him I felt like purring.

'Then I take you to Denmark. You not know *Hamlet* till you see it performed at Elsinore.'

I tucked my hand into his on our seat against the wall. 'You spoil me,' I said.

He touched my cheek. 'I like to spoil you, I want make you happy. And I not see enough of you now you have new secret job of work.'

I knew that I would spend the night with him if he asked. It would be our first, and God alone knew what

I would be like, but I desperately needed someone to be close to. I wanted to be hugged, clutched to a warm chest, kissed with loving lips. Now that I knew about Marcus, well, things were changing. It was the beginning of the next part of my life, like it or not . . .

Two letters from the States were through the letterbox next morning when I arrived home. Two messages were on my answerphone, and the telephone was ringing. I picked it up.

'Is that Annie Lloyd?'

I hesitated and nearly asked, 'Who?'

'Yes, speaking.'

'I'm Edward Anderson from Boston. Sorry for the delay in calling, I had to make a trip home.'

'Umm,' I said, after a short silence while I tried to get my mind around the name.

'Priscilla from Introductions for Discerning People said I may call you. Have I reached you at an inconvenient moment?'

'Oh yes, right, no. I mean, it isn't inconvenient at all.' What a voice. He sounded like a young John F. Kennedy.

'Well, gee, that's great. Can I meet you for drinks, tonight?'

I checked my nervous giggle in time. 'So soon?'

'Why waste time?'

'I'm busy tonight,' I lied. 'Can we make it tomorrow?'

I hadn't slept a wink in Gus's bed and I needed an early night. It had not been Gus's fault, he was tender and attentive. But for me it was like committing adultery.

'Sure,' Edward Anderson said. 'Shall I pick you up?'

Was he kidding? No way, with a pseudonym I was not yet used to was I going to reveal my address.

'It would be better for me if I meet you somewhere. I have a business meeting.'

'Where?'

'Knightsbridge,' I quickly lied. It was far enough away to be safe.

'Okay, then, 59 Basil Street,' he drawled, Bostonianlike. 'It's a cute wine bar.'

'How shall I know you?' (God, was this really me talking?)

'I'll be the tall, good-looking guy in a grey suit, a sombre tie and a blue shirt.' (Was he making a joke, expecting me to laugh, or was he being forthright American?)

'You forgot to say a modest, good-looking guy.'

'I like your humour. What will you be wearing?' (His voice was to die for.)

'Um, oh dear, let's say a beige dress and a brown jacket' (and let's hope the jacket is ready for collection at the dry cleaner's and that the gob of cream has been successfully removed).

'Can't wait to see you,' he drawled. 'Bye bye.'

I returned the call made by a lady called Lydia from Marriages Made in Heaven.

'Annie, dear,' the treacle-voiced Lydia said, 'I just wanted to know if I may send your particulars to a lonely sheep farmer in New South Wales?'

'Why not?' I answered, feeling safe with Australia being on the other side of the planet.

'If he likes the look of you, you'll have to go over there. Naturally, he will pay your fare one way. And you never know, you might like him so much you won't want to come back.' (Lydia, oh Lydia, if you only knew.) 'I'll read you his particulars. He's six feet tall (aren't they all?), slim, and fair-skinned' (in case I thought he was an aborigine?). 'Oh,' she continued, 'and he's divorced. So no problems with a dead wife who'd be a hard act to follow.'

I knew that I must say something, anything really, just to make myself sound genuine.

'A sheep farmer?' I said.

'Yes, dear. But don't worry, he doesn't have corks round his hat.' She laughed. (Corks round his hat? Was that meant to be a joke?)

'He's handsome, I assure you.'

'Oh, you've seen him?' (I wasn't going to forget Viscount Ludgrove in a hurry.)

'No, Annie' (patiently), 'our agent in Australia has interviewed him. He says he's quite cultured, for an Aussie.'

(No kidding, the sheep farmer would be pleased to hear that.)

'Oh, and Annie, I've just read on these particulars that he likes candelit dinners for two. So you see, he sounds romantic.'

'Either that or he doesn't have electricity.' (Was it my tiredness that was making me so scratchy?)

'His grandfather came from Somerset, England. That's probably why he likes English women,' Lydia volunteered.

'Either that, or he thinks they're less likely to make a run for it than a cute little lady from Sydney.'

'I don't follow?'

'You know, twelve thousand miles and most of it water.' (Forget I ever mentioned it, Lydia.) She was not bringing the best out in me, patronizing cow.

I returned Diana's call.

'Hello, Milla. Just checking that you've forgiven your best friend.'

'No, I haven't.'

She blew out smoke with such force I wanted to move away from the receiver. 'But you will. You seem to have been busy, your line's engaged all the time. Maybe you need a second phone.'

I switched to my freephone and walked with it to the kitchen in order to make a badly needed mug of coffee. 'I'm attending to our business, like the boss said.'

There was a second of silence. For all her business-woman front, she didn't really like me sounding cold. 'That's good news, tell me about it.'

I tucked the telephone into my shoulder and filled the kettle. 'There's a lonely divorced sheep farmer in New South Wales wants a châtelaine.'

'Did you say randy?'

'No, I said lonely. If he was randy I would already have passed him on to you.'

She ignored the trivial slight. 'So when are you leaving?'

I spooned coffee into the pot. 'We won't know if he likes the look of me till he gets the photographs. And I'm not going at all unless I'm guaranteed my own bed on arrival, and assurance that I won't be asked to help muster the goddamn sheep. And I get my return fare paid by you.'

I could almost smell the smoke this time when she exhaled.

'But supposing he wants to send you a first-class ticket right away? I'm sure they've faxed your particulars to him. It costs a lot of money to get to Australia, you know.'

Good old Diana, she thought God himself owned a fax machine. I poured boiling water on to the coffee. 'And a lot more to get back. Especially if the donor doesn't want you to leave.'

'But, Milla . . .'

I took a new mug off the hook on the wall. 'No, Di, a deal is a deal. You provide my ticket or I don't go.'

Diana backed off. 'So what else have you to tell me?'

I took my time. 'Well, I've had replies from two of Ms Pilbeam's men in the States. Haven't had time to read them yet, though, I'll do that when we finish talking. And tomorrow night I'm dating the young man from Boston I told you about.'

(If my kids could only hear me now, I thought. Socialite dinners were one thing. But blind dating in wine bars, their mother? They would have apoplexy.)

'Did he phone you?'

'Yes.' I poured out the black, steaming brew. The aroma made my throat tingle.

'How was his voice? Sexy?'

'As John F. Kennedy's.'

'My God, I wish I was the one going to meet him,' she said with envy.

I took my mug to the kitchen table, and pulled out a chair. 'You can go in my place if you like, you'd be good at blind-dating a younger man. Good at visiting wine bars, too . . .'

The first letter I opened was from Charlie Diamond in Carolina. I did not like the tone of it. Ms Pilbeam would be getting a call from me . . .

The second one spewed out a heap of snaps, and a short note saying he would write again soon, and instructing me to be sure to read the details on the reverse sides. There was Bradford Delman strolling in Central Park, in the snow, unless the light had played tricks. And then there he was painting at his easel, black French beret *et al.* A sideways-on closeup, a smiling-into-the-camera pose, wearing a funny hat at a Christmas party . . . it just went on . . . (but I thought he'd said he looked like Clint Eastwood?).

I parked my car and found the wine bar. Bodies were packed in wall to wall, smoke hung in a yellow smog just above the crowd, and girls screeched into each other's ears. All the men looked like City whiz kids and most of them wore dark grey suits, sombre ties and blue shirts. Every glass in sight contained red wine, and apart from a gay barman I was sure that I was the oldest person there.

An extremely young man came towards me out of the gloom. He had the figure of a male model and the face of an angel. 'Annie Lloyd?' he asked.

At that moment I felt really old, older even than I was. And what about my dress, nearly to the knees? All the Sloane Rangers propping up the bar wore skirts so short they resembled pelmets.

'I'm Edward, Ed if you like, but don't let my mother hear you.' He offered his hand in greeting. 'One hell of a crowd in here tonight.'

I licked my drying lips. 'Yes, it is rather a crowd.' (Especially for an old broad like me who's not used to places like this.)

'Why don't we stroll to the hotel bar up the road?' he said. 'It will be more pleasant for you there.' (Since you are so old and your skirt is so long?)

Later, I puzzled whether it was three Brandy Alexanders I drank in each bar we visited, or only two. Whichever, I had drunk too much. He put me in a taxi for home, and paid the driver. Now I would have to get up early and go back to collect my car.

I made a late-night snack, not having eaten in twelve hours, in the hope that it would save me from a hangover. What a heavenly boy he was, I thought with my first mouthful. If only I were younger. If only he were older.

'You're not thirty-five, are you?' I asked him in the second bar we visited.

Without flinching he said, 'If I had said I was twenty-five and preferred older women the agency would probably not have taken me on. And then I would not have met you.'

It was probably the first time I'd been called an older woman to my face, but he said it so warmly I found I didn't mind.

'And now, here we are drinking happily together. So you see, I was right not to tell. You're very attractive, Annie.'

Why did I get the feeling he almost added 'for your age'?

'So are most of the young girls you see around,' I said. 'And they don't need to worry about using moisturizer.' I sipped my drink.

'You have a very good figure,' he said. (He really did feel I needed boosting.)

'Better if I took up jogging.'

'Do you play tennis?'

'Yes, yes,' I said enthusiastically, 'I used to play for my school and I've kept it up ever since.'

'Good, we'll play at my club.'

At his club? In that case, I would need to buy some new tennis shoes. Shirt as well. Oh, yes, and my shorts were pretty ragged . . .

'My mother says having me ruined her figure,' he said. 'She hasn't eaten a thing since I was born.'

I could just see her, the anorexic American pampered wife. The Nancy Reagan of the East Coast.

In the street he said, before hailing a cab, 'Can I see you again, Annie? I really do like you.'

I was light-headed, I hadn't eaten since my breakfast cereal. And now, thanks to alcohol, I couldn't remember questioning him for my report for Diana. And come to think of it, I hadn't remembered to switch on my secret mini-tape recorder either.

'Can you afford me?' I asked with the boldness of a drunk. 'Sometimes I need to eat, you know.'

He blushed. 'Oh my, I'm sorry, I forgot. My mother would be so ashamed of me. Would you like dinner now?'

I felt unsteady on my feet. 'Next time, I really must go.' I was sure that I was slurring my words.

He called to a passing taxi, and as it executed a tight U-turn in the road he said, 'I'm not short of money, the folks have plenty, and I work for my old man. He's in oil.'

What a catch for a nice young girl, I thought from where I slouched in the back of the taxi. Perhaps I should introduce him to Katie. We could do with some money in the family.

Surely it was the middle of the night? The telephone was ringing. While I worked out first who I was, then where I was, the answerphone took over.

Nursing my aching head and worried that it might mean trouble (mothers always think of disaster in the night), I staggered to my office and listened to the message. After atmospherics and a short silence a deep, sexual voice said, 'Hello, this is Bradford Delman at twenty-two hundred hours New York time. I hope you received my reply to your letter. I will be calling again. *Ciao.*'

I staggered back to bed.

It was a happy sort of a dream. Church bells were ringing and Katie was walking down the isle in a froth of white lace on the arm of Edward Anderson . . .

I woke up just enough to feel the hammers pounding in my brain, and I opened my eyes with caution. The bells were still ringing. I made a grab for the phone and knocked it clean off the bedside table. I could have fought off an elephant at a watering hole for a long cool drink. And if this call was from Dizzy Tits telling me it was time I was up and getting on with my day, I would certainly kill her.

'Hello, is that Annie Lloyd?'

'No, it's her sister.' (Who the hell was this?)

There was a pause and noisy static on the line. 'I think you're putting me on. You Brits have a strange sense of humour. This is Bradford Delman, but you can call me Brad.'

'What time is it, Brad?' (What a stupid question to ask someone in New York whose phone was eating dollar bills.)

'Well, here in New York I have three in the morning. Guess that makes it eight for you.'

'I thought it was the middle of the night. I was having this lovely dream . . .' (Get your head together, woman, and say something intelligent.)

'Lucky you, honey. Would you like me to call back later? I get the feeling you just don't have it together yet.'

I was awake now. I sat up straight and wished I could ask him to wait while I fetched water. 'Yes, I mean no' (he'd called twice already without getting me). 'It's nice of you to call.'

'I have your letter here beside me. I like your turn of phrase, and you look cute in your picture.'

Cute, indeed. I'd never been called that before. And what should I talk about? I already knew that he didn't actually look like Clint Eastwood. So was it likely that he really had an open-plan apartment with a view of the Hudson River? But he did have a voice like Burt Reynolds', as it happened. Not that I much cared, if I couldn't get to water quickly, I might pass out.

'May I call you back? My, um, doorbell is ringing.'

He was laughing, and that sounded like Burt Reynolds too. 'May you? Gee, honey, you Brits sure have a quaint way of talking. Sure you can. I'll expect your call. *Ciao*.'

Things were really happening now, and I was very busy. Marcus telephoned to ask me out to dinner, to show we are now friends, like intelligent people, he said.

Intelligent people my eye, I wasn't going to fall for that one. Much more likely he was tiring of the poison dwarf

and it would look smart to have an ex-wife on his list
of new conquests. But he'd drop me pdq when the next
big-eyed blonde came along, now that he was in bimbo
mode. And no way could I handle it, now that I was trying
to keep my love for him down to a sensible level. And,
anyway, I was beginning to see him differently since all
was revealed by Diana.

I promised to return his call when I'd consulted my
diary and moved a few appointments, I said. I was rather
busy at the moment . . .

He couldn't stop the sarcasm that entered his tight,
sharp laugh. Be sure to make the call to the office, he
said. Not on your life, boyo, I thought. Not after the way
you've made me suffer. I'll write you a letter to your flat,
and say I've no time to have dinner at the moment, but
thanks. And serve him right if the awful Angie opened it.
She was probably the type who would. I could just picture
her with the envelope held to the steaming kettle.

And all my juices were flowing as I listened to his voice.
Was there no justice?

Then there was Edward. He wanted to take me to bed
and, dare I tell you, I wanted to go. He was virile and sexy,
and what more could a woman in her forties ask for?

But hold it there, just for a moment, ma'am. Whatever
happened to the woman who only three months ago
would have joined a holy order rather than contem-
plate sex with anyone but Marcus? And what had
happened to the constant nag that if he ever found
out about another man he would never come back?
I couldn't answer that but I genuinely wanted him
to come back to me. So maybe it would be better
to think about it next week. And in the meantime,
surely, sex with a younger man would help me to
decide?

Well, hold on then again for a spell. This was just a
job of work, I wasn't compelled to sleep with the clients,

and hadn't I made it clear to Diana that I would not be doing that?

But Diana had said I was to do it my way. And I didn't intend to sleep with the clients. Jesus, there were six of them over in the States, and at least one in Australia. No way would I sleep with any of them.

Just with Edward, he was here, in England, and he was different. And we both agreed, it didn't feel as though we'd met through an agency.

As for Gus, he was just a dear friend, and that was different too. I was so lucky to have met Gus, he was healing me. And I probably would not sleep with him so very often . . .

My latest report for Diana was due to be faxed by mid-afternoon, and I had invited the kids over for supper. I had to tell them, just in case, that I was working on an away assignment, not saying what or where of course. Supper meant buying food, going to the wine shop, and, mustn't forget, going to the pharmacy. I had to go back on the Pill, and fast . . .

But first, I had to telephone Ms Hands Across the Sea Pilbeam. I switched on my tape recorder and attached a suction-pad mike to the receiver.

She spoke into the phone in her usual holy whisper. 'Annie, what can I do for you?'

'I would like you to listen to this letter I've received from one of your American Gentlemen, Charlie Diamond in South Carolina. You said he was a particularly lovely man. Personally, I find his letter pretty offensive.'

There was a long silence. Obviously Ms P. was not sure that she wanted to hear it. 'Oh, surely you must be mistaken, Annie?'

I took a long breath. 'This is what he wrote:

' "Dear Ms Lloyd, I dunno who you think you are, some smart-arse writer calling me Charlie and making like you already know me. I know about women like you. I guess it's because I was married to one for thirty years, an then y'all know what she did? She ran off with a preacher. An' as if that weren't bad enough the goddamn preacher was a nigger. I'd a had him strung up a few years back. In all probability you're a gold-digger too, just like she was. Money was all that one ever thought about. And they got some from me right enough, her and that nigger a'hers. The judge shoulda been shot, thought about it myself for a whiles. But you won't get nowheres with me, Ms Lloyd. No, sir. I'm gonna tell that goddamn agency they can stuff their two-timing sassie Englishwoman. Dunno who y'all think you are over there. An' I'll tell you this much, before I'd ever consider having you as a bride, I'd need to know the surname you was born with, what town and what county and where your mother was born. I'd be checking up on you real good. For all I know you could have nigger blood in you. You looks pretty damn dark to me in that picture. An' another thing, I'd be needing a recent negative Aids test certificate before I'd be touchin' you with a punter's pole.

"Yours truly, Mr C. Diamond, Senior."'

The silence on the end of the line was heavy. So, Ms Nofirstname Pilbeam, what do you intend to do about that, when you've recovered enough to speak?

'Do you not think it a strange way of communicating?' I asked into the quiet. 'That this man, who takes the trouble to join an agency, should write in this manner to a woman he has never met?'

Ms Pilbeam spoke in her controlled whisper but I knew that she was shaken. 'Yes, it is a little strange. Obviously your letter did not bring out the best in him.'

I was boiling. 'That's rubbish. My letters were all the same, and from everyone else I've had a pleasant reply. This man's a fruitcake. He should have been vetted more carefully.'

Ms Pilbeam's voice switched to bordering on joyful, the cool cow. 'So you see, Annie, he probably liked you really, and your letter reached him on a stressful day . . .'

I was getting mad. 'Stressful my eye. I'm stressed, everybody's stressed. This man is plain unpleasant. He's an ace bigot, and a weirdo. Didn't someone interview him? You told me that an agent always interviewed clients who lived abroad and whom you didn't see personally . . . Miss Pilbeam . . . are you there?' Even saying her name made me feel like throwing up, and Ms P. didn't know it yet, but she could live to regret her attitude.

'Yes, yes, I'm just checking the gentleman's file. Of course our agent went to see him, those are the rules. Ah, yes, I see here that he found him very pleasant.'

'Bullshit, Ms P.'

I knew she would have a hand on her bosom, such as it was. 'Really Annie, you mustn't speak to me like that.' (At least her voice had become normal.) 'I agree that there has been a small mistake, and I shall look into it.'

'Please do,' I said, 'and I shall expect one-sixth of my money back.'

She even had the gall to laugh. 'It isn't the end of the world, you know, Annie. And we do not return money. It says so on the bottom of your contract.'

It might be the end of your world, dear, I said under my breath, when you see it reported on your TV screen. Or was she one of those stupid people who considered any publicity was better than no publicity at all?

I put down the telephone and turned to my word processor. Like it or not, Diana would have to admit that I was on the case and going strong, when I faxed her my report.

I went to my bathroom mirror and studied my reflection. I noticed I wasn't wincing the way I had been doing when I looked at myself.

Wouldn't it be nice if I could start liking myself again? I hadn't liked myself when I was trying to hang on to Marcus's coat-tails after he left me. Nor when I stayed at home to lick my wounds. Or when I was always crying, and certainly not when I was using the children to prop myself up.

But (studying myself more closely) I had to do something about my hair. Straight, squeaky-clean, tied-back, shoulder-length hair had gone out of fashion while I wasn't looking. Now it was time for a change. Selina Scott looked divine with the new feather cut when I saw her picture in a recent magazine. Maybe that style would look good on Annie Lloyd too.

For my part, having the children round to supper was not a raging success. It was my guilt feelings, of course. And family talk was stilted because at the last minute Kate had asked if she could include a new boyfriend. He was a bit quiet, and he didn't drink (a recovering alcoholic, perhaps?). His lack of ease was made worse by Emma describing what happened at her ante-natal classes. At one point she actually got up from the table, squatted on the floor and gave us a demonstration of puffing and pushing. Husband Gareth continued to stuff his face throughout it all, having lived through the scene several times before and seeing it as a great moment to help himself to more food without being noticed. The ears on the new boyfriend turned red, and out in the kitchen Kate begged me to shut her sister up, by whatever method I could think of. I pulled out all the stops – had I explained to them that I would soon be going abroad on a new assignment? They merely nodded yes. I would give them a full itinerary and plenty of warning before leaving. Naturally, they said. What did new boyfriend do for a living, I asked him, all friendly and motherly. I mean, what sort of career – doctor, dustman, lawyer, layabout?

Name it, sonny, for God's sake, we're about to sink. The urgency was wasted on him. He didn't yet have a career, he said, sorry. He was just a student. But he didn't say of what. And I was too exhausted to care. Wills didn't say much all evening. But when they left he squeezed my arm and whispered in my ear, 'Never mind, Mum. You tried hard.'

SIX

At seven o'clock he telephoned. I came out of a deep sleep, and a dream about being driven along the Champs-Elysées in Paris with Marcus, and fumbled for the telephone as it rang unwelcomingly in my ear.

'This is your morning wake-up call,' Brad called down the line, amazingly clearly. 'Not too early, I hope?'

I stretched and, half-asleep, felt good hearing a man's voice. 'Not at all, and it beats the hell out of an alarm clock.'

'I stayed up late especially,' he said, 'and I've written you a letter. I've included some more photographs, so you can see how I look not being formal. There's another one of me in my studio, painting a nude. It's good.'

He had already sent me nineteen snaps, how was that for vanity? I couldn't even blame it on American egotism, since Hunter Lee McNab from Chicago had not sent me a single one. I ignored the remark about the nude painting.

'Thank you, that's very nice.'

'When are you coming over to visit your aunt? I'm kinda getting impatient to know you.'

I used the aunt story for the American men. It gave me a reason for going over and not accepting offers of a ticket.

'I'm waiting to hear from her. I'll let you know, but I'll

probably visit her first.' (My plans were fast forming in my mind.)

'Call me soon, honey. I like to hear your voice. *Ciao.*'

I was in the shower when Edward Anderson called me. 'Just checking that it's still on for tonight. You said you weren't sure if you had to visit the family?'

Did I say that? I must have been trying hard to resist him. 'I'm just out of the shower, I'll call you back. And yes, I'm free tonight.'

'Annie, will you stay with me?'

I tried to wrap a towel around me while I rubbed at my wet, newly shorn head.

'Yes, Edward, I'll stay.' (I had better phone Emma and head her off. She had taken to calling me late, then telling me she stayed awake worrying if I was out.)

The next call was from the travel agent. She had booked a first-class return ticket beginning in Los Angeles, then to Chicago and terminating in New York in fourteen days' time. Would I like insurance (yes, I would) and who would be paying? I gave her Diana's number.

I was at the end of a letter to Tod Bradshaw in Los Angeles when I received a call from Hunter Lee McNab in Chicago.

Hunter was a lawyer. His first wife had divorced him and his second wife had died of cancer three years earlier at the age of forty, he said. His conversation was brisk and to the point and conducted in the manner of delivering a brief. But he seemed nice. He was the only man so far that I felt bad about deceiving. Except perhaps Edward, but he was young, the experience would do him no harm. Hunter said he was pleased that I was coming over, yes, he would get me a hotel room of the best quality and he would meet me at the airport from the Los Angeles plane after I'd been to see my aunt in Beverly Hills, and might he have clear flight details.

The telephone rang again, it was Lydia from Marriages

Made in Heaven. Would I like to go that very day to lunch with an Australian who was passing through London on his way to Ireland? No, he was not the sheep farmer, he was a corporate man from Sydney.

Well, it was my job, and for the sake of the story I got my rear into gear (which included putting a new battery into my tape recorder) and beat it to Soho and the Italian restaurant that was the client's choice. Clue number one, he knew his London.

The name was Sean O'Donnell and he was waiting for me. His bum scarcely left his seat as I was shown to his table, and the nod of his head did not shower me with warmth, but at least he extended his hand and his grip was encompassing and firm. He was good-looking in an Irish way, long upper lip and black curly hair, and when he allowed himself to smile, he was definitely attractive. Conversation with him was not difficult, he had not lost the Irish gift of the gab and he had acquired the Australian forthright approach. It became clear before too long that he was an IRA sympathizer, and he wanted to know where my feelings lay. I managed not to reveal them.

Towards the end of the meal I plucked up the courage to ask him (after all, I was still a new girl at the job) why he was looking for an English wife, when it was obvious he hadn't much time for the English.

'How do you know that?' he asked with a curious expression.

To keep things lighthearted I answered, 'Your ears go pink when you mention them.'

In a childlike way that defied his demeanour, he felt one ear, but he did not smile when he did it.

I tried to work out his angle, and I had got as far as his needing a cover for whatever his business was in Australia. Taking back an Irish bride might seem too convenient, and he did not want to risk getting involved with Australian women. Then he said, 'You'd have a good life out there. I'd settle money on you, not be demanding. But I need a wife, looks better, you know.'

I didn't dare to check on my recorder for fear he might get suspicious, he was not the kind of chap to make angry, but as there was no doubt that here we had good copy for the programme, I had to keep the conversation flowing. I would need to see Sydney, I said, and I couldn't travel for a week or so. I was about to use family commitments when he said, 'You don't have commitments, and all that stuff, I hope.'

'No, just my job. I'd have to give my notice in.'

'How important is your job? What do you do?'

I managed to look him in the eye (I was learning fast). 'Just a secretary. But I wouldn't like to let the boss down. I would have to find a replacement.'

He gave a slow smile, then actually patted my hand and said, 'That's okay, Annie,' and then, as an afterthought, 'I like that.'

It was only after we'd said goodbye, and I had promised to give a quick answer to Lydia at the agency, that I realized I still had no idea how he made his money. Still, Diana would be pleased. She might want to send me to California via Australia. And a few flight details would need to be changed, a few men would have to be given new arrival dates.

Edward moved towards me across the bed as if in his sleep, then he turned me on my back and ran his hands slowly across my naked breasts. My stomach contracted and I moaned with the expectancy of sex.

We were fully awake now. I turned my head towards him and he placed his parted lips over mine, forcing my mouth open with his tongue. I could feel his erection pressing against my thigh as it grew. Then he lifted himself over me.

'I'm sorry about last night,' he whispered in my ear.

I touched him with the tips of my fingers. 'It's all right.'

He was breathing heavily, and his breath was tickling my shoulder. I found it arousing. (Marcus knew about this and used to do it on purpose and watch me squirm while begging him to hurry.)

'No, it isn't all right,' Edward said, 'but you excited me so much . . .'

(And you're so young, my dear. It can happen when you're young.)

'I'll try not to let it happen again,' he said.

I pulled his face on to mine and licked the dent in his chin. He moaned, I spread my legs. My back arched and I gave a small cry as I gave myself up to him.

I said a bright good morning to the boy delivering my newspaper as we arrived at my door together, feeling sure that he knew I was wearing last night's clothes.

I let myself into the flat convinced that there would be a judge and jury, including my children waiting for me in the hall. But Kat running towards me gleefully was the only sign of life. Thank heaven Irish Rose was in hospital, I could not even imagine what her reaction would have been.

I went straight to my office. Gus was on my answer-phone. Had I been away overnight? he asked. He worried when I didn't return his calls. Could he see me for dinner? And would I bring my diary, he wanted to arrange the trip to Hungary he'd promised me, and would I like to go to Paris with him for two days next week?

(Paris? Would I be able to handle Paris yet? I thought not.)

Katie's was the next message. Emma was driving both her and Wills mad because, she said, I was never at home and it worried her. So what was going on? Would

I please telephone before Emma got the flying squad involved.

Diana was on the tape too, bitching about another report being due, and would I move my arse and fax it to her pretty damn quickly.

The weeks were running away with me. Men were on my telephone, men were packaged and coming through my letterbox. Some I would never see but I had, at least, to talk to them or to answer their letters. The agents insisted on it for the good of their reputations. And Diana insisted on it for whatever reason she could think of at the time. Bossy bitch.

I had no idea there were so many lonely men out there. Up to the present I had thought that loneliness only happened to women. A few were cranks, as with Charlie Diamond (and Diana had the gall to say that I should visit him, it would make good copy for the programme), but most were your average Mr Nice Guy, or so it seemed to me.

In the bath the first call I made was to Edward at his office. I used his private line.

'Darling,' he said intimately, 'I've been trying to call you but I only get a busy line.'

'Yes, the phone has been a pain. I'm sorry about calling you in the office. I just wanted to say hello, and to thank you for dinner.'

He gave a small laugh. 'Annie, you're always sorry about something. I love it when you call me. I was only doodling, and thinking of you.'

'Nice things, I hope.' I was thankful I'd mastered the art of suppressing the nervous giggle. 'Why were you trying to call me?'

'I wanted to say thank you ... you know ... for everything.'

I rearranged the bubbles in the bath while I thought

about how to phrase it. 'We did have a nice time, didn't we? But, Edward, do you think we should see one another again?'

There was silence before he answered in a shocked voice, 'Annie, what on earth are you saying?'

'I don't know really. But I'm too old for you, Edward. It must be obvious to everyone.'

'Annie, I'll be the judge of that, and who cares what other people think?'

'I have children nearly your age.'

'Annie, stop it. We're perfect for each other. And you know I've fallen in love with you.'

'No, you haven't,' I said quickly, too quickly. What if it happened to me too? I couldn't handle any more heartbreak. 'I'm sure it will go away, like measles,' I said inanely.

And so much for my resolution not to see him again, I then said yes, I would like to go walking on the Yorkshire moors next weekend, but please, no more talk about love, it was much too soon in the relationship.

'Okay,' he said, like a child.

It was only my second attempt at sex since I'd last slept with Marcus. True, I had enjoyed it, and surprisingly the guilt was not there. But it was wrong, Edward was so young. None the less, I was finding the prospect of going away with him for the weekend rather intoxicating. Imagine the joy of spending Sunday being close to someone, having hugs and laughing at silly jokes. I probably wouldn't sleep for the rest of the week just thinking about it.

Gus lifted his glass of Château de Belchier 1978 and held it towards me. 'To us, dear Milla,' he said, 'I want to have you in my life for always.'

'Same here,' I answered, and looked into his eyes and meant it. What a dear friend he was becoming, what an absolute stroke of luck that I had met him. He had helped to heal my open wounds, he had taught me how to live with an ache in the heart and how not to fight the things I could not change. What a joy it was to have a true male friend like Gus. And he was the only man of recent times who knew my real name. Would he be shocked when he heard what I was about to tell him, I wondered.

As if reading my mind, at which he seemed to be particularly good, he said, 'What is this work you are doing that you try not to tell Gus about? You are a spy?'

I laughed, and used the time to arrange my thoughts. 'No, I'm not a spy. I wouldn't be brave enough for that sort of work.'

'Is it, then, to do with your writing?'

'In a way.' Diana would have me minced and made into dog food if she ever found out I was blowing our cover. But I was disinclined to let her meet Gus anyway, since she would do her best to steal him. And it was becoming important to me to confide in someone. The secret was a burden, and as I said, I am not brave.

'Secret writing?' he asked.

I took another sip of wine. 'It isn't writing, Gus. And it's only secret because it's for a TV programme. So you mustn't tell. You have to cross your heart.'

Gus placed a hand in the appropriate place. 'I cross my heart not to tell.'

I leaned towards him and lowered my voice. 'It's to be about dating agencies. Finding out why men use them really, everyone knows why women do.'

'So, you interview men?'

I thought of Edward. Gus should only know.

'Sort of. I go out for a drink, or have lunch. Or dinner even.'

'Do they know you are reporter? You have a notebook?'

I smiled at him. 'Of course not, silly. They have to

think that I'm a fellow member. But I do carry a secret
mini-tape recorder.'

Gus took my hand across the table. 'It is safe, you
think?'

'Oh, perfectly. I don't give my real name. And no one
knows where I live.' (Except Edward.)

'What unreal name you use?'

'Annie Lloyd. It will all be over in a few weeks. So you
don't have any need to worry.'

Gus did not press me, but he became thoughtful. A
waiter poured more wine. I was happy to change the
subject.

'I won't be able to do Paris, not yet anyway. But I shall
look forward to it. And can we leave Hungary till I've
finished this job?'

I packed my case, then tipped it out and tried again. I
couldn't take too much with me, only the middle-aged
travelled heavy. And I had no idea what kind of car
Edward drove, most likely a two-seater sports with a
minute luggage compartment.

He'd probably have the hood down as it was such a
perfect day, so I'd best take a sweater and something to
cover my hair. (No, not the latter, silly, that would be
naff, and make me look dated.)

What hair? I looked in a mirror. In the salon the new
style had looked a real treat. Made me look years younger,
everyone said. A mere child, Gus had said over dinner,
and under dim lighting, so how on earth old did I look
before?

What had gone wrong, I wondered. Pieces of hair meant
to lie flat stuck out at conflicting angles. Every morning,
fresh out of bed, I looked like Worzel Gummidge. And I
wasn't at all sure that I liked the highlights. It made me
look fair, but I would always feel dark, and seeing my
reflection gave me a shock.

I changed the suitcase for a holdall, so much younger-looking than a suitcase (especially the one that I'd won in a raffle, with wheels), then proceeded to discard unwanted clothing. No way would I need a dress, or even formal shoes. I'd travel in jeans and sneakers and take shorts and T-shirts for if the weather stayed good. Pants and shirts for evening. Not too much make-up (Edward seemed to think that I didn't use it). The book previously packed was discarded, it wasn't likely that I would be reading in bed!

William had agreed to sleep over for the sake of the cat. He would be less curious than Katie, but I did call the agencies to tell them not to phone till Monday if they needed me as I was unavailable, and I took good care to lock my work away.

Guilt pricked me when I told William that I was invited to a writers' conference in York. But what the hell, he probably lied to me about his carryings-on all the time.

'Oh, is that all?' he said. 'I thought at least it would be a dirty weekend.' (I very nearly confessed.)

Two o'clock arrived too soon. My face was on fire, and the icepacks were not working. It was a hot day, eighty-two degrees in London. I was waiting for Edward to arrive. The rule about my address had to be broken in his case, I could hardly meet him on a street corner, with luggage.

I was starving, having lived on lettuce leaves and grapefruit for most of the week so that my stomach would be flat. I was halfway through ravenously munching on a water biscuit when the doorbell rang.

'I'll be right down,' I called to Edward through the whistling of the apparatus, as I watched him on the closed-circuit screen. I was afraid that he might be looking smartly dressed, but he was wearing the same sort of clothes I was, jeans and a T-shirt. So there was a God after all, I thought, and hugged the cat goodbye.

Edward greeted me with a kiss on the lips and took my bag. 'My, you travel light,' he said.

He headed towards a dark green Rolls Royce. I thought that it was a joke and waited for him to laugh and veer away towards, it so happened, a rusty old sports car parked behind.

'My dad thought that his Rolls would be more comfortable than my sports for a long journey,' he said over his shoulder. He opened the enormous boot and placed my small holdall alongside his large suitcase. 'You should only see what my mother takes with her for a weekend,' he said. 'And I'm not much better.'

I longed to ask if I could run back and get more clothes. 'That was very generous of your father,' I said as he held open the front passenger door for me, and I wondered if his father would have been so generous had he known I was a Mrs Robinson. 'Won't he be needing his Rolls?'

'Oh no, he'll use the other one,' he said casually, and secured my seatbelt.

I noticed a large hamper on the back seat as Edward climbed in behind the steering-wheel.

'I popped into Fortnum and Mason's, thought a champagne picnic on the way might be fun,' he said, then he started the engine. Not that I would have noticed if the car hadn't moved forward. It all happened without noise.

'You can adjust the seat, if you wish,' he said, 'up, down, forward or back, the buttons are on the passenger's panel.'

I placed my sunglasses on my nose and smiled to myself. If Marcus Cage could only see me now . . .

Edward turned on the air-conditioning and the tape-deck, and asked me to tell him my favourite piece of music so that he could press the button that would select it from the bank of tapes stored alphabetically in the boot. Maybe he meant classical, but I asked if he had any Herb Alpert of the 'seventies. Can you believe, he had, and he selected my request, 'This Guy's in Love with You'.

It carried me up and away, to when Marcus told me to meet him in his flat soon after our romance began, and gave me the keys to let myself in. I'd never had a key to a man's flat before and the guilty feeling heightened the excitement.

In the middle of the carpet in his very modern all-black living-room lay a note. For a Girl Called Milla, it was headed. Play the tape on the deck. Just press it in. It says it all, Marcus . . .

For the first week after he left me all those years later I played it every waking hour and wrung myself dry with tears. Kate took it from me in the end, and although she gave it back to me later I had not listened to it since.

I think Edward knew that it was nostalgia time. When the tape was finished he reached over and silently took my hand.

I was humming to myself. I'd been doing that for the three days that followed the weekend in Yorkshire. I could not believe how quickly the time was going, and I slept like a rock every night. It was a luxury that I had forgotten.

The air on the Yorkshire moors had felt like silk after the fume-filled stuff we breathe in London. The country house hotel had been an old hunting lodge and smelled of beeswax polish and leather. The huge four-poster bed we slept in had a mattress like a cloud and fine linen sheets that were changed daily. Country garden flowers filled our room and sherry in a decanter stood on an antique table near the bed. We rode the horses from the stables and cantered across the moors. Edward cosseted me with love, enveloped me with attention and contented me with sex.

I tried to cancel the lunch date I had with my daughters,

I didn't need them disturbing my reverie, but they would have none of it.

After Pasta Neapolitano in a working-girls' café, and during a cappuccino, Kate said, 'Dad tells us he saw you coming out of the Savoy the other night. He seems worried about you.'

'He should be happy for me,' I said quickly before emotion set in. 'How can you worry about someone lucky enough to have dinner at the Savoy?'

'Who were you with?' Emma asked, never the one to mess about with the diplomatic approach.

I resisted the temptation to ask what it had to do with either of them, or their father.

'I was with the man I met at the dinner party you so kindly treated me to,' I answered sweetly.

Emma leaned back in her chair and placed her hands on her swollen stomach, as though to remind her mother that she must not be caused any worry during her pregnancy. 'So you're still letting him take you out?' she asked.

I controlled my voice to hide the aggro I was feeling. 'I thought that was the idea, someone to have dinner with to alleviate my loneliness? Or was it supposed to be just a one-off outing – sorry sir, I won't be able to see you again, my children and my ex-husband would not approve?'

'I'm happy you're dating, Mum, really,' Katie said, looking awkward and glancing at Emma, 'and Dad wants you to find a mate too, I'm sure . . .'

'But we don't want you overdoing it, and you are out an awful lot,' Emma cut in, her hands still resting on her stomach.

'Overdoing what, mating or dating?'

Emma was tense. 'Mother, be serious.'

'I am being serious.'

'You're being flippant.'

Why was it, whenever I answered back, and was not just passive, my family accused me of being flippant?

'Sorry, I don't mean to be.'

Emma looked at her sister. 'Tell her,' she said.

'Let it go,' Katie answered.

'No, we have to tell her. You promised you would do it.'

I was beginning to feel serious annoyance. 'Now what?' I asked.

Kate looked down at her coffee cup. 'Lucy Bainbridge was standing at a bus stop in Bayswater and saw you in a Rolls Royce with a very young man.'

'So what? Was she jealous?'

Katie smiled. 'Probably.'

'Mother, be serious,' Emma repeated.

'What, again?'

'And you told Wills that you were going to a conference when you wanted him to stay with Kat.'

'So, I went to a conference in a Rolls Royce with a young man. Give over, Emma, I've had enough.'

'It's just that we worry about you,' Katie said. 'So does Dad.'

I reached into my handbag to find my wallet. 'He wasn't so worried about me when he dumped me and left me all alone. And believe me, girls, he does not worry about me now, unless it's worrying that I might be having a better time than he is. Let's get the bill, shall we?'

'Well, promise us you're not hopping in and out of bed. I mean . . .' Emma said.

'Why? So that you can pass the good news on to your father?' I was fuming and the girls were wondering if they had gone too far. 'I'll tell you what to do to make yourselves feel better,' I said hotly, 'ask your father if he would like to come back to me. If he says yes, then telephone me with the good news. If it's no, then I suggest you all get off my back.'

I reached into my wallet and put a ten-pound note on the table. 'There's my share. I'm off, I have a lot of work to do this afternoon.'

'But you will be careful,' Emma persisted, rotating a hand ever so discreetly on her stomach.

I stood up and pushed back my chair noisily on the tiled floor. They should only know the half of it. 'I shall heed your advice and I shall do my best to be careful. Rest assured I shall only go out to dinner with gentlemen, and I shall carry plenty of condoms with me at all times.'

'Mother!!' Emma screeched, looking around her with horror written all over her face.

I did not kiss them goodbye, which hurt me more than it hurt them. But I glanced at Kate as I strode from the table. I felt sure she was longing to laugh, and I'm certain that she winked at me.

So much for getting myself to Australia to pretend to be a potential wife. The sheep farmer turned up on my doorstep and gave me the fright of my life.

I looked into the closed-circuit screen after the doorbell rang and saw a man standing down in the street with a suitcase beside him. I decided that he had pressed the wrong button. But the bell rang again as I watched him, and he didn't take his finger off the button.

'All right, all right, is there a fire or something?' I called into the answerphone. (It had been a trying morning.)

'Takes you long enough to answer the bloody door,' he answered with similar impatience.

'Who are you?'

'Harry Smith. How about letting a bloke in?'

Harry Smith? Had I heard that name before?

'Do I know you?' I asked a trifle more pleasantly.

'Course you bloody know me, unless you're not Annie Lloyd.'

'Are you from an agency?' (What the hell was going on? He sounded Australian, but that wasn't possible.)

'No, I'm from fucking Australia, and I've just flown in from Sydney.'

I seriously know now what it means when people say they nearly died from shock. My first reaction was to say that Annie wasn't in. But then he'd expect to be asked up to wait for her after a gargantuan journey of twelve thousand miles, and things would go from bad to worse. And I couldn't bear to imagine the confusion that inventing a twin sister would cause.

I realized that my phone was now ringing, but in my dilemma I did not consider it a priority and I let the call go on to the machine.

'Look, Annie,' his voice boomed up from below. 'It's frigging raining and I'm getting wet. Can't you let a bloke come up?'

'Yes, of course, come up,' I said in a quandary, and pressed the button that opened the street door.

I rushed to my office and quickly put the mini-recorder in my jeans pocket and switched it on, concealing the tiny button-mike under the lapel of my shirt. I could hear Lydia from Marriages Made in Heaven talking urgently into my machine, telling me of the unexpected arrival of Harry Smith and suggesting (or was it more like begging?) that I should be nice to him. (What did she think I was going to do, beat him up?)

Harry stood in the open doorway and the top of his rather shorn head was level with the lintel. I swear he caused a dark shadow as he filled the space, and boy, was he ever handsome, in a rugged sheep-farmer-from-the-outback sort of way. He grinned and showed two rows of perfect teeth, ducked his sun-bronzed head and walked in with hand extended.

'Sorry if I gave you a shock,' he said, putting his suitcase down, throwing his Qantas bag on top of it and almost breaking every bone in my fingers between his as he shook them till my whole arm juddered. 'Only made up my mind to come over two days ago. Bloody long flight, that one, I'm knackered.'

I stepped back a few paces to ease the angle of my aching neck as I looked up at him. 'Yes, you must be, after flying all that distance.'

'Too right,' he said. 'Nice place you got here.'

'Yes, it isn't bad.' (But you can't stay in it, Harry Smith.)

He smiled again. 'Just being friendly, don't expect you to put me up. But I reckoned you'd know of somewhere good I could stay. Don't want to put you to any trouble, mind.'

I warmed to him at that moment, and I smiled at him for the first time. 'Come in properly,' I said, 'and have tea or beer, or whatever it is you Aussies like best.'

'That's better,' he answered, not moving. 'I thought you were never going to smile.'

I laughed. 'You certainly know how to make a girl feel she's not hospitable. But it's tea or coffee or wine. I don't have any Foster's.'

He took off his crumpled jacket, revealing an equally crumpled shirt. 'I think Foster's stinks. But I'll take you up on tea. Strong, a lot of milk and four spoons of sugar.'

He followed me to the kitchen and watched as I filled the kettle. 'All right if I take my tie off?' he asked, already tugging at the knot. 'I hate these bloody things. Never wear one at home.'

'Of course,' I said, not really listening. We had a crisis. I'd given the last of the milk to Kat.

'And can I use the toilet?' (Well, at least he didn't say the dunny!)

As I directed him to the bathroom he said over his shoulder, 'Oh, and Annie, sorry I was bad-tempered in the street. I reckon I must be tired . . .'

A quick glance at the cat's drinking bowl revealed some left-over milk. I snatched it up and poured it into a jug.

Kat loved him, and showed no grudges as she watched him pour her milk into his tea. She leaped up onto his knee as the two of us sat at the kitchen table.

'She likes you,' I said, taking the lid off the biscuit tin.

'Yair, I like cats, got a couple back home. I like dogs too but I only have them for working. They like it better that way, stops them getting crook.'

He reached into his back pocket and pulled out a few loose pictures. 'That's my dogs,' he said with pride. I took the picture and made suitable enthusiastic noises while he held out another. 'And that's the station. I'm just building on two more rooms. For the boys.'

The one-storey house looked ordinary, but large and not unfriendly. 'It has a tin roof, doesn't it?' I asked, a bit aghast.

'Sure, nearly all homesteads have tin roofs back home. That's my boys. Pair of devils, they are.' He handed me the last snap.

I looked at the two young men Lydia had omitted to tell me that Harry had sired and wondered how I would have felt if I really was hoping to marry him. They looked like a couple of convicts, as tall as their father but bigger, with bulging muscles and shoulders like ox-yokes. 'Good workers,' Harry said. 'It's time they had their own bedrooms, though. They fight a lot, things get broken.' He laughed. 'And they're too big now to clip around the ears. Most likely they'd thump me back.'

I had to get rid of Harry, though he seemed to be a very nice man. While he was drinking three large cups of tea in the kitchen and I was quietly toying with a glass of wine, I heard first Gus and then Edward on my answerphone, even though I had turned the volume down. Plus someone from the States whose name I didn't catch, and a man from the Emirates, whom I had no intention of seeing again, demanding my attention. Then, Lydia from M-M-I-H was there again, enquiring if Harry Smith had found me and asking me to telephone her soonest about something hush-hush. For both items she should have used a quieter voice. I had to cough myself silly, and it caused Harry to thump me on the back and pour me a glass of water. But it was either a coughing fit or a clog dance, and the latter seemed a bit over the top.

Harry was dragging his feet, maybe it was jet lag. I practically had to push him and his luggage through the door when we left to find him an hotel room. I was liking him more all the time. He was refreshingly blunt, humorous, and totally in touch with himself.

'I sent the wife packing,' he said, without malice, in the car. 'She had an affair with my head man, told me she loved him. I just sacked him, the boys did the rest.'

'How awful,' I said, not quite knowing what to say for the best.

Harry scratched his head. 'Not really, I couldn't blame her. You can't help falling in love, can you? And she'd had a tough life on the station before we went into profit.'

He tried to stop the porter at the hotel of my choice from carrying his bag from the car.

'It's heavy, and I'm bigger than you,' he said when the man insisted.

At reception I said to him, 'I would have liked to take you to dinner tonight and have shown you my city . . .'

'You don't take me to dinner,' he cut in, 'I take you. No woman's going to spend money on me.'

I touched his arm. 'No, Harry. What I mean is, I cannot see you tonight. I have to see someone else. Business you know . . . work.'

'Well, cancel it,' he said flatly, handing over his passport to the clerk.

'I'm afraid I can't do that. It's important, and I didn't know that you were arriving.'

The receptionist handed him the plastic card with which to operate his door. He looked puzzled. 'Funny place this. Don't they know about keys?'

'It's safer than a key, Harry, and it's destroyed when you leave. Just try not to lose it.'

I held out my hand in goodbye and Harry crushed it once more. 'Too bad about tonight,' he said. 'Still, I'm pretty bushed, I'll probably sleep the clock round. Just don't forget to come for me tomorrow.'

'I won't, Harry,' I said, 'I'll pick you up at eight.'

'In the morning?'

'No, Harry, the evening.'

'Jesus, that's late for eating dinner,' he said. 'How about six o'clock?'

(This is London, Harry.) 'I'll split it with you. Make it seven . . . in the bar.'

SEVEN

I treated myself to a new black dress with a deep V at the back, having always considered that my back was better-looking than my front. I hoped that Gus would like the image. I had mastered the new short hair-cut, at least for that one night, with help from a heated roller and lots of gel. I'd managed to singe my ears and burn the tip of one finger, but that was par for the course. And everything, I've long decided, has its price.

I applied my makeup with care, but that was the nice thing about dating Gus, I didn't need to try to look younger. I would feel the same way too when I went to dinner with Harry Smith, I was sure. Nice Harry, he'd phoned me to say that he'd discovered room service, and was having a (T-bone) steak on the bed, and watching television. And I was to have a bonzer night out and not to worry about him.

The new fine smoky-coloured tights I'd invested in improved the look of my legs no end and I remembered I'd not worn that colour since going to a gala performance of the Kirov Ballet with Marcus five years back. What a heavenly night out that had been, I dreamed about it for a full ten minutes before getting back to straightening my tights.

Gus rang the bell, and I slipped my feet into my new black suede shoes. By the time he was inside the building and the lift was rising slowly to the sixth floor, I had put the ice-cold birthday-present champagne and two frosted glasses on to a tray and taken it all to the sitting-room.

He took my hands and we kissed in the doorway, he looking handsome in his dinner jacket and black bow-tie, I blushing as he looked me over 'You are a truly lovely lady,' he said (I'd dimmed the lights), holding me away from him and smiling with pleasure.

The £100-a-ticket reception and slap-up dinner that followed was in aid of the world's starving children, which struck me as odd. Surely stale bread and thin soup would have been more in keeping?

While being introduced to the wife of the Prime Minister of Australia, I found myself thinking of Harry and hoping that he was sleeping soundly and not feeling abandoned in a large lonely city, where he knew no one except me.

Every time I glanced across at Gus he was looking at me. He would smile, and ease his way towards me. At dinner we were seated together and he held my hand under the table through all the boring speeches and quite disgusting coffee.

When we managed to sneak away through the grey haze of cigar smoke, we went for a walk and a quiet drink in a plush place on the river. Gus ordered brandies and then he took my hand. 'How is my favourite lady coping with her merry men?'

'Annie Lloyd aka me is coping, I think. I'll now need to go down-under as well as to the States.'

He looked quite startled. 'Down under who?'

I laughed. 'You know, to Australia.'

'Oh, there, oh really so?' he said. 'I hope soon you finish with Annie Lloyd's work.'

'I shall be finished after the States.'

'I know a good idea,' he said, his eyes twinkling. 'How if I meet you in New York when you finish? We could have nice time, I used to live there, I know lots of good restaurants.'

'Brilliant,' I said enthusiastically. 'That to look forward to would make the trip so much nicer.'

'We could motor up to New England for weekend to see the trees in the fall, is beautiful.'

'Oh yes, I'd love that. I have an aunt who lives up there in Connecticut.'

He gave me a funny look.

'No, truly, I have a real aunt who lives there. She's wonderful and she would love us to call on her.'

He released my hand, reached inside his jacket and held a closed fist towards me. 'Milla, darling, I wanted to give you a present. Is only tiny, but it comes with all my love.'

I felt real panic. Not a ring? I couldn't possibly accept a ring. I was still hoping to get Marcus back, wasn't I? A ring could ruin everything.

'Is not a ring,' he said, watching my face. 'I think you are not ready for ring. But it still comes with all Gus's love.' He placed the small box in my palm.

I kept my eyes on his face. 'You shouldn't buy me gifts,' I said.

He leaned over and opened the box for me. Inside, tucked into pale peach satin, sat the most elegant pair of antique diamond earrings I had ever seen. They were breathtaking.

I leaned over and kissed him. 'They're gorgeous, how can I possibly thank you? I've never had such a fabulous present.'

He beamed with pleasure and shrugged his shoulders, trying to look casual in the Continental way.

'Can I try them on?' I asked, not waiting for him to answer. I looked into my small handbag mirror and saw them sparkling in my ears.

'You look like a princess,' Gus said.

'It's surprising what a pair of expensive earrings can do for a girl,' I answered, feeling shy of his attention.

He touched my cheek. 'And you make me feel like a prince.'

I laughed. 'But beware. When I take them off I'll just be ordinary me again. Like Cinderella.'

I invited him home for a nightcap, and knew that I would not send him away. I needed to have him with me that night.

In the lift I put my arms around his neck. 'Thank you again for my lovely present. I shall treasure them always, and keep them safe.'

Gus kissed me on my parted lips. 'They for special occasions,' he said as he took my keys and unlocked the door. 'Not to wear all the time.'

I smiled at him, reached up and kissed his cheek. 'Just for special occasions with you. And never to wear on Sundays.'

'Sundays?' he repeated after me, looking puzzled.

I walked into my hall, thinking it was the first time that the door had been unlocked for me since I'd lived in the place.

'Nothing,' I said, 'it's just me being silly.'

It was not that I hadn't enjoyed spending the afternoon with Edward, but it was five o'clock and I had to meet Harry Smith at seven. And, as I had discovered on our first dinner date, Harry was one hell of a strict time-keeper.

Not only that, most of my morning had been taken up seeing Lydia in her office. The hush-hush assignment, if I could carry it off, would be enough to give Diana an orgasm on the spot. And as my handsome salary was beginning to look like less of a gift and more like forced labour, that was a good thing.

A South African man of the cloth wanted a wife. Someone to run his home, organize the entertaining (we had to be aware that His Eminence had connections in the Government, and was a very important personage). Lydia and I nodded and smiled our understanding of the situation. And my smiling became genuine when I heard that sex would not be involved. The holy man had three grown-up children all living at home, and a wife who was long since buried, so I reckoned he had a mistress in his bed, who could not be seen in his drawing-room.

His Eminence, Dr Lawrence Voorberg by name, had sent his aide to London (looked more like a boxer's manager to me) to sort out the best in likely females to be had on the market. Lydia convinced him that was me, and he need look no further. He made miles of notes in longhand in a book, even though Lydia tried to cut it short by saying that she would have it all typed out in a trice. And then, if you don't mind, horror of horrors, he produced a camera and proceeded to photograph me, head and shoulders, from all angles. His boss would need to describe me to his friends, he said, since we had recently met at, and he had proposed to me at, a religious conference in London. I never was sure if that made me a lady of the cloth or not.

I would give it my best shot, I told the aide and Lydia. He said that I was never to use that expression in South Africa, and what date would I like for my first-class ticket?

As I said, Harry Smith was fanatical about time-keeping. On that first evening, he'd greeted me with 'You're late, Annie. I've been sitting here waiting.' He was propped up on a high bar stool with a Coca-Cola in front of him.

I looked at my watch. 'Only fifteen minutes late, Harry. The traffic's hell out there.'

'A person shouldn't be late,' he answered, finishing his drink with one gulp. 'I thought you'd stood me up.'

'Oh, Harry,' I said with genuine concern, 'I wouldn't do that.'

He started to walk away, it was obvious he was not going to ask me to join him in a drink. 'Well, I didn't know that, did I? Things like that give a bloke a turn.'

I caught up with him and put a restraining hand on his arm. 'I'm sorry, Harry, will you forgive me and let me take you on my special guided tour?'

'Do I have a choice?' he asked, not loosening up. But he did let me go first through the swing-doors, then hung back while three large American ladies clutching theatre tickets and wearing see-through raincoats pushed their way through with the force of charging rhinos.

In the car I thought that he was sulking, and I was about to suggest that I had better things to do than drive a sullen Aussie who had landed in my life unannounced around London, when, as we reached the Embankment, he looked at me and said, 'I'm not really mad at you, Annie, or anything like that. But this bloody town is just plain scary. I reckon a bloke at that bar was trying to pick me up. Kept giving me the eye. He was a faggot, wore a pink shirt. Fair turned my stomach.'

I laughed. 'Stop worrying, Harry. It was probably a female prostitute in male drag, we're a bit kinky like that over here, haven't you heard?'

He gave me a very funny look.

I took him everywhere that we could pack into one evening. Going past the Tower of London, as I recounted some of the heads that had fallen to the chopper, he said, 'Must have been pretty bloody dark inside there before electric lights, reckon they'd have had a few miss hits, don't you?'

On Tower Bridge when I explained how it held up the traffic and caused chaos when the bridge went up to let tall ships through, he said, 'I saw a film once where a car managed to jump the gap as the bridge was going up.

Bloody good film that, only took me an hour to fly to the nearest cinema in the old two-seater, wouldn't mind seeing it again.'

Standing looking at the tiny, misshapen Old Curiosity Shoppe, he measured the door, which came to his chest, and said, 'Not very big were they then? You ever read *Great Expectations*, Annie? Writes a bloody good book, that Dickens.'

Going past Buckingham Palace he said, 'Ugly bunch, that royal family. Apart from Diana, that is, she's a cracker.'

'They work very hard,' I said, feeling the need to defend them as I eased our way in the traffic around Queen Victoria's statue.

'Yair, you're right,' he said ungrudgingly. 'Specially the old girl, and that Princess Anne. Pity about the looks, though. But Di, she's the tops. And she did name her son after me, so she can't be all bad.'

There was something about Harry that made me want to smile all the time. He was totally without malice, he spoke his mind and bore no grudges (except perhaps where the gay in the pink shirt was concerned).

'Don't drive so bloody fast, girl,' he said as I vied for position at red lights in Trafalgar Square. 'You're scaring the living daylights out of those bloody pigeons.'

'You never get anywhere driving slowly in London,' I answered, revving in readiness for a quick getaway.

'But you go so bloody close to everything,' he yelled.

I threw him a quick glance. He looked a little white, I thought, so I slowed down a bit. 'We don't have the room to spare that you have in your country.'

His knuckles showed white as they clutched at the door-handle. 'We won't have much room in our coffins either. Where's this bloody restaurant? Reckon I'd like to get out . . .'

But walking up St James's, after I'd abandoned the car

on Harry's assurance that I shouldn't let the bloody police intimidate me about parking, he put his arm around my waist and his long fingers dug appreciatively into my ribs. 'I couldn't drive like that, you're a bloody marvel,' he said. 'Hope you won't find Australia a bit quiet.'

I decided not to comment. '*I* couldn't shear sheep,' I said, 'so that makes us quits.'

He looked down at me. 'Bet I could teach you about sheep in next to no time.'

I looked up at him and smiled. (Bet you couldn't, Harry Smith, I said to myself.)

As we walked into The Caprice the sound of people having fun was deafening. 'I think you'll like it in here,' I said quickly, not giving him time to find fault. 'It's a fun sort of a place.'

'Screw the fun,' Harry answered, 'can you eat the friggin' food?'

At the table he closed the menu without seriously looking at it. 'Surprise me, Annie,' he said. 'But no kangaroo steaks. I hate roos, dead or alive.'

It was the first time since McDonalds, little kids and hamburgers that I had drunk Coca-Cola with hot food. Harry did not approve of alcohol and thought that women, especially, should not drink it.

'My boys swig beer,' he said, 'and it makes them nasty. When they were shrimps I used to belt them for doing it, and smoking too, but as I said, can't do that now.'

I found myself wondering what his chances of finding a bride prepared to put up with those boys could be. About ninety to one against, I would have thought.

When the rare roasted marinated quail arrived, Harry speared a bird with his fork, lifted it up, turned it over and stared at it. And though he didn't actually do so, I felt sure he was going to smell it. He cut it in half, bones and all, and picked it up with his fingers.

'This isn't restaurant food,' he said, crunching on bones, 'this is bush tucker.'

I looked at him enquiringly. 'Bush tucker?'

'Yair, the stuff you have to look for to cook when you're caught out in the bush and you're bloody hungry.'

I laughed. 'How soon can I come and eat in your country, that has to beat the hell out of paying these prices?' There went my big mouth again, and no hope of taking it back.

Harry carefully put a freckled brown hand right next to mine on the table. 'You can come over and take a look as soon as you want, I liked you right off. The next lady I have to see will need to be real special, you'll be a hard act to follow, Annie girl.'

I hoped that my expression had not changed, and I swallowed the fatuous remark that embarrassment was about to lead me into. It was a strange feeling, being on a list of marriageable possibilities.

I checked that my recorder was switched on. 'Why come all this way to find a new wife, Harry?' I asked. 'You have some great women in Australia, I'm always reading about them.'

He stretched his long frame and rocked the chair on to its back legs. I feared for its life as it creaked menacingly.

'Oh, I dunno, townsfolk don't reckon with the bush back home. I thought with the bloody awful climate over here and all the violence, a nice English girl who'd had a basinful might want to go for it.'

I had to agree, he had a point.

'Edward, I must go,' I said, easing myself from under his arm.

He lay on his back and watched as I headed for the bathroom. 'Must you go out with your son tonight?' he called after me with emotion in his voice. 'Mother arrives tomorrow, and that means I won't be able to see you.'

I turned on the taps and stepped into his luxurious shower, big enough for six. He joined me, and as water streamed down my face he kissed my closed eyelids. 'Did you hear what I said about Mother arriving from Boston?'

'Yes,' I spluttered. 'And Edward, don't suggest that I meet her, please.'

'Why ever not?' he asked, aggrieved.

'It may not have occurred to you, but she wouldn't approve of me.'

Water splashed over our bodies. 'You're wrong,' he said, 'Mother will love you.'

I stepped from the shower and grabbed for a towel. 'No way, Edward. Trust me, she would not approve of you having an affair with an older woman.' (Whatever age she might be she'd probably look younger than I did, with all the surgical help that money could buy over there.)

'Annie, don't be difficult.' His voice had raised in volume.

'I'm not being difficult.' Mine raised an octave.

I was sure that Edward was about to cry, when he wrapped me in a large towelling robe and carried me into the bedroom, setting me down on the edge of the bed. 'I'm going to speak to my folks just as soon as Mother gets here,' he said. 'I want to marry you, Annie.'

I leaped from the bed, knowing that there was a look of horror on my damp face. 'Edward, you can't possibly. Don't be silly.' I was stunned, the tone of my voice was the one I would have used to William at the age of seven.

He looked hurt and confused. He moved away, and stared at me like a devoted puppy as I dressed.

'I have to go, right now,' I said, anticipating there was more to come.

He came towards me and placed his boyish hands on

my shoulders. 'Can I catch up with you later, after you've seen your son?'

I slung my bag on my shoulder and fished my car keys from my jacket pocket. The lie about William did not sit well. 'No, Edward. I'll be too tired. Really.'

He followed me through the mirrored hall, holding a towel around his waist. 'When, then?' He opened his front door while he waited for me to answer.

'How long is your mother over for?'

'About two weeks, I guess, then she's going on to our house in France.'

The odds were I would never see him again. I would have to write to him just before I left for the States.

I kissed him on his cheek. 'So, see you when she's gone.' I looked at the towel draped around him. 'Better not come any further,' I said, trying to make a joke, 'you might frighten the residents.'

'I shall miss you, Annie,' he said forlornly.

I turned as I hurried silently along on thick-piled carpet, and my eyes lingered on his handsome young face. He blew me a kiss as I rang for the lift.

'I love you,' I heard him calling as the lift doors opened and the bell-hop touched his cap and said a clear 'Good evening, madam.'

Marcus was persistent on the telephone. He simply had to see me, he said. If I didn't agree, he was coming round to my flat. It was family stuff, important.

'Is something wrong?' I asked, concerned. 'Is it the children, are they keeping something from me?'

'No, nothing like that. How about lunch on Sunday? We'll motor into the country.'

A woman's scorn touched me, lightly. 'Wow, I get to have a ride in your hot-shot car. What happens if the poison dwarf finds out you're being unfaithful?'

'Bin it, Milla,' he said. 'Just tell me if you can come.'

'I shouldn't really,' I said, knowing that I would, it being a Sunday and all. 'I have an awful lot to do, at the moment.'

'Even on a Sunday?' He sounded disbelieving.

'Okay,' I said slowly, 'phone me on Saturday and I'll tell you if it's possible.'

Let him stew till then, I thought.

Brad Delman lifted the receiver on the first ring, just as I was about to replace the telephone having remembered that it was 5 a.m. in New York.

'I'm most terribly sorry,' I said, embarrassed. 'This is Annie Lloyd, I didn't mean to wake you. I'd forgotten about the time difference.'

He gave his Burt Reynolds laugh. 'No need to be so terribly sorry, Annie Lloyd. Gee, I love the way you talk. I haven't retired yet.'

'You're not in bed? Why ever not?' (As though it were my business.)

'No big deal, I'm stuck in my studio all day painting, so sometimes I go out at night. Jog in the park, go get the morning paper hot from the press. Stop off at the all-night deli for pastrami on rye with a pickle.'

'How terribly brave of you. Are you not worried about being mugged?'

The BR laugh came again. 'Don't be silly, dear, I'm one of the muggers.'

'Brad,' I screeched, 'how can you say such a thing?'

'Only kidding,' he said. 'When are you getting your buns over here? I can hardly contain myself.'

I quickly opened my shorthand notepad, no time like the present for some relevant mating agency information. 'I bet you say that to all your transatlantic conquests.'

'No, I usually correspond by letter. It's your sexy voice that makes me want to talk to you.'

'Have you corresponded with many of us?' I asked, trying not to sound like an interviewer.

He laughed again. 'Sure.'

'How many have you met that way?'

'A couple.'

'So what happened, Brad? Didn't they like you?'

'Sure they liked me.' He sounded miffed. 'They both fell in love with me. But one wanted to live in California and the other didn't like sex.'

(Well, I like sex, Brad Delman, but not with you, I think.)

'Hey,' he said, 'you promised to tell me when you're arriving.'

So I had, but things were changing.

'I hope to be in New York in about four weeks' time. I shall let you know.'

'Great stuff. Where are you staying? You can bunk in with me if you like. I'd just love that.'

'I'm staying at a place called 79 Park Lane. Do you know it?' (I ignored the bunking-in invitation. No way, Jose.)

'Sure, it's the hotel for women. Well, I guess I'll have to court you properly and get permission to call on you.'

I could hear him breathing, it was uncanny across all that distance. 'Brad, I must go,' I said urgently, 'or I'll be bankrupt.'

'Okay, I'll call you next week. I love you, Annie.'

Americans were truly weird, I thought. I'd heard about it, everyone touching, and saying I Love You to total strangers. They spread the love word around like honey running over hot buttered toast.

I tried to concentrate on my reports, but the telephone would not stop ringing.

'Hello, Diana,' I said into the receiver. 'I'll be faxing them in half an hour, I promise. This cannot possibly be a social call, you have your office voice on.'

'Got it in one,' she said aggressively. (So what else was bugging her?)

'The bill has come in for your airline tickets. Jesus, they're expensive.'

'Yes, aren't they?' I said sweetly.

The lighter clicking told me she was not about to go.

'Anything more?' I asked.

She took an enormous drag. 'I've had a call from Marcus. He was asking about you. Says he's trying to see you.'

'Why should Marcus call you about me?' I tried to keep resentment from my voice.

'He says he knows you're working on something, and suspects it's to do with me. I told him he's wrong.'

'It's none of his business,' I said crossly, standing up and getting impatient for her to go.

'I don't think you should see him just yet,' she said.

What business was it of hers, how dare she try to tell me how to live my life? She'd already had her turn and she wasn't about to get another.

'Not unless you're desperate for a man in bed,' she said, when I didn't answer her. 'Because that is where he'll want to take you.'

I collapsed into my office chair. Desperate for a man in bed, did she say? Well, hardly, I ask you . . . !

No sooner had I replaced the receiver than the wretched telephone rang again.

'Darling, how nice to hear from you,' I said at the sound of Emma's voice, cradling the telephone on my shoulder as I attempted to concentrate on my keyboard while she talked.

'Mother,' she said dramatically, 'the doctor says that I'm not well.'

I stopped typing. 'Why, whatever is wrong?' (I should have known better than to ask, but suppose it was something genuinely terrible, what then?)

'He says it's stress, and it's affecting the baby. They may have to do a caesar, and bring it early.'

'Oh, Emma, I hope not,' I said, hating the thought of it. 'Natural is so much better. What is it that's causing you so much worry?'

'Well, you for one thing, Mother.' The words tumbled out of her mouth, it was instant cleansing of her frustrations.

'Me? You don't need to worry about me. I'm kept busy and sometimes I'm even happy.'

She sighed. 'That's what is worrying me, Mother.'

'You are worrying because sometimes I'm happy?' I hoped that she was sitting down to support that extra weight, this was turning into a long conversation.

'Don't be silly, Mother. It's just that you're acting strangely and you're never at home.'

'I'm at home now, and deep into work at that. Or rather I was until you interrupted me.'

'Are you seeing a lot of men still?'

'No, next question.'

'Are you seeing a lot of that man you met at the dinner party?'

I took a deep breath to stay calm.

'Emma, he does have a name and you know that it's Gus. Yes, I do see him quite often. But don't worry, you're not going to have a stepfather.'

'Oh, Mum,' she said, 'I can't tell you how happy you've made me. I had a terrible feeling you were going to marry him. And it would absolutely kill Daddy if you married again.'

I laughed, but not humorously. 'Really, Emma, it wouldn't even come close to killing him. But I'd better tell you, I am seeing someone for lunch on Sunday.'

'Oh, Mother, no, who? Another stranger, I suppose?'

Smart answers came to my mind, but this was not the

time, or with the right person. 'No, not a stranger exactly. Your father.'

'Oh, Mummy, that's great news.' (It was also enough on the subject of men.)

'Did I tell you I'm off around the world in two weeks' time, on an assignment?' I knew that I hadn't told her but it was an opportunity to bring it into the open. And Emma was just the person to tell.

'Oh, how lovely, Mummy.' (I smiled to myself, noticing how I had progressed from Mother, to Mum, to Mummy as she began to feel safer. 'Is it an important assignment?'

'Yes, quite.' (Well, to me it is, and the pay is good.)

'Will it be in the papers?' (Jesus, I hope not.)

'Shouldn't think so, darling, not unless my bag is snatched on Fifth Avenue and I stab the snatcher in the heart as he tries to get away.'

'Will you bring some of those adorable American baby clothes back?'

'Yes, darling. But only if you promise not to have a caesar while I'm gone.'

'I promise you, Mummy. I shall absolutely refuse.'

'Good girl,' I said. 'You do that.'

As it was not likely I'd be asked by Harry to have wine at dinner, I decided to down as much white as I could while I bathed. I liked Harry and was genuinely sorry that after tonight I might never see him again.

'You look like a tall Paul Hogan tonight,' I said when we met and he shyly kissed my cheek.

'Come off it, lady, he's a bonzer-looking bloke,' he said.

'So are you, Harry,' I persisted. (My wine at home had come in several very large goblets.)

'Pull the other one,' he said, and blushed.

After a musical at Her Majesty's Theatre, during which

Harry fell asleep and snored, and an unmemorable dinner at a tourist restaurant of his choice, during which I had to excuse myself to go and throw up (Coca-Cola on top of all that wine, no doubt), I found myself whisked to his hotel room for talks.

'How about marrying me, Annie?' he said without preamble, as I placed my bag plus recorder in a strategic position. 'I like you. We'd have a good life together and you'd soon get used to the station.'

'I thought you were seeing other women. Are you asking us all the same question?' I said facetiously. 'Maybe you should line us all up and do Eenie, Meenie, Minie, Mo.'

'Are you listening, girl?' he said, taking my coat off. 'You're not very good at listening, Annie.'

I moved away from him. 'I'm not sure that I would get used to the station, Harry. It's so huge, and I know nothing about life out there.'

He came over to me and placed his hands on my shoulders. 'It isn't big, Annie, it's only a hundred square miles. That ain't big. Don't you like me?'

'Oh yes, Harry, I do,' I said quickly, looking into his face.

That did it. He started to kiss me. I always was a sucker for kisses, and Harry, well, he could certainly kiss. I pulled away and disconnected my mini-mike.

'Maybe I should go,' I said, regaining my breath but not showing much enthusiasm for leaving.

'Annie,' he said, picking me up and taking me towards the bed, 'cut the crap and stop talking. Jesus, you Brits can't listen but you certainly can gab.'

It was wonderful sex, quite remarkable. He knew much more in life than how to rear prize sheep.

'Come back with me,' he said from under the sheet.

I stroked his arm. 'I need time to think,' I said, feeling trapped now that I'd been to bed with him.

'Maybe I could come for a visit, you don't have snakes, do you?'

Was I becoming promiscuous, I asked myself at home, alone. Or was this what the young referred to as casual sex? I wasn't required to be monogamous because I had no husband, but hadn't I always told the children it was morally wrong to have more than one mate at a time?

That was it, then. No more men for me in bed, except Gus. If I could fit in a quick trip to Harry's sheep station while I was visiting Sean O'Donnell in Sydney, I would definitely not sleep with him.

The lunch with Marcus turned into dinner. I had work to finish, I said. Whether this was entirely true or whether I wanted the last word, I was not sure. But Marcus seemed pleased, almost as though he preferred dinner but did not think I would go for it.

The sixteenth-century inn where we dined was the one he took me to on my thirty-ninth birthday. The dining-room was still lit exclusively with candles and the whole place still smelled of wax polish and wood fires. Ducks turned slowly on the spit just the way I remembered.

Marcus had taken care, and dressed the way he used to. A smart grey worsted suit had replaced the designer jeans, and he wore a discreet tie, a Dior one that I had given him before he left me.

He bought Dom Perignon champagne at great expense, then asked my opinion on the red wine before he ordered (an unheard-of move when we were married). 'I think we should do this more often,' he said, raising his champagne glass.

Somehow I was not impressed. I looked across the table through the flickering candlelight and wondered if I could ever trust him again. I had dreamed up moments like this in the bad old days when he first left me. Often it was what had kept me going. But now that it was happening it seemed different.

'Perhaps,' I said slowly.

He topped up our glasses. 'You look good,' he said, 'young, too.'

I stared at him. 'Why are we here?'

He leaned on his arms and looked into my eyes. 'I realize I still love you.' I did not answer. 'Do you still love me?' he asked. 'You said you always would.'

I felt tearful and emotional suddenly. Here I was sitting across the table from the only man I'd ever intended to have in my life, and it was not the great lover-returning dream. 'Six months ago if you had asked me that question I would have fallen into your arms,' I said quietly.

He kept his eyes on my face. 'So what has changed you?'

I watched the bubbles in my glass. The children would love it if we got together again, I knew. Didn't I owe it to them to try?

'Learning about your other women hasn't helped.'

After a short silence he said, 'They were not important, and I'd never be like that again.'

(Didn't all men say that? But wouldn't it be nice to be rid of Annie Lloyd, and Dizzy Tits, and lonely Sundays?)

'You broke my heart.'

'I know,' he said. 'I'm sorry.'

'You'll never know what I went through those first two years.'

'I didn't think that you would take it so badly.'

'I'm a different woman now.'

'I realize. You go out with a lot of men.'

Gus would understand if I took Marcus back, I thought. He probably expected something like this to happen. And of course I would return the earrings.

'So you think that makes us quits?'

He was silent, but soon he would ask me if I'd slept with other men. I'd have to be truthful. Would he be able to handle that, I wondered.

The wine was going to my head. 'I've been so lonely.'

He reached for my hand. 'I could change that, if you would forgive me,' he said.

(Gus could never satisfy me the way Marcus did. Edward could, but he was too young. Harry did, but he lived in Australia.)

'I'm drunk,' I said over coffee in front of the wood fire.

'So am I,' he said, 'let's stay the night.'

'I can't sleep with you, I'm not ready.' (I've been sleeping around too much, it isn't right.)

'So I'll sleep on the floor.' He was laughing.

We walked in the garden, perfume from night-scented stocks made me light-headed.

'Does Angie know about tonight?' For some inexplicable reason I was shaking from head to foot.

'We've parted,' he said. 'Didn't I tell you what happened?' He knew he hadn't. He put his arm around me as we slowly walked the narrow cobbled path. 'The ex-husband's just died from Aids. He must have had it for years. We both had the test and it was negative. But somehow, I couldn't perform after that.'

Why did he think he could tell me stuff like this, and it would all be all right? I felt sick.

'I want to go home,' I said. 'You shouldn't drive. Can we hire a mini-cab for me?'

Someone knocking on my flat door could only be the porter. The street door was always locked and no one was showing up on the screen from the other side of it. I opened the door without even looking through the magic eye. My expectant smile slipped when I did not look into the eyes of a porter, but those of a very smartly turned-out lady. The grooming was sensational and the clothes spelled out filthy rich. The red hair was lacquered to perfection, it would have been a formidable gale that could have unleashed it. The wide, mascara-coated deep green eyes and the parted red lips had possibly never known defeat.

'Miz Lloyd?' the talking waxwork asked, and didn't I just know exactly who she was? My voice deserted me.

'Miz Annie Lloyd?' she asked, a little less casually. 'Ah think you may know why ah'm heah.' (Edward had not told me his mother was from the South. He was such a Boston man himself.)

My voice returned. 'You had better come in . . .'

Her perfume was only overpowering in the sense that it reeked great expense, 220 dollars' worth a bottle, I assessed. Brain-waves moving about in the strange way they do, I found myself wondering whose make the scent could be, instead of concentrating on how not to be crucified.

I showed Barbara-Jean ('I can't call you Mrs Anderson all the time' – 'The name is Barbara-Jean') into my sitting-room, which seemed more modest than a moment before, and wished that I was dreaming and would shortly wake up.

'Would you like tea?' I asked, praying she wouldn't. I couldn't even remember when I'd last seen the teapot, and she was not a tea-bag-in-a-mug sort of lady.

'No, thank you.' She sat down and the tight skirt of her sage-green suit showed an unreasonable length of sheer nylon-clad magnificent leg.

'Wine, perhaps?'

'Ah don't drink alcohol.' Of course she didn't, you could only look like she did on straight water irrigation.

(And hey, you don't need to say it in that tone, as though I, Annie Lloyd, invented crushing grapes and leaving them to ferment. Edward knocks the sauce back without any encouragement from me.)

'If it will make you feel better, ah'll take a Perrier, with a twist of lemon.' She was so at ease as she prepared to destroy me it was frightening. (Move over, Scarlett O'Hara, you have a rival.)

I was relieved to scurry to the kitchen, snatching up my recorder and button mike from the office as I went. If this could be used, Diana would be delirious with joy and I might even get a bonus. I prepared her drink meticulously, using my one remaining hand-engraved crystal water glass and hoping that she would never know that the brew was Highland Spring and not the requested Perrier. I even overcame the wicked desire to spit in the glass the way the slaves did in the bad old Deep South days.

I placed the glass on my one and only low table, and moved it in front of her.

'Ah thank you,' she said, and took a tiny sip.

This Mother of Edward was truly something else. I found myself wondering if she ever used the bathroom without locking the door. Did she ever give in to a scream? Have an orgasm? Burp? And, God forbid, admit to needing deodorant?

'I don't want to cause embarrassment,' I said quickly. 'I've already decided not to see your son again.'

Her expression changed not one iota, her face could have been cast in bronze. She spread her miles of fingers, red-tipped, nails shaped like almonds, along her beautiful knees.

'Ah'm not embarrassed,' she said, her eyes on my face. 'Ah'm here to tell you never to try to see mah son again.'

I bridled, but I'm sure the iron lady did not notice. 'I've told you, I'm not going to see him again.'

'Mah son's impetuous,' she said, as though I hadn't

spoken. 'Ah have to be strong with him, his fahther being a weak man, also.'

(Weak enough to lend us his Rolls Royce for a week-end's pleasure! Scarlett should only know. I felt like telling her, if only to discover that the statue had hidden cracks. I overcame the desire for the sake of Edward's father.)

'I'll write and explain to Edward,' I said, and I might have enlarged on this improbable idea had not Barbara-Jean put down her Highland Spring in mid-sip, narrowed her eyes and said, 'Ya'll do no such thing. He's mah precious boy and ah'm here to protect him from women like you. You stay out of our lives, ya hear?'

With that she opened her Chanel purse, took out a cheque and placed it on the low table. 'For you,' she said, and stood up. 'Thank you kindly for the water.'

I never did look to see how much the cheque was for, and I certainly could have put it to good use. But as I let her out of my front door I tore it up in front of her and pressed the pieces into her cool white palm.

She fixed me with a glassy green eye. 'Mah husband said ya'll would do that. Good day to you, Miz Lloyd.'

Good manners prevailed and I stood at my open door until the lift enclosed her. But then I couldn't help rushing to a window, jumping on to a chair, looking down and watching as a liveried chauffeur helped her into the back seat of the same Rolls Royce in which Edward had taken me to Yorkshire.

But I never did discover who had let her into my apartment block without alerting me. She must have tipped that porter well.

EIGHT

Only four days remained before I left for my world trip, and I wished that I need not take the journey at all.

It had been a bad day from the moment I woke up. The night had been fretful too. There was a monkey on my back, and he intended to bring me to my knees. What on earth, he wanted to know, made me think that I would be any good at this assignment? No woman with half a brain would have agreed to do such a thing. Only a dimwit would want the job.

But wait, I asked him. I hadn't wanted the job, not at first, at any rate. Only desperate loneliness, shortage of money, reluctance to look a wimp in front of Diana, and a deep in-built desire to please had made me agree.

He leered at me, and clung on. He wasn't done with me yet. He still wanted to point out that maybe I was a no-good person, that perhaps my life was useless, hopeless and pointless.

I'd obviously been no good as a wife, or Marcus would not have left me. In all probability, any man would have left me. And had I wondered, ever, if I was much use as a mother either? After all, when the children were small, hadn't I been a party to keeping them out of the bedroom merely because of carnal lust? Shouldn't a physical activity like sex have been secondary to the love and attention little children needed? Men didn't know about these things, it was up to the woman to point out that children must come first. And irresponsible of her if she didn't.

And surely I should take a good look at myself now? Here I was, leaving to go around the world, on an assignment I could have left alone, something I was only doing for money. Should I not be standing by my child in her advanced stage of pregnancy, like any other mother would?

I like to think that I may have picked myself up around then and weakly fought back, but that demon monkey saw the danger in letting me get off easily. So he pressed down on my back a little harder with his clawed feet. He wanted me to have a really bad day, not merely an averagely bad one. And so there was more to come.

Look how I hadn't told my lovely family the truth about the TV job. And had I ever considered that I should confess about my affair with Edward, or about sleeping with Harry Smith? If I kept it to myself, not being religious and all, wasn't that very wrong of me?

He'd got me on my knees now, and I cried out to him to find some pity. Was I never to be allowed points for trying, I asked. I always had tried. I was still trying.

I could accept that I was an average person, with average ability, an average brain and average looks. I knew that I was not a genius, an academic or a great beauty. But I'd always worked hard, and like I said, I'd tried. Wasn't it a fact that life was more hard graft than natural genius anyway? And I'd never shirked hard graft.

That monkey was not impressed . . .

The porter rang my front-door bell and called my name. It necessitated action and I hauled myself together.

When I opened the door he handed me a large bunch of old-fashioned pink roses, my favourites. I kept him at the door long enough to read the card and to discover, not with surprise, that they were from Marcus. I explained to the porter that I was going on holiday very shortly and asked would he care to give the roses to his wife?

He looked into my face with the cunning of a man who thinks he has the whole world sussed, and asked wouldn't the friend with the surname Lloyd who was staying with me, and getting so much mail, like them for her bedroom?

I said that she was leaving too. So he lowered those wicked eyes, said that his wife was up north visiting her ailing father, and would I mind if he gave them to his girlfriend? It was as though he saw me as a partner in crime.

I wanted to say that I would not have minded if he put them in the nearest garbage bin, apart from making the innocent roses suffer. But I said, 'Please do,' and he left a happy man.

I closed the door and tore up the card sending me Love from Marcus in two. It was my first positive act that day, and it led me to getting rid of not only the monkey but the framed pictures of us taken together through the years. I filled a box to distribute between our children, and kept back just two. They stayed out long enough for me to savour before they went on to the back of a high shelf in a dark cupboard.

One was taken on the deck of a friend's yacht when we went sailing with them in the Mediterranean. It was a long time ago, but it felt like yesterday. The wind was blowing our hair and we were laughing. My face was turned towards the camera and Marcus looked down lovingly at me, his arm around my shoulders. We looked so sun-tanned and healthy, and oh, so very happy. Small wonder it was that our friends told us how wonderful we looked together, and how much they envied us. The Perfect Couple they called us, they said.

The other picture was my favourite photograph from our wedding collection. It showed just the two of us, taken outside the church. The wind blew my veil and rippled my newly curled hair as I looked up at Marcus.

As I gazed I remembered how, later, at the reception, he made his speech. He said wonderful things about me, assured my parents and the whole assembly that he would love and protect me for ever. I was the most wonderful girl in the world, he said, the most of everything good and lovely that came to his mind, and then he handed me a golden brooch set with tiny pearls in a circle.

It was all too much for me. I had to be excused to go to the bathroom to shed tears of joy and to savour his words, knowing that I would never forget them. I clutched the brooch to my breast and said aloud, 'Thank you, God, for bringing me such a wonderful man to love and to cherish.'

Now it was over, trophies of our love story were no longer visible, no more lapsing into dreams for me, simply by seeing a picture in a frame. No more musing, no more fantasizing, the end of reverie. The best part of my life was being locked away in a cupboard, and that was that.

I tried not to dwell on the pictures that I'd taken of him with our children, it only reminded me of how foolish I had been to have felt so secure, and so certain that I knew my life's future pattern.

I saw the one with him holding William, aged two, with his tiny arm in plaster and pain showing on his small white face. He'd grown a lump on the bone in his forearm, it all happened so suddenly. One day he was playing and happy, the next he was in hospital having major surgery for the removal of a malignant growth. Marcus and I clung to each other at night and both of us wept most of the time. We were assured that there was nothing we could have done to prevent it happening, but it was small comfort. The ugly treatment that had to follow, William's sickness, the hospital visits was agony for all of us, and it was five years before we knew that he was totally in the clear.

Now I knew for certain seventeen years later that I would never willingly see Marcus again, not after – well – everything. And not after the casual way he told me how the awful Angie's husband had died from Aids, as though it could have been a bad dose of flu.

That night, after dinner together, we'd gone from our walk in the hotel grounds to the reception desk to ask for a room for Marcus and a car and driver to take me home. I could not stop trembling, and while we waited in the lounge for my car to arrive, Marcus drunkenly insisted on giving me a summary of his sex life with the poison dwarf. I hated myself for listening and I hated him even more for telling, but a dreadful fascination gripped me and stopped me from walking away.

She dressed up for sex he said, even in bed, black suspender belt, sheer stockings, high-heeled shoes, very titillating.

'What, no knickers?' I asked, aiming at sarcasm to hide my embarrassment and, perhaps, my jealousy.

It served me right because Marcus looked me in the eye and said, 'Oh yes, she wore knickers, black frilly ones, very French. But she cut a hole in them underneath to make room for me. All very exciting.'

Was I upset at the baseness of it, and that he felt the need to tell me, or do you suppose that I was put out because he had never asked me to perform like that for him? I might not have been any good at it, I might not have wanted to, but I'd not been given the chance, and I had the distinct feeling that this was not the first time he had taken part in that sort of sex.

I grappled the monkey from my back, left him at home to cool off, and went shopping to cheer myself up, the way women do, and I let a reluctant credit card take the strain. I bought a new suitcase and matching flight bag, and hunted for a few clothes suitable for different climates, and especially for California.

Tod Bradshaw had said, 'We'll have a heavy schedule of parties, Annie. The Oscars will be on, so bring something ravishing to wear.' (No wonder I wished that I wasn't going.) When he insisted that I stay at the Beverly Hills Hotel, all expenses paid, I told him that I couldn't possibly.

'Why not?' he asked with surprise. 'You're my guest.'

'But we may not like each other.'

He laughed, and simply said, 'Tough.'

I was not sure what he did for a living – company director was all it had said in his agency details and he had given me no further explanation. He seemed a typical Californian man on the telephone, brash and full of himself. But I had to get enough information on him in two days to keep Diana happy, and if that meant going to parties, then so be it.

The children were coming round for a farewell supper and I had to make myself think about food. My stomach was a mess and anything solid did not want to stay down. When I thought about it, it had not been right since Barbara-Jean's visit. That Mother of Edward must have put a hex on me.

Back home I tried to discipline myself into making a list of things to pack, but something held me back. It was as though with my bag not packed on time I would miss the plane and then I need not go at all. Just a normal reaction to something one would rather not do, I supposed.

Irish Rose who did for me was out of hospital, walking strangely, looking thinner than ever and holding her stomach in position with her hands. She was moving in with Kat when I left, to rest and recuperate in peace, away from her husband. Piles may have been causing him discomfort in his back passage but their presence did not affect his virility, and poor Rose was a very used woman. I think that she looked forward to the prospect of staying in my flat, away from the sex machine.

Emma and Gareth, Katie and William came round to supper and to collect written details of my whereabouts while I was travelling. Emma tried to make me swear on her unborn baby's life that I would not have any affairs with strange men, not go out after dark, not carry a handbag to encourage robbers and not ever talk to anyone I did not know, no matter which country I was in. I tried to tell her that the latter would be impossible in America where everyone was so verbal. She would have none of it, so I mumbled something incoherent about not seeing men anyway, and shied off swearing that I would not carry a bag, it was too much of a burden on the baby, I said.

They all loved the mystery of Annie Lloyd and promised not to breathe a word to anyone. They wouldn't keep that promise, of course, the moment my back was turned, but as they did not know what I was actually doing, I could see no harm in it.

William whispered in my ear, 'You find someone nice to have dinner with, Mum, Emma need never find out.'

'The Academy Awards will be on when I'm in LA,' I said, 'so it should be exciting.'

'Brilliant,' Kate said. 'Imagine, our mum might get on the telly. You might see Kevin Costner in person now.'

'Tom Hanks would be better,' Emma said. 'How on earth did you find an empty hotel room?'

'I haven't,' I said. 'I've got to share with three strapping chaps, I hope they're good-looking . . .'

They all laughed except Emma. 'Very funny,' she said sarcastically.

Then, while we were ploughing through nursery-type bread-and-butter pudding and cream (by special request, they must have really been feeling insecure about their mother travelling – they should only know the half of it, as I've said before), William looked at Kate, his soulmate, and said he wanted to tell us something.

'As long as you're not getting married, you can tell me anything,' I said, without thinking, and not meaning to hurt someone I loved so dearly. He was the favourite child we mothers are not supposed to talk about having.

Kate looked down at her plate and Wills looked slightly gutted. 'Well, you see, Mum, I just might be getting married,' he said in his usual quiet way. 'The point is, I've fallen well and truly in love.'

'Bad luck, old man,' Gareth said, and Emma glared at him.

Kate said, 'Isn't it brilliant, and she's pure heaven to know.'

'So how come you've met her and we haven't?' Emma asked Kate, petulant as ever.

I put my hand over William's in his lap. 'That makes me very happy, it really does,' I said. 'Sorry about the thoughtless remark.'

William put down his spoon and looked serious. 'There's just a small complication, Anna is pregnant. Neither of us knows whether she should have an abortion or whether we should get married.'

We all gave him our silent attention while we separately tried to ascertain if he wanted our opinions or knew exactly what he was going to do and would tell us any moment.

'You may regret an abortion,' I said, as a mother should.

'Pregnant is not the way to start a marriage,' Emma said.

Kate looked defensive and said, 'Anna's lovely, Wills would be a fool to let her go. Show Mum her picture.'

The remark was arranged – it was a let's-get-it-all-over-at-once agreement between the two of them. William, in a flash, produced a picture from his top pocket, and I looked into the eyes of the most beautiful black girl you could ever imagine.

I could feel Katie's unblinking eyes upon me, and it had nothing to do with Anna's colour. 'She's very lovely,' I said. 'What age is she?'

William shifted in his seat and said quickly, 'That's it, you see, Anna is thirty-eight and her clock is running out, she's never had a child before.'

Many emotions flitted over my brain, but fear stuck. My God, Edward's mother had just given me the hardest time over her son, and now I was facing the same situation.

'But you don't mind about her being older than Wills, do you, Mum?' Kate said assertively.

'I bet she does,' Gareth cut in, and I gave him my fiercest look. That boy always managed to say the wrong thing.

'That's too old,' Emma said to William. 'You'll regret it, marrying her, that is. She should have an abortion.'

William's face had become the colour of uncooked dough. I longed to take him in my arms and rock him.

'I'm sure you have both talked it out,' I said.

He looked at me then and his face showed fear. 'We talk about nothing else, Anna knows that everyone will say she's too old for me. She wants to have the baby quietly without marriage and then wait and see how we feel about each other later.'

'She sounds wise,' I said thankfully, thinking maybe there was hope yet.

I thought that I saw tears in William's eyes. 'But I love her so much, Mum. And the baby is mine.'

Was I, perhaps, thankful now that I was going away? William's situation was a little too close to home for comfort. Still, he had proved to me that he was a nicer person than Edward who, predictably, had not put up a fight for me. But then, I think *he* was in love with his mother.

I received a letter from Harry next day. It went like this:

Dear Annie,

You don't have to marry me if you don't want to, but why don't you come over to stay and we can see how you like the station? You would find everyone very friendly, even the snakes! (Only joking.) My boys have been talking to me and they think that they should hop it, go and do some travelling and see what is out in the world, maybe never come back to sheep farming. I never did think that their hearts were in it really. It would be just you and me in the main house, and the hands in their own quarters. They've got their own Abo cook, so no problems, you won't have to do it. (Ha, ha.) I won't be away for more than a few days at a stretch and in no time you can learn to fly and have a real good life. I'll also buy you a new four-wheel-drive truck and I'm already looking at a beaut stallion who would be just right for you. He's not difficult like some of them and he likes to be ridden hard.

I came back to a bloody awful bush fire, it had started before I got here, you might have read about it or seen it on the telly. The back-burning we had to do as a precaution went wrong on account of the wind changes and one of my men was burned to death when a flaming tree fell on him. Leaves a missus and four nippers up in Darwin, and that's not good. Fairly broke me up. But we only lost two buildings, which was lucky, and the water tower collapsed. What with that, and the firefighters' hoses, the mud has been bloody awful, up over the top of the old boots. We lost a lot of bush animals, especially koalas, poor little buggers were trapped when the fire went around in a circle. Some of them died stuck to the branches of the gum trees, but I've saved a few. You should come over real quick and help to look after them. Reckon you'd like that, and I don't have a lot of time for putting ointment on tiny burned paws. I've burned my arms a bit and the backs of my hands too, but they'll be right in no time. It's a bit painful writing but not too bad, otherwise I wouldn't be doing it. I think about you a lot, Annie, and know you're the girl for me. Just say you'll come and I'll send an air ticket right off. No promises, no packdrill. Just come and look and enjoy.

Yours very truly, Paul Hogan's lookalike (I wish).

I very nearly wrote Harry a confession, I almost could not bear to think how I'd deceived him. I wanted to tell him that my name was not Annie, but I liked the way he said it and he could call me Annie if he wanted to. I wanted to confess that I was not looking for a husband but I liked him very much.

Couldn't I pretend that it was all a joke, I wondered. That I'd done it for a dare? At my age, come off it. A man like Harry would think I should be put away in a secure place. Anything at all, then? Except the truth, that is. I couldn't tell him about the programme, he'd be so angry he would blow its cover right away. But I had a bad conscience about him, and as I said, I rather specially liked him. I wouldn't have minded visiting his station and staying for a while, sans plane and stallion, of course.

So, wait a min, if I was now going to Australia to find out what Sean O'Connell was up to, maybe I could work in a quick trip to the station. Sort of surprise him. Just stay for a day or so. (And sleep in his bed again, you mean? No, no, nothing like that. Just to say hi, and stay friends!)

The day before I travelled was frantic to the point of me throwing up, and I had no time at all to dwell on second thoughts and ifs, buts and maybes. I didn't even have time to varnish my nails.

Diana telephoned me five times, and each time contradicted what she had said previously. I carried my freephone around stuck to my ear as I did not have time to sit down, and I ignored most of what she said. Apart from screaming at her once, that is, to say no, I would definitely not go to see Charlie Bloody Diamond and that was final. (You can see how some part of Harry had brushed off on me.)

I packed my files into my overnight bag to study on the long flight to Johannesburg. Rose moved in with her suitcase and I took my car to the garage for repairs, asking them sweetly to send the bill to Marcus.

I packed and repacked three times, but that was just par for the course. I stayed awake all the previous night, and should have varnished my nails in bed as I tremblingly watched, at 2 a.m., a terror-rated blood-curdling thriller.

Then, all of a sudden, it was time to leave, and Gus was at my door with transport. Rose clung on to Kat, and Kat clung to me. At the lift door I turned back to ask Rose if she would take Kat home with her and cherish her for ever if anything happened to me and I did not return. She burst into tears, and Gus pushed me into the lift.

Under the Passengers Only sign at Heathrow he took me in his arms and asked me to marry him, third-party vocabulary of course.

'Gus loves you so much,' he said. 'He can only think

of having you for his wife. He make you very happy for always.'

I promised to think about it. I knew that I could never be safer than I would be as Gus's wife. And maybe I'd stay wise and not run the risk of losing him by telling him that I'd slept with Edward, or that I'd slept with Harry and that he, too, wanted me to marry him. Along with a South African God person, an Irish Aussie, and six yet to be blind-dated Americans.

'We could marry in New York,' he said. 'That way no one is around to tell you no.' (I wondered who he had in mind?)

I promised again to think about it, we hugged and kissed goodbye, and I waved till he was out of my sight.

It was exciting travelling first-class. In the preference lounge I was plied with champagne. All the males wore classy suits, looked like successful businessmen and had their briefcases open importantly. It was no place to try to varnish my nails.

There was only one other woman in the hushed lounge, and before she turned and smiled at me my heart missed a beat, and I wondered what excuse I would need to leave the lounge and refuse to travel that day. She had flaming red hair and from the back she looked for all the world like Barbara-Jean. Still, maybe if it had been her we could have had a mutual understanding, now that I knew what it was like to be worried sick about the welfare of your only son.

NINE

I was proud to be travelling British Airways. Up front in first class they had picked them well, those stewards and stewardesses. By computer magic they knew my name, took my flight bag, showed me to my window seat, explained how to turn it into a bed, plied me with cushions and a blanket, hung my coat on a hanger in a cupboard in the nose cone and gave me a glass of ice-cold vintage champagne of which Marcus would have been jealous. And all of that in the first five minutes. So much room did I have it was a mighty long stretch to the container pocket on the seat-back in front of me. I examined everything carefully, like an inquisitive child, checked that they were telling the truth about the location of my life-jacket (as though it mattered, how often have you heard of anyone being rescued alive from a jet crashing from thirty thousand feet?).

I'm altogether childish on planes, I like to sit with my nose glued to the window, even when there is not much more to see than clear blue sky and the occasional vapour trail left by another plane. And looking out while still on the ground, watching the luggage and food activity, gives me quite a thrill, there's such a sense of purpose in preparing a plane for a long-distance flight. A steward once told me that the calmest place while still on the ground is on the flight deck, but I am not in a position to verify that remark.

So I was slightly miffed when a rather handsome chap disturbed my rêverie as he was seated beside me. The head steward was giving him special attention and almost pulling a forelock. In wonderment I watched, and it was then that I noticed the passenger had a leather metal-bound bag chained to his wrist. With the steward's help he unchained himself from the bag, took off his jacket and gave it to the steward and then rechained the bag to the inner metal leg of his seat, tucking it firmly in front of him and putting his feet on it. I tried to see what he did with the key but his sleight-of-hand was ahead of me. Then, from his briefcase, treated much more casually, he retrieved a cashmere sweater and pulled it over his head, fished the *Financial Times* from under some typed papers, loosened the tastefully patterned tie snuggled up to the collar of his blue silk shirt, and turned towards me with a friendly nod and a smile on his nicely tanned face.

'Well, that was more riveting than watching food trays come on board,' I said, reckoning that if he had not wanted to speak he would not have looked at me. 'Can I expect an encore?'

'I have been known to extract an egg from my ear, but if I do, don't applaud,' he said, humour showing at the corners of his mouth. 'Fred here doesn't like sharp noises.'

'Fred?' I echoed, knowing that was what he wanted.

'Yes, he's my viper.'

'In your bosom?' I asked as a joke.

'No, in my pocket. I carry him to protect me.'

'From women?' I asked incredulously.

He smiled. 'Who knows? But don't worry, he's in the outside pocket, not the one next to you.'

He had to be joking, of course, but he left the words hanging in the air, as was intended. The steward brought him champagne, and refilled my glass.

'I'm Greg McLaren,' my companion said to me and

held out his enormous, well-manicured hand for me to grip.

'Camilla Cage,' I said, feeling good at using my real name. 'Are you going all the way to Johannesburg?'

With a dead-pan face he looked straight into my eyes and said, 'I think I should, don't you? The plane doesn't stop anywhere else.'

I blushed and hit my forehead with the heel of my hand. 'It must be the champagne, I think I should keep quiet. Would it upset you if I varnished my nails?'

'Not at all,' he said. 'Would it upset you if I read my paper?'

I retrieved my varnish from my bag, relieved at last to be using it. 'Not if you don't read it aloud. I hate commerce, and the giants of industry who get their pictures in the press never look like giants to me, more like fat gnomes in glasses.'

As I looked down and concentrated on not covering too many things other than my nails with varnish I felt sick, and the small gnawing pain I'd suffered for a few days previously started to nag. I had to close my eyes and put my head back. God, I thought, I hope I'm not getting an ulcer, that's all I need.

Doors slammed shut, seatbelts were checked, overhead lockers double-checked, and excitement mounted as the crew were told by a mystery voice to take their seats. In no time at all we were rushing down the runway and the centrifugal force effect on my stomach was not nice. In the air, I felt better. There was no turbulence and once the plane had banked in the right direction, cut through the clouds and into clear blue sky, climbed to the prescribed thirty thousand feet and the captain had lulled us into sublimity at the mere sound of his voice, apart from a slight headache I forgot about any pains. Anxious to feel totally well, I asked for an aspirin, and when the stewardess brought it she assured me that lots of people get headaches on jumbo jets, a sort of air-sickness, she said, but it would pass.

After cocktail orders had been taken and canapés served together with the smallest paper napkins I have ever seen, elaborate menus were handed out. Between then and dinner I dozed off into half-sleep and had the weirdest dream about Tod Bradshaw in Los Angeles. I didn't of course know what sort of house he had in California, but in my dream, after getting out of a London taxi high up in Beverly Hills I'd dragged a cabin trunk full of ball-gowns up his short front drive, straightened a large and unlikely straw hat I was wearing, and pressed his doorbell.

A man in drag answered and I knew from photographs that he was Tod. The large dark moustache did not go well with the heavy makeup and the red silk dress he was wearing, and, if you can believe it, on his head rested, at a comic angle, a hat identical to mine.

'Annie darling,' he yelled as though I were across the street and not two feet in front of him, 'you're just in time. Come and have a quick snort and I'll take you to the pool to meet the others. We're skinny-dipping . . .'

I was not sorry to wake up.

Greg McLaren asked me during dinner if I was on a business trip. I very nearly told him the truth, it happens I think with complete strangers in the isolation of the skies, but common sense prevailed and I said that I was on a world trip, visiting friends and relations as I went. He asked me which major cities I was taking in and I told him, dates and all. Really gabby, I was. I asked him what he did, since he would not have expected me to see him as the usual sort of traveller, considering his unusual sort of luggage.

'Well, I can't confess to being a captain of industry after what you've said about them, so let's say that's what I'm not.' He went on to regale me about himself for fifteen minutes, and it sounded for all the world as though he was giving me his life history, except that at the end of the entertainment I was none the wiser about what he actually did for a living. If he was not a spy he should have been, so skilful was he at verbally ducking and diving.

'I actually live in New York,' he said. 'Dirty, violent and brash, but I love it.'

'Oh, I thought you were English,' I said. 'Sorry, I mean Scottish.'

He laughed. 'I am Scottish. I live in London too sometimes, and lots of other places. But my main base is in New York.'

'Do you like Los Angeles?' I asked him.

'No, I hate it,' he answered quickly. 'Everyone conning everyone else. The place is full of pseuds.' It was a good thing I hadn't actually been going there to meet a prospective husband with a view to living on that sun-soaked coast for the rest of my life or I might have become extremely depressed.

With dinner over and plates, cloths and coffee cups removed, he excused himself. 'Fred wants a drink of water,' he said. His eyes were full of merriment, but then perhaps they should have been – he had consumed a few jars of merry-making liquid.

As Greg left, the chief steward came up and took his seat and stayed there without so much as a glance in my direction until Greg returned. Could they perhaps have thought that left alone I might have used a pocket-sized jemmy to open up the chained leather bag and spy on the contents?

I was just deciding that I would answer Harry Smith's letter and express it to him from Johannesburg, when earphones were given out and blinds were firmly drawn down. It was film time, like it or not. I wondered what right they had to assume that everyone needed in-flight entertainment. As I said, I get a kick out of watching blue skies, or the stars. It's like dreamtime with your eyes open. And if it's daytime and good visibility you can see the ocean too, way, way down beneath you, and that's an added bonus.

We were settled in by the BA nannies, our feet coming up and our seat-backs reclining, blankets tucked in and pillows placed whichever way we liked them. I would have read my book but it was made clear that the use of the personalized overhead light was frowned on by others, so I swallowed a little blue sleeping pill with my last mouthful of wine to ensure that I did not stay awake staring at the bulkhead all night.

The full force of what I was embarking on began to sink in before the pill took effect and I didn't much like the feeling, especially after my weird dream earlier. I was a long way from home, and I was committed up to my neck to see the job through properly if I hoped to get paid.

Still, I had a great six hours' sleep. Greg McLaren said the second film was terrible so he had only watched it for a short time. He said teasingly that he watched me instead, and thought that I looked sweet when I was asleep, which was embarrassing. A strange man watching you sleeping seems immoral somehow, and what if your mouth drops open or, God forbid, you snore?

I felt queasy again when my breakfast grapefruit was served – this air-sickness stuff was not funny. And then it happened.

Without warning of any kind, no particular turbulence, no fasten your seatbelt announcements and no bells ringing, the plane dropped bodily out of the sky. No nose-dive, no noise change, just dropping without, it seemed, any means of support at all from the engines.

Stewardesses were tumbling down the aisle, people were screaming, breakfast trays were flying around, and so were scrambled eggs, coffee, croissants and toast. I do not know how long it was before the monster stopped falling but it seemed like an hour. Continuing forwards happened so naturally that without the chaos around it could have been an impossible dream.

I removed my arms from around Greg McLaren's neck, and noticed that he looked as grey as I felt. My throat hurt, and I knew I must have been screaming. A young steward lifted himself up off the deck, blood streaming down his face from where a flying tray or something had caught his forehead.

The captain didn't even bother to use his calm-making voice. He went straight in with 'We're all right now, ladies and gentlemen, but wasn't that a dreadful experience? It was air disturbance of the worst kind, but I must say I've never had it happen to me before in twenty years of flying. Please accept my apologies. Now you know why we suggest that you keep your seatbelts fastened at all times, and I hope that you all had them firmly done up when that happened.'

Greg McLaren poured coffee out of one of the shoes he'd discarded for the night in favour of the airline slippers, and I picked two segments of grapefruit out of my hair. It sounded like Bedlam in the economy section and all the first-class staff ran aft to help. The co-pilot came to check on us privileged mortals and said that the captain would speak to us again soon. I was relieved to see that he too looked like a ghost, his face was so white. He asked me if I needed anything and I dumbly shook my head. I would have liked to ask how soon I could get off, would the electrical system be affected by all the escaping liquid, was he sure it wouldn't happen again? But I couldn't find my voice.

He whispered something to Greg McLaren and left us to our nervousness. The cabin staff returned and cleared up as best they could. I didn't know that tears were running down my cheeks until Greg told me not to cry, he was sure that we were safe now.

'I'm not crying,' I said. 'I'm just wishing that I was safely at home, with my children.'

He reached across and patted my hand. 'I envy you the children. When I thought that we were going to die my only worry was for my old mother. I'm all she has.'

'Did you think we were going to die?' I asked. 'I'm glad I didn't know, you seemed so calm I was getting my strength from you.'

'Oh, I certainly thought we might die,' he said. 'That wasn't calm, it was paralysis.'

The chief steward came along, said something to him and took his place as he left his seat, as usual. He saw me looking at him.

'Mr McLaren has gone to the flight deck,' he said unsmilingly, and left it at that.

It was an obvious relief to us all to land safely in Johannesburg, somehow coming down seemed more dangerous than usual after our brush with death. Then we had to wait while casualities were taken off. Two men and one small boy in economy had broken wrists and fingers, one woman was threatening to miscarry and was taken off on a stretcher, and the injured steward went off to have his head stitched. We made a motley caravan when we left the plane, more like a defeated battalion of troops returning from war than a plane-load of fare-paying passengers. Not one person, including the crew from the captain down, looked well. We all carried the same pallor, pale grey, and the only smiles were those thin ones of relief.

I don't know where Greg McLaren went. We were kept in our seats till well after he had disembarked, his leather bag rechained to his wrist and a messenger carrying the rest of his gear. Before the chaining took place he handed me his card.

'That shows where I live in New York,' he said, 'and that's when I expect to be there,' pointing to his handwriting on the back. 'If you feel like company when you're passing through, give me a ring. I'll be someone to have dinner with.'

I thanked him and said that I would like that and we could celebrate being alive.

He looked at me strangely for a moment. Then it seemed to dawn on him that we had very nearly been in serious trouble together and he nodded, rather absently. It must have been some huge assignment he was on, to control his mind so successfully. Speaking for myself, I knew that I would remember that trip for ever.

I had to connect with a flight to Cape Town. Needless to say, I had missed it. Immigration took for ever. Luggage materialized with unbelievable slowness, and Customs (seriously) were on a 'go-slow'. No ready smiles abounded, no helpfulness was shown, and forget concern for a poor beleaguered traveller. It was as though everyone had been struck dumb. If I asked directions of someone, even another traveller, because nervousness was making me blind, a finger would be pointed at the sign already pointing a finger. It was hard going, shoving my trolley with only three working wheels up the narrow steep slope that led, with a cunningly bad design, to Internal Flights, and when a frail old man in front of me gave up the struggle with his over-loaded cart halfway up, and stepped nimbly aside to let it go into reverse, no need to tell you where that left me.

I was late, the bossy female with the Afrikaans accent told me. I knew that, I said, but it was not my fault, the plane I was travelling on very nearly . . . Was I not aware, she demanded to know, that it was a public holiday tomorrow, and everyone was trying to get to Cape Town for the weekend? . . . No, sorry, I said humbly, I didn't know that. But I had my ticket from London, England, to Cape Town. To get there today, and it was paid for . . .

'Virry sirry,' she said, in that strange South African idiom of the English language, 'but so has iveryone ilse paid for a ticket, you aare wait-listed. Sit down over there till you aare called.'

'No, thank you,' I answered bravely, 'my luggage is too heavy for me to keep moving it. I'll stand here and wait.'

'No, you cannot—'

'Yes, I can.' (Just watch me.)

She didn't stand a chance, not after what I'd been through. It only took a quick glance for me to establish that the six wait-listed passengers, obediently sitting where they had been sent, were all very large young men with long legs and no luggage, and my overstrained three-wheeler appendage would make me no match for them in the final dash.

She had one more go as the one to be obeyed. 'You can leave your luggage h'yar. Then go and sit down.'

'No, I absolutely refuse,' I heard Annie say on behalf of Camilla, in a voice far stronger than she was actually feeling. And not only that, Camilla didn't take her eyes off the gauleiter's face for the next ten loaded minutes. Though she did stand aside to show a vestige of respect.

The bossy bitch caved in eventually, and beckoned me over one split second before her sidekick picked up his loudspeaker and invited all the wait-listed passengers for Cape Town to come to the desk. She processed my ticket, handed me a boarding card, and almost smiled. 'Virry sirry about your plane,' she said.

I made myself smile. 'It wasn't your fault. Just bad luck,' I said, all friendly. Well, at least she'd talked to me, and no one else had.

It was an overloaded one-class plane, more like a bus really, with very little room for our knees. The black lady sitting next to me was extremely large, and oozed over on to my section of seat. She also had a crawling-age baby squirming on her knee. He was a nice little chap, but fed-up, like me, and he gave her some grief. After take-off he managed to break free, and his goal was my lap. His mother was anxious, I told her not to worry, he could sit there for a bit, give her a rest. Instantly at ease, he smiled beguilingly into my face from his new resting place, fingered the gold chain around my neck, blew a few bubbles, pressed on my nose with a tiny brown finger, giggled . . . and then peed.

A uniformed mahogany-faced giant held aloft a card with Annie Lloyd's name on it, and I can tell you, I felt overwhelming relief. I was tired, dirty, and wet around the lap. Being winter out there it was kind of chilly, even though the sun was huge, and the sky a vivid blue. I smiled up at the man, and though his expression did not flicker, a teenaged fair-haired girl who was with him smiled back and extended her hand.

'You have to be Annie,' she said with enthusiasm. 'I'm Amelia Voorberg. Welcome.'

A nice friendly voice at last, and I very nearly wrapped my arms around her neck. The uniformed driver relieved me of the trolley, and Amelia put her arm through mine as we walked, and it was a comfort.

The two of us burrowed into the back seat of the large Mercedes Benz, and the driver, whose name I now knew to be Sylvester, drove us slowly and sedately, by the scenic route for my benefit, Amelia assured me, to the house that was to be my home for the next four days. She put her hand into mine, and seemed genuinely pleased to have my company. Like a child, she asked if I knew the name of the flat-topped mountain that dominates Cape Town on all the picture postcards.

'Table Mountain,' I answered obediently, and she squirmed with delight.

It was beautiful everywhere, colourful, and so clean.

165

And it was greener and more lush than I had imagined. For me, used to London, there seemed a shortage of people, and not much traffic, although Amelia assured me that it was the rush hour.

Eventually we turned into a virtual oasis of beautiful homes, and paddocks, woodland and lawns. There were huge gateways, high flowering hedges almost hiding low, sprawling homes, and an abundance of enormous trees. Sylvester indicated that we were turning left, though no one was around to heed it, and a pair of electric wrought-iron gates opened on their own. As we drove between them, four enormous Rottweilers bounded out from a hidden place, bellowing as they ran.

Amelia gave me a sideways look as she heard my intake of breath. 'Don't worry, Annie,' she said. 'I shall tell them that you are my friend, and a guest in the house, and that they must be nice to you.'

I found myself hoping that they listened to what she said, and preferably before I alighted. I was not averse to the odd dog around the place, I even liked them. But I had a healthy respect for other people's canine pets, especially if they were the size of ponies and used as guard dogs.

Both Amelia and Sylvester (it was the first time that I had heard his voice, and it had the depth of distant thunder) roared orders at them.

'Okay, stand still,' Sylvester said to me, 'let them see you don't mean them no harm.' How about me, Syl, old chap, I wanted to ask. What assurance do I have that they don't mean me no harm, neither?

'This is Mo,' Amelia said, calmly and gently pointing at them, now that she had assumed a semblance of control and the dogs were circling, but slowly. 'And that is Flo. They're husband and wife. And these are their two sons, that one is Best Boy, and this one is Wilfred.'

I didn't really give a toss what their names were and I didn't give Amelia my undivided attention as I was sniffed at, and seriously, by four noses attached to four heads the size of black motorcycle helmets. And especially as Best Boy (or maybe it was Wilfred) became excited at the patch of baby-pee around my crotch, and his willie showed up bright pink and assumed a life of its own as it unsheathed itself.

Of course, as this was the first leg of my new assignment, and it was my exterior only that gave off a semblance of calm, it was comforting to find that His Eminence Lawrence Voorberg had a lovely daughter and (or so it seemed) a very nice home.

My luggage and Sylvester disappeared up a wide staircase and Amelia showed me around. Floor-length windows in the drawing-room revealed a large garden, acres of green lawn and huge flowering shrubs, and a temptingly large swimming-pool – heated, she assured me, as her brothers needed to swim daily to keep them extra fit. I might have asked if I could pop out and take a quick dip myself, had not M and F, BB and Wilf been staring in at me, and salivating, from the other side of the glass.

The kitchen was vast, with a huge wooden table in the middle of it, and open wooden shelving revealing large amounts of china and pans.

'Don't be worried by the size of the kitchen,' Amelia said as we prepared to depart it, 'we do have labour-saving devices, not like the old days.'

Why should I be worried, I wondered. In theory I was moving in as lady of the house, the châtelaine, the one who held the keys and gave the orders. I wasn't coming here as a paid housekeeper.

It was then that I noticed two long handwritten lists covering most of a cupboard door at eye-level. One was headed 'Week's Dog Rota', and for a second I thought I saw Annie Lloyd's name on it. The other one was headed

'Week's Cooking Rota', and her name was definitely on that one.

Amelia saw me looking and said, 'They're emergency lists. The servants are unreliable now, with all the changes. No one has come in today, except Sylvester, not even the gardener. I shall have to give the dogs their evening meal.' And then she laughed, but not particularly humorously, and added, 'And you need to be strong for that. My brothers should do it, but they always cheat.'

She took me upstairs then, and showed me her room first. It was plain and did not look very comfortable. She had just one picture on the wall, a large painting of a good-looking, fair-haired lady. 'That was my mother,' she said, and came close to me, and took my hand. 'I can't show you my brothers' rooms, they keep them locked,' she said, 'so we'll do Daddy's room. You'll just love that one.'

It was large and opulent, but not lovable. The bed was around eight feet wide, and had a heavy, brightly coloured ethnic cover on it, and over it hung a wooden cross almost the size that Jesus had needed when he was in trouble. If it had fallen on Daddy in the night, it would have stapled him to the bed for keeps. The shag-pile carpet came over my shoes, and the heavy Spanish-type furniture had cruel and ugly corners just waiting to deliver leg injuries. The en suite bathroom was tiled in deep blue. The large square bath, and all the other fittings were red, like blood. It was hideous.

And then Amelia took me to my room. It was across a narrow passage and opposite Daddy's room, and it was the size of a closet. Honest to God, with my luggage in the middle of the floor, where Sylvester had left it, I could go no further. I could see a hanging cupboard large enough only to accommodate child's clothing, and a bed from which my feet would surely protrude. And weary as I was, I could have cried. What sort of a welcome was this, for a woman who was supposed to be the Master's intended?

Amelia watched me. 'It's a little small, I know,' she said, 'it was our nursery, when we were babies and Mummy was alive. So it has nice vibes, because she was a very special person. Sometimes when I'm sad I creep in here to sleep. And I can feel her beside me.'

I didn't actually get to meet the Very Rev until just before dinner. I was summoned from a much-needed nap in my minuscule bed by Amelia, looking red in the face, smelling of cooking and wearing a huge black sacking apron. Daddy was awaiting me in the drawing-room, she said, looking, I thought, a tad nervous.

Earlier, I'd risked a swim in the pool while Amelia promised to keep cave on the dogs. I don't know what went wrong, but as I dived in and lost my breath at the coldness of the water, heated or not, a thumping great Rottweiler dived in too, right beside me. And could he ever swim. I did the fastest four lengths of my life (it took me that distance to work out how I could safely stop swimming), and there he was, pacing my every stroke. The finish was a dead heat. I armed myself out breathlessly and sat on the edge of the pool with my eyes closed, waiting to be eaten. Nothing spectacular happened, except that I got drenched with freezing cold dog-smelling water as the beast shook himself, and then all I could hear was heavy panting. It must have been Best Boy, because he ended up leaning on me with a friendliness that could only have been brought on by his memory of the smell of delicious baby-pee on me earlier, when I'd got the first going-over.

I put on my best and tamest dress, had a few practice runs with my mini-mike, and took myself down to the drawing-room, working out as I went how not to stay for four whole days and nights in such a wacky household (and that was before the rest of it revealed itself). As I walked in, and the Very Rev looked up from his paper and over his glasses, I got the distinct feeling that he'd expected me to knock. But he graciously folded his paper, hauled himself to his feet from a huge leather chair, and came at me with both hands extended. His heavy chain and cross swung like a pendulum and his long, faded purple gown (or was it robe?) clung to his ample thighs, showing that he wore long underpants beneath. Not that I blamed him, it was a chilly night, even though a large log fire roared away in the big black hearth.

It surprised me, because Amelia was so fair, that his skin was coffee-coloured, and his white thinning hair clung to his skull in tiny tight curls.

'Virry pleased to meet you,' he said, almost as though I was an unexpected but not resented guest. 'Would you care to join me in a scotch and soda?' Would I ever. Those were the best-sounding vowels I'd heard all day, Afrikaans clipped or not.

He grinned a lot, and his cowlike eyes sparkled behind his thick-lensed glasses, giving him the look of someone who is not quite all there. He poured my drink from a side-table, handed it to me and returned to his armchair, still smiling. We sipped in silence, but then, when he caught me looking at him, he said in a whisper, 'You are aware of course that everyone thinks you are my fiancée? Must you go away again?'

'Yes,' I said, rather more quickly and forcefully than intended. He scratched at his crotch, which wasn't very attractive, and he saw me looking.

'Virry sirry,' he said, like everyone did, no matter for what reason. 'But you will return quickly? I have to get a wedding organized, or you won't be able to stay in my house. You understand?'

With fingers crossed I promised convincingly that I would, adjusted my mike and congratulated him on having such a lovely daughter, to get us off the subject. He grinned even wider, and seemed childishly happy. Well, until his twin sons joined us, that is. But then, at the sight of those two, Pieter and Paul by name, the smile would have left even the face of Jesus. If they weren't neo-Nazis, then I've never seen pictures of the old Gestapo. They wore tight jeans and sleeveless white T-shirts that accentuated their bulging biceps, and their blond hair stuck out from their skulls like golden spikes. Both had hideous scenes tattooed on their arms, wore studded leather belts at their waists, and heavy black shoes with metal tips.

Daddy introduced them to me, but neither acknowledged this. Both selected the best armchairs, one of which was the one their father had vacated to stand up and greet them, and threw their booted feet over the arms. It was all too gross for my liking and the pain on their father's face was heartrending.

At the dinner table he told us to pray, putting his hands together dramatically and closing his eyes tightly. Actually, the rest of us were not required to do any more, because he intoned without stopping for quite some time. I for one crept upstairs to fetch a cardigan, and when I returned he was still at it, going on about God being everywhere, sitting with us (oh, please, tell me not in the bathroom too?), helping us to be good, and kind, and honest, and true (not that He'd had a heap of success with the two Nazis on my right, I thought). Then, just as I was preparing to say Amen because dinner was in danger of solidifying, he ranted on about how everyone was God, we were God, the trees were God, the greens and potatoes were God. It was all such a lot of tosh that I was expecting the new Third Reich warriors, who were definitely not God by a long chalk, to get up and carry him out.

After serving us tough turkey, grey greens and thin

gravy, Amelia, bless her heart, attempted to join us with her plate of food.

'What d'you think you're doing?' Pieter asked, chewing as he talked. 'You can't serve us and eat at the table at the same time.'

'Yes she can,' I said without thinking. I loathed those two so much it just slipped out.

Amelia looked across at her father for support. But the Rev looked up from his plate vacantly, said nothing, and looked down again. However, she held her ground, put her plate on the table and pulled out a chair. But I noticed that her eyes were full of tears, and when she eventually looked across at me, I was able to blow her a quick, silent kiss, and at least it made her smile. It was not my place either to get up from my seat, walk over to the monsters and thump their large ugly ears, but the idea of doing so was very tempting.

So engrossed was I, trying to get my teeth into the turkey, and thinking of the succulent birds I had once cooked at home, that I jumped when the Rev asked what the rota was for the following day. Both boys spoke together and both said that I was scheduled for kitchen duty and Amelia for dog duty.

Bearing in mind that I was supposed to be a guest, I was ashamed and surprised to find myself being relieved that I got the kitchen to do and not the dogs. If anyone in that house thought that I would ever take out those beasts they were mistaken to the point where I would pack and leave.

From a distance in my head I then heard one of them say, 'You get dog duty next day, Annie Whatever-Your-Surname-Is.'

The Rev did the wisest thing. He stood up, pushed his chair back, and as he was leaving the room said, 'Excuse me for a moment.' Then he made a sign of the cross in the air and intoned slowly as he went, 'Lit us all be friends, shill we? God is with us . . .'

A pox on that, I thought, and as he quietly closed the door behind him I turned on the monsters. 'I won't ever be taking those dogs for walks. Don't even consider it a possibility.'

They both laughed nastily into my face, and Amelia looked tearful again. 'Not walks, you idiot woman. Guard dogs don't go for walks. You take a bucket and shovel and get up their dirt.'

I laughed then too, pleased to be sharing a joke. A sick joke, granted, but at least it showed P and P had a sense of humour which hadn't been obvious previously.

'Don't worry,' Amelia said quickly, 'I'll help you. I don't mind.'

'You will not help her,' one of them said, and looked at her menacingly.

I was fuming fit to catch fire. Getting up dog doos, indeed. I hadn't ever been asked to do that in my own country. And foreign dog doos? . . . No way, Jose . . .

'I don't remember seeing your names on any rotas,' I said, coming over all English-schoolteacher-visiting-the-Colonies.

Both said, 'We don't do stuff like that.'

'Oh, come now,' I said, amazing myself, 'surely you two Bettys can do a bit of shit-shovelling? You'd probably find you are good at it. Personally, I wouldn't give you house-room in the kitchen. But in the garden, dealing with dog dirt, now that strikes me as right up your strata . . .'

Amelia put her hands to her face. I think she expected them to get up and hit me. Myself, I was sure they wouldn't. I was old enough to have seen bullies at work before.

Pieter, or maybe it was Paul, turned to me with a very red face and ears. 'You better wash your fucking mouth out, you white bitch'! he shouted.

Amelia ran round the table, put her arms protectively around my shoulders and said, 'Leave her alone, you – you – awful things. Hilton may come in to work, and then we won't have a problem.'

'That motherfucker won't come in to work ever. He knows he'd have to face us,' one of them said as the door to the dining-room opened and in came the Rev, can you believe, with his hands still together.

He sat down slowly as if in a trance, and looked around the table. You could have cut the silence with the pudding spoons, forget the red-coloured jelly and acid-yellow custard for which they were intended.

'Let us pray,' the Rev said, closing his eyes.

Both boys stood up. 'We're off to our meeting, Dad, sirry.'

'Good,' I said under my breath. But I knew they'd heard. And I found myself hoping that there was a key in my door that I could turn when I went to bed.

I said Amen for the Rev at a pregnant pause and prepared to stand up. Maybe he intended to carry on, end up with a psalm, perhaps, who could tell? But me, I'd had enough.

Not surprisingly, I did not sleep well, in my too short bed and with my allotted bathroom located miles away. When I used it I wanted to repeat the process the moment I got back from it, and I had those pains again. (Brought on probably at the thought of meeting the hostile villains en route.) So most of the night was spent doing serious thinking.

There was no such luxury as a bedside lamp in my room, and it was as I was groping for the wall switch beside the door, so that I could make a list of important things to do – such as how to find a way of using the phone, and how to phone the airlines for an earlier flight without being found out – that I heard hushed voices coming from the Master Suite, this being quickly followed by a female giggle. So I crossed the narrow passage and listened blatantly.

The Rev was obviously being given the time of his life. He moaned and he groaned and he sighed, and he didn't once mention God. The lady in question said something about looking after him plinty, and would he be liking some more? You bet your sweet life he would, and she came up with it quickly, judging by the renewal of high-rising ooohs and aaahs, and the thumping of the kingly bed against the wall. He must have had a very understanding relationship with Jesus, I thought, carrying on like that right underneath his cross, the way he was. And no wonder the old dog was not going to make sexual demands on the lady he hoped to choose for a wife. It seemed that he was getting more of what he liked best and than a Very Rev could possibly need, almost every night of his life.

Amelia brought me strong tea and cold toast in bed next morning. She must have cried a lot during the night because her eyes were seriously swollen. And as she sat down uninvited on my tiny bed, they filled with tears again. 'You can't marry into this dreadful household, Annie,' she said.

I took her hand and held it tight. 'I know.'

She looked intently into my eyes. 'I'll help you to leave, if you like.'

It was more than I had hoped for, but I needed to be careful. What if she was tricking me? What if she'd been forced into it by those terrible boys?

'My brothers are evil,' she said. 'My mother killed herself because of them.'

I was sorry, but I really didn't want to hear any more. I wanted to have already sent my report to Diana. I wanted to have packed. And more than anything I wanted to be on a plane tearing towards the end of the runway with its nose pointed towards the sky and as intent on leaving as I was.

'Annie,' Amelia said suddenly, 'would you take me with you . . . ?'

I was saved from giving an answer by the ringing of a distant telephone. Amelia rushed off to answer it, which, with luck, meant that there was no one else in the house, and I could start to activate my plans. I got hurriedly out of bed and into a robe as Amelia called my name and said the call was for me.

Kate shrieked so loudly into the receiver that I had to demand she calmed down and give me the bad news slowly to save me from going into shock.

'Mother!' she screamed. 'The problem is not this end. It's you. What about that plane you were on? You could be dead now.'

'How do you know about that?' was the first, and typically womanish, thing I could think of to say.

'It's on the television news and in the papers. It says that the plane dropped ten thousand feet. I was so worried I phoned the airport to confirm that it did land safely. Oh, Mum, you could have been killed.'

Holy shit, ten thousand feet! 'Yes, I know, darling, but I wasn't, so don't upset yourself so much,' I said in my mother's voice, feeling quite emotional that she cared so much.

'You seem so calm!' she yelled. 'Weren't you scared?'

'Of course, out of my wits. I hung on to the neck of a totally strange man. People were injured, it was all very frightening.'

'Oh, Mum, I do love you,' she said, calmer now. 'Everyone's been phoning me for news. You didn't tell Daddy where you were staying' (you bet I didn't) 'or Gus' (gosh, did I not?). 'And Emma said she thought that she was going into premature labour from the shock' (but she didn't, of course). 'They all send their love' (even Marcus? Come off it).

'That's nice,' I said, 'now, no more worrying. I must get back to my breakfast' (and several other things too).

'Mother!' she screamed all over again. 'How can you talk about food when you could easily be dead . . .'

I did not feel good about Amelia. What an unhappy little girl she was. She risked a lot to deliver me to the airport, secretly getting the car out of the garage and quietly taking my luggage out of a rear entrance.

Of all days, the Rev returned early from wherever he went in the daytime. Amelia said that it had never happened before. He and I passed on the stairs. I tried to look normal, and inquired after his health.

That was a bad move. Shortly after, he summoned me to the Master Suite. This time I knocked and was bade to enter. He had his back to me and was staring up at Jesus's cross.

'You are a good girl, Annie,' he said in his holy-type voice. 'I wish to ask you something.'

Well, it had to be different from what Amelia had asked me because he didn't know that I was leaving. So good manners decreed that I had to invite him to spill his load. 'Anything,' I said rashly.

'I wish to propose to you properly,' he said, and my only wish right then was that he'd turn and look at me instead of using the cross as a mediator. Actually, it would have been better if he'd stayed facing the cross.

'That's very nice of you,' I answered, all English middle-class manners, 'but really, it isn't . . .'

He turned then, slowly, for maximum effect, the usual leer that posed as a smile across his face, his magnified eyes shining like full-beam headlamps behind his glasses. His expression propelled me to look slowly down the length of him, and when I saw that rolling pin, or

Philippa Todd

whatever it was that caused such a mound under his frock, I promise you, my departure preparations went into a major fast-forward.

Amelia drove to the airport like a professional on a winning streak. My luggage was transported to the plane's hold without so much as a we must see if you're overweight, madam. My first-class ticket to Sydney was processed at the double, and Amelia pulled rank and came with me right to the aircraft.

'Will you send for me?' she begged, and I felt such a heel.

'How old are you, Amelia?'

'I'm seventeen,' she answered, honestly.

'You must be eighteen before I can ask you to stay with me. Otherwise I could be in trouble for attempted kidnapping.' I hated myself. It all came out so pat, she must have known that I had rehearsed it.

'But when I am eighteen, will you invite me then to London?'

'Yes,' I said, and this time I meant it.

'I don't have your address,' she said, pushing a notebook and pen under my nose.

I was trapped. I couldn't give her my address, Annie Lloyd had to be buried long before then. I couldn't give the dating agency address because before too long, with the advent of the programme, I would be persona non grata in that department. That left, now let me think, only Diana. What a brillant idea! She would unload the communication on to me very smartly. And so I would be sure to know. And if it were at all possible, of course, dear, sweet Amelia, you can come and stay with me.

TEN

O n the long flight to Sydney, once I'd caught up
with much-needed sleep, I did my office work
like a professional. It was no time at all since I'd left
England, but it felt like a lifetime. I had made a good
many mistakes in that short time, and there was a lot of
procedural tightening up to do, or I would land myself in
trouble. In most ways, so far, I had behaved like a dork
through lack of forward thinking. From now on, things
would be different. I had been lulled into breaking the
rule about not having my fares paid by clients and staying
in hotels that were not paid by them either, because I'd
felt a sense of security with Lawrence Voorberg being a
man of God (though his job description should have read
wacky man of God). And as he had a family, and as he
wasn't going to make sexual demands on me, staying
under his roof made such good copy. That, though, was
not going to happen again.

Sean O'Donnell was there to meet me at Sydney airport.
It was a glorious winter day, the climate being upside
down from us, same as South Africa, but the blue of the
sky was even more radiant than in SA, and the people,
well, they smiled a whole lot more.

He greeted me as though we were betrothed, and it
crossed my mind that he might suspect he was being

watched (or had I been reading too many thrillers recently?). In casual but expensive clothes he looked quite handsome, and I noticed that he had acquired an Australian accent that had not been obvious in London.

In the car, a smart BMW coupé, he asked me what I had been doing in Cape Town. Thanks to my homework and my recent decision to be more efficient, I calmly answered that I had acted as an official courier for a human-parts pool. I had delivered a kidney. Urgently needed, I said. I doubted he could ever check on such an errand, and he seemed impressed with what I had done.

'You work in medicine, so it seems?'

'Yes, in a very humble way,' I lied.

We were approaching Sydney now. 'This is a lovely city,' I said, intent on leaving Cape Town behind.

'I want you to like it, Annie,' he said earnestly. 'I've been thinking about you, you seem a nice lady, even if you are English.'

I looked across at him quickly, but he was smiling. 'That was a joke, sure it was,' he said, giving his Irish accent the full treatment.

For the sake of the programme I asked him casually, wanting to get it over, 'Are you seeing many of us, women for wives, I mean?'

He reached over and patted my knee. 'None of your business, Annie.' That put me in my place right away.

'Regent Hotel, was it?' he asked, forcing his way into a right turn. 'Nice place, the Regent, central, view of the Harbour, all that. My house is just down on the water, and you'll see it soon. You look tired, Annie.'

Punchy was more like it. 'I am,' I said, 'I didn't sleep well last night.'

'Where did you stay?' he asked.

It was an instant lesson on why one should never over-talk. If I hadn't mentioned sleeping badly, he might not have asked where I stayed.

'I know Cape Town well,' he was saying, 'business takes me there.'

Stick with the truth then, girl, I told myself. He isn't likely to know Lawrence Voorberg. 'With friends of friends,' I said quickly, 'it wasn't very successful, I had to sleep in the nursery and the bed was too small.'

We were at red traffic lights and he was looking at me. 'Where did you have to deliver the kidney?'

'It was collected from me at the airport. All very efficient.'

The lights changed to green. We moved off with the traffic.

'Some nice restaurants around Cape Town,' he said.

'So I believe.'

'But you didn't get to visit any?'

'Not a single one. Oh, look, what a lovely view of the Harbour bridge.'

'Pity to have to go all that way and not see anything of a country,' he said. 'Still, maybe you'll go there with me one day. And then I'll show you all the things you missed.'

We pulled up at the door of the Regent, and a man in uniform opened my door. 'That would be nice, Sean,' I said, relieved that we had arrived.

Alone in my high-rise room with its spectacular view, I unpacked slowly, lazed around a bit, gazed out of my window and admired the view. I felt a touch homesick and vulnerable and I chanced a late-night call to Kate. She greeted me with enthusiasm, so I asked her to run the risk of having her ear chewed off and chance a late-night call to Diana, asking her to telephone me. 'Tempt her with my having interesting information,' I said.

'Golly, Mum, your assignment sounds great,' Kate shrieked. She should only know the half of it, I thought.

While I waited for Diana's call, I made a decision. I

would try to see Harry Smith. Why not, I argued, as was my way if guilt was hovering, as if expecting someone to say no, you can't do that. After all, I said, to no one at all, he had invited me over, had he not? Not just for a few days, I knew that, of course, but maybe he'd be happy to settle for that. And it could be a short rest for me. Wasn't I now Camilla-loadsa-money-Cage? Had to be, with ten thousand big ones in the offing plus expenses. I certainly didn't have to ask permission from anyone when I wanted to pay a visit to a friend.

So why was I in Sydney, he would ask me. I couldn't pretend it was just for him. Maybe the kidney would have to be re-routed? He might want to know if I was seeing another prospective husband, so I must have an answer ready. So, well, was I or wasn't I going to tell him the truth?

I could have talked myself out of contacting him, so before nervosa major took over I dug out his telephone number. After an age the receiver was picked up, and a woman with a strong Aussie accent asked me who I wanted.

'Mr Smith,' I replied.

'Which Mr Smith, dear?'

Oh yes, he had sons. Damn, I'd hoped they would not be there.

'Harry.'

There was a very long pause, a few words on the side, something that sounded like a sneeze, and a deep-throated cackle posing as a laugh. 'Harry Smith, you said?'

'Yes, I did.' She was beginning to get on my nerves.

'Don't reckon he's there.'

What did she mean by that? Surely she'd know if he was home or not?

'He ain't answering, dear.' But wasn't that the faint voice of Harry I was hearing in the background? 'No, wait on,' she said, with the earnestness of a film director. 'I tell a lie, he's come good.' Then at the top of her voice she screamed, 'It's for you, Harry.' Then, more sotto voce for me, 'Go ahead, dear.'

'Who's that?' Harry asked quite clearly.

'Annie,' I said, smiling broadly down the phone at the sound of his voice.

'What, orphan Annie from London?'

'Yes, that's the one.'

'Well, bugger me.'

'I couldn't have put it better myself,' I said, all relaxed now, and ready to curl up in a chair and chat to a friend.

'Where the hell are you?'

'Sydney, passing through.'

There was a pause. 'Nobody ever passes through Australia, mate. You either come here or you don't.'

I simply could not take the smile off my face. 'Don't knock it, Harry. I'm here, but only for a few days.'

'You holed up with some bloke? Bet he's not as good-looking as me.'

'I wrote you a letter,' I said, declining to answer. 'Didn't you get it?'

'Nope. But then I haven't collected mail for a week or so.'

'I'm pleased you weren't waiting anxiously for my reply.'

He, in turn, ignored that. 'You coming out to see me, Annie girl?'

'Tempt me,' I said, flirting a bit now (well, I was off duty).

'Well, you can't drive, less you're pretty damned cracked, that is. Reckon I'll have to come and get you in Lovely Lady.'

'Don't tell me, you've got a camel.'

'Yair, with wings. But a girl with a nice tough name

like Annie Lloyd won't mind a bit of rough flying, now will she?'

'Oh, Harry Smith, you say the most outrageous things . . .'

I sat in the glass-covered sun room of Sean O'Donnell's house with a drink in my hand, looking out over Sydney Harbour. It was late afternoon, calm on the water, just before dark, and the last few small racing yachts were making a dash for home. And what a sight it all was. Stars were appearing in the dimming sky, a jumbo jet was flying low, headlights on, making a slow approach to the airport, an ocean liner was inching up the harbour to an allotted berth, and traffic glided over the bridge. It was like a colour travel brochure come to life. If only winter was like this at home, I thought, there would be far more smiling faces between November and March.

'Make the most of it,' Sean said, not mincing words. 'I'm taking you to the Hunter Valley tomorrow. I have to do some business with a friend of mine who keeps a winery. He's got a nice wife, I'm sure you'll like her.'

'That's great,' I said, wondering if we'd be returning at night, and not wanting to ask.

'They'll put us up for the night,' he said. 'Do you like ballooning, Annie?'

Not quite sure if this was the latest position for sex, and I should invent a grumbling appendix, I remained silent in order to think.

'Ballooning?' he said again. 'Going up in a hot-air balloon?'

'Oh, that,' I answered, relief relaxing my nerves. 'I've never been up in one.'

Sean showed the most enthusiasm I'd seen in him yet. 'Great stuff,' he said. 'I've done a lot of it. The peace is unbelievable, takes you right away from this whole stinking world.'

Maybe now he would tell me what he did for a living, I

thought, and I looked down at my lapel without meaning to. 'You don't seem to do so badly out of the stinking world. In fact, you seem to do quite well,' I said.

It didn't work. 'I keep my balloon down at the winery. It's shamrock-green with golden stars. Will you come up with me?'

As I thought about it, quite suddenly I felt sick, and the gnawing pain gave me quick hell before it faded. 'If you think I'll be a good passenger and won't throw up.'

'You won't throw up,' he said with confidence. And I wondered then, as I watched him, if he might be a spy. I had never before seen a face that could close down and show nothing, of an instant, like his could.

We drove to the winery, stopping for a picnic provided by Sean on the way. It was a glorious day, warm in the sun, and he sang Irish songs.

'My great-grandparents were dirt poor,' he said, pulling on a blade of grass. 'Forced by the famine to emigrate. It was wicked.'

'So you have relatives in America?' I said, not knowing quite how to answer.

'All over America. Some successful. Some still Irish layabouts.'

He broke into song again then. A mournful, heartrending ballad that brought tears to his eyes and depressed the hell out of me.

Cahil and Maeve, who ran the winery, were a great couple. Maeve was descended from convict stock, she said with a laugh that lit up her green eyes. Rumour had it that one of her great-great-great-grandfathers stole a loaf of bread, she said, though personally, she was pleased. But Cahil now, he'd arrived voluntarily aged eighteen, she added with a toss of her long red hair, and I would notice, would I not, that his Irish accent had not left him?

He and Sean were obviously great friends, and greeted

each other with a hug, and a special look that did not go unnoticed, and went off together for quite some time. Maeve showed me round and explained how wine was made. Then we sat down at her vast kitchen table with two large slabs of cheese and a hot loaf and sampled some of the red. She was a lovely woman, and I felt guilty that she obviously believed Sean was in love with me, and that I was his intended. It also put paid to my plan to enlist her help for having a bedroom of my own.

The men returned and joined us over the wine and cheese. Then a bottle of special brandy was opened and I ceased to worry about the sleeping arrangements. Maeve played Irish tunes on the piano. The men sang, and then they danced Irish jigs. They got very drunk, and Maeve and I had to put them to bed. It couldn't have worked out better had I planned it. The trouble was, I'd been drinking too, and my bed wouldn't keep still. To get any sleep at all I had to sit up . . .

Standing beside the hot-air balloon I was amazed at how big it was, for which I was truly thankful. I would have liked to decline, my head was killing me, but Sean was not the kind of man you chickened out with. Maeve piled extra clothing for me into the basket that was to be my home until our (please Lord) safe return, along with wine, hot coffee in a huge Thermos, sandwiches, hard-boiled eggs. I began to wonder how far we were going. Then she gave me an empty screw-topped jar.

'For emergencies,' she said. I looked at her. 'You know. If you're dying for a pee.' I went on looking at her. 'You just turn your back on him, pull your knickers aside and, well, just go.' Then she laughed. 'To be sure, don't forget to screw the lid back on.' What a funny lady, I thought, thinking I would do a thing like that.

I climbed aboard. Cahil took a picture of us, Sean with his arm around me and kissing my cheek. Then suddenly, we were up and away, and they seemed a long way down on the ground, waving goodbyes up at us as though we were going to cross a few oceans and end up in China.

Once I had allowed myself to settle down, and had become interested in how Sean made it all work, I began to enjoy it – the freedom, and the silence, and the swish of cold air. I fed Sean hot coffee, and was surprised that he did not seem to be hung-over. Myself, I only started to feel better after one of Maeve's ham sandwiches.

I was putting on a third sweater and watching the Hunter River and the thick forest beneath us when Sean said close to my ear, 'You going to marry me, Annie?'

The major opportunity had arrived and I spoke quickly before chickening out. 'But I know nothing about you. I don't know if you've been married before, how old you are. I don't even know what you do for a living. Though I can see that you are very successful.' (Flattery usually helps with a man.)

He became thoughtful and Irish-intense for a short time, concentrated on flying the balloon. Then he said, 'God bless the woman's mind. Much more practical than the male. You going to marry me, do you think?'

He was watching me. So I smiled up at him. 'I might,' I said.

He said, 'Let's have another coffee. Put some brandy in it this time.'

I obeyed, it was an important moment for my assignment. With hands wrapped around the hot mug while I topped it up with brandy, he said 'I'm forty-three, and I'm an international arms dealer. I'm kind, and I don't beat up old ladies.' He smiled then and added, 'Ask my mum.'

Now, Sean was not a man to be toyed with, and coyness was not to be considered. Nothing, in fact, should I say that might ignite his short Irish fuse. But what did arms dealer actually mean? Dealing meant buying and selling, arms meant guns, and guns meant war. So did he organize wars? Was he a mercenary? Did he make his money from war? He did have a sinister side to him. So did his friend Cahil. I was sure they worked together, and I didn't mean at making wine, though it was a perfect front. I wondered if Maeve was privy to their arms dealing. I supposed that I would never know, and that would be safest. I stopped thinking about it.

He was watching me. 'You got a problem with any of that?'

I shook my head and sipped my coffee, thankful that I'd given myself a quick slosh of brandy too.

Soon after, he relaxed and said, with the ease of someone telling me to have a nice day, 'Which position do you prefer for sex, Annie?'

To my credit, I went on sipping, as though mulling over the answer. It would be smart of me to say I preferred it lying down, because that couldn't take place in our present laundry-basket premises. I could be unsmart and pretend I hadn't heard, but a man like Sean would just repeat the question. I couldn't dive overboard for a quick swim in the river to change the subject, but if we'd been a bit lower I might have considered it. And I couldn't say let's talk about it later when you haven't got your hands on the wheel, now could I?

'Have another sandwich,' I said. 'These liver pâté ones are delicious.'

He took one, unfazed, took a bite, and waited till he'd finished it. 'D'you have a favourite fantasy, Annie?'

I tried to look worldly and thoughtful. 'Not really,' I said over my shoulder.

'Know what one of my favourite fantasies is?' He didn't wait for me to invite him to tell me. 'Making love to a woman all clothed,' he said, 'like they did a hundred years ago. In bed she'd wear a long voluminous nightie, like a shroud. Makes it real exciting getting under all that cloth, much better than nudity.'

That at least was a relief. The thought of being asked to take my clothes off in those temperatures would have put me off sex for the rest of my life.

'And what about all those petticoats under those long rustling dresses?' he said. 'It would take a man for ever to find where to go. The anticipation would drive him mad. Any more coffee, Annie?'

You bet there was, anything to oblige and hold up the fantasies. Brandy too, and thanks to Maeve (d'you think that girl knew something?), lots, and lots more sandwiches.

'If we'd lived then,' he continued, sipping, chewing, watching the skyline, 'you would have had to call me Mister. You know, like wives did?'

'Oh, yes,' I said, 'they did, of course.'

'Come to bed now, woman, I'd say, in the middle of the afternoon. I want to have you. Of course, Mr O'Donnell, you'd say, putting down your embroidery willingly. I'm yours at your command. I'll have another of those pâté sandwiches now, Annie love. You're right, they are good. Maeve's a good girl, so she is.'

Sweet Jesus, I thought, what a life those poor women had. And no contraception to boot. Every time your skirts got lifted you ended up counting off the weeks in your diary.

'And can you imagine, Annie, the excitement for a man? When I had you in the bedroom, let's say you were . . . wearing a crinoline. I would unhook the waist and you would very carefully step over the hoop' (how come he knew so much about it, I marvelled). 'Then there would be petticoats to come off, lots of petticoats, all white and starched and smelling of clean laundry. And then the stays . . . oh, those stays, they would drive me mad.'

I didn't speak, I just held out another sandwich.

'And then, of course, I'd get to the knickers. You know, those knickers with legs in them, and frills round the ankles. But they didn't call them knickers, what was it they called them . . . ?'

'Drawers,' I said, without thinking. What on earth was I doing helping him out? It was his fantasy, not mine.

'Yes, drawers, that's it. They didn't have a crotch in them, did they? They just sort of folded over, so they did. You wouldn't be able to pull your knickers down to go to the lavatory, wearing a crinoline, now would you?'

Come to think of it, I supposed you wouldn't.

I'll never know why I looked over the side right then. Maybe it was something to do with the captain having gone back a hundred years, and judging by the look on his face, enjoying it in his trousers. But look over I did, and there we were about to graze the tree-tops in the jungle.

A large cockatoo, white and bright blue-crested, almost crashed into my face as he fixed his terrified eyes on mine. Then he flew off, squawking at the very top of his lungs, in fear of his life, hotly pursued by his wife and several next-door neighbours.

'Sean!' I screamed. 'We're crashing.'

He looked so calm, I felt a fool. He did a few tricks, I threw a few leaves and branches back overboard, and then there we were, slowly gaining height, and Sean was saying, 'Sorry about that. Now, where was I . . . ?'

'Please, can we go back?' I asked.

He looked surprised. 'You had enough?'

Was he kidding? I was cold. I was stiff with shivering. I'd had enough brushes with death of late to make me permanently nervous and I had a full bladder fit to burst which I wasn't about to empty into Maeve's portaloo. Sean looked as though he might mistake my old blue jeans for an Edwardian skirt with train and mink edging, and suggest a quickie in the basket. And then where would I be?

But, let me tell you, if I could persuade him to get me back safely on to the ground, preferably back at the winery, hopefully to a roaring log fire and lots of mulled toddy, flannel shroud in place over woolly vest and nice thick socks, he could have me, any whichway he wanted.

I felt much safer up in the clouds with Harry than I had with Sean, but then, Harry's airborne means of travel had an engine.

'Bloody hell, Annie,' he said when he saw all my luggage at the check-out desk, 'you'll have to leave most of this behind. My plane's a tiddler, not a fucking jumbo jet.'

I burst out laughing as he scratched his head. Now I knew for sure that I was back with Harry.

Sean had been better than I thought he would be about my leaving. I just told him that I wanted a few days with a friend to work things out, and that I'd be back. He asked me to promise that I'd let him know whatever my decision was, and I promised. To keep things on the light side, when I kissed his cheek in goodbye I said, 'Don't let too many young girls in crinolines flirt with you. They might get you into trouble.' But he looked at me strangely, with his black curly head on one side and a puzzled frown between his eyes, and said, 'Come again?'

So I patted his arm, and got the hell out.

It was a dreadful sight, looking at the burnt earth below us. Mile after mile of it. And blackened trees, sometimes only half a trunk left standing. But surprisingly, as we came down lower preparing to land, I could see that almost everywhere green shoots were poking through the black. Harry told me later that it was what nature intended, and how else would the earth get fertilized?

It was a bumpy landing, and I'd never seen a strip so

full of holes. But Harry seemed to be happy with the conditions, and who was I to complain? Harry made you feel like that.

My heart sank when two huge young men came out to greet us. They were so obviously Harry's sons. And I'd had enough of other people's grown-up sons to last me a lifetime.

They were nicer than the Very Rev's pair, though, even if they didn't look it. They both had an earring in their right ear, and their heads were shaved. They were tanned, and had nice teeth. And both of them shook hands nicely with me, with the hand that wasn't holding the tankard of beer.

'These two are about to leave,' Harry said, pointing to a jeep laden with luggage and black plastic bags. 'Time you got going, fellas.'

'We was just waiting for you to come back,' one of them said, but quite friendly. It was obvious to me that Harry had been a good father, things were relaxed between them.

'See you then, Dad,' one said as they got into the jeep. 'See you then, Dad,' said the other. Harry punched them both on the arm, and then they were just a trail of dust. It was as quick as that.

'When will they come back?' I asked.

'Bloody never, shouldn't wonder,' Harry said casually, but his eyes were sad.

I think I can say that those next three days were without question, as far as I can recall, the best three days' holiday I have ever spent. Of course they were different, too, from anything I had done before.

Harry took me in through the front door when the dust trail was out of sight on the flat land. I only knew it was the front door because he told me it was. Actually, it was at the side.

'This is a very large house, Harry,' I said, standing in the main room the size of a tennis court. Well, almost. And thinking of how the polished wood floor would look such a treat in England.

'Well, no need for small, now is there? Space is what we've got most of.'

It was a surprise, under the vast tin roof and exposed wooden rafters, to find such a beautiful room. Full of old settees, side-tables, extra chairs, and, can you believe, a grand piano with a huge old vase on it, a silk fringed cloth and endless photographs in old silver frames.

'Do you play the piano?' I asked, fully expecting him to tell me not to be bloody daft.

'Yair,' he said, 'when I have the time. But Joan, she was my wife, she was better at it than me. Real good, she played some lovely stuff, especially when she was sad.'

I knew it was her in a picture, taken with the boys. 'Is she happy now?' I asked, to bury her ghost.

'As a tick in a warm bed,' Harry answered. 'This here picture's of my old mum. Real special lady she was. Strong as an ox, and talk about a worker. Had ten nippers too. What a woman.' His eyes shone as he put down the picture.

'Who's that?' I asked, looking into the face of a pretty girl smiling out at the camera.

'That's Gracie when she was young, she's my favourite sister,' he said. 'Let's go and make some tea now.'

The kitchen was huge too and had the same polished wood floor. I could tell that Harry had no idea how lovely the inside of his house was or how beautiful the floors looked. We sat at the enormous kitchen table and Harry drank gallons of tea, poured from the biggest teapot in the world. He could not believe that I drank one half-inch of tea in the bottom of my mug topped up with a mugful of water. And no milk. 'That's not tea. That's pee-water,' he said. 'Tea's like mine, nearly black, and milky.' I suddenly felt sick at the thought.

We went outside at the sound of a truck engine. Men in dusty clothes and large hats were jumping out of the back of a large old lorry and calling greetings to Harry.

'They been checking fences. Come and say hello,' he said, and led me over. I met Sam, Dick and Terry, to name but three. And they all crunched my fingers to the bone in greeting, shuffled their feet, pushed back their hats and looked at each other. Then they disappeared around the back of a building called the generator shed, with huge metal drums stacked beside it.

'That's where their quarters are, back there,' Harry said. 'They won't bother us none. Come with me, I'll show you where my best friend lives.'

'I know, your dog,' I said.

'Course not a dog,' he said as we walked towards the kitchen door. And there, on the ground beside the door, in a very large nest, was a creature that looked like a baby alligator, one eye trained on us. I jumped back as it lifted its head at the sound of Harry's voice. 'No cause for worry,' he said, 'he's just a lizard. I rescued him from the fire. Paws were all skinned. Never leaves me now.'

'Does he come in the house?' I asked, and hoped I sounded casual.

'Nope, no more than the dogs do. They all know the rules.'

Three horses galloped up then, and were reined to a rapid halt by the drovers on their backs. And two black and white sheep dogs bounded up, saliva everywhere, and tails wagging at Harry.

He cooked dinner that night, wouldn't let me do a thing. Roast lamb, and enough roast potatoes for an army. It was great, and I got a bottle of red wine all to myself. He even let me give him a glass of his own with a small amount of wine in it, and decreed it to be not bad for vintage Ribena.

'You going to sleep in my bed?' he asked, no preamble, when he noticed my eyelids drooping, and he'd played a few tunes on the grand piano.

'Where else?' I said as I listened to the distant laughter of men, horses snorting, dogs barking, wild animal noises I could not identify, and the silent presence of a very large lizard outside the back door, who loved Harry enough maybe to want to see the back of me.

'Let's go then, girl,' he said, putting the piano lid down, 'and take the strain off the generator.'

Being in bed with Harry was so wonderful, I felt for a moment that I wouldn't mind if I died then and there. The bed was huge, the mattress stuffed with feathers, the sheets old-fashioned linen, the blankets thick and woolly. And Harry, well, Harry was a darling friend, and Harry was a terrific lover. I decided that night that making love with a lover was not half as good as making love with a very best friend and not being in love. It was so much more peaceful, and free of drama and tension. I reached the heavens every time he laid a hand on me. And he was rare content too. I suggested that I wouldn't care if we stayed in bed until it was time for me to leave. But we didn't. Harry only laughed, said I had no respect for his age, and traced a line down to my navel, before kissing me there.

I can't remember all the things we did. But next morning he took me to see his front gate. It was miles away, and with the return journey as well took all day. And then we were in lovely bed again.

Next we rode horses. I was terrified because they were so frisky. But Harry said I wasn't frightened at all, I just thought I was. And his wise words worked.

But like all good things, my visit had to end.

'You don't have to go, Annie,' Harry said over break-fast, 'not unless you really want to.'

I put my hand over his. 'I have to go, Harry,' I said, but truth is, at that moment I couldn't think of a reason why. I could ditch everything, forget the money, give up on the world. What did I need it for, when I could have all this?

'We both know it wouldn't work,' I said.

He stood up and poured himself more tea. 'Well, that's where you're wrong, Annie girl,' he said.

But he said no more, and he didn't try to stop me leaving. Like the gent he was, he flew me back to Sydney, and stayed with me till I boarded the plane for Los Angeles. And he asked no questions.

ELEVEN

D on't let anyone ever tell you that the United States of America are not efficient. One and a half hours after entering Passport Control I still had not reached the Customs hall, so long were they taking carefully checking on each and every visitor. If you were an ex-convict, or indeed someone attempting to hide any information whatsoever, when those immigration officials open those tomes of doom to verify that you are or are not 'in the book', the faint-hearted would breathe their last. I had written that I was a tourist on my all-important form, and questions to the contrary would have had me spilling out the truth in no time, no threats necessary.

I knew that it is an offence in America to pay over money to find a husband (or a wife) for entry into the country if the deal includes the obtaining of a coveted green card. I was carrying not just photographs of possible husbands but details as well, so how was I to get out of that one if challenged? For some reason I kept worrying about what the children would think if they knew, and wouldn't it all look terrible in a front page column in the British press?

'You wrote here,' the immigration official said to me, when at last it was my turn, and she was checking my documents, 'that you was born in England. You was specifically told on that plane to write UK.'

'I don't remember that,' I said in a small voice.

'But you was,' the raised voice said. 'England, Great Britain, GB, all that stuff wastes our time. Don't you think we got better things to think about? Remember in future, UK only. UK y'hear?'

The prospect of a term in gaol kept my lips firmly buttoned until the rubber stamp being banged aggressively on the relevant pages of my passport brought me relief. It wasn't until the twenty-stone black person dealing with me told me in a totally different voice to have a nice day that I had the courage to look up and see that the balance of my expectation of a future happy life had been in the hands of a goodlooking and happy housewife.

The Customs Department was just as nerve-racking. Greg McLaren had certainly been on to a good thing having his bag chained to his wrist and knowing the secret code-word in the genre of James Bond. My humble case was emptied down to the lining, by a man this time, my toilet bag was unceremoniously tipped on its head, and two Tampax rolled the length of the trestle. I was asked what I had in my pockets, then I was looked in the eye and asked if I was absolutely sure that I was not, repeat not, carrying any forbidden substances anywhere, repeat anywhere at all. As I was being watched on the sideline by a female Zulu warrior who could have been the twin sister of the immigration official, I was not at all happy. I started to feel unwell again and wished that I was at home, in bed with a good book, and with Kat curled up on the pillow beside me.

I cheered up, however, when I eventually emerged into the relative bliss of the Arrivals hall. A lovely-looking boy of about seventeen with blond hair and the obligatory LA tan came forward hopefully, bearing aloft a board with my name on it – well, Annie Lloyd's actually, but you know what I mean. 'Beverly Hills Hotel' was written on his pale grey cap in gold and 'Jed' was printed on his lapel badge. With generous lips framing perfect teeth into a fascinating smile, he took over my baggage trolley and the tickets that would get it through the last set of doors, and told me to leave everything to him. I began to feel almost human again.

In sunshine so brilliant it had me groping in my bag for sunglasses, Jed steered me towards a three-rooms-and-kitchen pale grey stretch limousine that might have been twenty feet long and had black windows. He opened the rear door and I stepped into an interior that was big enough to house a sofa and armchairs, and it very nearly had them. It certainly had a cocktail cabinet and a TV set, and (wait for it) three pink gladioli in a fixed vase. The pale grey carpet covered my shoes, which I thankfully kicked off and sank my swollen feet into soft, silken pile. The only trouble was, in that land of air-conditioning, it was freezing cold inside and it stayed that way, even though I begged to be warmed up all the way to Beverly Hills, and Jed assured me that he was doing just that, ma'am. He was the soul of decorum, spoke only when spoken to, and then in the well-paced, low, breathy drawl of a hopeful young actor.

He apologized regularly for the heavy traffic, which didn't look particularly heavy to me, used as I was to the scrum of driving in London. But it certainly did move slowly, even when there was no need. A detour was necessary, owing to the most recent earthquake, he said, adding quickly that it wasn't so bad really and he was sure it was the last. But I would have preferred not to be reminded that I was in the earthquake belt.

In what seemed to me time almost as long as the flight across the Pacific, I saw the pink stucco and the name of the Beverly Hills Hotel before me, just as it looks featured in films and expensive holiday brochures. Unreal, and unlikely, but marvellous. I found myself wishing I was seeing it for the first time with Marcus – not the man he became, but how he was before he fell out of love with me. The place was too romantic to be staying in it alone.

We swung into the drive and up to the canopied entrance. Jed handed me and my luggage over to a distinguished doorman, told me to have a good day and hoped that he'd see me again real soon. I panicked in case I was supposed to pay him, but I was glad I didn't try or I might have been drummed out of Southern California for being a nebbish. You could have cut the sophistication with a knife.

My room was a delight, but freezing cold of course, and my first positive action was to turn off the air-conditioning. Decorated in pale blue and primrose yellow with touches of biscuit, it had fresh flowers to match, a canopied balcony, a mattress eighteen inches deep on the king-sized bed and a marble bathroom. And there was a basket of fruit on a low table with a handwritten note, compliments of the manager.

I unpacked, had a bath into which I tossed all my complimentary toilet goodies, all smelling of apple blossom and elderflower, then climbed into a large, soft and lovely pale blue towelling robe, with mules to match. I knew that the moment I sampled the bed sleep would be instantaneous, so I had to face the part I'd been trying not to think about – telephoning Tod Bradshaw. Major jet-lag had taken over, and as it was evening on that coast, I had the perfect excuse at least to put off seeing him in person till next day.

I punched out his number with a feeling of trepidation and waited for an age for the phone to be answered. If it got to fifteen rings I'd decided I would be justified in replacing the receiver, but on fourteen it was picked up.

A male English voice said, 'Jeeves speaking.'

'May I speak to Mr Bradshaw?' I asked.

'Unfortunately no,' he said in a prattish voice. 'This is his butler, may I take a message?'

Jeeves . . . the butler . . . from England? He had to be kidding . . .

'This is Annie Lloyd . . .'

'Ah, yes, Ms Lloyd,' he cut in, 'the master said to tell you to call on him in the morning, and to be prepared to accompany him in full evening dress in the evening, which as you may or may not know, is Oscars night.'

I was so relieved to hear the news from Jeeves, and I thanked him quickly and replaced the receiver. Suddenly I was not tired, but I was starving hungry. The menu told me that room service went on for twenty-four hours, covered whatever I fancied out of around two hundred dishes, and my mouth watered non-stop till my chosen hamburger and French fries arrived in a heated trolley, together with enough pickles on the side for six starving refugees and a side-salad for ten. I have never tasted a hamburger like it in my life, all pure moist ground beef and herbs, and the chips surpassed even the very best of French. I cleaned my plate, expecting complaints from my stomach, but not a bit of it, I felt fit, well and ready to face whatever would befall me.

I sank into the mound of pillows on my king-sized bed, flicked the remote control of the twenty-inch-screened built-in TV set and mindlessly watched whatever it was, battling for recognition, between the advertisements. Haemorrhoid creams discussed at cocktail parties between handsome men I took in my stride, but when the ads reached how to obtain the best pessaries on the market for vaginal thrush, I felt the need to turn off the set and leaf through one of the magazines fanned out prettily on a low table. Then I called it a night and pressed the button that simultaneously deadened all the soft-hued lighting in one go.

*   *   *

The driver sent by Tod Bradshaw was either taking the scenic route up into the hills, or the whole area was routinely manicured and forced to blossom to perfection. He pointed out to me the homes where various film stars lived, and pretty lush they were too.

I tried to bring his boss into the conversation several times before asking outright what he actually did. He looked a bit bemused and I knew my question would be discussed in Tod's kitchen when he called in for his coffee and a gossip, but he was a nice young man, and said politely, 'Oh, he's still a film producer.'

I was back to the old argument I had with myself of what was a man capable of being a film producer doing paying money to find a wife. He must surely, even if he was five feet nothing with pigeon-toes and wore a rug, have women falling at his feet?

We drove high into the hills and my ears were beginning to pop when we stopped in front of a pair of twenty-foot-high wrought-iron gates and my chauffeur inserted a card into the remote-control box on the handsome stone pillars, then punched out a few numbers. The gates opened in total silence and the red gravel crunched under our tyres as we crawled up the tree-lined drive and, as requested, went Dead Slow. The sign added Dangerous Dogs Patrolling, and as you can imagine after my experiences with Mo, Flo, BB and Wilf, for me it was instant freak-out.

However, I saw no sight and heard no sound of patrolling dogs as I bravely rang the doorbell (chimes, actually) on the studded nuevo gothic-shaped heavy front door, after assuring myself that the driver would take me back to my hotel when I requested he did so. After all, if I was going to be jumped on by dogs, or fed cocaine by the owner, or both, I wanted to know that I wouldn't have to walk down those winding hills.

If I had not known that John Gielgud was appearing on

stage nightly at the Adelphi in London, honest to God, I would have thought he was posing as Jeeves the butler as some sick joke. I'd seen the film *Arthur* several times, and this was like an action replay. The voice was horribly different, but apart from that you have the picture.

He showed me into the 'Master's study' and then left, hardly managing to hide a smirk as he quietly closed the magnificent mahogany double doors behind him. I got the feeling that Prince Charles does not have a study at his country place like the one in which I was standing. I tried to get to a rough total of the books lining the walls by counting across and then down, but was interrupted by one half of the double doors crashing open, and a fair-haired six-foot-tall female stick-insect in major disarray stood before me, pink silk-slippered feet akimbo. Her hair had not been combed for quite a while and she wore a low-cut pink silk nightdress under an open and free-flowing pink silk robe. Well, it was only midday, and in Beverly Hills maybe that's quite early for getting out of bed. She had obviously eaten breakfast, meagre as it may have been for the sake of her figure, because some of it had stained the front of her expensive nightie.

'Yo,' she said, not unpleasantly.

'Hello,' I said, 'I'm Annie Lloyd.'

She looked at me slowly from down to up, took in my tan loafers, my tan Armani linen pants that cost too much, my white cotton shirt, and my face. I felt like a runaway orphan looking for a cleaning job and wondered why I had spent all that money getting suitable new clothes and a salon sun-tan back in London.

'I know,' she said. 'I'm Peaches, his wife' (inclining her head irreverently towards the door).

I was quite proud of myself for neither letting go of my bladder nor being sick on the Aubusson rug, but I could have done both. You know the feeling, when bladder or stomach collapses with shock, and the one person not in control is you? Brave I think I can be when life depends on it, but right then I just wanted to get the hell out for several good reasons. Tod and the agency had failed to tell me that he was married, and I was not about to make an enemy of a wife, especially a six-foot-tall one who was most likely a judo expert to boot. So, with head held high I made for the door.

Peaches started to laugh and hauled me back bodily by the sleeve of my shirt, confirming that she was no physical slouch. 'No problem,' she drawled, 'we're in court next week, it's over, I'm his fifth, he stinks, you're welcome to him . . .'

I don't know how I managed it but I flicked the switch on my recorder by reaching in my pocket for a tissue, stayed calm and smiled at her. 'You don't seem to be in love any more,' I muttered for something to say, hoping that I sounded sincere and not just barking mad.

'In love my ass,' she said. 'I never did love him, but he was a way into motion pictures.'

'Oh, you're an actress,' I said, weakly, 'how lovely.'

'Double-crossing sonofabitch didn't help me much anyway. But we've got a little kid now, so, well, you know, I kinda stuck around for a bit.'

As though on cue, the sweetest, most angelic, blonde curly-haired three-year-old girl ran into the room. She wore minuscule bikini bottoms in pale blue, had beautifully tanned skin and enormous china-blue eyes.

'Mommy,' she screeched, 'that awful new governess says I can't go in the pool without company and no way is she coming in. You better come quickly and sort her out.'

'Honey baby,' said Peaches, attempting to hold her still, 'this person is going to be Daddy's new wife. Now say hello to her nicely.'

The blue-eyed princess gave me a look fit to kill and

turned to her mother. 'Did you hear what I said?' she asked in a high-pitched shout. (Whatever happened to baby-talk, I wondered, could they possibly have done away with it in California?)

Peaches looked at me helplessly across her shoulder as the tiny monster, who didn't even reach her knee, turned her around and dragged her roughly towards the door. 'Ain't kids the same the world over, though? See you later,' she called above the wailing that Honey baby had perfected in the year or so that she'd been around, guaranteed to break up any hope of conversation between adults. Since everyone I had met in the short time I had been in LA had told me on leaving that they would see me later, I was unable to assess if she meant it literally, and we would all be together that night as one happy family, or if I'd never set eyes on her again.

Left alone, I tried to work out my next move. It came as no surprise to find that I felt sick and had indigestion again, and prolonged jet-lag was making me a little light in the head. It only needed the master himself to come in dressed in the drag I had dreamt about and I would be through that mock-Gothic front door, out into the drive and climbing into the pale blue sedan before he had time to suggest as much as a quick snort.

He came in looking a bit strange, but not so bad really unless I was just getting used to Beverly Hills. He had on a tight black stretch cat-suit that zipped on from the crotch to the neck. He had left the zip unclosed from mid-chest up, to reveal a fair amount of black curly body hair. He should have been wearing a cod-piece, though, and being Jewish his circumcised penis showed head rather unattractively instead of lying in a smooth mound of repose. His stomach was flat, luckily, his biceps were large and he obviously worked-out regularly. But he was wearing a rug, expensive no doubt, the best you could buy, but an obvious rug none the less. I thought for sure he'd look better without it, but as I was only passing through and not going to be slotted into his future, and certainly not going to be around when he removed it for bed, it would have been an imposition to comment.

'Good to know you, Annie,' he said seriously, taking both my hands in his and kissing me right on the mouth. He held me off and examined me, even turned me round, and when he lingered on my rear I got the embarrassing feeling I'd sat in something.

'You got a nice ass,' he said, turning me back to face him. 'Nice teeth too. Not many English women have good teeth.'

I felt like a filly up for sale in an auction and that at any minute he would tickle a fetlock and ask me to show him my trot. 'Nice place you have here,' I said benignly, to change the subject.

He gave a dismissive gesture with his hand. 'It's okay. But we can live someplace else if we make it together. All this crap cluttering up the place is Peaches' idea of what the furnishings in a British stately home look like. Siddown.'

I gratefully sat, or rather sank into a long low settee, whereupon a maid in frilly pink apron and low-cut dress straight out of a 'fifties B-movie came in with lemonade in a crystal jug and chocolate-chip cookies on a silver tray. She stooped bunny-girl fashion to deposit the tray on a low table and looked at me warily. I could see that her ample breasts were as bronzed as the rest of her, and I wanted to tell her to stick around and not to consider giving her notice in, that I wasn't permanent and with a bit of luck she could be the next Mrs Tod Bradshaw.

Tod sat down opposite me on a matching settee and broke a cookie in half, leaving one half on the tray. 'We gotta talk,' he said, 'I ain't told nobody how I found you, none of their goddamn business anyhow, see whad I mean?'

'Why on earth did you come to an English agency to find yet another wife?' I asked, suddenly remembering why I was there. 'Surely you are surrounded by possible future wives all day long?'

He stretched out his legs, leaned back on the mighty cushions and folded his arms behind his head. I wished he hadn't struck that pose because, try as I did to control my eyes, they kept swivelling to his crotch.

'I've had it with American dames, they don't have no class. There's nothing broads won't do for money in this town. You gotta have class, you look like you might have class, Annie.'

There was no answer I could give to any of that.

'Course, we'd have to work out the finances before marriage, but our lawyers would do that. I ain't a mean man.'

'I'm sure you're not,' I said for no apparent reason, since there was no possible way that I could know the depths of his generosity.

He sat forward again and poured us both some lemonade. I grabbed at the glass gratefully and drained it in one go. No old-fashioned home-made lemonade had ever tasted so good. He smiled for the first time and his heavy black moustache stretched across his rather cluttered features. But his smile was nice.

'You'll know it's the Academy Awards tonight,' he said as a statement.

'Yes,' I answered. 'I was surprised you were able to get me into an hotel. I've never been amongst so many glamorous people.'

'Isn't anything I can't fix in this town,' he said matter-of-factly. 'I don't have a movie picking anything up, so we'll be going to a party to watch the whole goddamn circus on television.'

He paused and picked up the other half of his cookie. 'It'll be dressy, though, and it's the most prestigious party

207

in town, and later we'll all be going on to the best restaurant around for late dinner. You'll have a ball, Annie, this city will be full of beautiful people tonight.'

A prestigious party yet, with the most beautiful people in town? Another first for Little Annie, Camilla too, come to that.

'I'm sure,' I said, feeling rather nervous at the thought of all that glamour.

'We'll get to know one another in the next three days,' he said, standing up. 'Then I have to fly to Japan.'

I stood up too, recognizing that I was being dismissed. He put his arm around my shoulders and showed me to the door.

'Whadd'ya think of Jeeves?' he asked. 'Ain't he just something else?'

'Yes, he is,' was all I could think of to say.

'Sonofabitch earns too much money, though. Whadd'ya think he would earn in the UK?'

'I've absolutely no idea,' I answered quickly, not wishing the wrath of Jeeves to descend upon me before I had the chance to get out of America and safely back home.

'Find out,' Tod said, pressed his chocolate-chip-cookie-and-lemonade-flavoured moustache firmly on my lips, patted me on the behind and handed me over to the driver.

'Pick the lady up at six-thirty,' he said. 'Oh, and by the way, Annie, a hairdresser is booked for you at the hotel for four o'clock. I thought you'd like that, and they've all been booked up for weeks.'

What a truly thoughtful man, I decided.

Honey, the monster-angel with the adult diction, came rushing through the front door trailing a towel behind her. 'Daddy, Daddy,' she screamed at full throat. 'Come and swim, you promised.'

'I didn't promise I would,' her daddy answered with love in his voice.

'You did, you did,' she hollered, 'you're a liar.'

Tod picked her up and she squirmed in his arms and slapped at his face.

He looked at me helplessly. 'It's a good thing you know about bringing up kids,' he said. 'See you later, Annie.'

I bundled into the car before she waged war on me too, thankful that I was not going to have any part in bringing up that particular kind of kid.

I nursed my pain and my nausea all afternoon and seriously wondered if I should ask to see the hotel doctor. But as hysteria had reached a peak in the front hall, and having a sensible conversation with the telephone operator was practically impossible, I took a few pain-killers and lay down to rest. I nodded off and dreamed of Honey (it was more like a nightmare, really). I have often said that it is not easy to love other people's children, and that little monster had done nothing to make me change my mind.

Tracy the hairdresser's knocking woke me. She kicked off her shoes as she came through the door and threw her enormous work-bag on to the floor before she collapsed into an armchair with a heavy sigh of fatigue.

'Coke?' I asked, feeling she must need some refreshment, she looked so bushed.

She looked at me with a hopeful expression. 'Coke, you got some?'

'Or Pepsi,' I said quickly, 'you know, something to drink.'

'Oh yair, thanks,' she said. 'Pepsi sounds great. Can I use the bathroom?'

She was gone for a long time, but who was I to comment? It would be fair to say, though, that between sneezes she performed magic on my hair. She poured on pints of stuff I didn't recognize, twisted it, blew it dry, hot-rollered it, damped it down again, twisted it again, and the result was brilliant. I looked as though I had three times the amount of hair that I actually have (so now you know how the stars accomplish it). Furthermore, it stayed that way for two days, and I didn't as much as touch a single tendril, so good was the casual tailoring. No one in London would have recognized me when I was ready to go out.

Tracy said that I was her last client and would I like her to make up my face. You bet I would, I said, and talk about glamour, even I had trouble knowing that I was me. When I told her that I was going to the celebrations with Tod Bradshaw, as she helped me into my slinky black gown with shoe-string straps, she nearly flipped. I felt I'd found a friend and tipped her way over the top, from one working girl to another. When we both took one last look into the mirror as they rang from the desk to say that my car had arrived, Tracy said that Tod should offer me the lead in his next movie. It was a case, I felt, of move over, Meg Ryan, here comes Annie Lloyd, the dame with star potential.

In the front hall photographers looked over the guests hopefully for a recognizable face, and one chap blinded me with his flash as I passed.

'Who was that?' I distinctly heard his chum say to him.

'Nobody,' he answered.

Outside Tod's house photographers were also gathered.

'What's happening?' I asked my driver.

'Just six people coming over for drinks and they want to know who they are,' he answered.

He performed the usual magic with the gates, and faces pressed to the windows to look at me before their expressions took a dive at my unknown countenance.

'Who's coming next?' one chap asked.

'Fuck off,' the driver answered as we drove through, but not with malice.

Tod introduced me as his fiancée, and I couldn't help wondering how jealous Diana would be when I told her about all this glamour. I was faxing her copy of it all, in a code that we had worked out before I left London, but neither of us knew it would be quite like this. I also wondered if Tod might set the local Mafia on to me when I disappeared, like Cinderella, the day after tomorrow.

No one smoked tobacco, it was something I noticed everywhere. A few lines of coke were stretched out on the hall table, though, and a few short straws lay beside them.

'Help yourself,' Tod said after greeting me.

I can't say that I wouldn't have liked to, but I was just too plain scared, always have been. Most other people, however, were not.

Peaches made a late entry looking like a Greek goddess, marched over to me and kissed me on both cheeks before circulating and kissing other guests. It was such a generous gesture that I gave her a quick hug.

When we moved on (Peaches taking a quick snort as she passed the hall table) in two stretch limos to the most prestigious party in town, the thing I'll remember most was the friendliness shown by everyone towards me. We hear and read about the bitchiness of Hollywood, and no doubt a lot of it is deserved, but speaking as I found it, everyone was great – laid-back, warm, witty and kind.

The party was co-hosted by Tod and he repeated the introductions to at least twenty people, almost all of whom were faces I recognized from films and the newspapers. Some of them were big stars whom I'd never expect to mix with, never mind hold hands with, and they were mega-friendly. The mini-celebrities were

Philippa Todd

naturally the more insecure and therefore more stand-offish.

We munched on tons of caviar into which we dipped mother-of pearl spoons (forget the toast or the biscuits, there weren't any). We drank only champagne and it was vintage French (what a waste, thought I, when some very fine grapes produced most palatable wines only a very few miles away in the local vineyards, or wineries as they call them).

There were three TV screens in the basement viewing-room of the vast and lovely villa and they were huge, with incredible definition. (I even spotted a tiny zit on the end of a heart-throb's nose, which I'm sure did not show up in his magnified bathroom mirror.)

Then it was let's-get-off-to-the-restaurant time, where, I was assured by Peaches, all the most important people in town that night would be eating. And so they were. At one glance I saw Tom Cruise, Nicole Kidman, Ellen Barkin, Kenneth Branagh, looking lonely, and, though they did not appear to be on speaking terms, Hugh Grant and Liz Hurley.

Someone tall and handsome whom you all know (and whose name I won't mention in case he told his wife he was working late at the studio) patted me on the head while feeling my bum and whispered in my ear, 'Hi, baby, haven't we met someplace before?' When I turned round to face him he said a quick 'Sorry, I thought you were . . .' and disappeared into the crowd. The girl he thought I was truly missed a treat that night.

I cannot remember what I ate for dinner, and it doesn't matter, because when I tottered up to my room in the hotel, in the early hours, boy was I ever sick. I groaned and vomited for what was left of the night, and braved the mosquitoes and propped myself up on a lounger on my terrace, to get the maximum of what passes as fresh air in that city. It was a hangover, only worse, and I made up my mind to send for the hotel doctor as soon as the hangover part had departed. I just knew that I had an ulcer.

He was charming, the doctor, a real film star (I learned later that he was married to a minor star). He recorded all my symptoms and took notes too. Then he stretched me on my bed, covered my body with a sheet and felt my tender abdomen. I jumped around no matter where he pressed, and he began to look puzzled and not at all happy.

'What about periods?' he asked.

'What about them?' I wheezed through gritted teeth.

'Well, for starters, when did you menstruate last?'

'I haven't had regular periods for nearly two years,' I said, feeling instantly inadequate and sorry for myself. 'My GP in London said it was because of my mental state over the breakup of my marriage, and not early menopause.'

He nodded his handsome head in agreement. 'It can happen. Have you a history of ulcer symptoms or any other gastric problems?'

I shook my head. 'Not that I know of.'

He held my towelling robe high as I left the bed and I squirmed into it, fearful that I might cry just because he was being so nice. I would have been more assured with the good old British health service crone who would give me a prescription big enough for ten patients and throw me out of the surgery without a single smile or a tender word.

'I think you should see a gynaecologist and a stomach specialist,' he said, and pulled out his mobile phone.

The gynaecologist agreed to see me that evening at six, the stomach man next morning. The doctor said he would look in later, and left.

In trepidation I telephoned Tod and told him that a major hangover was gripping me and please could I be excused dinner at his place. I need not have worried.

'No problem,' he said, 'we've got a lifetime left to us. You just rest and I'll pick you up for brunch tomorrow at eleven-thirty . . .' (Well, it made a change from dinner.)

T. J. Towning's 'office' was in a white stuccoed house with a manicured lawn and lots of statuary. As I rang the bell I realized that the statues were either of pregnant Virgin Marys or women with the same expression nursing babies. Thankfully there were no name-tabs attached. An incredibly pretty nurse in a white cotton trouser-suit, white doeskin shoes and 'Tammy' written on her breast smiled into my eyes and asked me into a waiting-room fit for royalty. The white lilies in a huge vase on a low centre table must have cost a mean dollar but were wasted on me as their perfume made me feel sick.

A white-clad receptionist took me into an ante-room and recorded my details on to a computer screen. Before I had time to really settle into one of the gently reclining armchairs in the waiting-room, pretty Tammy ushered me into T. J.'s office, but not before handing me a sweet little tray with a cloth over it, a corner of which she removed to reveal a tiny glass container and tiny swabs in a dinky dish, and heading me into a luscious lavatory with a request for a urine sample, after which, she said, she would be taking blood from my arm.

T. J. Towning treated me like a princess and discreetly did not ask what I was doing in Beverly Hills. No doubt he had decided that with a temporary address such as mine the settlement of his fees was in good hands, so what else mattered? He should only have known!

I could see a printout of my particulars and a letter from the hotel doctor on his desk, into which he buried his head while Tammy helped me undress, get into a fine white cotton robe and stretch out on the gynae examination couch. She then smiled assuringly and gently insisted that I relax, while she put my legs into the stirrups and covered the relevant parts with a tiny white diaper.

I don't know what T. J. did with his finely gloved fingers, but it hurt like hell and literally squeezed tears through my tightly clenched lashes. But in no time at all he discarded his gloves and Tammy had me dressed and seated before his black and chrome designer desk.

'Let's have coffee, shall we?' he said to Tammy and she brought in a daintily arranged tray before quietly leaving. T. J. looked at me without speaking for what seemed like a considerable length of time.

'Have you any idea what might be wrong with you?' he asked at last, his eyes not leaving my face.

'I hope you're not going to tell me I'm starting the menopause,' I answered. 'It's not exactly something I look forward to.'

'You're pregnant, Camilla,' he said quietly (I'd given my real name as a safety precaution against anything medical going wrong).

For some reason I started to laugh. 'That's impossible,' I said, 'I'm forty-three.'

He sipped his coffee slowly. 'A very well-known patient of mine is forty-three, on her fourth marriage, and pregnant for the first time.'

'But I'm on the Pill.' I was aware that my heartbeats were becoming more pronounced.

'It can happen,' he said.

Hysteria could not be far away, I knew. I stared at my hands as they clenched together in my lap, and they were shaking. 'My God,' I said.

'Can you remember throwing up for any reason shortly after taking the Pill one day, say, a few weeks ago?' He said it so casually.

Only once could I remember being sick before it became a habit. I had a sore throat and didn't feel too good but Harry Smith was expecting me to go out with him in London, so I took two aspirin and went. I was thirsty, and knowing that Harry didn't drink alcohol, I asked for a Coca-Cola on meeting him. I drank it too quickly and was sick when I went to the loo. We had sex that night.

'You can call the father from here, if you wish,' T. J. said, gesturing towards his telephone. 'Will he take the news kindly in the middle of the night? I assume he's in London?'

'No, he isn't and no, he wouldn't,' I said, and my voice seemed to come from way off.

'There is a possibility that you are threatening to abort the foetus. Hence the pain,' T. J. said.

Panic had not set in, which surprised me, but lethargy had. My arms and legs felt like heavy weights, my eyelids wanted to close, and I wished I was at home, with Kat, and my own bed. I wanted to go to sleep so badly.

'Don't worry about the lack of emotion or the absence of tears,' T. J. said as though he were looking into my soul. 'They'll come later.'

I looked into his face. 'Are you sure I'm pregnant?' I asked.

As though on cue, his internal telephone rang and he casually picked it up and listened. 'Thanks,' he said, replaced the receiver and looked back at me.

'Your urine agrees with my diagnosis.' He smiled. 'There is no doubt, Camilla. At this moment you are going to have a baby.'

Suddenly I felt incredibly sad. Harry was such a nice person, but I might never see him again. And expecting his baby would only complicate our friendship even if I was going to see him again.

'Not convenient at all,' I said quietly. 'My daughter gives birth to her first child at any moment. She would never forgive me. I'm divorced, and I'm old. And the father lives in Australia, and he mustn't know.'

T. J. looked patiently thoughtful, and was silent.

'I'm all alone on this one,' I said, and wondered why I didn't cry.

'If you are considering abortion you must think it over very carefully,' he said. 'As I said, I do not consider the foetus to be stable.'

'I must have an abortion, anyway,' I said quickly. 'Would you do it for me . . . please?'

'Are you insured?' he asked tentatively. 'I'm sure you know that medicine costs a bomb out here.'

Thank God I had done something right for once in my life – I'd bought medical insurance to cover my trip.

'Yes, I have insurance,' I said. 'If you would say that I was in danger of miscarrying I'm sure they would pay. When would you do it?'

'If you're miscarrying, it must be quick,' he said. 'We'll need the backup of the hotel doctor. Tomorrow or the next day latest . . .'

TWELVE

I have no memory of getting back to the Beverly Hills Hotel. My first recall is of lying in the ample bath with a head fit to burst, a mind full of turmoil, a dull ache in my lower abdomen and a painful burning behind my eyes.

There was no point in feeling sorry for myself, and no one knew it better than I. If you are female, healthy and fertile, don't indulge in sex if you want to be 100 per cent certain of not getting pregnant. I once had a journalist chum with iron ambitions that propelled her to the office an hour earlier than everyone else, and who made certain that the boss never forgot her first name. She was on the Pill, wore a diaphragm, made her boyfriend use a condom in the days before the big scare, and still became pregnant.

The fault was 100 per cent mine, but unreasonable anger with Marcus overwhelmed me. I hadn't wanted to sleep with other men, but *he* had broken the code, *he* had made me vulnerable. He'd abandoned me, forsaken our bond, thrown me away. I was only human, I needed male comfort like everyone else. But if men had come into my life via my work I would not have gone looking for them. Eventually I might have met someone, when I was really ready, had an affair, or even a marriage, been loved again, and treasured. But now I would never know.

I had to make my mind focus on the details of the

next few days; remorse, grief and emotion could come later. I couldn't throw the assignment away, I needed the money. I had to keep everything secret and careful planning was essential. I had to face the fact that there was no one I could lean on, cry to, ask for a comforting hug, or even scream at, and I would never be able to talk about it to anyone, ever, and I'd better face it.

I was drying myself when the telephone rang, and I picked up the bathroom extension.

'Feeling better, Annie?' Tod Bradshaw asked.

'Yes, much, thank you,' I lied, without thinking.

'Good, I'm coming round. Plans have changed. I fly to Tokyo tomorrow. Gotta see you.'

'I can't possibly eat, Tod,' I said quickly. 'I still feel queasy.' (I'd better start using my head if I intended to lie myself out of my present peccadillo.)

'No sweat,' he said. 'We'll go into the Polo Lounge, just have a drink, a snack maybe. I'll call up from reception in half an hour. Bye bye, Annie.'

I was out of the bath in a hurry, weighed down with anxiety and in a major panic about Tod. But still, all things considered, it was best this way and it would get it over with. I would check out of the hotel tomorrow and not cause more expense.

I dressed in a daze in something I hoped looked okay, made up my face to cover stress the way Tracy had explained, and took one minute off to write a list of important and immediate things to be dealt with.

As I sat opposite Tod in the Polo Lounge (a place I'd always wanted to visit, and now the bustle seemed brash and anything of interest eluded me), he reached across for my hand.

'You don't think you're sickening for something, Annie, do you?' he asked. 'You don't look too good.'

Dear God, I nearly burst into tears, he was the last

person in the world I would have expected tenderness from.

'No, Tod, honestly, I just had too much to drink last night and more rich food than I'm used to. It's nothing, really.'

He patted my hand. 'Good girl, you're a real straight-up lady, Annie, we'll make a good team, and you know what? I could get real fond of you.'

Before I could think of anything to say he handed me a card. 'Go see this lawyer tomorrow. He'll tell you what I've proposed through my attorney, you tell him what you want out of it and we'll do a deal. Why don't you stay on till I come back?'

My head was whirling like a vortex. 'No, I can't do that,' I said, a little too quickly again. 'I must see my aunt and then head home, my daughter is about to have a baby. I'll check out from here tomorrow.'

'Only if you want to,' he said, and I knew that he mean't it. 'Say, why don't you move into my place? Take your aunt, enjoy the pool and my kid. Teach her some tennis, it said on your spreadsheet you play tennis. I bet you're a good swimmer too and none of those dames up there want to even risk getting their hair wet.'

The horror of it could have shown on my face but he didn't seem to notice, and I promised to think about it.

Back in my room, which right then was sanctuary (it made me feel safe and protected, like a holy place), I telephoned T. J. as arranged and spoke into his answerphone, saying that I would like to have the abortion next day, and would be checking out of my hotel. Within half an hour he returned my call. He said that I was doing the right thing and that he would take care of everything. He explained that I would have an epidural anaesthetic, it was safer than a full one, and I would remain conscious, and I should stay in hospital overnight.

Oh, and by the way, he said sweetly, would I settle all accounts on arrival at the clinic, the receipts and his diagnosis would ensure I was successful with insurance. An English cheque would do, he said, anticipating my question, provided I gave a name of reference in America. After that he said a very tender goodbye.

I checked that I had my chequebook with me, now I only had to hope that there was enough money in my current account to honour it. I added the bank manager's name in London to my list of phone calls.

Dear God, I thought, let's hope the insurance company pays up, or my entire salary could be blown. I rechecked my list, making sure that I had covered every eventuality. One small thing overlooked now could result in a full-blown enquiry of my whereabouts.

I called room service and asked for one small chicken sandwich and a pot of camomile tea; my nervous state was making me hungry. Then I packed my clothes, leaving out only enough items to cover my stay in hospital. I telephoned the airlines and rebooked my flight to Chicago for two days later, and likewise my flight from there to New York. Then I sent Western Union telegrams at unbelievable expense to Hunter Lee McNab in Chicago and Brad Delman in New York, stating my change of arrival dates. This seemed like less hassle than telephoning and being asked for an explanation.

The room-service trolley arrived, bearing a sandwich on which you could have fed four starving children, a mega side-salad and a huge pot of camomile tea with a tiny burner underneath it to keep the tea warm. I took the repast to my bed, switched on the TV and tried to make my mind blank out in the interest of my sanity. After flicking through twelve channels I settled for a rerun of *Upstairs Downstairs*, knowing that seeing a bit of England would help me, even if it did represent the bad old days. And wouldn't you know it, the episode was about the maid who had the illegitimate baby by His Lordship's son, and was dismissed into exile in the depths of the country for her sins.

At midnight I telephoned Kate, to speak to her before she left for work, British time. My heart swelled with emotion when I heard her darling, happy voice.

'Mum,' she screamed, 'I was just thinking about phoning you, I dreamt about you last night, how are you?'

We were both laughing, and I was crying too. 'I'm well, and happy, and having a great time.'

'Brilliant,' she called out. 'How were the Oscars? I looked for your photo in the press.'

'You have no idea how glamorous I looked,' I said, 'your mother would have stunned you.'

'You always stun me,' she called out generously.

I dried my eyes and tried not to sniff. 'Katie, before this call bankrupts me, can I ask you to do me a favour?'

'Anything.'

'There's a slight change of plan and I'm leaving this number tomorrow. Give the news to Diana and tell her everything is going well and I'll be making contact very soon. If I call her myself she'll never get off the line. Oh, and Gus too, if you don't mind.'

'Of course I don't mind, I'll do it from the office and bugger the consequences.'

'You're an angel,' I said. 'I love you. And give love to your siblings.'

'I will. Mum,' she called. 'You haven't asked me what my dream was.'

'So tell me, but quickly.'

'I dreamt that I was a little girl and walking beside you pushing Wills in his pram. I told you that you looked lovely and all happy, and you said it was because you were going to have another baby ... bye, Mum, hugs and kisses ...'

Philippa Todd

When I'd finished crying and blown my nose, I telephoned my bank manager with news of a suspected ulcer. He said that my cheque for expenses would be honoured and he was sorry about my medical problem, and how could anyone afford to be ill in America? And he was sure that the expense would be dealt with successfully by insurance, he said. (From his lips to God's ears.)

I asked him not to mention my call to anyone (with Marcus in mind) as I did not want to worry the family. He enjoyed the secret we were sharing, and it was one more load off my mind. I had to wait longer before telephoning my real aunt on the East Coast to ask if I could give her name as a guarantor for my cheque.

I doubted I would sleep, but to be on the safe side I asked for an alarm call at six o'clock, then put out the bedside light.

The dream I was having not surprisingly escapes me, but I do know that it did not include an express train thundering through my room. But that's what was happening as wakefulness dawned, and it scared the hell out of me. Where in God's name was I? It was pitch-dark, even the faint glow under the door from the bathroom where I'd left the light on for comfort was not showing.

Simultaneously something crashed on to the floor in my bathroom and my bed convulsed. Sweet Jesus, it was an earthquake, and yours truly was terrified. I fumbled for the light switch, having remembered that the bedside lamps were fixed to the console tables, which were fixed to the wall (and now I knew why). Nothing happened, other than that the deafening noise persisted and my bed still gyrated. It was too dark to consider trying to find the door, and though I thought maybe I should see if there was room for me under the bed, I was too paralysed to try. If only the rooms had not been so soundproofed maybe I would have heard a shout or even a scream, or the sound of glass breaking – anything to show that I was not the only person left alive in the world would have been welcome. My fear was so great I actually thought that maybe I would miscarry and wouldn't need an abortion after all.

I must have become accustomed to the deafening roar because I do not remember it stopping. But the bed slowly settled down and then I nearly died as a light concealed in a corner came on. It was dim and didn't show much, but nevertheless it was magical light. ·

I heard voices in the corridor and then there was a tap on my door. I shot across the room to answer it, not giving a thought to being sparsely clad. A seven-foot black security guard asked me in a very small voice if I was 'okay, ma'am' and assured me that the quake had passed. He said it had only measured five point three on the Richter Scale (you could have fooled me) and not to worry if there were any aftershocks. His exact words were 'They ain't worth losing no sleep over'. I must say that I felt better for the human contact and wished that I could have asked him to stay for a chat to delay his departure.

It was five o'clock in the morning, there was not a hope in the world that I would go to sleep again, and thinking about lying in a bath full of lovely hot water and scented bubbles was the most comforting thing that crossed my mind right then, but fear of being drowned by a tidal wave stopped me turning on the taps.

Knowing that now I would have to start telephoning again to allay fears and future phone calls from back home, I tried to begin, but the line was dead. I did manage, however, to get the hotel operator who promised to consider a call to England a priority whenever she had success with the lines. I was lying on my bed, tense and still frightened, waiting for another rumble, when Tod called on his mobile phone.

The reception was bad and I could barely hear him. He was checking that I was okay, he said, and hoped that I was not too frightened. I think he was worried that I might have second thoughts about living in LA, and a wicked thought crossed my mind that now I had a legitimate reason why I couldn't marry him. Who in their right mind would go to live in California?

'I depart for the airport in five minutes,' he said. 'There's no damage out there, planes are flying.'

'But what if the roads arc damaged?' I asked naively. 'Your car might fall into a crater.'

He laughed. 'No sweat,' he said, 'I'm using the 'copter . . .'

At the desk I had difficulty making them believe that I was a leaving early because of an emergency in my family and not because of the earthquake. But as a precaution I had the hotel car drop me off at the Beverly Wilshire Hotel where I said I was having a business breakfast before leaving LA. Then I waited for the driver to depart before telling the bell-hop struggling with my luggage that I'd forgotten something and had him call a cab. Talk about intrigue and double-cross, it was wearing me out, and I was not cut out for it.

Whether or not it was considered a small earthquake there was damage, and to my inexperienced eye, lots of it. One overpass was closed and huge cracks were showing underneath. There was plenty of broken glass and workmen were boarding up windows and repairing broken gas mains, and fire-engines and ambulances were dashing about to the tune of screeching sirens.

The shock of the quake had weakened my paranoia about the abortion, and although I noticed the words Medical Center over the main entrance of the clinic and remembered the immaculate uniforms of the staff, and writing out a cheque for several thousand pounds in a room marked Accounts, I was in my bedroom and undressed before rational thought came to the front of my mind. It was then that I began to tremble and experience a fear that matched the night before, and the stark reality of what was about to happen to me replaced all else.

I was given a shot in the arm of something to calm me and stop the chattering of my teeth, then I was put into OR gear and asked to confirm my name and age written on two name-tabs before they were clamped to both wrists. I was then placed on a trolley and silently rolled away by two enormous hunks in uniforms of the type we see in hospital soap operas.

T. J. met me in what was labelled its Anaesthetic Room, kissed my hand and introduced me to a lovely-looking female anaesthetist.

'I'm Clover Johnson,' she said reassuringly in a heavenly drawl, 'you're not worried, are you, Camilla?'

She shouldn't have been so nice because it caused my eyes to burn and my lashes to get wet. I shook my head and she patted my cheek.

'You know about epidurals, I'm sure,' she said, showing that she considered us intellectual equals. Little did she know that right then I didn't as much as feel the intellectual equal of an ant.

'Yes, I think I do,' I whispered.

'I'm sure you do,' she purred. 'I shall give you a tiny shot in your spine to stop any pain before I insert the larger needle that will deaden everything unpleasant from your waist down.' (As in paralysis, but the word was not used.)

Two OR attendants turned me on my side and bared my spine for Clover, who then inserted the tiny needle, and thank God I was not going to feel the larger one because the pain was excruciating. I began to sweat and a nurse with perfect black skin like velvet wiped my brow and my cheeks with an ice-cold cloth. She also held my hand and smiled reassuringly at me, and I'll never forget that lovely face.

I was beginning to feel as though it was all happening to someone else and I was merely an onlooker, when Clover delivered the important injection that was to seal my fate. By the time I was wheeled into the Operating Room and lifted on to the gynae table I was a helpless lump with only arm and eye movement and no doubt a voice though I didn't try to use it.

Soft classical music played in the background and people talked quietly to each other. I think there were four of them behind those masks, but I kept my eyes closed because when I tried looking around I distinctly saw pink worms wriggling up a pale green wall. I knew that they couldn't be for real, but watching them unnerved me. I was aware that my legs had been put into stirrups but south of my waist belonged right then to T. J. and all events were out of my control. The die had been cast and there was no going back.

The trouble with local anaesthetic is that you know what is going on, and in the States, where everything has to hang out, they explain procedure to you as they go along. Clover sat beside me, held my hand and watched the monitor to which I was attached. My heartbeats were fascinating on the screen and rather fast, but steady. I tired of watching them, though, and closed my eyes again. If this was the real world I wished that I was not in it. I wanted to be a small child again, cosseted, adored and most of all protected. This was all much too grown-up for me . . .

Eventually T. J. told me that it was all over and I'd been a very good girl (it would have been difficult to be otherwise). Clover said it was time for me to take a nap, and I didn't feel her give me anything, but heavenly sleep overcame me in a natural way, and like a baby I did not wake when moved.

It was getting dark when I woke up back in my room some time later, with sensation and movement restored to my lower half. It was a relief to test my legs and then my toes and to find I was once more in control.

Between my legs was a different story, I was sore, and my lower abdomen felt hot. I had a major headache and could not bear the light, but I felt a sense of relief that it was all over, and I was sure that I'd soon feel strong enough to get up, get out, and start the battle with the rest of my problems.

A charge nurse said that my headache was natural after an epidural and that if I was hungry I could eat something. I could have sunk a bottle of cold white wine and a plate of prawns, but I settled for soup and a hot buttered muffin.

It was cosy in my room and I felt protected. Soon all that was to end, but right then, alone in a strange country and with a deadly secret (for me, anyway), it was a necessary sort of accouchement.

At about four in the morning I awoke and began to make plans rather than trying unsuccessfully to get back to sleep. I had to get to Brentwood to meet a man I would rather not have bothered about. But Diana was expecting me to see him, and I had to face the fact that he would probably make good TV material because he sounded so weird. I went to sleep again about an hour later and awoke at eight o'clock. As I opened my eyes I burst into a flood of tears and uncontrollable sobbing. I sat up in my bed and bawled into my raised knees.

A nursing assistant came in with a breakfast tray and departed swiftly when he saw the state I was in. A staff nurse hurried in, then sat on my bed and held my hand. I couldn't stop crying, it was hopeless to try, but she didn't seem to mind. My behaviour was perfectly natural, she said, and most patients would have reached there more quickly than I had. She brushed damp hair from my eyes and said that she would organize an hour's counselling before I departed.

'I have to leave soon,' I sobbed.

She told me to drink my coffee, eat my English muffin, and by the time I'd finished a counsellor would be with me. True to her word, that's the way it happened. This tall man knocked on my door and walked in, looking more like a male model than a counsellor.

'Hello, I'm George,' he said, taking my hand gently in his after I'd hidden a few damp tissues down the bed.

'Hello,' I said, convinced that there was some mistake. 'I don't wish to be rude, but I think you're in the wrong room.'

'Why so?' he asked, smiling and showing gorgeous teeth.

'You can't help me,' I said in an unfriendly way. 'I've had an abortion and I'm all to pieces. You can't possibly know how awful that is.'

He removed my tray, pulled up a chair, reached for my hand and said, 'You're right, I can't know. I'll go if you like, but I think that I can help you. The abortion itself is only part of your distress, more of a shock to the system really. But trauma is different, and I do know about that. Why don't you try me? Whatever we talk about is absolutely confidential.'

He smiled again and buzzed for fresh coffee. I cannot remember what we talked about, but George certainly made me feel better. I remember him giving me a hug at some point, and telling me not to be so hard on myself. He gave me a secret list of things to tell myself and said to be assured that I was a nice person really and not the harlot I was intent on painting myself. He made me learn a private prayer, and little did I realize then how useful it was going to be for me on more than one occasion, agnostic that I was, or not.

I was in my hospital bathroom showering once again and wishing that I would stop bleeding because it would complicate my life while travelling and reminded me constantly of what had just been done to me. It took me back to the real births I had had, and though I know I imagined it, I even had the empty feeling that followed my bringing full-term babies into the world. I fixed my mind on George.

But I was brought out of that with a cruel jerk when a late tremor rocked the clinic. I was standing on one leg at the time and fell out of the shower cubicle, knocking my head on the lavatory. What a way to go, I thought, having forgotten about aftershocks and small tremors. My body would be reported as being found in a hospital ruin where I'd been admitted for an abortion, and my children would finally know what kind of a parent their mother had been. I quickly said the private prayer that George had taught me, and picked myself up. I knew I had to get out of that godforsaken city as fast as I could.

THIRTEEN

B efore I left the hospital the nursing supervisor, a good-looking girl in a designer dress and black court shoes, gave me a few written instructions on aftercare, prudently sealed into an envelope, and a few gratis tablets for the headache I was suffering. It happened sometimes after an epidural, she said, but it was nothing to worry about. It might last for a few days, though, she added. And it did.

I took a hire car to Brentwood, a sub-tropical suburb if ever I saw one. If you didn't run a car yourself in Los Angeles, hiring one seemed to be the only other means of transport. I should have kept it waiting (the cost of such luxuries is so much less than in England) as a stroke of good fortune enabled me to leave for Chicago later that same day.

The lunch date that I had arranged was with one of the strangest men I had ever met, and it did not go well. He was a casting agent, and not too successful I'd say, judging by his bad attitude. He lived in a small house (by LA standards) the interior of which was totally decorated in jungle scenes and camouflage patterns, the sitting-room alone boasting a wall-to-wall mural of leopard hunting gazelle, right down to the gory kill and the eventual bloody tearing apart of the carcasses.

Even the garden, viewed head-on through a glass

wall, was planted to look like authentic jungle, and some enthusiastic landscaper had made a pretty good watering-hole out of the swimming-pool, where a large plastic but realistic alligator dozed in the sun. Well, I assume he was plastic, since I did not see him breathe. There were also two life-sized warthogs, one a female with the male mounted by his front legs on her back in the mating position. I assume they were plastic too, since I did not see top warthog give any copulating thrusts. Well, that is, not until the casting agent (call me Bernie), with a deep-throated laugh that did nothing to make him more lovable, flicked a switch, presumably for my amusement, and to the faint humming of a tightly sprung coil, male warthog availed himself of his mate to a frenetic coital rhythm.

To me, Bernie was a weird misfit, but to himself he was the most successful talent scout (his actual words) in the United States. Obviously he did not consider that I had enough of what he specialized in to bother about, even as a wife, and we both knew that we would never meet again when I declined to stay the night and he asked me for my portion of the lunch check after a mediocre snack in a local fast-food diner.

But I'd turned on my tape recorder and despite my aching head and sore groin I did my best to cajole him into spilling his beans, which was no big deal since the Californian man's favourite subject is himself. He did not particularly like women, he said, and when pressed into why he bothered to blindly join a foreign dating agency if that were the case, he muttered about wanting to find out if females were any more likeable in the Third World than in fucking California, and why didn't I cut the crap.

I began to say that the UK was not considered part of the Third World, but gave up when I noticed two red patches appearing on his cheeks directly under his eyes that looked ominous. And when his head developed a slight irregular twitch towards the left, I decided it was time to leave, and if Diana thought I was short on material she could go take a jump.

He had depressed the hell out of me, and free of him, and longing to leave Los Angeles, I took another car, and begged the driver to go a touch quicker than the permitted forty miles an hour, in the hope of finding an imminent flight.

A Chicago-bound plane was just leaving, I was told as I panted up to an outside receiving desk, more like a bus station really, and my luggage was grabbed by a stick-thin tall African/American (no more using the word Negro or black for me after that trip) who, in his dark brown uniform, resembled an animated Hershey bar. And with 'Move it, lady, or you'll miss the flight' he pushed my luggage through a hole in the wall, while fear of missing anything that would carry me off from that coast propelled me on trembling legs at breakneck speed along miles of moving walkways.

I was the last passenger to board the aircraft, the gay steward tossing his blond fringe haughtily from his pale eyes and fixing me with a long-suffering expression as he slammed the door shut on my heels, obviously as anxious as I was to leave the City of the Stars. Right off we were taxiing down the runway, and as all current enthusiasm for flying had left me, I fastened my seatbelt and closed my eyes, not only to pray for an uneventful flight (which I think I might be doing for several years to come) but to discourage myself from spilling all my secrets into the lap of the very fat man in tartan Crimplene trousers and pink socks next to whom I had been seated. My angst was dangerously near the surface, I had never felt the need to blab and let it all hang out more strongly than on that journey, and a total stranger would have done me nicely.

It seemed a long flight for staying in the same country

Philippa Todd

and not leaving a coast behind, but I slept fitfully through most of it, only waking briefly with a rapid heartbeat and wet palms at any change of engine noise, which before my falling-out-of-the-sky experience would not have bothered me at all. Not to labour the point, I just did not feel particularly well, and I was fighting a sadness that was doing its best to consume me. I wished that I was going home, I wished that Gus was around to give me a hug, and Kate to make me laugh. And I comforted myself by vowing that I would telephone them both the moment I reached my hotel room in Chicago.

I simply did not want to pretend that I was interested in any more men from an agency, whether they were wealthy professionals or handsome hunks or downright marriageable pillars of the earth. To me they were depressing, lonely, insecure and sad, and too serious about themselves for their own good.

Talking of handsome, the first man I saw on entering the Arrivals hall in Chicago made the celebrities of Oscars night pale into insignificance. Now, there was a good-looking man for you, tall, slim, dark-haired with a touch of grey above the ears, a beautiful tan and wearing his casual clothes to perfection.

He smiled briefly when he saw me looking at him. 'Annie Lloyd?' he asked, and with that I stumbled over my flight bag and landed clean in his arms.

'Now, that's what I call a greeting,' he said. 'Is this the way you do it in the old country . . . ?'

Seated next to him in his dark green Cadillac I began to relax. This man seemed so well put together it defied all that I had been thinking about misfits and marriage bureaux.

'It was kind of you to meet me at the airport,' I said, hoping I sounded well brought up and sophisticated.

He laughed. 'Kind, my eye. Just good manners, surely?

Couldn't have a lady picking up a cab late at night around here, it just plain wouldn't be safe.'

Hunter Lee McNab was easy to be with, and I wondered how soon I could connect my recorder and begin my 'Whatever made you go to a dating agency?' routine.

'Do I call you Hunter or H. L.?' I asked, getting used now to initials for names.

'My colleagues call me H. L. My wives called me Hunter when they lived with me and sonofabitch when we got divorced.' He flashed me a wicked look. 'You can choose, I answer to them all.'

Outside the Drake Hotel, while my luggage was smartly removed from the Cadillac's obscenely large boot, he handed the keys to the doorman. 'Keep it handy,' he said with style, 'I'll just see the lady checked in.'

This man had class, and it only served to confuse me further. Why would *he* need the services of a dating agency?

The entrance hall was huge and busy. It was late at night but the people around me moved purposefully and happily. Was everyone in a hurry, I wondered, or had laid-back, dozy Beverly Hills rubbed off on me more than I knew?

'Sit there, Annie,' Hunter said. 'I'll have you checked in in no time.' And he did. I was grateful.

He returned with a member of staff and took my hand as I stood up. 'This young man will take you to your room,' he said, pressing something into his palm. 'I'll call you in the morning. Sleep well, Annie, I can see you're tired.'

Next day we met for lunch, and we also met for dinner. I recorded our conversations, as usual, and I replayed them that night in my room. He did not sound like any of the others (excepting Harry Smith, but I saw Harry as a one-off person and not just because he'd made me pregnant). Hunter simply seemed different, and almost as though he were interviewing me at times, instead of the other way around. So what could his angle possibly be?

'Don't leave tomorrow,' he said over dinner, taking my hand. 'I'd like to take you out on the lake in my boat. You do like lakes, don't you?'

Lake Michigan had looked so lovely from my windows it was too tempting to pass up. I felt relaxed, and well, why not, I thought. It was less than a week since Oscars night but it felt like a year, and a year of pure hell at that. A day on a lake would be good for me.

'I'd love to come on the lake,' I answered. 'And I'm crazy about boats.'

The Italian import motorcruiser with the lines of a bird in flight had a crew of three, a sun-deck completely covered in lounger cushions, and an after-deck equipped for dining.

Lake Michigan is spectacular and huge and, can you believe, has beaches. The weather that day was brilliant in every sense of the word – cloudless skies, a gentle breeze and low humidity. We were on the water all day, and put in to a small harbour just once where our cook shopped for food and Hunter helped me to shop for presents to take home.

We dropped anchor way out and lunched on the after-deck. The girl member of the crew, a French Canadian, was a very good cook and I ate shellfish the like of which I have never tasted before. I was beginning to feel well again, the trauma of the abortion was lessening. But I had work to do, and I mustn't forget it . . . I checked on my recorder.

'Hunter,' I said as we sunbathed on the upper deck after lunch, 'you do not seem to be the type of man who would pay money to meet a marriageable woman, so what's your angle?'

He stared across the water for some considerable time, then looked straight into my face.

'You shouldn't be doing this either, Annie, paying out money to meet a man, I mean. It's dangerous, this lonely hearts stuff.'

I examined my toes. I'd been thinking the same thing myself, but I wasn't in a position to say it. 'Loneliness, I suppose, drives women to do it,' I said. (I'd read that somewhere.) 'It's a stronger emotion for desperate women than fear is.'

After another stretch of silence he leaned across and took my hand. 'Annie,' he said, 'you'll probably never forgive me, and I'm sure that I shouldn't tell you, but then, you're different from the other women I've seen . . .'

'Hunter,' I cut in, taking my hand from his, 'let's not go through that routine. If you're trying to say that you don't like me, that's okay. You're the one who wanted me to stay an extra day. It's no big deal, honestly.' I could scarcely hide my embarrassment.

He took my hand again. 'It's not that, Annie. I'm having trouble with my conscience. You see, I'm not looking for a wife . . .'

My heart stopped for a second. We were riding the swell in the middle of an enormous stretch of water, suddenly no other boats were around, the crew were so quiet they had to be taking naps. What was he going to tell me? That he was a serial killer and I was about to be his eighth victim? If so, I'd better scream to wake the crew, and quickly.

I was wrong, but on the right tack, if you see what I mean.

'I'll refund your fare,' he said. That was good news, it meant he wasn't about to kill me.

'But?' I said, aiming at sounding casual. Can you imagine if I had really been husband-hunting and had met a man like Hunter, I might have thought I'd died and gone to heaven, until he talked about refunding my fare home.

To his credit he never once looked away. 'I'm researching for a book,' he said. 'I'm not looking for a wife.'

Maybe it was suppressed anxiety coming out, maybe it was tension, or maybe just relief. All I can say is, if I'd been wearing a hat I would have thrown it in the air and whooped with joy. I burst out laughing.

'What's so funny?' he asked, looking confused.

'I'm researching too,' I answered. 'I'm not looking for a spouse either.'

His eyes went wide. 'You're kidding. For a book?'

I shook my head. 'No, for television, back home.'

He stared. 'Are you wired?'

I nodded. 'Yes, are you?'

'Yes,' he answered.

Well, we laughed then until we both collapsed. His stomach was heaving and my face ached. 'I'll take mine off it you'll take yours off,' he said, choking on his own joke. Then he excused himself and tottered off across the cushions in bare feet, getting into his shirt as he went and still shaking his head. He spluttered, 'I'll be right back,' and laughed and coughed his way down to the galley.

He returned with a bottle of champagne and two glasses. It seems that Hunter Lee McNab (how could he fail as an author with a name like that?) was tired of being just a trial lawyer and wanted to write books. 'They say you must write about what you know,' he said, 'and I know a lot about the law, courtrooms, criminals, stuff like that. I'm a criminal lawyer.'

'A budding John Grisham?' I said, sipping my vintage champagne (and because, as I told you, I can never drink champagne without thinking of Marcus, I wished that he had known where I was and what

I was doing, because he too liked boats, almost as much as champagne, and hopefully he would have been jealous).

'I wish that was true,' Hunter said, 'but the idea of writing a thriller excites the hell out of me.'

I stretched and leaned back on my cushions. 'Tell me the story-line,' I said, like a seasoned scribbler.

He leaned back too, sipped his champagne and stared out beyond me. 'There's this serial killer on the loose. He travels around and reads lonely hearts columns in down-market magazines. He dates poor lonely females, then tortures tham, rapes them, keeps them locked up, that sort of thing, then he kills them, slowly. Sometimes he cuts them up. The police just can't catch him, mainly because women who advertise like that don't keep the evidence around and don't tell anyone what they are doing. It gets a bit boring for him because killers get a kick out of avoiding capture. So, he gets a little bolder and contacts dating agencies in Britain. Are you following the plot so far, Annie?'

I looked at him. 'I certainly am. And I'm waiting to hear that this novel has no peculiar twist. You *are* the prosecuting attorney and not the serial killer, aren't you? A girl can't be too careful.'

He refilled my glass. 'No problem, I'm a regular lawyer. I suppose Annie Lloyd is not your real name.'

I shook my head, and was surprised by an unexpected hot feeling behind my eyes. 'My real name is Camilla Cage.'

'That's a nice name,' he said, 'but I was beginning to feel real comfortable with Annie Lloyd.'

I knew that he was watching me, and I tried to control myself, but quite suddenly, without warning, like a haemorrhage, I was crying. Not ladylike feminine distress and a few gentle tears, but real racking sobs and a heavy watershed. I do not know how long I continued but when I resumed just normal weeping, Hunter was sitting beside me hugging me to his chest, and the front of his shirt was wet.

'Cry all you want,' he said, patting my back. 'Then if it would help, you can tell me all about it . . .'

It was the secret of the abortion, of course, that I had to exorcize, and my psyche was telling me that isolated in the middle of a lake the size of a sea, with a sympathetic stranger beside me, was as good a place as any to spill out the guilt and sorrow that was eating at my guts.

'I had to have an abortion in Beverly Hills. I didn't know that I was pregnant before I left London.'

He rubbed his hand up and down my arm. 'You poor kid.'

'Kid nothing,' I sobbed. 'I have grown-up kids of my own back home. It's all so awful.'

'But not the end of the world, Annie. Sorry, Camilla. These things happen.'

'Stick with Annie,' I spluttered through my tears, 'it was Annie who got pregnant . . .'

He kissed the top of my head, and he asked no questions.

It was dusk when we walked down the gangway and on to the yacht harbour. Hunter put his arm around me. I was drained dry, but relief was beginning to wash over me.

'The Drake has some good restaurants,' he said. 'Let's have a late dinner.'

I nodded, I didn't want to be alone, and right then Hunter Lee was my tower of comfort. He looked down at me and smiled. 'And we'll celebrate your being my new best friend.'

I stopped and faced him. 'You won't put any of this in a novel, ever, will you?'

'Never, Annie,' he answered without unnecessary emphasis, and he didn't bother to change the name.

He took me to the airport next morning.

'I have to be in New York in a day or so,' he said. 'There's a literary agent there may take me on. Would you like to have dinner with me?'

I hesitated for a moment. I had to spend some time with Brad Delman, the New York client. Greg McLaren had asked me to contact him for a dinner date and I wanted to see him again because he'd be a great character for me to work into a book one day. And Gus had said that he would fly to New York in the hope that I would marry him. But Hunter was special to me right then and the thought of seeing him again was comforting.

'I'd love to,' I said and quickly scribbled down the telephone number of my hotel on the book of matches I had lifted from the Drake.

'Do I ask for Annie Lloyd or Camilla Cage?' he said with a smile as he took them.

We parted as best friends do, with a hug and a laugh and a promise to always keep in touch. Hunter Lee McNab had set me on my feet again.

This time I enjoyed the flight. It was my shortest one yet in the States, but it wasn't just that. I felt cleaner than I had in Los Angeles, and almost purged of guilt. Only one more client left to see, and I would never, ever take on anything so nerve-racking again, no matter how much I needed the money.

My mind was made up, probably it always had been, I was not going to marry Gus. I wasn't ready for anything like that. But he was a good friend, and it would be great to see him again.

FOURTEEN

New York was a shock to my system after the frenetic laidbackness of Los Angeles and the able style of Chicago.

Don't get me wrong, that city was not wasted on me, I found the way it throbbed and the paranoid speed at which it moved positively intoxicating. But when I went shop-gazing shortly after my arrival and in the space of a hundred yards I was called a fucking white bitch by a young black drug addict in need of a fix when I said no to the five dollars he demanded, and then a nigger-lover by a white punk in metal-rimmed boots when he saw me put a twenty-cent coin into the hat of a blind black beggar with a sad-eyed dog at his feet, I knew that it was time to take a tighter grip on my shoulder-bag, leave my gold neck-chain at home, and put my wrist-watch into my pocket.

Determined to deal with my final assignment with professional agility, I telephoned Brad Delman and suggested we meet that evening. He couldn't talk for long, he said, he was busy painting and his nude model was getting cold (meant as a joke, it was hot and humid), so could we meet in a Chinese restaurant near to where he lived, corner of Third and Ninety-third at eight o'clock? Love you, Annie. *Ciao.*

More as an exercise than with expectancy, I telephoned

my chum of near-disaster, Greg McLaren. I was speaking into his answerphone, over-explaining who I was (as is my wont), when he lifted his receiver and said, 'Hello, Camilla, of course I remember you, I was hoping you would call me some time soon.'

'No more travelling problems, I hope,' I said, unable to think intelligently on unexpectedly hearing his voice.

'No,' he said, 'but I was booked on that Russian plane that crashed in China two days ago, and luckily I missed the flight.'

'You have more lives than a cat,' I answered. 'Talking of animals, how's Fred?'

He laughed. 'You remembered. He's very well, just had a dead mouse for his supper.'

I was silent. Real or erroneous, a viper eating dead mice in a Manhattan apartment is a definite conversation-stopper, even for New York.

'Talking of supper,' he said, 'how about joining me for dinner tomorrow night?'

'I would like that.'

'Good, some friends are coming round for drinks at seven, why don't you join us and then you and I will go on to somewhere nice? I'll send a car for you if you care to tell me where you're staying.'

The yellow cab that took me to the Chinese restaurant where I was to rendezvous with Brad Delman was falling apart, and the driver's speciality seemed to be to drive up the rear end of everything in front of him, then, when they slowed down, slam on his brakes, point nine-eight of a second before sudden coupling. He swore under his breath all the time and hawked on his blocked sinuses in a most disgusting manner. I was pleased that we had a plate-glass screen between us.

'How much do I owe you?' I asked him through it as he screeched to a stop in the middle of the street. (A previous cab driver had straightened me out about paying while seated and the doors still locked by feeding dollar bills into the trap in the glass, unlike in a London taxi where the reverse applies.)

'Whadda matter, can't you read or something?' he asked in a strong Eastern European accent.

'Yes, I can read,' I said, tired by now of rudeness for the sake of it, and catching on fast. 'I can see too, but not when the meter is covered in a layer of grime. This is supposed to be a clean country, pity someone didn't tell you that when you got off the boat.'

With that off my chest, I gave him the correct amount in coins, no tip. He raised his eyes to heaven and made some guttural comment in Yiddish that I did not understand but knew what it implied, and he moved off while I still had one leg trapped in his goddamn cab. He gave me a swift two-fingered sign, and you would have been proud of me – I gave him one back.

Brad Delman stood in the doorway of the restaurant framed by two huge Chinese lanterns. He was recognizable to me only by his chubby face, though it was a deal chubbier than in the photograph of him I'd seen on his sheet of particulars at the Hands Across the Sea agency. The small white beard had been trimmed into designer stubble, which blended in with the stubble that covered his head. The piercing blue eyes were as I remembered them glittering out from the photograph, but tinier. A gold earring I did not remember noticing before was clamped into one tiny pink ear.

After that, his written description of himself fell cruelly short of the truth. He was small enough to resemble a dwarf and his tiny blue sandals revealed fat little toes that looked like a child's, and were dirty. He must have been sixty inches around the waist and did his best to disguise this enormity of girth with a loose-fitting, highly patterned short-sleeved Hawaiian shirt over dark trousers.

He smiled warmly in my direction and held out his short thick arms. I quickly switched on my mini-recorder as I approached him, and smiled back.

'You just have to be Annie,' he said. 'No way can there be two dames coming here tonight who look so English.'

I went to shake his hand, he went to swamp me with a hug, and we ended up in a human cat's cradle with me stretched across his girth and my chin resting on the top of his head. (All I could think of right then was thank God we won't be going on somewhere to dance.)

'A handshake is just a hug for fraidy cats,' he said as we untangled. 'Hug and love, I say, hug and love, hug and love . . .'

Excuse me, I thought. But did I just fly in from Chicago, or was I here on a weekend excursion from the moon? There was no answer to that, so I followed him.

Inside, the restaurant was dark, smelly, ice-cold from air-conditioning and throbbing with humanity. The waiters were rude, uncaring and in a hurry. But the food they brought in from the well-hidden kitchens that were probably a hot-bed breeding ground for cockroaches was so good I may always remember it. Their sizzling lamb was to die for.

Brad dropped an awful lot of it down him, together with the marinade from the spare ribs and whole chunks of chicken, caused mostly by his girth preventing him from getting near enough to the table, but made worse by the fact that his chair was not high enough for him. I wondered if I should offer to ask for a cushion, but didn't in case it appeared a little pushy. As it was, his tiny feet swung an inch or two clear of the floor. But he tucked his napkin under his chin, abandoned his chopsticks for his fingers and ate with alacrity. (I saw the worst table manners in New York than any other place I've been, and that's going some after the saga of the old viscount and his banana split in London.)

Brad leaned forward as best he could and reached with a short hairy arm for my hand. He had fascinating pointy cartoon elbows like Popeye's and his tiny hand was heavy in mine, and warm, and not overly clean, like his feet. Paint of various shades showed around the cuticles and under his nails. I wondered why artists, like musicians, never seem to have the long slender fingers you read about in the Barbara Cartland novels.

He laughed in the beginning at almost everything I said, throwing his head back and making his chair creak ominously. It was a fat man's laugh, the kind that Orson Welles traded on.

'Are you rich, Annie?' he asked me suddenly, still laughing.

'Hell, no,' I answered quickly and just as impolitely.

He didn't move his hand from mine or his eyes from my face, but he wasn't laughing any more. 'That's too bad,' he said, 'I told that agency I needed a dame with money and a large country house. It was a necessary condition.'

'They didn't tell me,' I said weakly, hoping I looked suitably concerned.

'Well, hell, Annie, that's not fair, and you've come all this way to see me. That's gross.'

He would have been right, if my hunting had been for real, I could have ended up one very distressed lady. As it was, I merely checked that I was recording such juicy material.

He stared at me sympathetically, then smiled hopefully. 'Are you putting me on, Annie?'

I shook my head.

Now at last he removed his hand from mine. 'You don't have any money at all?'

I wished he'd keep his voice down, people were beginning to stare, and that's not common in New York.

(Not until they pay me, is what I wanted to answer, but of course, I couldn't.) 'Not much at all,' is what I said.

'And no house in the country?'

'No, not even a one-up-and-one-down with outside lav.'

He didn't know what the hell I was talking about, but he knew that it was bad news. He ran a hand amongst his facial stubble and it made a grating sound that set my teeth on edge.

'Gee, that won't do,' he said. 'You see, I want to live in the UK. I'm tired of looking over my shoulder in this goddamn city, and it's safer there than here, isn't it?'

'Not so much,' I answered, remembering Bloody Sunday.

Brad looked as though he might cry, and I could tell that he'd stopped swinging his feet and had crossed them over each other to bridge the circuit, as a comforter.

'I've painted a real good collection of around a hundred nudes. I want to have a show in England when I get there. I have this dream of a large country-house setting. Stately home sort of thing, it's so classy. And I need a rich woman to provide the money, and I'll need to marry to be allowed to stay there. I'll be rich myself once the paintings are sold, of course. But to begin with . . .'

'Sorry I can't help,' was all I could think of to say, as I tried to imagine an exhibition of nudes taking place in a Queen Anne mansion, say, somewhere in Wiltshire.

'So there's nothing doing?' he asked, while managing to look half his original size, and that was not easy.

I shook my head.

He tossed back the dregs of his coffee and spilled some, not that it mattered, down his shirt. 'Maybe if I came over you could sort of introduce me around. You must know lots of people, even, maybe, a few dolls with money?'

I asked for the bill then, it was clear I'd have to pay. The waiter stared. 'She means the check,' Brad volunteered quite comfortably, no embarrassment there that the lady was paying.

'You know something, Annie,' he said as I counted out dollar bills, 'we could be friends. I'll need an agent when I make it to London. Come on over to my place tomorrow for lunch and see my work and talk about it. I'm a real good artist . . .'

'Okay,' I said, with Diana's programme and my fees in mind.

Outside on the street as I tried to hail a cab, he pointed to a deli on the opposite corner. 'Say, Annie, why don't you pick up two hot pastramis on rye on your way over? I live just down that street there so if you hurry on over they'll still be hot on arrival.'

I looked down at him and knew that I had to do it. He was the material of which TV producers dream. 'Fine,' I said. 'And you'll supply the wine?'

'Gee, Annie, I don't think I have any. But see that store over there, that's a great wine place. Ask for the inexpensive Californian Chardonnay, the one Brad Delman always gets for himself. They call me Toulouse-Lautrec in there. Shows they think I'm a good artist . . .'

A taxi stopped, nearly on my toes. 'Don't forget the pickles, and keep the pastrami hot. Love you,' Brad shouted as I slammed the door shut and collapsed painfully on to bare springs where the torn seat-stuffing was worn thin.

I slept late, then telephoned Gus. He greeted me with love in his voice, but I thought he sounded sort of edgy. I would meet him at Kennedy airport, I said to cheer him up.

I was not to dream of trying to meet the plane, he said. 'Is better my darling goes shopping, has good time. Check in at Pierre Hotel, nicer for you there, and Gus arrive in no time, and he loves you . . .'

I walked to Bloomingdales and tried not to worry about Gus's strange mood. Was I about to see a dark side of him, I wondered, while hoping I was not.

I bought as many adorable baby clothes as I could carry, plus an extra travel bag. I bought a tennis racket for William, half the price of in England, and designer jeans for Kate. Yes, the nice man in beige with Bloomies written on his chest said he would be happy to arrange to send my purchases along to my hotel right away. Now, that was the way to do shopping, I thought.

I stopped to pick up our lunch as Brad had instructed, and went next door and bought the wine. I found the run-down and rather grubby old building in which he lived, and pressed the relevant button while checking that my mike was in position.

'Hi, Annie,' he bellowed. 'Get your shoulder to the door, it's mighty heavy, and get your buns up here. It's eight flights and there ain't no lift.'

It was pretty scary on those stairs, dark too, most light bulbs that worked were covered in grime, and the rest were just smashed. They were bare concrete, the stairs, and they were steep. Graffiti covered the walls and some of it was quite graphic. There were two iron front doors on each landing with four security locks to each. It was my intention to stop for a breather on the fourth floor but a strange-looking man in underpants and murky vest peered out at me from the three-inch stretch allowed by his door chain and belched loudly.

Anxiety thrust me upwards and onwards as I clutched the paper sacks to my breast and climbed those stairs in a hurry. I reached Brad's level just as he was unbolting and dechaining his door. And what a picture he made. He wore an artist's black beret, a huge dark smock covered in paint, and baggy pink trousers that left his ankles and tiny feet bare.

As he grabbed the food from my grasp and I leaned against the wall fighting for breath, a tall dark girl resembling a hooker, in hotpants that snuggled into her crotch, and thigh-high shiny black boots, came into view, kissed him on the top of his head and said, 'See ya, toots' as a form of goodbye.

He felt the drum-tight buttocks that were almost level with his face with his free hand, found money in his trouser pocket and pressed it into her waiting palm. 'Say hi to Annie,' he told her, 'she's from the UK.'

She switched the gum she was chewing to the opposite cheek. 'Hi, Annie. I ain't never been to the UK. But then, chances are you ain't never been to the Bronx. So that makes us kinda quits, don't it?' She then clattered down the stairs on her raised platforms and four-inch heels without a backward glance.

Brad leered at her rear end, nodded his head in appreciation and said to me, 'Best model I ever had. Let's get this wine into the refrigerator. You only bring one bottle?'

His apartment smelled of artist's paint and cats. Tubes of the former were everywhere and three cats glared at me from a corner of a well-worn sofa in his rather small and airless living-room. It was dark too, there was only one small window and it looked out on to other blocks and their equally small windows. How on earth did this man see to paint?.

I knew, of course, before I actually looked, that the paintings on the walls would be of nudes. But when I began to study them while waiting for Brad to open up the food bag and drool at the sight of pastrami on rye and a side order of pickles, I got quite a shock. There were men as well as women, and just to give you an example, one large pair of canvases showed a full-frontal of a faceless man, naked save for a black fedora, with a large semi-erect penis framed by masses of curly black pubic hair and a faceless red-headed girl with a long black scarf tied around her neck sitting on the edge of a table with her knees up giving a graphic view of her labia area, framed by a halo of ginger curls.

I jumped as Brad put one hand on my behind and handed me a glass of wine with the other. 'Cheers, sexy Annie,' he said. (Sexy Annie? Come on. He equated sex to everything, even handing out a glass of wine.) 'Good, huh?' he then asked, nodding towards the paintings and pulling me back a pace, for all the world as if we were looking at important surrealist masters. Then he pointed towards the nude girl with the ginger pubes and said, 'Course, she ain't the girl you saw leaving. Ginger Curls here can only pose on a Tuesday. She's got four kids, and her husband takes Tuesdays off to stay home with them.'

My cheeks were already pink from the exertion of the stairs, and my knees were still trembling. I'm not sure what I would have said next, but luckily Brad didn't wait for any comments. 'Be right back,' he said, heading for his kitchen. 'Go look at the rest of my collection. There are some in my bedroom, it's behind the curtain. They're all over . . . just feel free to roam.'

And they were. Hanging everywhere. Mercifully the ones stacked in corners and leaning against the walls had their backs to me. In general, the rest of them were not too pornographic, just naked people in varying poses. But good art? Forget it. I should know, I tried to paint once and I cringe now when I think about my output. All were faceless and I guessed that this was because Brad could not paint faces and not because the models were coy. Only one that I saw was vaguely porno, and that was of a copulating couple on a bed, and they were both female. But I noticed on his easel a half-finished canvas showing men doing roughly the same sort of thing, but standing up. Willowy, tall men, with small hands and miles of fingers. More like women, really, and I think that Brad may have faked it with blush paint and a fine brush.

He served the sarnies nicely arranged, with lettuce leaves and chopped chives on the side and paper napkins neatly folded. I chose to sit with my back to the randy pair hanging on the living-room wall. Brad pulled up a tiny chair to a low table, tucked his napkin under his chin and didn't speak again until he'd eaten everything, right down to the last crumb of rye bread, helping to secure it with the tip of a licked finger. 'Good, huh?' he said again, this time meaning lunch, while unhinging pastrami from his teeth with the one very long little fingernail he must have grown for such a treat.

'I haven't finished mine,' I answered, looking away and in no hurry to find out what he had in mind for afters.

'No sweat,' he said, rubbing at his lips with his napkin and delicately wiping his grubby fingers. 'Gee, you're slow. If you can't finish all yours I'll finish it for you. Meantime, I'll go feed my cats.'

It was a relief to hear it, they were being a nuisance, and they were smelly. I thought of my handsome, fastidious Kat back home, who would sit so patiently at a distance, all smiley and appreciative, and who would rather die than be pushy, and I hoped suddenly that she was missing me.

But in no time at all Brad was back. He poured the last of the wine into his own glass, then climbed on to his sofa and settled back, facing me, his legs crossed and his feet not touching the floor, his head slightly on one side and his eyes floating over me. I knew with a degree of certainty that he was going to talk sexy, so I offered him my unfinished food, knowing that he was not likely to refuse it, and began to plan a possible route of escape with the sagacity of an SAS tactician who'd lost his compass in the sand.

'So you like my paintings, Annie,' he said, more as a statement than a question, as he tucked in to the remains of my platter.

I tried not to look at him. Those pale eyes of his were so penetrating. 'Yes, they're . . . um . . . interesting,' I answered, nodding my head too vigorously.

He wiggled his toes with pleasure. 'So, you don't mind explicit pictures. Say, why don't you model for me? I bet you look okay without clothes.'

I swallowed my last mouthful of wine. 'No, I couldn't, really.'

'No, I couldn't really . . .' he mimicked, shaking his head and trying to sound English. 'Jesus, you Brits are something else.' Then suddenly, not moving, and looking at me intently, he came out with 'You a tight arse, Annie?'

I felt my face going red. It was a question I simply could not confirm or deny. Luckily he lost interest in my silence, and jumped down from the sofa. 'I'll go make coffee,' he said, and as he passed a row of bookshelves he selected a paperback and threw it over at me. 'Enjoy yourself for five minutes,' he said, and smiled impishly.

Right, you guessed, it was pornographic. Well, not exactly, it was intended as a serious book on sex and sexual activity, a sort of Masters and Johnson tome with a liberal scattering of pen-and-ink drawings. And on the fly-leaf was scrawled large in red crayon, 'For Brad, who brought sex into my life (and how), Love Shelley'.

I flicked through a few pages. Shelley had underlined some sentences and a few of the drawings. One such sentence, with a little inked star beside it read, 'If the man does not seem to be penetrating you enough for your liking, bring your legs up around his neck.' At the bottom of the page Shelley had written, 'Now I do this all the time, just like the Master Fucker taught me.' A little further on, beside a sideways outline drawing of a man, she had lengthened his erect penis in red and underneath had written, 'Now, that's more like it, honey.'

Brad came in with two enormous cracked mugs brimming with steaming coffee. 'I'll just get cream and sugar,' he said, and went back again to the kitchen. When I heard him say to one of his cats, 'Get your head out of that cream, you monster,' I was pleased that I wanted mine black.

I closed the book and placed it as far away from me as possible. Brad deposited both cream and sugar on the low table and climbed back on to the same dent in the sofa. 'Good lit, eh?' he asked nodding at the book.

'Who's Shelley?' I asked as he slurped up his scalding coffee.

'My first ex-wife,' he said casually, leaning dangerously forward and dipping his finger into the cat-licked cream.

'How many ex-wives do you have?'

He seemed to think for a moment. 'Just four.'

'Sounds expensive.'

He licked his finger. 'No, nothing like that. Hell, they all had rich daddies, old money, you know the sort of thing. One of them makes *me* a modest allowance, provided I keep away from her. I would anyway, she's a miserable bitch, ugly too, now she's not getting enough.'

I wanted to leave but I had to keep the conversation going for a spell longer, it was such good material.

'Did Shelley marry again?'

'Oh sure, several times. She's a very successful attorney. Specializes in rape cases.'

There seemed no need to further that line, so I too sipped at my coffee.

Then Brad said, 'Anyway, Annie, I want to talk about you. Why don't we go to bed, get this sex thing out of the way? You'll be more relaxed then.' I had of course seen it coming, but the approach was somewhat different from what I had expected.

'English women are a gas,' he said, shaking his head. 'All tight-arsed and butter wouldn't melt in their mouths and never did it on the first date, don't you know. Then you get 'em into the sack and they perform like alley cats.'

But not me, buster, not with you, I thought. There was something about him, however, that made me not feel afraid. But as I had no intention of having sex with him I thought it best to put the 'I'll come back later' plan that I'd been hatching into action.

'You've gone quiet,' he said. 'I've read about English women like you. You're shy about sex, don't like taking your clothes off unless it's dark . . .'

(Marcus should only hear him, I thought.) I felt indignant, the way you do when you're abroad and someone attacks your race. But how could I argue, it was safer he thought that way.

'Right now I have to go,' I said, hatching my final porkpie. 'I have an important appointment with a publisher.' (Please God don't let him ask which one. I'll go to church on Sunday, I promise.) 'But I could come back later . . . and bring supper.' That got him (thank you, God, brilliant of you to think of allying sex to food).

'Not Chinese,' he said enthusiastically, 'we had that last night. I sure could fancy some Japanese, though. Bit more pricey, but I can see you're not a mean woman, Annie . . .'

I didn't feel good about letting Brad down, or his gastric juices. And for heaven's sake, he may even have planned to take a bath after I left in anticipation of post-supper high jinks. He'd be furious if he'd gone to such lengths as scrubbing his fingernails. But what was I to do? I certainly had no intention of seeing him again. And, as I reflected in the taxi going back to my hotel, it was exactly the way a man like Brad would have played it himself if our roles had been reversed.

I began to feel better.

FIFTEEN

I was dreaming, so vividly that the event was actually happening to me, and I was devoid of that sixth sense we sometimes get that lets us know when we are only dreaming, and tells us that, eventually, we will wake up from the nightmare.

Emma was in labour, and all was not going according to plan. I was summoned to the hospital urgently and then, can you believe, I was stuck in a large lift for half an hour with ten other sweating and nervous passengers, all with our adrenalin flow playing havoc with our overactive imaginations. One lady was crying and I was not far from joining her. One anxious young man whose claustrophobia seemed worse than mine kept up a hoarse cry for help from the Almighty and banged constantly on the doors with his fists.

The alarm bell, from whose emergency button a fat lady would not remove her finger, was our sole contact with the outside world, until suddenly the lift jerked twice, then moved. After an eternity so nerve-racking that I was sure we had gone clean through the roof and were flying into oblivion, it stopped, the doors opened and, with eyes shining and round with fear, we all fought our way out like released animals.

Marcus grabbed me roughly by the arm. 'Where the hell have you been?' he hissed demonically in my ear.

'I'm no good at this sort of thing and that stupid whats-hisname son-in-law of yours is on the missing list.'

I pulled my arm away roughly. 'If you'd taken the trouble to enquire, you would have known that I've been stuck in that airless lift for God knows how long. Not that you care, of course, and he's your son-in-law too.'

He pulled me along a corridor towards a pair of doors through which two nurses were rushing. As I slid on the polished floor I realized that I'd lost my shoes. They must have come off in that lift and now they'd be stolen. I hesitated, mumbled the fact to Marcus, looked behind me hopefully, and half-pointed like a simpleton towards the lift area. But he tugged me on and my shoes soon became irrelevant.

A mask was clamped around my face at the theatre door and then Emma's terrified eyes met mine from where she lay on the labour bed. 'Mum,' was all she said as she grabbed at me with wet and frantic hands.

The masked and gowned obstetrician glared at me from over his mask. 'We're about to do a caesarean section,' he said, much too loudly for the occasion, and as though he held me to blame. 'The baby is distressed. Sign here.'

Though a life probably depended on it, I could not remember my name. Marcus muttered, 'For Christ's sake, Milla,' and snatched the clipboard from me. It was no wonder I couldn't remember who I was, someone was ringing a bell directly into my ear and confusing the hell out of me. My God, it was torture.

I recovered consciousness slowly, dream changed to blurred reality, and soon I remembered my role in life. The bell continued to ring. Jesus, I thought, what am I doing in bed at a time like this? And where am I and where the hell is the telephone? I was halfway round the heavily curtained hotel room before my reluctant brain-cogs interlocked and told me that it was on the bedside table. I did a rugby tackle at it across the bed.

'Is she all right?' I shouted into the mouthpiece, my breath choking me and my heart fluttering in my chest like wings.

After a pause a voice said, 'It has to be you, I remember that voice. What in the world is wrong?'

'Who are you?' I asked, a touch more sanely.

'H. L. . . . McNab . . . Chicago . . . have you forgotten so soon?' The pieces began to fit together. It had only been a dream, and dreams are not precursors of doom, or so I've been told.

'Oh yes, Hunter,' I said weakly, feeling totally drained. 'I've had the most worrying dream. A nightmare, really.'

'Let me guess,' he said, and I just knew that he was smiling, 'your daughter was in premature labour. The baby was dying, you were late arriving . . . how am I doing so far?'

'You forgot about the lift.'

'Ah yes, the lift . . . I know . . . you were stuck in it.'

'Oh, very clever,' I said, getting back into bed properly. 'Not only are you a criminal lawyer and a budding thriller writer but a psychic too.'

'And,' he continued, 'they're going to do a C. section on your daughter and dear sweet Marmee has not been invited into the Operating Room and she's a touch put out . . .'

I shifted my pillow. 'I wouldn't have gone in anyway. And listen, this is my dream, not yours . . .'

I felt better now, but I had to get him off the line. I had to telephone Emma, just in case. And weren't mothers supposed to get premonitions of disaster with their offspring? Supposing something really was wrong?

'Are you still having dinner with me?' he asked. 'I've just arrived in New York, remember?'

No, I hadn't remembered. But I did now, and I had to do some quick thinking. I only had the next night free before Gus arrived. But I liked Hunter and I wanted to keep him as a new friend.

'I would love to,' I said, 'but it will have to be tomorrow night.'

'Not tonight?'

'No, sorry, I've said I'll have dinner with that chap I sat next to when I thought the plane was crashing,' I said, not needing to give a further explanation – I'd bent his ear in Chicago.

Hunter was silent.

'And guess what?' I continued. 'He was booked on that plane that went down in China last week.'

More silence, but I knew he was still there.

'You remember,' I said, pushing the point, 'he had the gladstone bag strapped to his leg? I told you. And another guess what, he has an apartment in Park Avenue. Sounds all right, eh?'

'Well, he would,' he said eventually. 'I'll pick you up then at a quarter of eight tomorrow evening . . .'

I telephoned Emma's number with trepidation, fully expecting to get no reply. She picked up the telephone immediately, excited to hear my voice. She was in the best of health, she said, though absolutely huge, and the obstetrician said the birth could be any time now. 'Oh, incidentally,' she said. 'Daddy asked me for your telephone number. I knew you wouldn't mind if I gave it to him. He'll be calling you. He said he has to be in New York himself and he'd like to take you to dinner. Wouldn't that be romantic?'

Romantic, my eye. I simply did not want to see Marcus, I felt much too vulnerable, and I did not want to be put into the position of having to make excuses to him. I couldn't think of any reason why he would need to be in New York. I was irritated now, so I said goodbye, did my usual act and ran a bath.

As I lay in it and slowly soaped myself I felt the need to be close to a man for the first time since the abortion. Around that time I decided never to go with a man again for the rest of my life.

I was pleased that Gus would soon be arriving and hoped that sex would not be painful and that I wouldn't be tense or show any signs of distress. I would never be able to tell him what had happened.

There was a stirring in my loins as I thought about Greg McLaren. He was a strange and unusual man, but sexual, and so very male. However, we'd be out with friends, and then he'd bring me back to my hotel and there was no way I could invite him to my room, so sex would be out. And Hunter wouldn't press the point, I felt sure. He was the kind of man who wouldn't rush things.

So I would wait for Gus. We were going to have such a wonderful time together it would be worth the waiting.

The limousine arrived on time for the short journey. The chauffeur was smartly dressed and extremely smooth and attentive. He turned down the air-conditioning when I asked him, which prevented me from arriving deep-frozen, but only just.

As we slid silently to a halt my door was opened and I was helped from my seat by a liveried doorman standing under a sand-coloured canopy that stretched across the pavement. Then I was saluted in farewell by the chauffeur, and ushered in by the doorman.

The entrance hall of the building was marbled and quietly opulent but tastefully done with its white marbled floor surrounding a huge inlaid Persian carpet, its large paintings of early city fathers dominating the panelled walls, and a scattering of baroque side-tables on which stood enormous ormolu lamps. I was shown into a mirrored and leather-upholstered lift, and didn't know

Philippa Todd

that we had moved until I was deposited on the ninth
floor outside Greg's apartment.

Greg opened the door himself almost as I touched the
bell. He looked handsome and immaculate in a dark grey
lounge suit and blue silk shirt. He kissed me lightly on my
cheek and showed me across his large hall and into his
drawing-room.

My first thought was what a relief it was to have left
my recorder in my bedroom, never having to use it
again. My second was to decide that without doubt this
was one of the most amazing drawing-rooms I had ever
been in. Clearly it was furnished for a bachelor, but the
brown silk-upholstered walls, the thick dark carpet, the
huge settees and the objets d'art were all in perfect and
expensive good taste. Large lamps standing on low tables
made softly glowing light. On a low square mahogany
table with darkly polished top, immaculate and newly
delivered canapés were arranged on an oval antique
dish, and standing beside it were four crystal champagne
glasses and a silver ice-bucket, dewy from the shards of
ice nestling around an unopened bottle.

After seating me Greg took the champagne from the
bucket and wrapped a white damask napkin around it
while he untwisted the wire from the top and expertly
eased off the cork with hardly any sound. While he
poured, with his back towards me, he said, 'The other
guests are going to be late. Baby's throwing up or
something.' He turned towards me with a glass of the
bubbling pale gold liquid in each hand and thrust one
towards me. 'I'm sure they won't be long. Cheers!'

I raised my glass to him and as the bubbles tickled my
nose I felt guilty that it wasn't until my third sip that I
thought about Marcus.

Greg handed me a tiny plate and a minuscule napkin,
American fashion, before inviting me to help myself to
the canapés. 'Might as well start,' he said, and wandered

over to the expensive array of sound-track equipment which immediately began quietly to play music of the 'twenties.

He sat down in a deep armchair opposite to me and smiled. 'You look lovely, Camilla. Women should always wear black.'

'I like black,' I said, smiling too much and wishing that I could be as cool and relaxed as he was.

He topped up my glass. 'Have you seen the musical *Crazy for You*?'

'No, I haven't. A friend and I are planning to go when I get back to London,' I answered, remembering that Gus had said he would take me.

'Cancel it,' he said, bending over me with the canapé dish. 'I shall take you, the week after next when I get there, if you will allow me.'

'It's terribly booked up,' I said naively as I bit into a miniature toad-in-the-hole.

He smiled, and said, 'That's nothing for you to worry your pretty head about.'

A telephone rang. Not the apartment number, that telephone was on a table beside me. But the ringing was extremely quiet and sounded muffled. Greg casually retrieved a mobile phone from under a large petit-point cushion, pressed a button on it and walked to the other end of the room.

I sipped my champagne and watched his face as he paced and listened attentively to the caller, eventually wishing him or her a very English goodbye and switching off. 'There go the best-laid plans of mice and men,' he said as he returned and picked up his glass. 'My friends can't make it. The baby seems really poorly and they've sent for the doctor.'

'Poor things, how worrying,' I answered, genuinely sorry that I was not going to meet them.

Greg sat down and looked thoughtful. I wondered if

Philippa Todd

he was annoyed with his friends. Then he looked over at me, smiled and said, 'We have a choice. I can send out for caviar and iced vodka and we can eat casually here, or . . . no, forget it, I'm sure that you would rather go to a restaurant. Now, where shall I take you . . . ?'

'No, no, not at all, we'll eat here,' I interrupted, for some strange reason (the old wanting to please, perhaps?). I much preferred the idea of dining out. I was dressed for it, and New York was such a throbbing city.

He leaned forward and looked concerned. 'Are you sure, Camilla?'

I smiled across at him. 'Yes, I'm sure. And I get the feeling that you would prefer to stay at home.'

His eyes lingered on my face. 'Only because I've had one hell of a day . . . and I could take my tie off . . . if you don't mind, that is?'

I shook my head. 'Of course not.'

He jumped to his feet. 'Then I shall telephone the ritziest takeaway in town. And naturally, I'll see you safely home later . . .' With that, as he reached a pair of double doors at the far end of the room, he turned towards me, laughed, and said, 'Just give me five minutes, I must feed Fred,' before disappearing and closing the doors behind him.

I stole another canapé, they were just so good, and amused myself looking out of the floor-length windows across Park Avenue to the luxury apartment blocks on the other side. Then I strolled the perimeter of the room admiring the paintings. Greg still had not returned when I'd done them all, but as I reached my seat I heard a door-handle turning.

Slowly I looked towards the double doors, rather surprised to see a large dark-haired lady standing in the shaded light. I was about to smile, and hope that she was not a wife, when I froze throughout my entire body, my heart stopped, I swear it, and my inert hands tingled in the palms.

'You don't mind, do you?' he asked, and calmly came across the room, sat down opposite me and picked up his glass.

I did not move. Paralysis was total as my eyes registered a pair of long, decidedly male hairy legs sheathed in sheer black stockings, large black court shoes with satin bows, a black mini-skirt and a cream silk blouse. The blouse was opened to reveal cleavage with chest-hair in it and a lace bra. A wig of shoulder-length black silken hair with a fringe framed the face, red lipstick applied skilfully covered the lips, and bright blue eye-shadow surrounded the piercing blue eyes of Greg McLaren.

I wanted to stay calm but firm, and get the hell out. But I knew, as sure as night follows day, that I was not about to handle the situation skilfully. I was frightened, embarrassed and paralysed.

'You mustn't be frightened,' he said. 'This is just my way of relaxing.' He crossed his legs slowly and revealed a large expanse of bare leg and black suspenders. Then he smoothed down the sides of his hair and tossed his head in much the same way a woman might. 'Cat got your tongue?' he asked, and I detected a slight camp harshness to his voice.

At last I stood up. 'I must go,' I said nervously, and reached for my handbag.

'Why on earth must you do that, dear?' He answered without moving. 'We haven't eaten yet. And it is ordered.'

I turned my head away. 'I'm sorry, Greg. I'm not good with . . . cross-dressing. It bothers me.'

He laughed then, and the large male teeth looked yellow and grotesque surrounded by the bright red lips. 'What a quaint way you have of expressing yourself,

Camilla. Cross-dressing I find a particularly ladylike way of expressing it.'

The doorbell rang, and a strange new fear gripped me. Was it the food, and if so should I make a bolt for it and go down in the lift with the delivery boy? Or was it more transvestites coming to a planned orgy?

Greg got up, adjusted his mini-skirt and casually walked out to the entrance hall with a particularly stable gait for a large man balancing on four-inch stilettos. I couldn't actually see him, but it was the delivery boy. He handed over a large box, for which Greg signed quite leisurely, put his hand into his cleavage and extracted a tip.

'Thank you, sir. Goodnight,' the boy said as the door began to close. So had he seen Greg dressed in drag before, I asked myself, or was this just New York life? Either way, I could not make my legs move, and my opportunity to escape had gone.

The moment the door clicked shut and Greg activated the security chain, of course, my legs obliged. I walked swiftly towards that exit as he placed the box of food on a side table. 'I must go,' I said, and fumbled with the chain. My knees were weak and my hands were shaking but I felt determined.

He took my hands firmly away from the door and stood close. I could smell perfume. 'You must eat first, my darling,' he said quietly, 'and I can promise you the food will be excellent.'

My lungs were not expanding properly, breathing was difficult and I was desperate for fresh air. 'I'm not hungry any more,' I said with difficulty. 'I cannot handle this, Greg, I'm sorry.'

He took my arm and tried to make me move. 'Don't make me cross, Camilla. Come and sit down and we'll talk for a while.'

'No,' I shouted at him, trying to free my arm from his grip. 'You have to let me go . . . I want to go, now.'

He was hurting me and his eyes suddenly looked cruel. 'I don't have to do anything of the kind, you know that as well as I,' he said quietly.

I was terrified now. There was more to this than relaxing in women's clothes and let's all be girls together. This had been planned; the friends, who, he said, had cancelled probably didn't exist. If there had been warning signs I'd missed them, and there was a big possibility that I could be in deep, deep trouble.

Now was the time to think positively and to change my strategy. After all, he probably wasn't dangerous, why make things worse for myself? And shouldn't I at least be feeling pity for him? It wasn't natural, was it? The man needed help. Diana once told me that lots of men liked to relax in women's clothes, and she had gone out with a fellow for two years who changed at home into a gymslip and black woollen stockings to relax.

My breathing settled down, and I wasn't trembling any more. Greg released his grip on my arm. 'That's better,' he said, not unkindly. 'Now, be a sensible girl and go and sit down while I prepare our supper.'

He obviously pressed a button somewhere because, to a quiet humming sound, three sets of heavily lined dark silk curtains closed across the three windows simultaneously, making the dim lighting dimmer, and more sinister.

'By the way,' he said as he lifted the champagne bottle and poured the dregs into my glass, 'I've deactivated all the bells and this apartment is soundproofed, so don't get any silly ideas. It would only upset me.'

While he busied himself in his kitchen and his high heels tapped on the tiled floor, I would like to say that I worked on a subterfuge for getting out, but I must have been in shock because my brain was numb. I tossed back the remains of my champagne in the hope that it would stimulate a few cells, but nothing happened.

Philippa Todd

I was not even sure how much time went by before he summoned me to the dining-room. But when I did not move he came over to me and firmly and silently pulled me to my feet.

SIXTEEN

When I regained consciousness I was lying between white satin sheets. My vision was blurred, but my brain was clear. My rapidly beating heart hammered painfully in my chest as adrenalin surged through my veins and fear clutched at the pit of my stomach.

I was not sure how or why I had lost consciousness. I remember Greg seating me at one end of an elaborate oval dining table. On a white linen cloth fine china was laid out for two. Four silver candlesticks stretched down the table and the glowing candles they held provided the only light in the room.

Vodka had now replaced the champagne in the ice-bucket, and Greg repeated the ritual and poured some of the silken liquid into my delicately tinted glass. Then he sat down at the opposite end of the table, lifted his glass to me, and smiled. 'What shall we drink to, my dear? A successful remains of the evening, perhaps?'

I was near to hysteria at this point. He was toying with my obvious discomfort and he knew that I was frightened. 'Drink with me, Camilla,' he then said quite forcefully, and I lifted the glass to my lips and took a large mouthful in the hope that the highly proofed spirit would give me courage. I had the feeling that he would like to see me cry. As I swallowed the neat vodka it took my breath away and I almost choked.

He waited till the spasm had passed, then lifted a
hand to his wig and slowly removed it. 'That's better,'
he said, drawing his hands through his own hair, 'these
wretched things are so hot, have you ever worn one?
Besides, I think that you will be happier when I'm not
wearing it.'

He was wrong. A man in full makeup and women's
clothes, I now know, looks even more grotesque wigless
in candlelight, with his short back and sides emphasizing
his masculinity and earrings meant to adorn a female
dangling from his large male ears.

He sat watching me as he waited for me to help myself
from the large crystal bowl of caviar placed in front of
me, and as I lifted a spoon from the dish I began to feel
a faint buzzing in my ears. It reminded me of when I once
had anaesthetic prior to the removal of my appendix. I
glanced down the table in his direction, terror obviously
showing on my face.

'You may count, if you like,' I heard him say. 'Back-
wards is supposed to be the most effective. Or you can
just quietly breathe deeply and enjoy what you cannot
change. Some people say it's quite a pleasant sensation,
and nicer, I'm sure, if you don't try to fight it.'

I do clearly remember trying to get up out of my chair
before the buzzing turned to a rushing sound and I lost
the use of my arms . . .

My eyesight was clearing, I had a bad thirst and I felt sick.
The room was somewhat dark because the drapes were
closed but daylight filtered through and I could detect a
half-open door which seemed to lead to a bathroom. The
knowledge of this reminded me that I needed to use it.
At this point I wondered if I had been raped. I did not
feel as though I had been man-handled at all, though
I was naked and there was a stickiness that needed
investigating between my legs.

I went to get out of bed, but I could not move my arms. I realized then, with a new kind of terror, that they were tied down at the wrists. Wide pink ribbon bound them, and the ribbon was attached to two short lengths of chain bolted on to the sides of the bed. Restrained from both sides, I could not reach the knots in the ribbon with my teeth, even if I could ever have untied them. Nevertheless, I tried until I was exhausted.

I was now sure that I was going to be sick and at this point I noticed a folded towel on the pillow beside me. How thoughtful of him to make sure that I would not mess up the sheets. I only threw up bad-tasting bile, but at least it landed on the towel.

I had no way of knowing whether or not I was alone in the apartment, but I called for help as loudly as I could until my throat hurt. There was no response, and the silence was heavy.

As my eyes became accustomed to the gloom I saw that a long table placed against the wall opposite the bed supported a glass tank, the kind you would have goldfish in. I could see some greenery and a large rock, but no water, and no fish. The tank appeared to have some sort of slatted top.

I was mesmerized by this tank and stared at it as though for inspiration. At first, when I thought I saw something move, I was sure that I had imagined it. But then it moved again. I squeezed my eyelids together, then opened my eyes wide for better vision. And as I watched, the occupant of the tank slid off the rock, raised itself up and waved its head, as snakes will, along the front of the tank. I was sure it was looking at me.

I was not too fazed by this, since it was not able to get out and I was nursing a good many other problems. Then, at that moment, I heard movement in the apartment. Keys were placed on a table, and I could hear footsteps crossing the marble entrance hall.

The bed on which I was imprisoned was behind the door that led into the room. The door was to my right and slightly ajar. I fixed my eyes upon it and held my breath as I waited.

I did not have to wait long before it was quietly pushed open, and Greg McLaren, dressed in city suit, smart tie and shiny black shoes, came into the room with the deference of someone visiting a sick friend. 'How are you, Camilla?' he asked casually as he walked to the window and pulled a cord that opened up the drapes.

It was sunny outside and I turned away from the light without answering. He walked over to the tank on the table and the snake went berserk. He tapped on the tank and made kissing noises. 'Yes, Daddy's home,' he cooed, 'but you know it isn't Fred's supper time just yet.'

Then he turned to me and stood at the end of the bed. 'Is there anything you want? You must at least be thirsty.'

I looked at his face, it looked so normal, so kind . . . 'I want to go home,' I said, and as I said the word home tears welled up into my eyes.

He ignored my request for all the world as though he had not heard it. 'Fizzy water would be nice, would it not? Perrier, perhaps?'

I nodded my head, it seemed pointless not to since I was extremely thirsty, and if I'd attempted to speak right then I would have cried.

He left the room. I shook the tears away from my eyes and craned my neck towards the window. It was quite large and stretched almost from floor to ceiling. But the apartment was too high up for an interior view from the street, and Park Avenue too wide to see into the buildings opposite.

He returned, bearing a small silver tray on which stood a large glass of sparkling water. 'I've put a little lemon juice in to help settle your stomach,' he said, removing, with a pained expression, the towel from beside me.

He held the glass to my lips and I gulped at the water, the bubbles going up my nose. He took the glass away. 'Not so fast, my dear, you don't want to be sick again, now do you?'

'I must go to the bathroom,' I said weakly, tears welling up in my eyes again.

He sat on the edge of the bed and looked at me sternly. 'You really must try to stop demanding things, Camilla. First you want to go home, then you must go to the bathroom.' He brushed back my hair where it was stuck to my cheek. 'Ask nicely when you have a request . . .'

I looked back at him and I knew that my lips were quivering. 'I'm desperate to use the bathroom,' I implored.

He patted my arm and stood up. 'Much better. I shall run a bath for you, you seem to be smelling a little.'

The snake went frantic again and his tongue shot in and out as Greg passed the tank. He repeated the kissing noises, tapped the tank with a finger and said, 'Who's Daddy's baby . . . ?'

When the bath was ready he carefully untied my bonds. Because I was naked I hesitated before getting out of bed. But he threw back the bedclothes and helped me to my feet quite forcefully. As I looked down I noticed red lipstick lines encircling my nipples. I broke from his grasp and hurried as best as I could towards the bathroom. I was sure that I could feel urine trickling down the insides of my legs.

Suddenly he let out a roar like an angry lion. 'How disgusting,' he yelled. 'Look at my sheets. You filthy woman . . .'

I turned back again, hurrying along with my knees together, my arms and hands crossed over the front of

me in bashful concealment. There, in the middle of the
bed, was a small pool of blood.

My hands flew to the sides of my face. 'You raped me,
you bastard,' I shouted back. 'And now you have the
nerve to blame me for the mess.'

'I did no such thing,' he screamed. 'I wouldn't enter
your body, or any other human being's, for all the money
in the world.'

'So what did you do with me?' I screeched, cautiously
watching his livid face.

'That is none of your business, you were fast asleep,'
he bellowed back. 'But as for rape, never.'

I looked down at myself. It was blood trickling down
my legs, and my humiliation was total. Even happening
before a man low enough to imprison me for his own
kicks and hold me in bondage, the embarrassment was
unbearable.

'I'm so sorry,' I heard myself say. 'I must be having
a period.' I had no way of knowing when a normal
period started after an abortion. This one could have
been brought on early by shock and fear. All I knew
now was that he was beside himself with disgust, and I
was frightened.

As I hustled myself into the bathroom I heard him say,
'And do not lock the door. You won't be doing yourself
a favour.'

There is no doubt, the warm bath-water helped to soothe
me. I was in a bad situation, to be sure. But if he wasn't
into rape, then things could be worse. I refused to let my
mind dwell on torture. And, as long as he wasn't into
murder, eventually even he would realize that he had
to let me go. Keeping people imprisoned against their
will was a serious offence of which I felt sure he would
be well aware.

It was essential that I keep calm and think only of

escape. After all, Hunter McNab would be wondering what had happened to me. (Had I told him where I was going last night? I really could not remember.) Tomorrow, or was it today, Gus was arriving and he would be looking for me. And, please God, if Marcus really had come to New York, even he might want me found.

Greg walked into the bathroom uninvited, carrying a large plain white T-shirt. 'You may wear this,' he said. 'Get out of the bath now, you will find Tampax and toothbrush and paste in the cabinet. I shall be waiting in the bedroom.'

I found deodorant, talc and a comb in the cabinet too, but closed my mind from thinking further about the permutations. Positive thinking and optimism about escape had to occupy my mind if I was to stay sane.

In clean T-shirt and with hair combed, I went to face him. He had changed the bed, and the same sinister ice-bucket containing champagne and two glasses was standing on the table beside Fred's tank, and a platter of small sandwiches. Greg, however was not in the room.

I dutifully returned to bed, and waited. It seemed so quiet, yet he couldn't have left the apartment or he would not have brought in champagne and he would certainly have tied me up.

Then thankfully, after what seemed an age, I heard a movement. It was strange how his absence was more intimidating than his presence. I looked towards the door as I sensed that he was on the other side of it.

Slowly a black gloved hand came round the edge, pushed it further open, and there he was standing in front of me. He wore a silver lamé cat-suit, open to the waist, with a mass of silver chains nestling into chest-hair, high-heeled silver boots, long diamanté earrings, black leather gauntlet gloves, a long red wig, and full makeup as before. The eye shadow this time was green. The batwing fluttering started up in my chest again and my mouth was instantly dry.

He walked across the room and went through the usual performance with napkin and champagne cork. 'You may sit in a chair while we drink,' he said, 'now that you are clean and are being a sensible girl. And let's try smiling, shall we, surliness does not become you.'

I wasn't feeling like smiling, but I did as he demanded for the sake of self-preservation. I looked up at him and smiled through my hateful thoughts as he handed me a glass.

'Can I risk drinking this?' I asked him. 'I don't feel like going to sleep again just yet.'

He laughed as he sat down, too heartily for my liking. 'That's what I like about you, Camilla. You have spirit,' he said, raising his glass to mine.

Little did he know how near to losing it that remark brought me. I had never felt less spirited, or more lacking in courage. I sipped my drink, half-expecting to feel a buzzing in my ears. Suddenly he jumped up.

'Oh, how remiss of me. I forgot to give you your sandwiches and you must be starving . . .'

I was rather hungry, but I nibbled without enjoyment. 'When can I leave?' I ventured, trying to smile again.

He slowly removed his wig, ignoring my question, and the same fear gripped my stomach as the night before. He resembled a giant monster. 'I'll have to stop wearing these things,' he said, and laughed at his own joke. Then, because my hatred of him was most probably showing, he became instantly serious. 'Your leaving depends on how nice you are to me tonight.'

I put down my sandwich plate and said quietly, 'What do I have to do?'

'The same as last night.'

'But I was not conscious then. Won't you tell me what it is you need?' (Did I really want to know?)

He walked to the ice bucket and returned to pour more champagne into our glasses. 'I can't tell you what I need until the time comes. But you don't need to be frightened. You won't be conscious the next time either.' He turned towards the tank. 'Will she, Fred?' Then, with finger raised, 'Ah, that reminds me, I prepared food for you too.'

On a sudden brave whim I followed him out of the bedroom, padding silently in my bare feet. I needed to refresh my memory of the rest of the apartment, and saw this as my only chance. But almost immediately he reappeared, turned me round and shoved me roughly back towards the bedroom. He was carrying, on a small plate, a tiny trussed mouse. He pushed me through the door. 'Get into bed,' he barked, 'and stay there.'

Luckily I could not see Fred enjoy the mouse because Greg was standing over me and preparing to tie my wrists. I could feel a buzzing in my ears. 'No, please, don't tie me down,' I begged. 'I won't move, I promise.'

He carefully made butterfly knots with the ribbon. 'Oh, believe me, Camilla, I know that you will not move. And don't be frightened, this time you won't feel sick when you wake up, I've used something different . . .'

The drapes were drawn but daylight filtered through as it did before. I knew, though, that it was the following day and once more I had been asleep for many hours. They had not been peaceful, either, not like before. It was true, I didn't feel sick, but the bed was a mess and my hair was half over my face. My throat was sore and my eyes burned.

I screamed as I realized that Greg was standing in the room looking at me. He was dressed once more in city clothes, every inch the professional man who only needed to pick up his briefcase to begin a normal new day, as he locked and bolted the doors.

'You've disgraced yourself, Camilla,' he said sadly. 'All that shouting and behaving badly. Obviously my special mixture did not agree with your psyche.'

I stared at him. There was nothing I could say, and keeping quiet seemed safer.

'You've forced me into making a few changes,' he said, as though it grieved him. 'You will need to lie very still till I return. If you move you will find that the lid of the tank will be released. And Fred is very jealous of you.'

Immediately I looked through the gloom towards the far table and I thought that I could see a cord crossing from the bed to the tank.

Greg came close. 'I have to go now . . . and what you are forcing me to do grieves me very much, Camilla. But it is important that you are not allowed to scream any more.' With that, he produced a reel of black masking tape, pulled a strip, and bit it off.

'No,' I shouted, 'don't do that . . . I won't scream . . . I promise . . .'

He slapped it around my mouth and stretched it under my ears. Then he patted one captive arm. 'I suggest you try to sleep, the time will pass more quickly.' As he reached the door, he turned towards me. 'Oh, I almost forgot. I've given you another companion. Even less friendly than Fred . . .'

He closed the door and it sounded as though he locked it too.

I simply had to escape, no matter how I did it, no matter if people were already looking for me and I would soon be found. I could not stay in that room any longer, because the occupant of the other, smaller tank was a very large black spider. It was the cruellest thing that I could imagine one human being doing to another when they knew that the one held captive was terrified of spiders. I clearly remember telling this to Greg McLaren when I sat next to him on that plane. My God, how he had drawn me out that day. He probably knew more about me than I could even remember telling him.

It looked to me as though the act of pulling up my knees and disturbing the bedclothes from the bottom would pull on the cords and open up the tank lids enough to let out the snake and the spider. It so happened, however, for reasons beyond my knowledge of the workings of the mind, that fear had left me and courage had replaced it. Only the need to free myself and take the tape from my face seemed important to me then. I felt sure that I would be successful at the rest.

When I looked down at my wrists, I could not believe my luck. My captor's over-confidence in the situation had caused him to tie the ribbon into bows, not knots as yesterday (or as far as I could see that was what he had done, no doubt to taunt me).

My enthusiasm waned when I realized that, of course, I could not reach either tied wrist with my teeth, even if I had had no tape around my mouth. However, I possess very long toes. It was a source of amusement in my family, and at school I'd won wagers on whether or not I could untie things with my toes.

I eased myself as far as possible into an upright position. Then, carefully and slowly bending my left knee outwards so as not to pull on the bedclothes, I brought my left leg up towards my right wrist. It took several attempts to grip one end of the well-tied bow between my toes. But once there, with the adrenalin flow giving me extra strength, I slowly pulled until bingo, the bow was open.

I could not see well enough to be sure that the first tie of tape was single and not made into a knot. I thought that it was a single tie, and I had to believe it, otherwise I might have crumpled with disappointment. It must have taken me an hour to get my toes around that tie, or so it seemed. Then I helped to loosen it with rapid wrist movements and eventually it became loose enough to get my long big toe between ribbon and wrist.

When you next see, in a film, masking tape ripped from around a captive's face without doing damage, do not believe it. I tried it, and caused myself great pain and bleeding to my lips, and I simply could not free them. But right then, it was a minor problem.

As I began slowly to get out of bed I saw the larger tank lid rise a little from the movement of the sheets. But Fred was sound asleep and I reckoned that a quick dash to the tank would secure the lid before he even woke. It was a happy moment to see that the spider tank lid did not move.

I tried the bedroom door, and it was not locked (my, how sure of himself Greg had been). The key was in the lock on the outside. I quietly and slowly removed it, though I felt sure I was alone, put it into the lock my side and turned it. It brought about an instantaneous feeling of safety from without. Next I had to go to the bathroom (small wonder).

I do not know why I took so long to open the curtains. Maybe it was the fear of stepping over the two cords attached to the bed from the tanks. Or maybe I did not want to find out how impossible my escape was going to be.

I solved the first problem by carefully rolling over the bed to the window side. My second fear was confirmed when I opened the drapes. The window, I discovered, was safely fastened with a security lock. It was also double-glazed. I thought of trying to break both thicknesses of glass. But with what? And if I succeeded, which was doubtful, what then? I certainly couldn't shout with sticky tape still around my mouth. And I couldn't make a slit in the tape between my lips unless I had a knife or a pair of scissors, and I had neither.

Unlocking the bedroom door and hunting in the apartment was unthinkable. The enemy might at that very moment be standing the other side of it, and the bedroom had become my refuge.

High up as I was, windows sealed and double-glazed, the sound of the police siren was muted. I dragged a chair over as far as the side of the bed, then, with a certain amount of effort, because it was heavy, I lifted it on to the bed, and pushed it towards the other side. Then I went over the bed myself, carefully got it to the floor and dragged it to the window, stood on it and looked down into the street.

Heavy traffic was moving at a steady pace but no blue lights flashed beneath me. The police car had gone, its purpose obviously not being to rescue me.

I cried then, and for some reason began banging on the windows with all my might. Tears ran over the masking tape and down my neck before I could mop them up on the hem of my long T-shirt. And as I cast a glance, as I frequently did, at the reptile and spider tanks, I noticed that my thumpings had agitated them. Both were excited, and looking at me.

It was while I was staring down into Park Avenue again from the vantage-point of the chair that I noticed two people, workmen maybe, standing at a large window with no hanging drapes, opposite to mine across Park Avenue. It was a long way over that wide street, but it seemed there were no windowpanes, as if the glass was being renewed. A wide piece of boarding had been secured to the lower half. My joy was complete when I saw that the two men were pointing over at my block, not at me, but their eyes were scanning various floors and they were pointing.

I frantically waved my arms and jumped up and down like a mad person. I vaulted over the bed and ran to the bathroom, grabbed a towel, leaped across the bed again, jumped back up on the chair and waved and waved. It was when I began jumping up and down as well as waving that one of them saw me. He looked away at first, looked back, then spoke to his companion. They turned away from the window, but kept looking back at me.

Then two other people joined them, as far as I could tell, a man with papers in his hand (an architect, perhaps?) and a blonde woman wearing a red outfit (the interior decorator, no doubt). She went back inside the room. The men stared down into the street, and over at the entrance to my block. But they regularly looked back to where I was.

The woman returned, having seemingly put on large sunglasses. Then she started to wave, and suddenly I realized that she was looking through binoculars. I pressed my taped face to the glass in the hope that she could see. She handed the binoculars to one of the men to look through, then all three took a turn, and every one of them waved at me.

The man with the papers waved a black object at me, stared at it and then very soon he put it to his ear. It was, of course, a mobile phone, and my cup was full. I was going to be saved . . .

SEVENTEEN

There were no sirens wailing, there were no blue lights flashing. I know, because I did not leave my perch on the chair by the window, and I did not take my eyes off the street. But they slipped in somewhere, and the result, for me, was very nearly disastrous.

I suddenly heard a loud hammering on the apartment door, and I mean a *very* loud banging indeed. This was accompanied by the use of a pair of lungs that should have been allotted to the Pope.

'Open up, open this door,' the voice yelled. 'Police, do you hear me in there? Open up, and freeze.'

You bet I heard, it was to be my salvation. And this was no moment to tell me to freeze. I leaped off the chair, gave not a thought to anything except getting to that front door before the NYPD either decided that it was a hoax, and left, or started firing. I hated guns with a passion.

The results of my fawnlike leaping were not good. I tore straight through the strings attached to the tanks, and brought them both crashing down, off the table and on to the carpet. Fred's tank did not break but the spider's did, and both lids came off. I cannot tell you where the animals went, but they were not as fleet as me as I unlocked that bedroom door, dived through, and, can you believe, locked it behind me, palming the key as I ran.

Philippa Todd

I was at the front door, planning my speech before it occurred to me that conversation on my part was impossible, and a new fear promptly set in. What if they thought it was some sick prank, what if they lectured me through the door about wasting police time and went away? Or, just as disastrous, fired at me through the door?

I banged on the door, kicked it too with bare feet, which hurt, and made closed-mouth noises through my nose.

'You all right in there?' a cop yelled.

'Mmmm, Mmmm,' I yelled back as loud as my nose would allow. (Hadn't they been told that my mouth was plastered?)

'Can't you talk?' he bellowed, in case I was deaf as well as dumb.

'Mmmm,' I answered, thinking, hell, Milla, why don't you grit your teeth and just tear the bloody tape off? But the blood I had on my T-shirt and the split swollen lips beneath the plaster to prove what happened when I tried it the first time sobered me up.

'Maybe it's her and she's gagged,' another male voice said with authority. So there were two of them, it was getting better by the second.

'Oh, yeah, you're right . . . Are you gagged in there?'

'Mmmm.' The lining of my nose was beginning to smart.

'Okay,' the voice of authority said. 'Just keep calm, there's nothing to worry about.' (He could have fooled me.)

They had a discussion in low tones with someone called Front of House Security.

'So why don't you have any fucking spare keys, Mr Front of House Security?' number one voice asked.

Security answered in a surprisingly soft male voice, 'Because the owner took them from me day before yesterday saying he wanted to get another set cut for a friend he was expecting. I already told you.'

'Hey, lady, you still there?'

I didn't waste my ailing breath on that question, I reckoned he was exercising the rule of Keep Talking to the Victim and didn't require the answer he already knew I couldn't give.

I could hear another side-conversation going on through a two-way radio to someone called Jim, which, please God, could mean that we were getting somewhere. I wondered what would happen now if Greg McLaren turned up. Wouldn't he be in for a surprise to step out of the lift in his damned city suit, to find guns at his head and handcuffs clamping his wrists? The fantasy cheered me up no end.

'My name's Sergeant Mel Kenning,' the first cop called to me. 'Just give one Mmmm for yes, two for no and three for maybe. Okay?'

We began. 'You by any chance the missing woman name of Camilla Cage? From London, England? Age forty-three?'

Going on sixty, I thought, was more like it, but I gave one nasal signal as requested, and even though that erstwhile bedroom door was locked, and the key was embedded in my left palm, I gave yet another glance in that direction. I had once seen a spider, not that big I grant you, climb over the top of a closed bedroom door in my grandmother's cottage and squeeze himself through the gap.

'I reckon whoever did this to you ain't in there?' I reckoned it warranted two Mmmms.

'Well, it's like this. This here's a security door. Not much hope of breaking it down.'

I gave a prolonged Mmmmmmmm, going lower at the end to show disappointment, like I was once taught during a very short period of youth when I was stage-struck.

'Excuse me?' he said politely.

'Get on with it, Mel,' his superior said. 'The lady's worried.'

'So, Camilla, this is Mel,' Mel said, and his voice took on a new kindness. 'If you get yourself back to that room at the front, the Fire Department is coming around to lift you to freedom. Okay?'

I went ape. I beat on the door, I jumped up and down and Mmmmmmed, without sequence, until my nose began to bleed.

'Ma'am, you trying to tell us something?' Mel asked.

'Mrs Cage . . . Camilla,' his superior said. 'Try to stay calm. Why don't you look around for a pen and notepad and write down your problem? You can push it under the door.'

Why hadn't I thought of that myself? I turned towards the drawing-room, but the thought of lingering in it gave me the creeps. And how did I know for sure that the eight-legged thug and his slippery friend were not lying in wait for me in there?

I turned to the hall table, but nothing was on top except china objets d'art. (They looked priceless, so I swept them to the floor theatrically with my forearm.) I snatched at a shallow centre drawer, which moved so silently and easily it nearly came out altogether. I couldn't believe my eyes when the first thing I saw was a revolver, though why I was surprised I cannot imagine. Then I saw a pen, just an ordinary biro, and amongst a few more bits of drawer-type flotsam, a plain envelope. The pen wouldn't write until I tested it so hard it tore the envelope. I had to sound sensible about Fred and the spider being the reason I couldn't go back into the bedroom. Bad as it had been, I didn't want to swap it for a hospital room in a place for the mentally sick.

The door was so well-fitting the envelope didn't go under easily, but we managed. 'Jesus H. Christ,' I heard

Mel say, 'he has to be a fucking psycho.' His superior talked again into his receiver, and his voice had lost the just-a-day-in-the-life-of-a-cop calmness. It now sounded worried and urgent to bordering on frantic.

It was all taking such a long time. I was losing heart again. Supposing Greg came out of the lift? What would happen then? Would the police start shooting? What if I got caught in the line of fire? (Through a security door, are you kidding? Well, you can't be too sure.) Oh God, please make them hurry.

It seemed like a brainwave when I grabbed the revolver from the drawer and turned towards the drawing-room doorway ready to fire on spider or snake if they as much as took one step or slither towards me. I had never held a gun before, much less fired one, but the cold smoothness of it gave me courage, and it was time to prove that I was a fast learner.

'Okay, Camilla, this is Mel,' Mel said again. 'Go and see if you can get into the room next to the one you were kept in.' I made more Mmmmm noises to say that I couldn't, and he picked up my fear.

'Be a brave girl now,' he said like a father, and I nearly broke down. 'We'll be right here.' (But you can't get to me, I would have screamed if I'd been able.) 'And we'll shoot the locks off this door if necessary to get to you,' he added, like a thoughtreader. 'Just go and take a quick peek, then come back and tell us.'

I reached deep down for that last morsel of courage that seems to settle in the base of your guts when you are frightened, took a deep breath and with gun held out before me, as they do in the movies, got it over with quickly. The door was ajar. I kicked at it with my foot ready to run to God knows where or maybe even fire if Greg McLaren was standing in there waiting to strangle me.

It was a large room with a huge bed in it, and tasteful,

as everywhere was in that evil place. It was unoccupied, apart from a huge man in fireman's clothes and a hard hat looking at me from the other side of the window, and standing on a mobile platform. When he saw me pointing a gun, instead of being terrified, he inclined his head and smiled at me. Then I knew for certain that I made a comic sight.

I ran back to the front door and made my usual signal.

'So you saw him?' Mel asked. 'Remember, one only for yes.'

I gave my most meaningful Mmmmmm.

'Great stuff, Camilla, his name's Mike. Now, stay where you are, don't move.'

As he said this there came from that other bedroom three almighty deafening crashes, followed by several smaller ones, like aftershocks. Defying Mel, I ran to look.

Through crunching glass and quiet humming came the most wonderful sight of my life. It was Mike, his badge assured me, from the NY Fire Department, and I will remember his big, beautiful, red and shiny face to my dying day.

I ran to him, and can you believe, in my blood-stained T-shirt that only just covered my naked behind, sticky hair plastered around my face and masking tape dangling from my cheeks, I reached up and threw my arms around his neck, and buried my face into his hard padded jacket as though I were five years old and he was a long-lost father returning from a war. He gathered me up before I cut my feet.

Everyone I know wants to hear what it's like to be lowered to terra firma from nine floors up. But I can't really tell them, I've blanked it out. I do remember Mike wrapping me in a blanket, maybe in the interests of modesty more than to keep me warm. Then he picked me up again as though I weighed nothing at all and tied me to him with a harness. We crunched through the glass, then in a sing-song voice that I'll never forget he said, 'Close your eyes and hold me tight.' After that he went on humming . . .

I felt the fresh air and I heard another male voice, but nothing would have prised my eyelids open . . . absolutely nothing at all. As far as I can remember I kept them closed in the ambulance too. I know a woman was driving it because they called her Lucy, and I remember hearing our siren all the time.

'Hey Lucy, can't y'find a few more potholes to go over?'

'Shut y'face, O'Shaunessy, y'big ape.'

'You okay, ma'am?' To me, different voice. 'I'd make a little slit in that tape for you. But with Lucy driving this veehickle I'd be in danger of cutting your head off.'

'In your face as well, Brubecker,' yelled Lucy.

I nodded my head. It was the only part of me I could move, the rest was held firm, and trussed, in blankets and leather straps.

'You can open them eyes, you want.'

I shook my head vigorously.

'Best you keep 'em closed,' O'Shaunessy said. 'Rick here ain't a pretty sight . . .' Lucy seconded that opinion.

'Not long now, lady. The ER will sort you out, no trouble at all.'

We came to a halt with a screech of brakes and the switching-off of the siren. The doors were flung open by two other people, the stretcher slid out and I was wheeled at a running pace into what was called the Emergency Room but had the acoustics of Carnegie Hall. My eyes stayed glued shut along with my mouth.

Someone put a warm hand on the top of my head, and I jumped. 'You okay?' a man's voice said. 'Don't worry about a thing. We'll soon have that gag peeled off. In the meantime I'll just make a small slit between your lips to make you feel better soon as we get there.'

At the very mention of peeling off and making slits I began to panic. Who was this sadist looking for kicks? I opened my eyes fast as soon as we stopped, to take a look at such a monster.

'Hi,' he said, and smiled at me from a distance of about two feet. 'Stay very still, this isn't going to hurt one bit. Just a little slit.'

My eyelids shuttered down right away, even though he had a confidence-boosting voice. Five seconds later he said, 'There you go. That should give you a bit more comfort while you wait,' and swabbed out my mouth with something resembling a drumstick that was ice-cold.

I breathed in through the small open gap and it was bliss. Then I heard an old familiar voice, the voice I'd once trusted, the voice that had been the core of my existence.

'What the hell have you been doing?' it said, as though I'd played truant and come home covered in mud. My eyelids came open fast.

'Dear God, you're a mess,' he said. 'Don't you know better than to go to the apartment of a stranger? Are you mad?'

How typical, I thought, how absolutely like him to patronize me in front of people. He probably had not even told the hospital staff that he was my EX-husband. I felt tears forming, and was mad with myself.

He looked beyond me to someone I couldn't see. 'How long before this stuff can be taken off her mouth?' he asked with authority. 'The police are waiting to question her. Surely it will only take a few minutes?'

Tears flowed out of my eyes at the very thought of anyone trying to free my mouth in a mere few minutes.

Marcus of course misinterpreted them. 'And don't shed tears now that you are safe. Not unless you are going to tell us how you got yourself into this mess.' He was standing over me like a dentist who questions you when he has your mouth wide open. The tears ran sideways into my hair.

'Leave her alone, for God's sake,' a male voice I'd heard before said. He was half-hidden behind Marcus. It was Hunter Lee McNab, and as he spoke he came around the side of Marcus, pushing him slightly out of the way. I removed a hand from my wrappings and held it towards him. He took it, leaned forward and kissed my forehead. 'Hello trouble,' he said, winked, and smiled.

My tears came in greater volume, and I spoke my first words, not very clearly and somewhat painfully. 'Hunter, please, don't let them tear this gag off. My lips are raw underneath.'

He stroked my matted hair. 'No sweat, I won't.'

'But no anaesthetic. I couldn't face being put to sleep again.'

'Milla, for Christsake,' Marcus snapped. 'Don't be such a whinge.'

Hunter gave him one hell of a look. Marcus turned his back and walked away.

'Hunter,' I mumbled, 'is there any news of Gus? I was supposed to meet him in the Pierre Hotel.'

Two nurses came to wheel me off. Hunter kissed the hand he was still holding. 'I'll go phone and find out. Don't worry about a thing. What did you say his last name is—?'

Things happened fast after that. I tried to question the intended method for removing my gag. After all, it was my face, and my pain, and I'd been through as much as I could take. They all smiled, and patted me, and still did it their way.

'Close your eyes, honey,' a dark-eyed nurse said from behind her mask. 'This won't take no time at all. You sure ain't the first we've had with this little problem.'

The whole of my face swiftly went ice-cold and numb. The only pain anywhere was in my upper arm. I opened my eyes in panic.

'Okay,' she said. 'Just a little prick. Stops any infection.'

Someone was cleaning my face. 'It's gonna be sore for a few days. But you won't have no problem . . .'

Marcus came to claim me, holding some clothes. God, he'd even been into my suitcase, I thought ungratefully.

'We have to see a lawyer,' he said without preamble. 'We meet with the police in half an hour.'

I walked towards the showers on very weak legs. As I went I turned back to Marcus bad-temperedly. '*I* meet with the police,' I said, stabbing at my chest with a finger. 'Not us . . .'

Hunter was approaching. He looked at my sore face without comment, and touched my cheek with the back of a hand. 'Gus has not arrived. There's a letter waiting for you. I'll go pick it up. See you later.' He strode away without a glance in the direction of Marcus.

In the shower room I looked at myself in a long wall mirror. And what a pathetic mess I saw reflected.

The lawyer, Sam Speak by name, managed to make me feel as though I'd made the whole thing up.

Was I sure, he said, that the gentleman in question wasn't a blind date? Of course I was sure, I'd just told him, had I not, that we met on a plane.

Was I sure the airline would verify our names on that flight? They sure as hell ought to, we damn nearly crashed. It was hardly a run-of-the-mill flight.

He couldn't see any real marks on my wrists, he said. Had I, maybe, enlarged on that information about being

tied to a bed? I certainly had not. And what the hell was
going on? Wasn't he supposed to be on *my* side?

The police would ask me worse things than that, he
said, best I was prepared. He was not kidding.

I began to feel threatened. When they were kind I was
afraid to speak because of what I said being used against
me. When they came over heavy I knew that I'd been
right to think as I first did.

'So, Mrs Cage, do you often take trips alone?'

'No, not often.'

'Do you make a habit of blind-dating strange men?'

'He wasn't a stranger. I've told you, we met on a
plane.'

'And you slept with him on your first date?'

'I didn't sleep with him. He drugged me, he tied me
up, he left me locked in a room.'

'Sure . . . what a bitch . . . bet you were really half
scared to death . . . mean to say, ladies don't like that
sort of thing, now do they?'

It was a frightening experience. Steadily I was becoming less of the victim and more of the instigator. I looked
at my lawyer, Sam Speak, who looked at his notes and
ignored me. I wanted to ask if Marcus could come in, I
felt so lonely, even his presence seemed attractive. Then
I remembered how he'd treated me at the hospital, and
decided against it.

Suddenly everyone stood up. 'Okay, Mrs Cage,' the
lead cop said. 'Go and get rested. We'll talk again when
your face is healed.'

At the door of the interview room I turned and faced
him. 'You cannot possibly believe that I would gag myself
with sticky tape?'

He turned his palms forwards and upwards, and
hunched his shoulders. 'Who knows?' he said with a
barely disguised smirk.

Philippa Todd

Then the other cop placed his hand on my shoulders and pushed me through the doorway. As he did so he managed to nudge me in what resembled a come-on.

'Must be something to do with that name, Camilla,' he said. 'Seems to be making a few waves in your country, for one reason and another, don't it . . . ?'

EIGHTEEN

Marcus and Sam Speak armed me back to my hotel as though they were my gaolers. They talked across me and about me as though I were deaf or, indeed, not there at all.

An English reporter from the *Sun* newspaper was waiting in the street outside the Police Department to fish for information, in the pushiest of ways. The lawyer made short shrift of him, but intelligently, and Marcus was downright rude. This did not seem overly bright to me, since the man was only doing his job, and judging from the frayed edges of his shirt he was not being paid a fortune, but who was I to have an opinion? I was only the thick-lipped, sore-faced, embarrassed and ignored, heavily guarded victim, being frog-marched along like a criminal in a scene from a B-movie. Even the oversized blacked-out sunglasses Marcus had produced as part of my disguise fitted the part.

My lips were not the only part of me that was sore and swollen. The probing I'd had to endure to rule out rape and what was termed as serious sexual assault, had left me ragged and demeaned. There had, of course, been some kindness shown along the way, but not by the police doctor or by his assistant. Understanding, by anyone other than Hunter, had not been shown, and, like any other major personal trauma, it had only happened to me, and no one could truly understand how I felt. I was offered counselling, but I refused on the grounds that the best counsellor for me was Gus, and I would soon be seeing him. But right then, I wanted nothing as much as I wanted to be alone, and in a bath, in my hotel room.

I was there, though not in the bath, having got rid of Marcus and Sam Speak, when Hunter found me. He it was who hand-delivered the couriered London–New York letter from Gus. He it was who, after the first two lines had sent me into shock, held my hand and read it aloud for me.

I was not heartbroken at what Gus wrote, just unbelieving. And at that time it did not take much to shake my foundations. It felt as though the world had gone mad, and that nothing for me would ever be the same again.

I was his dearest Camilla, Gus assured me in his letter. And he was most terribly sorry but he had misled me, and now he must slink away out of my life because he could not face me. He lied, he said, because he wanted me so badly from the moment he laid eyes on me, and he hoped it would become the way he had pretended. It seemed that his unhappily dead wife wasn't, but was equally unhappily alive, the victim of a rare palsy and unable to walk (if he is to be believed on this one, that is).

Oh, and there was more, almost in the form of a postscript. He also was most dreadfully sorry to tell me that neither was he a psychologist (well, it could have been worse, he could have posed as a gynaecologist). But he most truly loved me, and he might never get over having to give me up. I was not, however, to worry about him, and I was to have nice time in New York, and be happy for rest of life . . .

I took to my bed, thinking that I would not sleep. In fact, so Hunter informed me (he knew, because he had become my unofficial minder), I had slept for twenty-four hours. And when I awoke, my lips were so stiff, I had to Vaseline them before I could eat.

The New York Police Department managed to convey to me on my second interview that they considered I had been a willing participant in a kinky sex ritual that had gone mildly wrong. There were absolutely no signs of rape, they said, or of grievous bodily harm. And if I had been tied to a bed, well now, honestly, why were there no marks on my wrists? I tried to repeat that he had used ribbon for just that purpose. I was tired and humiliated at having to watch them all look at each other and smirk. A smirk that told me experience had taught them that kinky ladies came in all shapes and sizes. Oh, and, the lead cop said, looking at his notes as though he had very nearly overlooked a most important piece of information, on physical examination signs had been found that I had recently been pregnant and the foetus had been aborted. And I, Camilla Cage, was, after all, an unmarried lady. They would be considering, therefore, pressing charges against me on the grounds that I had entered the United States of America for dubious reasons, as documents found in my luggage would prove to be true.

I tried to turn to Marcus for support, but he was so embarrassed at having an ex-wife who had done him the injustice of getting pregnant by another man that he punished me by siding with everyone else.

Greg McLaren had not been arrested. He hadn't even been found. And I suspected that no one was actually looking for him, unless it was to testify against me.

At a final meeting in the lawyer's office it was suggested that I should, with police permission, fly back to London as soon as possible, having relinquished all rights to press charges, and in return the police would not press charges against me. Two strange men who looked more like diplomats from the Foreign Office than, as I was told, plain-clothed policemen from Scotland Yard, sat watching me throughout in a most unnerving way, and did not speak.

But it was when Sam the lawyer handed me an account of his fees, together with my passport and my redated plane ticket, both of which had been taken without my knowledge or permission from my hotel bedroom, that I wanted only to escape, and to get back home to London.

They had turned me very cleverly from victim to perpetrator, and it had become obvious to me that Greg McLaren was a protected species – an important operator in world politics, needed by all countries, a go-between, a trouble-shooter, even maybe an assassin. And no one, anywhere, intended to rock such an important boat. Certainly not over an inconsequential nobody like me.

It was not easy, being back in London, and I went through a lot of trauma. The kids had to be told the truth, and their father had beaten me to it with his dubious version turned factual.

Kate and William were a great support, totally loyal and believing, though scared to death at what I had taken on without their knowledge. Emma lectured me on my stupidity, especially at my age. This hurt, because there was truth in what she said. But luckily, a few days later she gave birth to a large and lovely boy, pointed out that he was the very image of his father, named him Marcus, and completely forgot about her mother's particular trauma in her ecstasy.

Diana had the gall to ask, after listening entranced to the full and painful details of the exercise, and excited by the thought of her pending dramatic production, if my New York experience was true. Or had I perhaps invented the story for the sake of the programme? Not of course that she would object. She then became instantly annoyed when I told her that my captor was not a client, and even tried looking shocked that I was casually blind-dating when I should have been working.

'And a stranger too,' she said, as though she would never do such an unwise thing.

I'm not sure where the next few weeks went. I had a feeling of being trapped in my own head, isolated by the sordidness of my experience. I was desperately tired but I couldn't sleep, and Kat ate more than I did. In bed, out of bed, daytime, night-time, sitting at my desk, answering the phone, it all blended into one, and my brain dealt with it by switching off. I was unsmiling, mechanical, tired and lonely.

Going out held no magic. Strangers who saw me in the street, I thought, would never have any idea that I was different from them. Different because I, not they, had been locked in a room, gagged, threatened, held in bondage, and made to sit in fear for my life with a pervert in female drag, a snake and a very large spider. The people who knew what had happened avoided bringing up the subject. Those who wished they knew brought up the subject and I avoided telling them.

My fax machine was giving birth to a letter from Harry one day as I put my key in the door after returning from a harrowing session with Diana, and nursing a tiredness that made my legs feel like lead. And for sure I was not expecting anything good to happen to me for the rest of the day. It was thanks to Harry's sister Gracie running a fax centre in Sydney that my day improved.

Harry was spending a couple of days with Gracie while attending some wool sales when he saw my picture in the *Sydney Morning Herald*, and a short article giving my real name and the pseudonym I was using, it said, for dangerous journalistic work in America. The article was headed 'The Dangers of Blind Dates'. It worried Harry enough for him to tell his sister. She suggested that he try to telephone me, and when he did I had my fax machine on, and all he got was the high-pitched whistle. Bright Gracie made him write a few lines on paper for her to send by fax.

It didn't say much, typical of Harry. Just, 'Are you my Annie Lloyd? I hope so, Camilla Cage is such a bloody stupid name to get landed with. Do you really want to lead such a dangerous life? If the answer is no, and you are the Annie I think you are, and not just somebody who looks like her (it wasn't a very good likeness in the paper), come on over and spend a holiday in the sun with your favourite Aussie, Harry.'

It gave me a turn, of course it did, that my picture had been in a Sydney paper, but apart from that, someone caring enough to send me a fax, someone I had deceived, cheered me up.

Diana had been really annoying. She was all right to begin with, wanted my opinion on the name changes and altered locations that she was making for everyone's protection. And I had to sit in on the auditions of actors to give approval of similarity of looks and accents for the mock studio interviews.

It was when she told me of her plans to turn Greg McLaren into a blind-date client that I hit the ceiling. The programme was supposed to be factual, surely, I said, on why men went to marriage bureaux to find a wife, not an unfair exposé on dating agencies?

She smiled at me patronizingly, lit a cigarette, and said that she couldn't see what possible difference it made to me. Then she weakened my argument by passing a well-timed and very handsome cheque, made weighty with extra expenses, across the table. I left it where it was for a bit, and continued discussions. But in the end I crossly left, ashamed that I was too weak and too broke to leave the cheque on the table, or to have torn it up. And I said as I went that I didn't give a damn what she did, I wouldn't be watching the programme anyhow.

She just smiled again and said, 'Don't be like that, Camilla.'

'Dear Harry,' I wrote, 'your letter gave me great joy and improved my otherwise traumatic day. But how can you want to know me again now that my cover is blown? It was only a job of work, but I feel awful about the deception, especially as we became good friends. And you were so nice, and I really liked you. Love, Annie.'

Ten minutes later he replied. 'Dear Annie,' he said, 'why are you wearing a hair-shirt? It doesn't matter a tinker's cuss to me how I met you, just bloody pleased that I did. And I wouldn't like to lose you again, you leave such hair-raising trails. So nod if you feel the same way I do. Yours, Harry.'

When I answered, after having hot tea and Marmite toast, and a cuddle with Kat, I did a strange thing. I told him everything. Everything, that is, except about getting pregnant and having an abortion. That would have to come later. But once I began writing I could not stop. I told him about how I felt locked in, how I couldn't sleep, and how when I did, I fought off spiders as big as plates and snakes with green venom dripping from their teeth. And how more than once I had wakened screaming and terrified because Greg McLaren's black-gloved hand was coming around my bedroom door and leaving blood-stains all over the paintwork.

By the time I faxed it, Australia was in bed. Next morning I received Harry's third fax. It had come in during the night, and as I slept well, with Harry's letters under my pillow, whispering at me that he cared, it had come in without my hearing the telephone.

It was brief, very Harry. 'Dear Annie again,' it said,

'better go to see your doctor, and ease the burden on Kat before she needs a feline shrink. Love, Harry.'

It was Sunday, and as you already know, that's the day I would like to get written out of the calendar. Kate took me out for a country pub lunch to ease my weekend blues and to show off her new car. She said that I was quiet and thoughtful and was I okay? I said that it was nothing, I was just tired all the time and that I loved her new car.

A good lunch and red wine loosened my tongue. I told her a bit more about my bad experience and about Harry suggesting I see a doctor. She agreed, took the next afternoon off and came with me.

The doctor made copious notes and called my disorder brain-overload. It had been a trying few years for me, he said (was he ever not kidding), culminating with near personal tragedy. And I needed a little help, a rest, some deep sleep, some tender loving care. It all sounded like bliss to me.

I woke up from an induced sleep four days after agreeing to go into a nice little nursing home for a week's rest. I had the major hangover of a tanked-up druggie and my pretty little room swirled around a bit. I could have killed for a large plate of deep fried prawns with French fries, and did I ever need to clean my teeth.

Oh boy, what a glorious sleep it had been. In my dreams I'd been serene all the while. Someone called Marcus came in and asked didn't I know him, he was my husband? I had him shown out. A blonde with a loud voice brought me flowers that wouldn't fit through the door, so I said to leave them in the hall, my room was full of blooms already. And a tiny little spider with a smiley face sat at the end of my bed telling me jokes and saying how sorry he was about New York.

I was rested and fit, if a bit unsteady and disoriented,

and wanted to get home as soon as possible to write a piece on the powers of deep and untroubled sleep.

The psychiatrist who came in to see if I was truly better, or only faking, was very large, with hands the size of hams and rough dry palms at which he kept picking. There were moments, when he tailed off an unfinished sentence and looked vague, that left me wondering which one of us was the patient. No way did I want to live in Shangri-La any longer. The picture on the wall in my room of happy little gnomes in a fairy-tale garden only made me want to get out and write children's stories. It was time for the real world.

Back home I flushed away the pills and asked the cattery to bring my soulmate home before dark. Of course the nights lost their euphoria and sleep wasn't always that of a baby, but you can't have everything. When dropping off easily evaded me, I read a book or, better still, got up and wrote a few pages of my own.

My saviour was Harry. He flew to England and rescued me. He arrived with flowers. 'Because you'd expect me to,' he said. 'But cut flowers don't bloody last, so don't expect them too often.'

He fed me up, he made me laugh, and he let me cry. He loved me, he said, always would. I was the greatest thing to happen to him since Coca-Cola was invented. And the sexiest thing since, well, never you mind.

I wasn't sure if I loved him, and I told him so. I would need to be sure, I said. Well, not to worry, he answered, he'd wait. Of course he'd have to go back to work on the station or he'd never be able to afford me. And this year's drought was no bloody picnic.

I was to send a fax to Gracie when I was ready, Harry said. Take my time, no sweat. Faxing wouldn't cost me as much as telephoning. And besides, all that static on the line when you tried to talk was enough to drive you barmy.

Thank God for Harry. Thank God for treatment. Thank God for feeling better. It all meant I was able to cope when Greg McLaren telephoned me. Nevertheless, my hand was fused to my mobile receiver, and I stayed in my chair without moving for an hour after the call.

'Camilla, this is Greg McLaren,' he said, for all the world as though we were friends. The tone was slightly miffed, but that was all. He sounded so close, and I was scared to death. I actually went to a window to look down at the telephone booth on the corner. It was empty.

'I must say I'm very disappointed in you, Camilla,' he said. 'You caused me a lot of embarrassment and pain.'

I could hardly breathe, and the pain in my chest was excruciating.

'You could have the courtesy to answer me,' he said, 'I know you are there.'

My voice would not come. I pulled out the centre drawer of my desk and groped for my recorder, the pin-head green light coming on when I pressed the switch to prove the batteries were working.

'I shall ring back, Camilla, if you do not speak now. What on earth is the matter with you?'

'How dare you telephone me?' I said quietly, it was the best I could do.

He laughed. 'Oh, please, do not be so dramatic.'

I had to be sensible. I had to encourage him to talk. 'I wasn't the first, was I, you bastard?' I said.

'There's no need to be lewd, Camilla. No, you were not.'

'But was I, perhaps, the first to escape? You murderer.' I wished that I did not feel so frightened.

'I'm not a murderer,' he said, his voice rising. 'And that is a very serious accusation.'

I couldn't handle it. I wanted him off the line. I didn't know where he was. He scared me half to death. 'I don't wish to speak to you,' I said. 'But if you have any soul at all, would you tell me what you did to me when you rendered me unconscious?'

He laughed then, a harsh, camp sort of laugh. 'Why do women always ask that question? It has to have something to do with females being unable to fantasize.'

I felt angry now. It was a better feeling. 'I find it hard to believe that you only sat and looked at me,' I said.

He sighed. 'I took a few pictures; of course. But before you ask, not of your face.' I felt sick.

'And of course, I masturbated. Much healthier that way.'

I felt sicker. 'I'm going to bring this conversation to an end,' I said.

'Do you know what happened because of your ravings?' he asked, his voice almost at a shout. I didn't answer.

'Fred was killed,' he said loudly, 'and it was all your fault. That wretched spider bit him to death.'

'Goodbye,' I said. 'I'm sorry about Fred. He was less of a snake than you are. And please, don't call me again.'

I knew that I had to allow him the last word. 'I probably won't, now that I've told you Fred died because of you. And I loved him. Oh, and by the way, Camilla, it won't do you a bit of good recording this conversation.'

While still a fixture in my seat, numb, and scared, I did at least telephone British Telecom to ask for a fix on the call. The nice man called Chris told me he would call me back. And when he did he gave me the greatest of news. He regretted, he said, but he could not help me. The call had come in from abroad.

NINETEEN

I woke up one morning, a week or so after Harry's departure, with an ache all over that you wouldn't believe. I was restless too, couldn't settle.

It had nothing to do with Greg McLaren's telephone call. I'd told no one about that, but in a funny sort of way it had helped to exorcize the horror of the events. Now I could healthily hate him. He was real again, flesh and blood, features intact, right down to the small brown mole on his left temple. Not someone I had invented, as a lot of people would have liked to believe.

This restlessness had a sort of pit-of-the-stomach excitement about it. As soon as I sat at my desk to try to work at notes for a novel I had decided to write, I'd remember that it was time for a coffee, and jump up again. Then it would be, had I turned the washing machine on? Maybe I should go and check it. Did I give Kat enough to eat at breakfast? Should I give her some more in case? Was it my turn to ring Emma?

Then a warm glow developed around my lumba region, and spread, slowly, to my groin, and my cheeks seemed flushed. Maybe I should take my temperature, I thought. I walked around the flat with an old thermometer stuck between my teeth while I put on the kettle for coffee yet again. When the mercury reading showed normal, and let me down, I abandoned my desk for a chair at the kitchen table, and comfort food of coffee and toast, while I thought seriously about it.

Between bites and sips I asked myself some questions, and Kat watched me warily as she checked out the birds that teased her from outside the window.

Was I feeling miserable? I asked myself. Absolutely not, chirpy as could be.

Happy then? Mmm . . . yes . . . sort of . . . but as I first said, restless.

Did I want to see the children? No way.

Was the glow still there in the stomach, like earlier? Definitely. It was nice.

Was anyone in particular on my mind? Mmm . . . yes.

Who then? Harry Smith.

I got up slowly from the table, leaving the last slice of toast on the plate, and moved to the window, to look out and place my hand gently on Kat's neck, which made her start to purr. A slim, pale moon was showing in the daytime sky, the way it sometimes does. It occurred to me that the very same moon was the one Harry would see on clear nights, and maybe daytime too, like this, at times, thousands of miles away in Australia. Then I knew in a flash what my symptoms were. They were withdrawal symptoms for one Harry Smith.

I went back to my desk to work and to put such fantasies behind me. Hadn't I already decided I didn't love Harry? Well, yes, I loved him, but I wasn't *in* love with him. Hadn't I already decided that I must pick up the threads again in London, get on with my book, be a doting grandmother who picked out new clothes for the baby instead of new tights for herself? And wasn't I going to be a sensible ex-wife, and go out to dinner with Marcus now and again? And forget about making new friends and concentrate on the old? All those things. Hadn't I definitely decided that was what I should do? And a woman had to be *in* love with a man to make a relationship work, I knew that better than anyone. My marriage to Marcus wouldn't have lasted half as long as it did, I now realized, but for my being desperately in love with him all that time.

So how did a woman, I mean a grown-up, mature woman, not a young girl, know when she was in love? Well, it was the same as when you're young, surely? So what *was* that feeling? Um, probably a warm glow in the pit of the stomach, restlessness, pink cheeks, thinking you have a high temperature when you haven't . . .

I got up from my desk slowly, knocking a few pages of script to the floor as I did so. Then I walked back to the kitchen to see if the moon was still there, a smile spreading on my face as I went, quite out of control.

Maybe the moon wasn't still there, but *I* certainly saw it. I stood and savoured the flutter of my heart, as Kat jumped down and began weaving her way around my ankles hoping for food, only to be startled and dashing to a safe distance when her mistress lost her mind, punched the air three times, and yelled, 'Yes . . . yes . . . yes!' at the top of her voice.

Then she did a quick jig, jumped around a bit, and hugged herself tight all the way to the fax machine.

Diana, of course, thought that I was quite mad. What sane person would want to go to live in Australia, she asked, even with somebody they thought they loved? And when she really thought about it, what sane person could fall in love with an Australian, anyway? Especially a sheep farmer. And especially when the programme was about to be filmed, and she'd spent all that time making a feature of how the researcher nearly lost her life. The spin-offs for that could be enormous for me, she said. And anyway, she had another project in mind, safer than the last one.

'Tempt me,' I said, curiosity getting the better of me.

Philippa Todd

'Researching on why a man is so guided through life by the size of his penis,' she said, for all the world as though I would find it simple and could start with the local vicar. 'Around the world again, first-class, of course,' she added, when she thought, rightly, that I was not taking her seriously. 'Some men won't even use public lavatories for fear the size of their penis will be noted by other men, and if it's small, reveal the torture in their souls.'

When I realized that she was serious, I made a thoughtful face and said, 'I wouldn't be good at that. You should research it yourself.'

'For example,' she said, 'did you know that a flasher is always a puny, introverted man with a large dick? And flashing it in public places is the only way he has of letting the world know that he's actually well endowed.'

'No, I didn't,' I said, 'but I'm not going round the world looking for flashers and big dicks. Not even for you.'

'I'll pay you more than last time,' she said.

But I think the closed look on my face did for me in the end. Because her last remark, intended to bite, was, 'You never did have a good sense of timing, Camilla.' Whatever that was supposed to mean.

Kate threw me a farewell party, and everyone came. Even Marcus.

'I don't think you should have sold your flat,' he said. 'You may want to come back.' What he really meant was, and how dare you get such a good price for it when the deposit was paid by me as the very least I could get away with when I deserted you? And now you are not even offering to share the profit with me.

The most heart-rending decision I had to make was not to take Kat with me. I'd been told, and I'm sure it's true, a cat has to be to the manner born to survive life in the Australian bush. But Irish Rose came to the rescue and begged me to let her take her to her little house with a garden in Essex. Himself had passed on a few weeks before and Rose thought that she would enjoy Kat in her bed much more than she had Himself. So Kat left before I did so that I could make quite sure she'd settle. And whether I liked it or not, she had. It was the garden that did it, I told myself.

I allowed only Kate to see me off, and her sense of optimism, assuring me that she would be over to see me in no time at all, stopped me from getting emotional.

'Mum, if I were you I'd do the very same thing,' she said. 'Come to think of it, I envy you. Here you are, going off on an adventure with a second amour, and I haven't even had one run-in yet.'

I felt like a scarlet mother.

It was an action replay for me, the ticket desk, the creeping of the staff because I was a first-class passenger (courtesy of the profit on the flat), the preferential lounge with champagne on tap. Only this time, I was a seasoned traveller (blooded, more like it). Now I knew that a girl has to keep her feet on the ground at all times. What is that saying? . . . 'There's no such thing as a free lunch' . . . how true.

But it didn't stop me when I boarded from going through the pocket in front of my seat like a child. Or watching the food come on board with amazement, or feeling pleased when a member of crew called me by name.

'Good evening,' the man said as the chief steward took his coat, and his briefcase, and his umbrella, and he sat down beside me with a sigh.

'Hello,' I said casually, trying not to take in his silk shirt or his hand-painted tie or the *Financial Times* he was tucking into the seat-pocket in front.

'Are you getting off in Singapore?'

'No, Sydney,' I answered politely.

'Oh, that's a long journey ahead for you. Singapore is bad enough.'

I didn't answer, I couldn't really be bothered. Those were all my lines he was using. The 'must be pleasant, can't be rude, and no, I'm not the least bit nervous' lines.

'I'm James Appleby,' he said. 'How nice to be seated next to a good-looking lady.'

I smiled at him. Well, you can't be totally rude, can you? Then I reached into the depths of my travel bag for my shorthand notebook and my pen. I must make a note, I thought, of a name like James Appleby for my book, before I forgot it.

'Let me guess,' he said. 'You're a writer. What an interesting flight this will be.'

I gave him a sideways look. 'Not really,' I said. 'It means that you'll have to keep quiet.'

Harry would have been pleased with me. He was sure that I'd pick somebody up on the way.

Harry pushed the luggage trolley with one hand. With the other he held me tightly round the waist, just the way he had in London.

'I've brought Gracie's car,' he said. 'It's over there in the shade. Special reason.'

He made me close my eyes and promise not to peek. Then he put the squirming bundle into my arms and said, 'He's so you won't miss Kat too much. You can open your eyes now.' And there, looking up at me, preparing to lick my face and wagging his entire rump, was the most adorable tan, black and white Jack Russell puppy.

'Oh, Harry, he's just perfect. But can he live indoors with us? Say that he can. I couldn't bear it if he had to live outside.'

Harry held up my chin and kissed me deep and sexily,

and the puppy tried to join in. 'Yair, reckon he can. Just make sure you house-train him properly. They're tough little buggers, these ones. He'll be running the show in no time.'

On the way to Gracie's place I said, 'I'm going to call him Flinders.'

'Bloody hell,' Harry said, 'Gracie'll have a blue fit. Captain Flinders was a hero . . . that bundle of tick-fodder's a mongrel.'

We stayed the night at Gracie's, and I don't know what she thought, but we didn't get out of bed for twenty-four hours. Flinders thought that it was great.

Harry and I made endless, passionate love. I was sated, satisfied, so unbelievably content. And, feeling the warmth from Harry, curled up against my naked back, our legs entwined, his arms enfolding me, I knew that I was ready to face anything and everything from now on, in my new life, with my new and loving man. Blissful drowsiness washed over me, and Harry seemed to have gone to sleep already.

'Like to go on a croc hunt?' he said into my ear.

'A croc hunt?'

'Yair, for a few days, before I have to get back to work. Gracie'll look after Flinders.'

'Where?' I asked slowly, while I tried to think.

'Northern Territory. We'll fly up to Darwin.'

'Is it dangerous?'

'Nair. Good fun, really. An old mate of mine runs a sort of lodge up there. Food's good too.'

'What's his name?' I still wasn't sure about the crocodiles.

'Charlie Tanner. Great-looking bloke. You'll like him. Only has one leg.'

I didn't dare ask how he lost the other one. 'That sounds like a great thing to do . . .' Well, what else could I say? I was ready to face anything and everything from now on, remember?

'Good on yer.'

'I love you, Harry.'

'I love you too.'

'Really truly love me? More than all the world?'

'Bloody right. Now go to sleep, will yer. We've got a big day ahead of us tomorrow.'

I told Harry about the abortion while we were on the crocodile hunt. I needed to get it over, I had to know quickly if he wanted to disown me.

Apart from clothes, I was smothered from head to foot in cream. Cream to protect me from the sun and cream to protect from mosquitoes, and I wished that I could look more glamorous.

'I know that I should have contacted you, told you what I was about to do. But I just couldn't.'

We were sitting with our backs against a huge tree, having a cold beer from the eskie. Well, I was having a cold beer, Harry was swigging from a can of Coke.

He looked out across the river. 'You poor kid,' he said. 'I don't like to think of you going through all that on your own.'

'You had a right to know,' I said.

He took my greasy hand in his and swatted away a fly. 'Nair,' he said. 'But promise me one thing, Annie girl. If it happens again, let things be. It's better that way.'

Of course not every day was perfection on the station, but most of them were. Harry was sometimes away overnight, looking at fences, looking for sheep, checking on water, and I had trouble getting used to that. Of course, there was always someone sleeping in the quarters, and I did have Flinders.

I don't know what I did to cause it, but once the kitchen

range blew up, and an iron oven door flew clean across the kitchen. It could have killed me.

And I thought that I would never master my fear of spiders. But I did, with Harry's help. He came home one day to find me quite hysterical. The yard-hand had told him before he came indoors that he was not likely to get me to bed that night unless he found the enemy, which had been on the bedroom ceiling one minute and vanished the next.

Harry sat me down and lectured me when I said that I was going to Sydney, even if I had to walk, and I would not come back until he'd found every single spider there was, and if he thought I didn't mean it, he would find my case in the hall.

'You going to let a spider come between us?'

'Yes, unless you find it.'

'But Annie, they eat the friggin' flies and mozzies.'

'I don't care. We can have screening at the windows and those bead curtain things at the doors. They sell all those things in Sydney. I don't need to be scared half to death all the time.'

He scratched his head. 'How d'you know they sell them in Sydney? You been talking to Gracie? Jesus H. Christ, bloody women.'

Snakes I was able to take in my stride, for one good reason, we don't seem to have any in our neck of New South Wales. Either that, or Harry has threatened the hands with dismissal if one gets to within fifty metres of the homestead.

I had four presents from Harry for Christmas. One was Kate, and I had no idea that she was coming over until she stepped out of *Lovely Lady* on Christmas Eve. She and Harry played that one close to the chest. The second was a beautiful horse. He's a bay, and his name is Oscar, and he now has me riding as if I was born in the saddle. He's gentle without being dozy, loves a gallop on the plains, and doesn't have a single bad habit. And best of all, he's respectful of Flinders, who loves to wind in and out of his feet and generally behave as though they are the same size as each other. The third is a four-wheel-drive jeep, with 'Annie's Vehicle' written on the roof. Harry says that's in case I break down when I'm combing the plains trying to find him. If he gets home before I do, he can come looking for me in *Lovely Lady* and guide me back to the homestead. And the fourth? Well, this one has me a bit worried. It's a course of flying lessons. Harry is convinced that I'll be good at it because I'm always advising him on what his next move should be when we're up there together.

Talking of Flinders, what a dog he turned out to be. He's so courageous, even Harry's pet lizard has respect for him, and he has the other dogs suitably tamed. He loves to play football too, and is the greatest goalie you could ever wish to see. In the evenings, he won't give us peace until we give him a game. He always comes with me when I exercise Oscar, and gets excited when we mount up. He's all over the place, and I'm always expecting him to get lost down rabbit holes. Sometimes he disappears near us, and surfaces a mile away. When it is very hot, and Oscar is longing for a gallop, I send Flinders back home. He puts down his little tail and runs off without a backward glance. I sometimes suspect he's not too sorry to be returning to a shady place.

The homestead is coming on too. I bought an electric sewing machine in Sydney and have renewed all the curtains and chair covers. Harry says it looks so posh, if the tax inspector pays us a surprise visit we'll be in 'deep shit'.

The regular hands have accepted me now. I think, when they watched Harry in those first few weeks, they thought the boss had gone soppy. All this worry about spiders, and the little woman who doesn't like to be left all alone. But one day, when I was upset about something trivial I've now blocked from my mind, and Harry was looking sheepish (forgive the pun) in the yard, and they were looking at each other, and stifling smirks, rather than running into the house to weep, as I'd done before, I put my hands on my hips peasant fashion and screamed, 'And you can all mind your own fucking business, and get out of my sight.' I've had no trouble with them since then. They call me The Missus now, and are respectful as anything.

The shearers are not so keen on me, though. But that's my fault, and they come and go when needed, so I'm not worried. They thought I was trying to be smart early on when I wanted to try shearing. And I realize now that I put Harry on the spot, and I'm sorry. Of course, I was not strong enough to hold the damned thing properly, and the sheep got away half-shorn. The shearers were contemptuous. I felt like a fool. Harry just went off on his horse to find it, scratching his head under his hat, and muttering, 'Bloody women, who needs them?' Well, he did for one, once I got him into bed, and we were speaking again.

The days are just not long enough for me. I was not disciplined enough for a long time, and I didn't devote enough hours to my novel. But not now. You see, I'm pregnant. Oscar's a bit put out, because at my age I'm scared to take him out for a gallop in case I fall off. But the book is doing fine. I've finished it, and I have a great new agent in London. (Dizzy Tits turned me out of her stable when I got involved with the NYPD. Not that, I think, she knew what it stood for. She just knew that it wasn't British.)

The arrival of the plane from Chicago, via Los Angeles,

was shown at last on the board in the Arrivals hall. A flutter of pleasure in my stomach showed on my face and tweaked at the corners of my mouth, causing an old lady waiting at the Customs' exit, as I was, to think that I was smiling at her.

It was almost two years since I had last seen Hunter, and a lot of water had flowed since then. I told myself that I hoped I would recognize him, but in truth I knew that I would. You don't forget the physiognomy of a man who looks like Hunter Lee McNab.

The first print of his book was out and on the market. It had the makings of a bestseller, and Hunter was beginning a world promotion tour. After putting himself about in Los Angeles on a signing spree, his next stop was Sydney, and he was spending a few days with us up on the station. Harry was looking forward to that, because Hunter had been my friend in New York and he had sent me as emissary to meet him.

I was really up in town to see my obstetrician, and to check with the hospital where I was to give birth. As an older patient, as they called me, I was monitored carefully. But all was going well, the baby was (to Harry's delight) a girl. I was the shape of a beer barrel, and the weight of a one-storey building. But everyone was pleased with me. I was moving into Gracie's place one week before the baby was due. And any small apprehensions I had, like every older woman having a baby, I kept to myself.

A tired young mother with three sleepy children accidentally disgorged baggage from her trolley in the Customs hall exit, almost legging Hunter up, and then there he was, looking as wonderful as ever, and smiling right at me. I launched myself at him and he gathered me up till my feet left the ground. Then arm through his, I led him out to the car park and the brilliant sunshine. It was a glorious day. Clear, sparkling and warm.

'You look great, Camilla,' Hunter said. 'Younger even than when I last saw you.'

I laughed. 'That wouldn't be difficult, would it? But you haven't noticed these six grey hairs.' I pointed to my temples. 'I keep pulling them out. But they come back again, relentlessly.'

'How is Harry?' he asked, as I started up Gracie's car.

'He's good,' I said. 'He told me to tell you that he has lots of interesting things lined up for you this weekend, and he hopes that you've brought him a copy of your book.'

We had so much to talk about that day. Over lunch on the Harbour, and while watching a seaplane coming in to land in Rose Bay, he reached for my hand and said, 'No sightings of that bastard McLaren, I guess?'

I opened my bag, took out and unfolded a newspaper cutting. 'That could be him, there, at the back, almost hidden.' I pointed at a foggy picture taken from a distance.

While Hunter read the editorial on the high-security summit conference in Japan, I stared at a large and lovely three-masted schooner sailing sedately down the Harbour towards the Pacific Ocean.

'I used to see him everywhere,' I said. 'I'd go around looking into the eyes of strange men who resembled him. I carried a knife with me for a time, but you are the only person who knows that. I wonder if I could have used it?' I still said nothing about the telephone call. The schooner turned a promontory of land and went out of view. I turned to look at Hunter as he took my hand.

'But you're over it now?'

'Oh, yes,' I said, meaning it. 'Good things have happened to me. I have the baby soon. I'm twice a grandmother. William is happy with Anna. Kate's getting married in London in September.'

'I'm halfway through my next book,' he said suddenly. 'It's kind of about you . . .'

I laughed. 'I thought you wrote horror stories?'

He laughed too. 'It's written as pure fiction. And Greg McLaren won't get away with a thing. He's going to kill someone, not you of course. And I think he'll end up in the electric chair. I've brought the manuscript for you to read so far, and, I hope, to approve.'

I placed my hand on his. 'I hope he'll recognize himself,' I said, thinking of the moment when Fred and the spider escaped and terrified me half to death.

'He will,' Hunter said slowly.

It was windy at the airfield, and Mike, who piloted *Lovely Lady* when Harry couldn't, said he'd like to get going. An electric storm was forecast, and we must be ahead of it.

Hunter looked pale as we folded ourselves into the four-seater and Mike taxied towards the end of the runway. 'This isn't a plane,' he shouted in my ear above the noise. 'This is a kite with an engine.'

I took his hand and laughed. 'Better not let Harry hear you say that,' I shouted back. 'He's crazy about her.'

There was plenty of turbulence all the way, and Hunter turned from white to green several times, and had his sick-bag at the ready in case. I held his clammy hand and looked out of my small window at the landscape I had come to love, below.

I could see Harry crossing the yard and coming towards the strip as we circled, all the dogs, with Flinders leading, making a tight line in his wake. There was no mistaking his long thin frame and that unhurried gait. And my stomach churned, just watching him.

We landed bumpily, and there was relief on Hunter's face as we slowed. Then we turned and taxied back towards where Harry was standing, hands in jeans pockets, open shirt ballooning in the wind, weathered face not giving away too much. As we came to a halt he ambled forward, opened the door on Hunter's side, and unfolded the steps.

Hunter alighted swiftly and gratefully, and I watched as they shook hands formally. I stood on the top step, bent over in the doorway, my back aching from my unnatural shape, my loose-fitting dress feeling cold and clammy in the wind, as Harry reached up and lifted me down as though I was light as a feather.

For a moment I looked up into his eyes. He looked down into mine, and I could have cried with joy at the sight of him. Then we hugged, and who would have thought we'd only been apart for two days? He kissed me, then held me off, and turned to Hunter. 'Looks like there's a lot of wind up there. Hope the friggin' turbulence wasn't too bad. How'd you think my wife's looking?'

We didn't have electricity in the dining-room, bit less work for the generator to do, Harry said. I was pleased that we didn't, it was a good excuse to fill the room with candles. No room looks more romantic than a room lit by candlelight, in my opinion, and I'd thrown out the smelly old paraffin lamps early on.

'Nice home you have here,' Hunter said with feeling, as he dipped home-made bread into home-made soup.

'Yair, she's made it real good,' Harry answered, meaning me.

'Great soup too,' Hunter said, smiling in my direction.

'Yair, she's in her element in the kitchen,' Harry replied, before I had time to show my appreciation. 'I'm a lucky bloke.'

I melted with love, as I watched his face, so ruggedly handsome in the candle-glow. The telephone rang then, and he pushed back his chair and unhurriedly went off towards the hall to answer it.

'I'm real pleased you're so happy,' Hunter said.

I smiled at him. 'I know you are.'

'Does Harry know that I would have liked you for myself?' he asked quietly.

I shook my head. 'I didn't tell him. There was no point.'

'I'm glad.'

'He has the biggest heart of anyone I've ever known,' I said. 'And I really love him.'

Hunter picked up his soup spoon. 'I know. He's a great guy.'

'The very best,' I answered as Harry strolled back in.

'That was the fax centre. Letter's a bit smudged, Gracie says. But it looks like you're going to be *the* Annie Smith.' He smiled then. 'That agent in London has sold your book . . .'

We took Hunter back to Sydney and waited while he caught a flight to Perth for another book promotion. He promised he'll spend next Christmas with us, and I really hope that he does.

I talked Harry into taking me to see a play at the Opera House. I think he fell asleep during the second act.

In the night, in the guest-room at Gracie's place, my waters broke. I had to shake Harry for quite a time before he woke.

'What's wrong now?' he said sleepily, preparing to turn over and resume his dream.

'I'm going into labour, Harry,' I said calmly. 'It feels as though it might be a quick one. Contractions are coming quite often.'

He dived out of bed and into his trousers, and hopped round the room wth one sock in his hand. 'Bloody hell, Annie,' he said. 'You don't give a bloke much time.'

'Sorry' (grabbing the emergency case I had packed and left at Gracie's place).

'Have you got the car keys from Gracie?'

'Not yet.'

'What time is it?'

'Quarter to two' (looking at watch while strapping it on).

'And where's my other friggin' sock?'

'On your foot . . .'